**Praise for *New York Times* bestselling author
Kathleen Eagle**

"A good man is hard to find, but a romance by Eagle
is a good place to start."
—*Kirkus Reviews* on *The Last Good Man*

"Eagle…delivers her signature energy."
—*Publishers Weekly*

"Eagle's smooth, sweet storytelling works magic
on the emotions of the reader who expects slightly
larger-than-life fantasy along with her romance
reading."

—*WNBC.com*

"Vivid descriptions, superbly depicted characters
at all levels, a touch of violence, and a beautifully
developed romantic relationship add credence to
this story of two wary, badly damaged people—a
loner with a guilt-ridden past and a mother who will
do anything to retrieve her son—who eventually find
healing, peace, and love. A poignant, heartfelt story."
—*Library Journal* on *Ride a Painted Pony*

D1374301

New York Times and *USA TODAY* bestselling author
Kathleen Eagle published her first Silhouette
Special Edition book, an RWA Golden Heart®
Award winner, in 1984. Since then she has
published more than forty books, including
historical and contemporary, series and single
title novels, earning her nearly every award in the
industry, including Romance Writers of America's
RITA® Award. Kathleen lives in Minnesota with
her husband, who is Lakota Sioux and forever a
cowboy. Visit her online at kathleeneagle.com.

Books by Kathleen Eagle

Harlequin Special Edition

Wild Horse Sanctuary

One Cowboy, One Christmas
Cool Hand Hank
Once a Father
Cowboy, Take Me Away
One Brave Cowboy
The Prodigal Cowboy

Other

One Less Lonely Cowboy
Never Trust a Cowboy

Visit the author profile page at Harlequin.com
for more titles.

Kathleen Eagle

Cool Hand Hank
&
Cowboy, Take Me Away

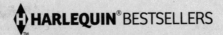
HARLEQUIN® BESTSELLERS

Recycling programs for this product may not exist in your area.

ISBN-13: 978-0-373-40110-9

Cool Hand Hank & Cowboy, Take Me Away
Copyright © 2015 by Harlequin Books S.A.

The publisher acknowledges the copyright holder of the individual works as follows:

Cool Hand Hank
Copyright © 2010 by Kathleen Eagle

Cowboy, Take Me Away
Copyright © 2011 by Kathleen Eagle

This edition published by arrangement with Harlequin Books S.A.

For questions and comments about the quality of this book, please contact us at CustomerService@Harlequin.com.

® and TM are trademarks of the publisher. Trademarks indicated with ® are registered in the United States Patent and Trademark Office, the Canadian Intellectual Property Office and in other countries.

Printed in U.S.A.

www.Harlequin.com

CONTENTS

COOL HAND HANK

For My Nieces and Nephews
and
To Honor the Memory of
Phyllis Eagle McKee

Chapter 1

Hank Night Horse believed in minding his own business except when something better crossed his path. A naked woman was something better.

Technically, Hank was crossing her path. He was about to step out of the trees onto the lakeshore, and she was rising out of the lake onto the far end of the dock, but the breathtaking sight of her made her his business. She was as bold and beautiful as all outdoors, and she was making herself at home. Maybe she hadn't noticed the moonrise, couldn't tell how its white light made her skin gleam like a beacon on the water.

At his side, Phoebe saw her, too, but she knew better than to give their position away without a signal. With all that skin showing, the woman looked edible. Phoebe was trying to decide whether to point or pounce. Hank knew his dog. He couldn't help smiling as the woman turned to reach for a towel hanging over a piling. She was slender but womanly, with a long, sleek back and a sweet little ass. If he moved, if he made the slightest sound, he would kill a perfect moment. It would be a shame to see her…

…stumble, flail, go down on one knee. From graceful to gawky in the blink of an eye, the woman plunged headlong into the lake without a sound issuing from her throat. Hank was stunned.

Phoebe took off like a shot, and their cover was blown.

Fall back, regroup, find new cover.

She had the water, and he had the dog. *Excuse my dog. She has no manners.* And the woman…

…should have surfaced by now. *Maybe the water had her.*

Phoebe was paddling to beat hell. Hank skittered sideways down the pine-needle-strewn path until his boots hit the dock, reminding him that whatever he was about to do, the boots had to go.

And then what? He was a man of many talents, but swimming wasn't one of them. If the adoption people had told him Phoebe lived for the water, he would have walked right past her and taken the Chihuahua in the next cage. Instead, he'd saddled himself with a big yellow bitch who thought she was a seal. Or a dolphin. Dolphins could rescue swimmers, couldn't they?

Dive, baby, dive.

Swish! The woman's head broke the water's surface like a popped cork. Phoebe paddled in a circle around her, yapping exuberantly as though she'd scared up some game.

The woman spat a water-filled "Damn!" toward the open lake as Phoebe circled in front of her. "Hey! Where'd you come from?"

"She's with me." The water sprite whirled in Hank's direction. "You okay?"

"Fine. Where did *you* come from?"

Hank jerked his chin toward his shoulder and the pine woods behind his back. "My dog—*Phoebe, get over here*—my dog thought I shot you."

The woman laughed. A quick, unexpected burst of pure glee, which Phoebe echoed, adding gruff bass to bright brass.

"Are you coming in, too?"

He hadn't thought it through. Hadn't even realized he was sitting at the end of the dock with one boot half off. "Not if I don't have to. It looked like you fell."

"I did." Eyeing him merrily, she pushed herself closer with one smooth breaststroke. Her pale body glimmered beneath the rippling water. "I have fins for arms and two left feet that want to be part of a tail." She looked over at the dog paddling alongside her. "I'm not dead in the water. Sorry, Phoebe."

"She thought you were flapping your wings. If you really had fins, she wouldn't've bothered."

"But you would have?"

He pulled his boot back on. "The way you went

down, I thought you'd had a heart attack or some-thing."

"Klutz attack." She bobbed in place now, her arms stirring the water just beneath the surface. She made not going under look deceptively easy. "The water's fine once you get used to it. Now that I'm back in I wouldn't mind company."

"You've got some." He glanced straight down. Booted feet dangled over dark water. *Damn.* He felt like he was the one caught with his pants down. Had to get up now. He'd recover his dignity once he had something solid underfoot. Needed something to hang on to, and words were all he had. *Keep talking.* "That dog won't hunt, but she sure loves to swim."

"And you?"

He scooted toward the piling. "I'm not givin' up the best seat in the house." *Until I can grab that post.*

"So you're one of those guys who'd rather look than leap."

"I'm one of those guys who'd rather watch than drown."

There was that laugh again, warm and husky, like an instrument played well and often. "And you were going to save me exactly how?"

"By throwin' you a life boot." He smiled, more for his hand striking the post than his wit striking her funny.

"No need to." Her voice echoed in the night. "My feet are touching bottom."

"You serious?"

"If I stood up, the water would only be up to my waist."

"From what I saw, that would make it about two feet deep."

"Come try it out." She dared him with a wicked, deep-throated chuckle. "Bring your depth finder."

What a sight. The strange woman and the dog he fed every damn day were treading in tandem, two against one. Phoebe should have known better.

"I've got a measuring stick." Hank grinned. "But it retracts in the cold."

"Speaking of cold…" She hooked her arm over Phoebe's shoulders. "If you're not going to join us, I'd like to take another stab at getting out."

Post in hand, he stood. "My feet are touching bottom."

"Not mine."

"Yours is wet." He laid his hand on the towel she'd left hanging over the post. "Bring it up here and I'll dry it for you."

"One free look is all you get, cowboy. A second will cost you."

"How much?"

With the pounding of her fist she sent a waterspout into his face. He staggered back as Phoebe bounded onto the lakeshore.

"Damn! You must have ice water in your veins, woman."

"Warm hands, cold heart. Go back where you came from, please." She assumed a witchy pitch. "And your little dog, too."

If he could've, he would've. Back to the little house in the North Dakota hills where he'd grown up, where his brother lived with his wife and kids, and where the only water anybody had to worry about was spring runoff. Even though he liked the Black Hills—what red-blooded Lakota didn't?—he wasn't big on weddings or wild women. But Hank Night Horse was a man who kept his word.

He touched the brim of his hat. "Nice meeting you."

So this was what a *real* wedding was all about.

Hank scanned the schedule he'd been handed at the Hilltop Lodge reception desk along with the key to a room with "a great view of the lake." He'd told Scott—the host, according to the badge on the blue jacket—he'd already had a great view at the lake. Scott had promised him an even better one at sunrise, and Hank said he wouldn't miss it. But a wedding was something else. He'd witnessed a few horseback weddings sandwiched between rodeo events, and he'd stood up for one of his cousins in front of a judge, but he'd never actually watched a guy jump through so many hoops just to trade promises.

Damn. A three-day schedule? His friend had claimed to be done with weekend-event schedules now that he'd hung up his spurs, but you'd never know it by the list Hank was looking at now. Social hour, wedding rehearsal, rehearsal dinner. He had to laugh at the thought of a rodeo cowboy publicly practicing his walk down the aisle. The sound of Western-boot heels crossing the wood floor brought the picture to life.

"What's so funny, Horse?" Zach Beaudry clapped a hand on Hank's shoulder. "You laughin' at me? You wait till it's your turn."

"For this?" Grinning, Hank turned, brandishing the flower-flocked paper beneath his friend's nose. "If you don't draw a number, you don't take a turn."

"My advice?" Zach snatched the schedule and traded it for a handshake. "Take a number. You don't wanna miss the ride of a lifetime."

"Here's two, just for you. Number one, I patch you cowboys up for a living. I know all about that *ride of a lifetime*. And number two..." Hank gave his starry-eyed friend a loose-fisted tap in the chest. No man wore his heart on his sleeve quite like a lovesick cowboy. "Nobody's askin' you for advice this weekend, Beaudry. It's like asking the guy holding the trophy how he feels about winning."

"Damn, you're a smart-ass. Be careful you don't outsmart yourself. Come meet my family."

Hank followed Zach through a lobby full of rustic pine furniture, leather upholstery, and glass-eyed trophy heads. Rough-hewn beams supported the towering ceiling, and a fieldstone fireplace dominated one wall. They passed through a timber-framed archway into a huge dining room—bar at one end, dance floor at the other, rectangular tables scattered in between— flanked by enormous windows overlooking the lake. Hank wondered whether the shoreline was visible from the terrace beyond the massive glass doors. According to the plaque in the front entry, the lodge and the lakefront were products of a Depression-era Federal construction project, and everything about them was rough-hewn, but grand.

"This is my bride," Zach was saying, and Hank turned from the windows to the woman linking arms with her man. "Annie, Hank Night Horse."

She was small and pretty, and her smile seemed a little too familiar. But the way it danced in her blue eyes didn't connect, didn't feel like it had anything to do with him. And her curly golden ponytail looked bone-dry. Hank held his breath and offered a handshake.

"Our wedding singer," the bride said in a soft, shy voice. "Thank you for coming, Hank."

"Sure." And relieved. He was sure he'd never heard the voice before, so he looked his buddy in the eye and smiled. "You did well, Beaudry."

"I did, didn't I?" Zach put his arm around his intended. "She's got a sister."

"You don't say." Hank lifted one shoulder. "I'm willing to sing for a piece of your wedding cake, but that's as far as I go."

"I'm just sayin', you got a great solo voice, man, but that solo livin' gets old."

"I'll bet it does. I know I don't like to go anywhere without Phoebe."

"She's here? Phoebe's here?" Zach's face lit up like a kid who smelled puppy. "Annie, if we can't get married on horseback, how 'bout we put Phoebe in the wedding party? She could carry the rings. She's like the physician's assistant's assistant. Hank's pretty good with his hands, but Phoebe's got heart. He's stitchin' a guy up, she's lovin' him up like only man's best friend knows how to do. Helps you cowboy up so you can climb back on another bull."

"He can't," Ann assured Hank. "We wrote it into the contract."

"That's good, 'cause I'm tired of sewing him up and watching him rip out my stitches in the next go-round."

"Where's Phoebe?" Zach demanded. "I'll bet she's not tired of me."

"She's outside. Caused me some trouble, so she's in the doghouse."

"No way. You tell Phoebe she can—" Zach glanced past Hank and gave a high sign. "Sally! Over here! I want you to meet somebody."

"Can he swim?"

That was the voice. "Sounds like I'm out of my depth again." Hank turned and hit her feet first with a gaze that traveled slowly upward, from the red toenails she'd claimed to be touching bottom to the blue neckline that dipped between pale breasts. He paused, smiled, connected with her eyes—blue, but more vibrant than her sister's—and paid homage again with the touch of his finger to the brim of his hat. Her short blond hair looked freshly fixed. "I like your dress."

"What's that? You like me dressed?"

"That, too. But clothes don't make the woman." He'd already seen what did.

"So true. I didn't catch your name."

"Hank Night Horse."

Ann looked up at Zach. "I have a feeling we missed something."

"I have a feeling this is the sister," Hank said as he offered his hand. Hers was slight and much colder than advertised. He gave it a few extra seconds to take on a little heat. He had plenty to spare.

"And this is the music man." Sounding as cool as her hand felt, Sally looked him straight in the eye. For someone who'd been laughing it up less than an hour ago, she sure wasn't giving him much quarter.

"Hank, Sally Drexler, soon to be my sister-in-law. Have you two already…"

"I took Phoebe for a walk right after we pulled in. She tried to retrieve Sally from the lake."

"Aw, you gotta love Phoebe," Zach said cheerfully. "Hank's part of the medical team working the rodeo circuit, and Phoebe's his bedside manner."

Sally's eyes brightened. "I've spent a lot of time around the rodeo circuit. I used to be a stock contractor. Zach delivered the thrills and I furnished the spills. But that was probably before your time."

"I just hand out the pills."

"He does a lot more than that," Zach said. "Pops joints back in place, sets bones, makes the prettiest stitches you ever saw. Plus, he shoes horses on the side."

Sally challenged Hank's credentials with a high-headed smile. "All that and a wedding singer, too?"

"First time." Hank gave Ann an indulgent smile. "I hear brides can be hard to please, and I'm a what-you-hear-is-what-you-get kind of a guy. I don't mind being the funeral singer. You get no complaints from the star of the show."

"You're listed on the program without the name of the song, which I really wanted..." Ann glanced at Zach. They were already developing their own code.

Good start, Hank thought. He and his former wife had never gotten that far.

"But we agreed to leave it up to you," Zach filled in.

"It's my gift. I want it to be a surprise."

Ann shrugged. "I promise not to complain."

"I promise not to sing 'Streets of Laredo.'" Hank glanced across the room. A handful of people were gathered at the bar. Two women were setting bowls of flowers on the white-draped table. He turned to Sally. "What's your wedding assignment?"

"Maid of honor, of course. It's a plum role. By the way," she reported to her sister, "more gifts were delivered here today. I had the desk clerk store them under lock and key. There's actually one from Dan Tutan."

Tutan. Hank frowned. He hadn't heard the name since he was a kid, when he'd heard it whispered respectfully, sometimes uneasily, eventually contemptuously around the Night Horse home.

"Or his wife," Ann was saying. "She takes neighborliness seriously."

"Dan Tutan's your neighbor?" Hank asked.

Sally sighed. "A few miles down the road. Not

close enough so we have to see him every day. But before I say *fortunately,* is he a friend of yours?"

"Nope."

"Well, he'd like to turn our wild-horse sanctuary into a dog-food factory."

"Why's that?"

"The horses like to mess with him," Zach said. "They know he's extremely messable."

"Tutan's had a pretty sweet deal on grazing leases around here for so long he's forgotten what a lease is," Sally said. "We're bidding on some leases and some grazing permits that he's held for years, and we've got a good chance at them because of the sanctuary. We're a retirement home for unadoptable wild horses. We give them grassland instead of a Bureau of Land Management feedlot. So Tutan doesn't like us much these days. How do you know him?"

"My father knew him." Hank glanced away. "Tutan wouldn't know me from an Indian-head penny."

"He'd know the penny," Sally said. "Damn Tootin' never walks away from any kind of money."

Zach clapped a hand on Hank's shoulder. "Don't tell him which one we picked up for a song."

"Damn Tootin'." Hank chuckled. He didn't think he'd heard that one.

"Were they friends?" Sally asked. "Your father and my neighbor?"

"My dad worked for Tutan for a while. Long time ago. No, they weren't friends."

"Good. I'm not good at watching what I say about people I hate." Sally linked arms with her sister. "I'd get the bomb squad to check out his gift if I were you. And then put it in the regifting pile."

"Tell us how you really feel, Sally," Zach teased. He winked at Hank. "I'm glad you're giving us live music. That's something she can't regift."

"I'm recording everything," Sally said. "Hell, if your singer's any good, I'll burn a few CDs for Christmas presents. The frugal rancher's three R's: regift, repurpose, recycle." She poked Zach in the chest as though she were testing for doneness. "But we can't regift your brother's trip, so you're going to use that one."

"We'll get to it. There's no rush."

"No rush to go on your honeymoon?" Sally flashed Hank a smile. "What's this guy's problem, Doc?"

"Can't say."

"You're ducking behind that confidentiality screen, aren't you?" She turned back to Zach. "Your extremely wealthy brother hands you the extreme honeymoon, the wedding trip of your dreams, the one you mapped out with your bride, and you're saying *we'll get to it?* Like *anytime* is honeymoon time?"

"Well, isn't it?" Zach held up a cautionary hand. "Hold on, now, I haven't said *I do* yet. I gotta go work on those vows some more, make sure we both say *I do it anytime. All the time. Rain or shine.*"

The bride blushed.

The maid of honor laughed. "Say what you want, cowboy. I figure a nice long, romantic honeymoon will guarantee me a niece or nephew nine months later. If you don't get away from the Double D, what you'll do is exactly what you've been doing, which is working your fool britches off."

"*Britches off* is step one, Sally," Zach said. "It's not much work, and it's no guarantee, but it's a start. Right, Hank?"

Hank answered his friend with a look. The conversation had veered into no-comment land.

"I can handle the Double D." Sally glanced back and forth between Zach and Ann. "I'm *fine*."

"We're here for a wedding," Ann said, "which is a one-time thing, and we're doing it up right. Right here. Right now. We're going to rehearse." Ann offered a hand for the taking. "Hank?"

"You want me to practice walkin' and talkin', fine." Hank took the bride's hand with a smile. "But I don't rehearse my songs in public. It's bad luck."

"Let's walk and talk, then. Help me make a list of reasons why Zach should ride horses instead of bulls."

Sally hung back, watching her sister walk away with two attractive men. Two cowboys. Lucky Annie. As far as Sally was concerned, there were only two kinds of men out West: cowboys and culls. She didn't know any men from back East.

Sally had been around a lot of cowboys, and most of them were pretty easy to figure. All you had to do was take a look at the shirt. A cowboy wore his heart on his sleeve and a number on his back. He lived day to day and traveled rodeo to rodeo, accumulating cash and consequences. He was addicted to adrenaline, and he'd paid dearly for his sky-highs with rock-bottom lows. By the time he'd filled his PRCA permit with enough wins to earn the right to call himself a Professional Rodeo Cowboy, he'd paid in some combination of torn flesh, spilled blood and broken bone.

Such was the story of Zach Beaudry. He'd been the up-and-coming bull rider to beat until he'd met up with the unbecoming end of a bull's horn. Like the rest of his kind, he knew how to tough it out. Hunker down and cowboy up. Put the pieces back together and get back on the road. Which had led him to Annie's doorstep.

Hank Night Horse had the look of a cowboy. He was lean and rangy, built to fork a horse and cut to the chase. But a full place setting required a spoon. Sally smiled to herself as she pictured his possibilities. He looked great going away. She could paste herself against that long, tapered back and snug her thighs under his, tuck his tight butt into her warm bowl and be fortified. She could back up to him and invite him to curl his strong body around her brittle one and make her over. It could happen. In her dreams, anyway.

Hank turned to say something to Annie, who turned to say something to Zach and then back to Hank again. Conspiring. Setting Sally up. She knew what they were up to, and she didn't mind as long as this crazy body of hers was working properly. The fall from the dock hadn't been a good sign, but she was back in control now. And Hank Night Horse was turning back, giving her another one of those rousing once-overs. *You and me, woman.* He was coming for her, and, ah! she saw how fine he looked coming and knew how readily and happily she would come and come and come if the table were set with a man like Hank Night Horse. It wouldn't matter how much time he had to spare as long as it was—what was the expression? *Quality time.* Remission from illness was like a blue space between clouds. Either make the most of it, or stay in your box.

"Care to join me in the back row?" he asked.

"Am I your assignment?" She threw her voice into her sister's key. "If you're not going to rehearse your song, could you keep an eye on Sally?"

"I didn't quite catch what they said," he claimed with a twinkle in his eye. "Something about *drink.* I'm supposed to buy you one or keep you from falling in. Either way, I could be in for some trouble. Are you a troublemaker, Sally?"

"I do my best. And I know you're lying, because I'm not allowed to drink."

"Anything?"

"Anything with alcohol in it."

"Who said anything about alcohol?" He gave her a challenging look, his eyes growing darker and hooded, his full lips twitching slightly, unwilling to smile. "And who makes the rules?"

"Sensible Sally." She gave the smile he denied her. "That was her alter ego down at the lake. Shameless Sally."

"She's got the right idea. Shame shouldn't be allowed, either." He tucked his thumbs into the front pockets of his jeans. "So, what'll it be?"

She looked at her watch. "Rehearsal in five. Can't hardly whip up a good batch of trouble in five minutes. Sensible Sally drinks green tea on the rocks with a twist."

Hank decided to "make that two," and they left the dining room, glasses in hand, no hurry in their feet. Sally felt a growing reluctance to catch up with the little wedding party in the lodge library. The lakeside setting for the ceremony would be set up tomorrow, so tonight's indoor rehearsal was literally a dry run. Sally knew her part. She'd seen it played out a hundred ways in movies, read the scene in dozens of books. Sensible Sally stayed in the house a lot. Shameless Sally couldn't go out to play until the unreliable body caught up with the willing spirit, and now that the two were working in tandem, she would go where the spirit moved her.

"Look!" She pointed to a window, grabbed Hank's arm and towed him out the front door on to the huge covered porch. A procession of trail riders passed under the yard lights on their way to the pasture below the lodge. "How was the ride?" Sally called out.

"Beautiful!" said one of the helmeted riders. "Made it to the top of Harney Peak."

"Let's go up there tomorrow," Sally said to Hank. "You ride, don't you? We should…" She turned to the riders. "Where did you get the horses?"

"We brought our own. We're a club."

"But there's a hack stable close by," said the last rider as she passed under the light. "Ask at the desk."

Sally looked up at Hank. "We could go really

early." She turned, cupped her hand around her cheek and shouted at the last rider's back. "How long did it take?"

"All day!"

Sally scowled. "I'll bet I could take a marker to the programs and change the time. The lake is beautiful this time of day. *Night*." She pointed to the white moon hovering above the ponderosa pines. "It'll be full tomorrow. Imagine Annie in her white gown, and Zach...well, he's wearing black, but can't you just see it? Moonlight on the lake?"

"I did, yeah. Beautiful."

"They don't need us. They wouldn't even notice. Look." She took his hand and led him to the end of the porch, pointed to the tall, bright corner windows that showcased the rehearsal getting under way in the library.

Sally could see Zach's niece and nephew perusing the bookshelves that flanked the stone fireplace. Zach was having a chat with his brother, Sam. Annie and the minister were poking through a sheaf of papers. "My baby sister's getting married tomorrow," she whispered. Hard to believe. The window might have been a movie screen, except that she knew these people—some better than others—and what they were doing was exactly what they'd been talking about for months. It was happening. Sally's little sister was getting married. "They won't notice anyone but each other tomorrow." She squeezed Hank's hand. "Let's do it."

"Do it?"

"Tomorrow. Let's ride to the top of Harney Peak."

"Zach's a good man. They don't come much better."

"Oh, I know that." She drew a deep breath and laughed. "But I love the smell of horse in the morning."

He laughed with her, and that felt good. Even better when he took control of the hand-holding and led her back into the lodge as though they were in this together, a two-part unit joining a group of two-and-more-part units. She could come to like this man much more than Sensible Sally would normally permit.

The first person they ran into when they entered the library was the wizened cowboy who would be giving Annie away. Hoolie was draped over a pair of crutches near the door, prompting Sally to ask gently whether his ankle was bothering him again, whether he was coming or going.

"Thinkin' about getting outta the way until they decide what they want me to do. One of them kids tripped and near busted my cast."

"It was an accident," the sandy-haired boy called out over the top of the book he'd been reading.

"Man, they can hear good when they want to, can't they?" the wiry cowboy muttered, glancing at Hank. Then he turned to the boy. "I know you're sorry, Jim. No hard feelings. I can still hobble."

"Hank, this is Henry Hoolihan, our foreman."

"Hoolie." He offered Hank his hand. "Nobody's

called me Henry since I was Jim's age. Who dug that up?"

"I don't know, but it's on the program," Sally said. "Jim and Star are Zach's brother's kids. Say hello to Hank Night Horse, Zach's doctor."

The children sang out as instructed, but Hoolie said, "Doctor?"

Hank glanced at Hoolie's cast. "I work the rodeo circuit as a physician's assistant. Zach's been a pretty steady customer the last few seasons." As one, the three turned their attention to the couple attending to wedding business on the far side of the room. "He's a good hand."

"Was," Sally said. "He says he's retiring."

"The body can only take so much," Hank said. "Some guys don't know when to quit. I'm glad Zach's not one of those guys." He looked at Sally. "He's still a good hand."

"We love Zach," Sally said with a smile. "Don't we, Hoolie? I'm being summoned. Let's get this over with so we can eat. And then on to the fun stuff." She touched Hank's sleeve. "Keep your program handy. We had one dull moment scheduled in, but then you came along and buffed it up, thank you very much."

"The pleasure was mine." He eyed her hand and then raised his dark gaze to her eyes as he leaned close to her ear. "Seein' as how the buff was yours."

Sally's neck tingled. An icy-hot shiver blew apart and streaked gloriously throughout her body. She stood still, waiting for the feel of another warm, magic breath.

"Sally, we need you!"

She let her hand slide to the edge of Hank's cuff where she could feel his working-man's skin. "Hold that thought," she said.

At dinner, Sally did her maid-of-honor duty by making the rounds among family and friends. Sally and Ann had lived on the Drexler ranch in South Dakota all their lives. But the family had been reduced to the two of them, along with Hoolie, who had come to work for their father before they were born, outlived him, and earned the privilege of giving the bride away. And now they had Zach, who brought his mother, Hilda, and brother, Sam, to the Drexler fold—hardly big enough to fold—along with Sam's new wife, Maggie, and their two children. But the Beaudrys made their home in Montana, and Zach had become a rolling stone until he'd rolled to a stop at the Double D. The wedding was Zach's reunion with the Beaudrys as well as his formal initiation into the Drexler clan. The Beaudrys couldn't contain their joy, and why try?

Duty done in the middle of the circle, Sally moved to the edge, where Hank had laid claim to the observer's station, a post she had come to know all too well in recent years. She had made her peace with it, while Hank seemed quite comfortable there. Maybe he could teach her something. He'd moved from the table where they'd shared dinner with Hoolie and Hilda to a corner conversation area near the bar. When he saw her coming, he moved again, from a big leather chair to a love seat. She was invited.

"They're all going on a moonlight hayride," she reported as she sat down. "I'm supposed to fetch you."

He smiled. "Good luck."

"Ready for another dull moment?"

"Looking forward to it." He lifted his arm over her head and laid it along the back of the love seat. "You?"

"I don't feel like changing clothes. When I take these off, that'll be it for the night."

"Big day tomorrow."

"Big day." She laid her head back and let it rest against his arm. "They're good people, aren't they? Why would Zach stay away from home so long?"

"Wouldn't know."

"But you know him well enough to vouch for his character."

"Yep." He shifted a little closer. "Tell me more about your mustang sanctuary. How do you support it?"

"We get some support from federal programs. Before my dad died, the Double D was one of the biggest cattle ranches in the state, and we still have a small cow-calf operation. We're also permitted to sell some of the colts off the wild mares."

"Is there much of a market these days?"

"They sell pretty well if they're at least green broke. Even better if they're broke to ride. But the market fluctuates with the rest of the economy, and right now it's tough. I have a plan, but I put it on hold for the wedding."

"Is that why they're holding off on the honeymoon?"

"Oh, no." She turned her head to give him a warning glance. "They don't know I have a new plan in the works. They're trying to put the honeymoon on hold because they don't want to leave me—" she raised her brow and gave a suggestive little smile "—to my own devices."

"Sounds like you have a reputation."

"I did, but I haven't been keeping up. A reputation is something you have to tend, just like a garden." She made growing, blooming, stepping-out gestures. "You want it to get big enough to precede you."

"Except when you get caught with your pants down."

"Depends on your perspective." She turned up the tease in her smile. "I can't speak for yours, but from mine, sooner or later you'll get my attention. It's better if you're not a *sooner.* Laters are generally slower and longer."

He shook his head, rewarding her with a slow smile. "You're a little smart-ass."

"Ah, but I grow on you."

"We'll see." But he crossed his near leg over the far one before she had a chance. "You can't hire somebody to help out while they're honeymooning?"

"Are you looking for a job?"

"I have two jobs," he reminded her. "I'm a farrier and a physician's assistant. My services are in high demand on the rodeo circuit."

"They'd be pretty handy around the Double D, too. If we had someone like you on staff, Zach and Annie would leave tomorrow. The day after at the latest."

"How big…how *many* on your staff?"

"Four, counting Hoolie. We get volunteers to work with some of the horses, but a lot of them are kids. Mostly from the reservation. Annie teaches at the high school."

"How long did they plan to be gone?"

"About three weeks. But then Hoolie got tangled up in some barbed wire and broke his ankle." She sat up and took new interest. "You wouldn't have to stay around the whole time. Seriously. You could be on call."

"That's why I'm not on any kind of staff. Been there, done that, found out I don't much like being on call. You work a rodeo, you're there for the weekend. The pay's good, and you get to have a life."

"Doing what? You have a family?" She hadn't missed something, had she?

"I used to be married. Had a son. He died."

"Oh. I'm so sorry."

"Yeah, me, too. But I got my life back, and I'm not short on things to do."

"Neither am I. It's time that's the kicker, isn't it?"

"I probably don't think of time the same way you do."

No kidding. "Not very many people do."

"A day is a day. You fill it with how you feel."

"That's interesting. I couldn't've said it better. Right now, tonight…" She stretched her arms straight and strong, crooning a saucy, "I feeeel good." She slid him a glance. "Hey, you're smiling."

"You're growin' on me."

Chapter 2

"Oh, Annie."

Sally's sister turned from the mirror, eyes shining like stars. Her golden hair was swept up from the sides and anchored by a pearl-encrusted comb and a cascading veil. The off-the-shoulder neckline and body-skimming lines of her elegant ivory dress were simple and stunning and perfectly suited to the woman who stood there, eclipsing all the dreams the two sisters had conjured over the years.

The photographer quietly snapped pictures, allowing the moment to unfold. Sally was dumbfounded. How many times had they gotten dressed together, given each other a last-minute review? Sally had helped Annie choose each piece of her wedding ensemble, had overseen the fittings and giggled with her over their memories of dresses and dates, new measurements and old tastes, the never-ending Double D "chest jest"—a size Annie had at one time nearly reached—and the ever-after girlish dreams. And now all the pieces had come together, adding up to a vision that came as no real surprise to Sally even as it brought rare tears to her eyes. This was it. Annie was the fairy-tale bride.

Blinking furiously, Sally handed over the bouquet of white calla lilies, drew a deep breath and blew a wobbly whistle. "Whoa. Wow. Okay, Hoolie thinks he can get by without crutches, but I know what it's like to fall on your face in front of an audience, so I think we should put my cane in his hand right when the music starts."

"It's not a long walk. A few steps. I'm almost there, Sally." Annie grabbed Sally's hand, and the camera hummed. "Why am I shaking like this?"

"They're big steps." Baby sister was taking big steps, and Sally was the only Drexler left to hold her hand.

She wanted to hug her, hold her a little longer, but she made do with squeezing her hand rather than making smudges or wrinkles or tears. Annie wasn't leaving, but life would be different after today.

"I wonder if *he's* nervous. Do you think he's shaking like this?" Annie laughed and shook her head. "Probably not. He's a cowboy. He rides...*used to* ride bulls for a living. What's a little—" she turned for another glance in the mirror, complete with bouquet, and smiled "—wedding?"

"There's no such thing as a *little* wedding," Sally said, speaking from her all-too-frequent experience as a captive TV watcher. "By the numbers, this one is little. But it's big by my calculations."

"I know. It's all Sam's fault."

"I'm not calculating in dollars. Zach's brother's money definitely falls into the easy-come-easy-go category, and since there's so much of it, why not enjoy the frills? I'm talking about *big,* as in big as life. This is your wedding, and it means the world to me."

Sally touched the simple strand of pearls around her sister's neck. They had belonged to their mother, whom Sally saw so unmistakably in Annie's big, soft eyes and bow-shaped mouth and dainty chin. Sally looked more like their father, but she was the one who clearly remembered Mom. Sally was the keeper of Drexler memories.

"I'll be kinda glad when it's all..." Annie gave her head a quick toss. "No, I'm glad now. I'm ready. I feel beautiful. And you look beautiful, Sally." Annie turned her sister so that the mirror made a framed portrait unlike any they'd taken together before. They'd been big and lively, little and sweet. One primary, one pastel. One ready to go first, the other pleased to follow.

"I love you so much," Annie whispered, and Sally had no doubt. But Annie was the one once meant to wait while Sally went ahead. And it wasn't that Sally was resentful of the reversal—she really did look good in her chic, fluid blue waterfall of a dress, Annie's gift of opals around her neck and studding her ears, fragrant gardenias in her hair—but she was unsure of her footing. Annie was taking a big step.

Where did that leave Sally?

"Me, too, you," she said as she squeezed that ever-dependable hand again. "Lest we spoil the makeup, consider yourself kissed."

"You know you're not losing a sister, don't you? You're gaining a brother. And we're not going anywhere. We're partners, and we're family, and we're going to—"

"—be late for your wedding. Listen. I am fine." She enunciated each word forcefully, willing her sister to make sense of three simple words and move on. "Look at me. No cane, no pain." *Enjoy this with me while it lasts.* She needlessly fluffed Annie's veil. "This is your day, honey. Take a deep breath. Your man is out there waiting and, yes, probably feeling just the way you are. When you take each other's hands…" Sally smiled, blinking furiously because she *would not cry.* "Tell me what it's like, okay? That moment."

Annie nodded as she pulled her hand free, placed a finger lightly at the outside corner of Sally's eye, caught a single tear and touched it to her lips.

Granite spires bound the crystalline-blue lake on the far side, the perfect backdrop for a hand-woven red willow arch decked out with a profusion of flowers. Guests were seated in white folding chairs. Zach's niece led the way, tossing handfuls of white rose petals on a path of fresh green pine needles. Sally followed, taking measured steps in time with the string quartet's elegant processional. Looking as handsome and relaxed in his black tux as he did in well-worn jeans, Zach waited for his bride. His brother, Sam—a little taller, a little darker, a little less at ease—stood like a sentry overseeing his charges. Daughter, son, wife, mother, brother—Sam's eyes attended to each one. He was clearly the Beaudry caretaker. *Funny,* Sally thought. *That's Annie, not me.*

Before she'd been diagnosed with multiple sclerosis, Sally had been the seeker, the doer, the risk taker. She'd cared passionately, but she'd never *taken care.* That was Annie's role. Careful, caregiving, selfless Annie.

Sally paused before the minister and looked the groom in the eye. *Be good to her, Zach. Be the man she deserves.* She pivoted and took her place, knowing she'd made her point. She felt Annie step up to fill the space she and Zach had left for her, but she couldn't quite turn to watch Hoolie place her sister's hand in Zach's. It was enough to see the movement from the corner of her eye, where Annie had touched her for a tear.

It was happening. Annie was interlacing her life with someone new, becoming someone else's next of kin. Sally clutched two handfuls of flowers and listened to identical promises exchanged in voices that complemented each other in a way she hadn't heard before. It was a pure sound and a simple truth. Annie and Zach belonged together.

And they stood together, hand in hand, while Hank

played an acoustic guitar and sang "Cowboy, Take Her Away" in a deep, resonant voice that was made for a love song. He'd said his gift was his song, and he sang to the couple as though no one else was there and every note, every word had been written just for them. Sally was enchanted. Her beautiful sister, her new brother, the music and the man who made it— she wanted to suck it all in and keep it alive within her in a way that the video camera could never do.

At the end of the song, Hank said, "Kiss her, Zach." And he did, cheered on by friends and family, who showered them with white rose petals as they retreated down the path. The guests followed, and the violinists made merry music at the back of the line as it wended its way up a gentle slope between stands of tall pines. When they reached the lodge's gravel driveway, Zach swept his bride up in his arms and carried her across the path and up the steps to the front porch, where he set her down and kissed her again. Women sighed. Men whooped. Cowboy hats sailed skyward.

Annie and Zach were hitched.

"You're a lucky man." Sally raised her glass of sparkling water in toast.

"Yeah, I know." Sam put his arm around his new wife, Maggie. "I hit the jackpot."

Maggie looked up at him. "*You* did?"

"Trusted you and got myself a whole family."

"I think Sally's talking about winning the lottery,"

Maggie said. "It's crazy. Real people don't win the lottery."

"Well, it was complicated," Sam said. "It was Star's mother's ticket—our daughter, Star—but she died before she could claim it. In fact, we thought the damn thing was lost in a car accident, but it turned up, kinda like..." He waved his hand as though words failed.

"Miraculously," Maggie supplied.

"To put it mildly," Sam said. "It's been a year, but it still doesn't seem real. We're trying to manage it sensibly. You don't want to go crazy. You want to put some of it to good use now, give some away, make sure there's plenty left for the kids. I've never known any rich people, never thought I'd like them much."

"He won't give up his job," Maggie said.

Sam laughed. "She won't, either."

"I'm part-time now, but our little clinic needs nurses, and I'm a good one. We just moved into a house we built on Sam's land. It's a gorgeous spot." Maggie made a sweeping gesture. "Kind of like this, but the lake is smaller and the mountains are bigger. You have to come for a visit."

"Where's Hank?" Sam asked, searching over the heads of the guests. "Man, that guy can sing. He about killed my brother with that song." He grinned at Zach. "He didn't leave yet, did he?"

Did he?

Sally hugged her new brother-in-law. "Where's Hank?"

"I'll tell you a little secret about ol' Hank. He don't

like compliments. He does his thing, and then he disappears for a while. He sang at a funeral once—bull rider, wrecked his pickup. Hank tore everybody up singin' over that kid. And then he disappeared. I found him playin' fetch with Phoebe." Zach glanced over the balcony railing. "He's around."

"Hey, cowboy." Annie joined the group, entwining her arm with her new husband's and beaming up at him as though he'd just hung the moon. "Take me away."

A skyward glance assured Sally that the moon wasn't up yet. The sun had slipped behind the trees, but there was still plenty of light for searching the grounds. She didn't have to go far. She found Phoebe first. The dog greeted her with a friendly bark, and the man followed, emerging from a stand of pines near a picnic table. He carried his jacket slung over his shoulder, white shirtsleeves rolled halfway up his forearms, black hat tipped low on his forehead.

Sally scratched Phoebe behind the ears and caught a little drool in the process. Hank tapped his thigh, and the dog heeled. With a hand signal, he had her sitting.

"Impressive," Sally said.

"She's willing to humor me because you're not as appealing as you were last night. If you were splashing around in the lake she'd be all over you."

"And you?"

"The only part that didn't appeal to me last night was the water."

"You were wonderful," she said, and he questioned

her with a look. "Today. Your music. You play beautifully, and you sing like—"

"Thanks." He swung his jacket down from his shoulder. "It's a good song."

"It's a *lovely* song. Perfect. I don't think I've heard it before."

"Aw, c'mon. You gotta love those Dixie Chicks. I had to change a couple of words to make it work."

"You made it yours. *Theirs.* Annie's and Zach's. That'll be their song now." Feeling a sudden chill, she hugged herself and rubbed her bare upper arms. "What a gift, Hank. That's something they'll take with them throughout their journey together. *Their song.*"

"You're layin' it on a little thick, there, Sally," he teased as he laid his jacket over her shoulders.

"Never. I'm no gusher. If anything, that was an understatement. My little sister just got married, Hank. If I could sing, I'd be…" She adjusted the jacket and began to sway. "You know what? I can dance." She did a tiny two-step, added a slow twirl, and then a more enthusiastic two-step and a spin. "I can dance. *I can…*"

She lost the twinkle in her toes, stumbled, and landed in a hoop made of two strong arms.

"Oops. I tend to be a little clumsy when I get excited. All I need is a strong partner." She copped a feel of his working-man's biceps as she steadied herself and eased up on him, catching a knowing look beneath the brim of his hat. He thought it a pratfall.

She smiled. "How about it?"

He took his time about tilting her upright, the corner of his mouth twitching. "How about I do the singin' and you do the dancin'?"

"They didn't set this up very well. The best man is married. What fun is that for a maid of honor?"

He bent to retrieve his jacket from the grass. "What kind of fun are you looking for?"

"The loosen-your-tie-and-kick-your-shoes-off kind. How about you?"

"If I start taking more clothes off, the party's over." He draped his jacket over her shoulders again. "I'll settle for a good meal and a little music."

"Ah, the quiet type. A challenge is always fun." She linked arms with him and made a sweeping gesture toward the lodge. "Shall we? Dinner's coming up soon. Right now the bar is open and the drinks are free."

"Free drinks would take away any challenge if I didn't have this booze-sniffin' bitch with me." The dog whined and perked her ears. "See? Phoebe don't miss a trick. No way am I goin' near any open bar, so just save me a seat at the dinner table."

"I've already arranged the place cards. You're next to me on the wagon." She had him walking now. Ambling. She was in no hurry. "Have you thought about my suggestion?"

"What suggestion?"

"Think of it as sort of a working vacation. Not hard labor, mind you. More like backup. Hang out with Hoolie and me. We can be quite entertaining. And according to Zach, you're unattached and somewhat flexible in your schedule." She looked up and gave a perfunctory smile. "I asked."

"Why would you do that?"

"Filling out your résumé. I didn't tell him you were thinking about applying for the job. So far, this is just between you and me."

"You're serious."

"Of course I'm serious. I want my sister's wedding to be perfect, and the perfect wedding includes a fabulous honeymoon." She gave his arm what she hoped felt like a winning squeeze. "I don't know what your somewhat flexible schedule looks like for the next few weeks, but you wouldn't have to miss any rodeos. Come and go as you please, but stow your gear with us for a while. That way there's another man around, and the honeymooners have nothing to worry about."

"What about the man? Should I be worried?"

"You don't strike me as a worrier."

"Long as I'm not hangin' with troublemakers, I got nothin' to worry about."

"No worries, then." She laughed. "I really don't make trouble. I fall into it sometimes, but who doesn't?" She looked up. "You?"

"Not lately."

"Maybe you need a little adventure in your life, Hank. Get out there, you know? Try new things. New people. I like to get while the gettin's good, but I'm always careful. You gotta be careful with the good stuff, right? Good people, good ideas, good times—there's a certain balance. A little daring goes a long way with a lot of careful." She wagged an instructive finger. "If we had an emergency, we'd call you."

"There's nobody crazier than Zach Beaudry when it comes to risking his neck, and you can tell him I said so."

"And he'll say he's changed." She stopped, turned, blocked his progress. "Will you think about it? What's three weeks?"

"How much time do I have to think about it?"

"About three hours." She pulled his jacket in tighter. "Do you have horses? I could pay you in horses. You know, the Indian way."

"Yeah, I know the Indian way. But you're talkin' Sally's way, and I'm goin' Hank's way. Nice try, though." He smiled. "I do like the way you swim."

"Dance with me tonight, and I'll swim with you later."

"For me, that's a whole lotta daring and not much careful." He slipped his arm around her shoulders. "Be damned if I'm not tempted to jump in."

Hank generally steered clear of big parties, but the Beaudry wedding was turning out to be a pretty good time. With beef for dinner and the prospect of Sally for dessert, he was happy to loosen his belt now and put his boots under her bed later. She hadn't been kidding about arranging the place cards. She'd given up her seat at the bride's table, supposedly so the best man could sit with his wife. She'd grabbed Hilda Beaudry and nodded toward Hoolie and Hank, who'd claimed a table on the sidelines and started

in on the bread basket. It was a good setup. Hank
wouldn't presume to guess where Hoolie pictured
parking his boots tonight, but he secretly wished the
old man whatever he could score. Hilda was definitely
enjoying the company.

"It's too bad you can't dance tonight, Hoolie,"
Hilda said, genuinely grieved.

Hoolie checked all his pockets. "Too many hidey-
holes in this monkey suit. I don't know where my
pocket knife went to. You got one on you, Hank? I'm
gonna cut this damn thing off."

"No nudity here, Hoolie." Sally winked at Hank.
"Wait till we're back in camp."

"Is that where you're hiding all the Double D's?"
Hank scanned the room. "'Cause I ain't seein' any
in this crowd."

"I'm talkin' about this mummy's boot I got on my
foot," Hoolie grumbled.

"How long you had it on?" Hank asked.

"About a month."

"About a week," Sally said.

"Sorry, Hoolie. You got a ways to go."

"I broke a wing before. Twice." Hoolie flapped
his folded arm. "But never a leg. Sure cramps a guy's
style."

"I'll request the Funky Chicken," Hilda promised.
"When the mother of the groom and the father of the
bride are both unattached, they get one of those spotlight dances. Right, Sally?"

"Absolutely. We make our own rules. Don't we,

Hoolie? I think I might have found us a sitter." She flashed Hank a smile. "Hank's almost convinced."

"What kind of a sitter?" Hoolie scowled.

"The kind who looks like he can keep the mice at bay while the cats go play. Hank's perfect, so help me put him over the edge." She laid her hand on Hank's shoulder and crooned, "Come on out to the big Double D, where the horses run wild and the cowboys live free."

Hank chuckled. "Yeah, that's gonna do it."

"Hell, yeah, we want those kids to have their honeymoon." Hoolie leaned closer to Hank. "You like horses?"

"He's a farrier," Sally said.

"Thought you was an MA or a PD or some kind of code for junior doctor."

"PA," Hank said. "Physician's assistant."

"For people, right? And you can shoe horses besides?" Hoolie grinned. "Yeah, you need to come see our place. You got some time? Say about—"

"Three weeks? They don't trust you to mind the store either, Hoolie?" Hank asked.

"They would if I hadn't gone and—"

Sally whapped Hoolie in the chest and nodded toward a paunchy silhouette in an oversized straw hat looming in the doorway to the dining room. "What's he doing here?"

Hoolie peered, squinted. "Don't ask me."

"Annie thought about inviting the Tutans. Double D diplomacy, she said, but after the last stunt he pulled—I know damn well it was him—I said it was him or me." Sally's hand found Hank's forearm again, but like Hoolie, he was zeroed in on the uninvited guest. "He cut our fence," she was saying. "We keep the old horses in a separate pasture, and Tutan cut the fence. He said he didn't, but it was definitely cut, and that's how Hoolie broke his ankle."

"That was my own damn fault."

"We have special fencing separating the young horses from the retirees and the convalescents. Those horses don't get through a four-strand fence without help." Sally slid her chair back. "I'm sure it was a trap. I don't know if it was set for the horses or for you, but I know he did it to cause us trouble. And he's about to get his."

"Hold on, girl." Hoolie's chair legs scraped the floor. "Not now."

"I don't want him anywhere near Annie's wedding."

"C'mon." Hank was the first one to his feet. "This is my kind of fun. Don't worry, Hoolie. We'll keep it civil." He smiled as he helped Sally with her chair. "But there's nothing wrong with showin' a little claw."

Tutan. The name ping-ponged within the walls of Hank's head as he took in the face for the first time. He kept pace with Sally, who had a point to make with every deliberate step. *No hurry. I'm in charge here.* His admiration for the woman's style grew with every moment he spent with her. And now, here was Dan Tutan. Her lease challenger. His father's leash holder. *Mr.* Tutan.

"We're on our way to Rapid City, thought we'd stop in and offer our best wishes. Did you get our gift?"

"We did. Thanks, but you really shouldn't have."

No *hello,* no *go to hell.* The way Sally was bristling and the man was posturing, Hank expected a little snarling. He was disappointed.

"We've been neighbors a long time, Sally." The man with the round, red face adjusted his hat, hitched up his pants, and finally folded his arms over his barrel chest. "We figured our invitation got lost in the mail."

"Annie wanted to keep it small. Family and close friends."

He eyed Hank. "Close friends?"

"Hank Night Horse." No handshake. A nod and a name were more than enough. "I've known Zach a long time."

"Night Horse." Tutan went snake eyed. "I had a guy by that name working for me years ago. Any relation to you?"

Keep looking, Mr. Tutan. "Where was he from?"

"I don't think he was from around here. Coulda been Montana. Isn't that where Beaudry's from?"

"Yeah, it is."

"I like that Crow Indian country up there. Real pretty. Is that where you're from?"

"Nope." *Crow country is Crow country.* "But Night Horse is a common name. Kinda like Drexler and Tutan."

"That guy that worked for me...there's something..." He kept staring, the rude bastard. But he shook his head. "No, if I remember right, he was shaped more like me." He patted his belly and laughed. "And he was a good hand. Except when he got to drinking. Fell off the wagon and got himself killed somehow. Hard to tell by the time his body was found, but they thought he might've been out hunting. That's one sport you don't want to mix with too much Everclear." He shook his head. "Tragic."

"Sounds like it." Hank stared dispassionately, kept his tone tame and his fists tucked into his elbows.

"Maybe that wasn't his name. Pretty sure it was some kinda Horse." Tutan turned to Sally. "You're looking fit. Some new kind of—"

"I'm doing well, thanks. *Very* well."

"Good. Good to hear." He tried to peer past Sally, but it was Hoolie who limped into view. "Good man, Hoolihan," Tutan enthused. "There's sure no keeping you down. Where's the bride? I just want to give her my best. I've known these girls most of their lives, and I want little Annie to know that the Tutans wish her well."

"She's on a tight schedule," Hank said. "We'll tell her you stopped in."

"This time tomorrow I guess the happy couple will be off on a nice honeymoon."

"That's the main reason I'm here." Hank drew a deep breath, steadying himself. "Zach and Annie won't have a thing to worry about. I'll be keepin' these two in line."

"You're gonna have your hands full, son." Tutan threaded his thumbs under his belly roll and over his belt as he moved in on Sally. "Tell your sister I wish her well. She and Beaudry would do well to get out of this crazy horse thing you've got going and live their lives. You and your wild ideas. You're just trying to keep your sister from leaving you without—"

Hank caught Sally in time to save Tutan from what undoubtedly would have been a nice right hook if she'd followed through.

Backpedaling, Tutan wagged his finger. "Your father's rolling over in his grave over what you've done to the Double D, Sally."

"This is a private party, Tutan," Hoolie said.

Tutan's angry gaze didn't waver. "Hell, girl, I'm sorry for all your troubles, but I ain't rollin' over. I've got a *real* ranch to run."

"Let me go," Sally grumbled as Tutan turned on his heel and stomped across the lobby.

Hank eased up, but he wasn't letting go until Tutan was out the door. "Marriage and murder are too much for one day."

She drew herself up and challenged him with a look. "You're the one who suggested showing some claw."

"A *little*."

"Night Horse," she said quietly. "He said the man worked for him."

"And you heard my answer."

"What I heard was…" She took his warning from his eyes. "Did you mean it? About helping out?"

"Actually, I was just sayin' it to help out, but then

he went and called me *son*." He gave a curt nod. "Yeah, if it'll make a difference, I'll stay."

"Let's go tell the bride and groom." She grabbed his hand. "You're just full of great gifts. They'll be calling you Santa Claus."

"You might be callin' me Scrooge. You kids won't be having any parties with me in charge."

"Actually…" She leaned in close, and he had half a mind to take that flower out of her hair so he could smell only Sally. She was giving him those eyes again, full of fireworks and mischief. "I'm looking forward to that part about the party being over."

He laughed. "You're the damnedest woman I ever met."

"Only when I'm at my best."

"Sally!" Glistening with bride shine, Annie burst on the scene, brushing Hank's arm as she reached for her sister. "Are you okay? Somebody said…"

"Everything's okay. Look. Not a scratch on me, and Tutan got off easy. Come with me to the bathroom." Sally put her unscratched arm around her sister's shoulders and wheeled her in the opposite direction. "I gotta go talk her down," she told Hank in parting. "Keep the big surprise under your hat."

For how long? Hank wondered as he watched the Drexlers head for the women's sanctuary. He'd be walking around with a bombshell under his hat until somebody took the detonator out of his mouth by whispering *Thanks, Hank, but you won't be needed after all.*

* * *

"It was nothing." Sally snatched a tissue from the box beside the sink and used it to dab a lipstick smudge from her sister's cheek. "Tutan said he was on his way to Rapid City and just stopped in to make sure you got his gift. Don't open it. It's probably some kind of curse on your firstborn."

"Did you put any scratches on him?"

"I came so close. If Hank hadn't interfered..."

"Then what?" Annie prompted. But before Sally's very eyes, the question of *what* took a mental backseat to the *who*. Annie smiled. "*Hank*. Zach was right. He said you two would hit it off."

"I'd like to see more of him." At least as much as he'd seen of her. Feeling good, looking fine—she glanced at herself in the mirror, just to make sure, yes—for now and however much longer, she would do her best to see and know, give and take with a man, *this* man.

She raised a cautionary finger. "Remember, Annie, I tell *who* I want, *when* and *if* I want. And for right now, I'm as healthy as you are. You haven't said anything, have you?"

"I hardly know the man."

Sally nodded. "I would have hit him."

"Hank?"

"No, Tutan. It would have felt *so good*. But Hank held me back." She smiled. "And that felt even better."

Annie gave her that what-are-you-up-to? look. She always recognized the signs. "You didn't sign us up for one of those reality shows, did you?"

"You mean like 'My Big Fat Redneck Wedding'?" Sally snapped her fingers. "Hey, we could have gotten some publicity for the sanctuary. I wish I'd thought of that." She laughed. "Just kidding."

"Seriously, you're having a good time?"

"I'm gonna dance my shoes off tonight, little sister." Sally fussed with Annie's golden curls. "You're so beautiful."

"You're giving me that look. What else have you got up your sleeve?"

"Are you kidding? I can barely hide my boobs in this dress." Sally winked. She could barely contain herself. "It's no wonder you're a teacher—you read me like a book. I do have a little surprise for you. I think. I hope. Like you said, we hardly know the man."

"Another song?"

"You want another song?" Sally leaned closer to the mirror and adjusted her décolleté. "I'll see what I can do."

Hank sang "Can I Have This Dance?" for Zach and Ann Beaudry, who waltzed alone in the spotlight, surrounded by family and friends smiling in the dark. Beautiful people. Sally's throat tingled. Her eyes smarted with happy tears. Her heart was fuller than she could have imagined in the days before the wedding, when her only sister was still a bride-to-be and Hank Night Horse was simply a name on a list. She wanted to catch the moment and slip it into a magic bottle, preserve it in all its sensory glory for a time when her senses would not serve and she would turn to memory.

Hank left the cheers and applause to the bride and groom and the music for the wedding party dance to the DJ. Sally smiled as the best man reported for duty, but by the time she was able to get a good look past Sam's nicely tailored shoulder, her private man of the hour had disappeared. She added his modesty to the growing list of his irresistible qualities and committed herself to leaving him alone for a few minutes.

But when she escaped to the terrace, her commitment fell by the wayside at the sight of the guitar leaning against the balcony along with the man seated on the top rail. A sinking feeling in her legs urged her to pull him down before he fell backward, but she fought her foolishness with a slow, deep breath. Strong sensation was good, even the silly, sinking kind. Anything was better than numbness, which would be slinking back sooner or later along with whatever other anomalies the erratic disease lurking in her body had in store. She threw back her shoulders and walked the planks, taking care not to turn an ankle over the kitten heels that had been her compromise to the killer spikes she'd longed to wear just this once and the safe flats Annie had tried to talk her into.

He watched her. He didn't smile much, this man with the breathtaking voice, but as the bright lights and music fell away from the starry night, he summoned her with his steady gaze.

"What took you so long?" he asked quietly.

"I've danced with Sam and his boy, Jimmy. I've danced with Zach. I've even danced with their mother. But I have not danced with you. Do you always sing and run?"

"Yep."

"If I didn't know better, I might have gone looking for you at the bar."

"But you do know better."

"I do." She stood close enough to touch him, but she laid her hand on the railing and reveled in the feel of the wood and the wanting. "You've been with Phoebe?"

"Took her for a walk. Had to keep her on a tight leash when some guy came along with something that looked like a giant poodle. Phoebe was ready to tear into that thing."

"Blessed are the peacemakers."

"You're right." He came down from the railing like a cat, languidly stretching one long leg at a time, pulled her to him with one arm, took her free hand and tucked it against his chest. "We should dance."

"Mmm-hmm. This is nice." She swayed in his arms, brushing against him just enough to incite sweet shivers. "Peaceful, but not still."

"If I didn't know better, I'd say we'd met before."

"In another life?"

"How many do you have?"

"Three at least, maybe more. But I'm sure this is the only one I've met you in."

He laughed. He thought she was joking.

"So far," she said, and he drew her closer. She rested her head on his shoulder and inhaled his zesty scent, wondering what he tasted like and how soon she would find out. "But I know what you mean. It feels like we needed no introduction."

"It was a jaw-dropping introduction. Maybe it wasn't necessary, but I sure wouldn't trade it for a handshake."

"You barged in on the life behind door number one. Good choice."

"Phoebe has good instincts."

If anyone but her sister had interrupted, Sally would have hissed mightily.

"Is this a private party?" Annie ventured.

Sally peeked around Hank's shoulder and smiled. "Not if we can wangle a private audience with the bride and groom." She gave Hank's hand a quick squeeze. "We have a proposition for you."

Zach laughed. "I told you somebody was getting propositioned."

"Tell them, Hank." Sally flashed him a smile, but he wouldn't buy in that far. She turned the smile on her sister. "You two are going on that honeymoon."

"Maybe this fall," Ann said. "Or this winter, or—"

"Maybe *this week.* I ran a little contest, and Hank won himself an all-expenses-paid vacation at the Double D Dude Ranch."

"Wait a minute," Hank said. Sally held her breath. "I thought you ran a little want ad, and I got *hired.*"

Sally exhaled a laugh, inhaled relief. "You didn't

qualify for the job, but all applicants were automatically entered into the drawing for a vacation, and you're our winner."

"What'd I tell you, Horse?" Zach clapped his hand on his friend's shoulder. "You come to my wedding, you're bound to get lucky."

"Sally, you didn't." Ann's eyes sparkled. She was on top of the world, but she would gladly make room for her sister.

"Didn't what? Award the grand prize already? He's not *that* lucky." Sally glanced askance, giving Hank a coy smile. "But the winner of the vacation may become eligible for—"

"No, no, no," Ann said. "It's the second-sweetest offer I've heard all day, but we can't go halfway around the world and leave Hank to take care of things at the Double D. It's way too much to ask. He has places to go and things to do."

"Which is why I'll be the one taking care of things at the Double D. All Hank has to take care of is your peace of mind. And he's happy to do that." Sally linked arms with Hank. He wasn't going anywhere anytime soon. "Right, Hank?"

"Absolutely. You two lovebirds enjoy yourselves. I'll stand guard over the nest while you're gone."

"Oh, Hank, we really appreciate the offer, but with—"

"But nothing," Sally said. "It's perfect."

"I have a couple of commitments to work around, but Sally's been telling me about the program you're running, and I'm interested. I can use a little—" Hank slid Sally a conspiratorial glance "—diversion."

"Can we trust these two?" Ann asked her new husband.

"I can vouch for Hank. Salt of the earth. Even if we had eggs in the nest, I'd trust him."

"Nobody's vouched for *you* yet," the bride reminded her sister. She looked up at Zach. "Is it safe to leave the salt of the earth with a shaker that doesn't always have her head screwed on straight?"

"I do like to shake things up," Sally said. She glanced up at Hank. "I used to be a mover, too, but that's a lot of work."

"I don't shake easy," he told her.

"Hank's the right man for the job," Zach said. "I'd even trust him with Zelda."

"You hear that?" Sally asked Ann. "If Zach's willing to leave the keys to his precious pickup in Hank's hands, you know your sister is safe."

"Can we still do it? I mean, we canceled the reservations, but we still have the tickets." Ann turned to Hank. "I don't travel that much, and I would've been happy with an extra night right here in the Hills, but Sam gave us this trip to Australia. *Australia.* I've always wanted to…"

"You go, Mrs. Beaudry," Hank said. "Live the dream."

"I owe you, man."

"Damn straight, cowboy." Hank waved a cautionary finger at the groom, but his warning was for the bride. "I don't ever wanna see this guy on my exam table again."

"That makes two of us. But, Sally—"

"Best behavior," Sally promised. "Pinky swear."

Chapter 3

Hank had never considered himself to be a cowboy, but he was a horseman. He owned two mares, pastured them at what was now really his brother Greg's place up north, just across the state line. Hank also owned some of the land, but Greg's cattle used it. All Hank asked in return was a room, a mailing address and a place to keep a few horses. He didn't take up much space.

Hank was no breeder or fancier, wasn't out to acquire pedigrees or trophies. He'd rescued the two mares from a farm foreclosure. They'd been bony and riddled with parasites, about as sad eyed and desperate as the old man who was losing all he had and looking for somebody, *any*body with a heart to take in the last of his stock. Hank had even offered to adopt the farmer, but his niece had shown up for that end of the rescue. Wormed, fed up, trimmed up and turned out on Dakota grass, the two mares had turned out to be pretty nice. Not the best of his rescues—he'd taken in a sweet-tempered colt that had gone to a couple looking for a friend for their autistic child—but they would make good saddle horses if he ever found the time to work with them.

Three hundred miles northeast of the Hilltop Lodge, Hank checked in at home and took care of his personal business. The next day he drove nearly the same distance due south to the Double D. Not that he was in a killing hurry to start his "vacation"—a vacation for Hank would have meant stringing together a few nights in what he loosely termed his own bed—but he had promises to keep and curiosity to satisfy. He cared a lot about his friend Zach Beaudry. He'd heard a lot about the Double D. He'd thought a lot about Sally Drexler. He had a bad feeling about her neighbor. It all added up to a sense of purpose, and Hank Night Horse was a man of purpose.

He called ahead to make sure he knew where he was going once he ran out of map markings. The two-story farmhouse was off the state highway at the end of about three miles of sparsely graveled road. He found Sally waiting for him on the sprawling covered porch. She came down the steps to greet him.

"Hey, Phoebe."

Okay, so she greeted his dog first. Unlike Hank, Phoebe was not above making a slobbering fool of herself.

"You just missed the honeymooners," Sally told him, her eyes unmistakably alight for him.

"You got time for TV?" He wasn't above grinning.

"I've always got time for a comedian." She took a hands-on-hips stance and gave his pickup with its custom long-box cap an appreciative once-over. The sleek, slide-in cargo box was outfitted for his business and his gypsy lifestyle. "You must have done just about what the newlyweds did. Grabbed your gear and run. Of course, they had a plane to catch. Are you hungry? Tired? Ready to rock 'n' roll?"

"I'll do anything that doesn't involve sitting."

She raised her brow. "Interested in reclining?"

"If I do that, I'm liable to be out for a while."

"Then let's walk and talk before we eat, drink and be merry." She gave a come-on gesture. "I'll show you around."

Her walk wasn't quite as smooth as her talk. He'd noticed it before, but it was so subtle, he'd dismissed it as another of her quirks. Sally wasn't your standard model female in any way, shape or form. She was special. Easy to follow, hard to figure, no doubt heavy on the upkeep.

Hardly the best fit for Hank Night Horse. He was an ordinary man who talked with a straight tongue and tried to walk a straight line. He understood most people—once you figured out what they wanted, for better or worse they were generally predictable—but Sally was like a horse he'd ridden for an elderly neighbor when he was a kid. Four out of five days the beautiful Arabian was smart, spirited, smooth-gaited, a dream to ride. But on the fifth day she'd likely take off with him and run like a hellcat until they hit some kind of a wall. She was four-fifths dream and one-fifth damned, but she was special. And four days out of five, she sure was fun to play with.

He wasn't sure about the hitch in Sally's gait. It was slight and oddly sporadic. An old injury wouldn't seem to explain it, and maybe there was no explanation. Maybe it was just Sally.

They entered the machine shed through a side door, which was propped open for ventilation. Hoolie looked up from a workbench and then slid off the stool before he remembered he wasn't going anywhere without his crutch.

He grinned anyway and reached for Hank's handshake. "Did you bring all the tools of your trades? My saddle horse could use corrective shoes, and I'll pay you to take this damn mummy boot off my hoof."

"Like I told you before, you take that off too soon, you'll pay dearly. Your horse is a different story. My pickup is a blacksmith shop on wheels. Phoebe!" The dog was headed for the door.

"Does she get along with other dogs?" Sally asked.

"Sure does. She's around dogs all the time."

A warning growl sounded outside the door.

"Well, that makes one of them," Hoolie said ominously as a black-and-white shepherd slunk across the threshold, teeth bared.

"Baby!"

Sally bolted for the door, but she fell flat on her face before she got there. Tripped over her own feet like one of the TV comedians she'd claimed she always had time for. She was doing a shaky push-up on the concrete by the time Hank got to her. She tried to wave him off, her attention fixed on the dogs.

Hoolie came on strong once he had his crutch in place. "Here, you dogs, you want a piece o' me?"

The clamor settled into a war of whines, both bitches determined to get in the last whimper as Hoolie and his crutch prevailed.

Hank found himself down on one knee beside a woman who was on her way up. "You okay?"

"Yes! Yes, of course." She laughed as she braced her hand on his shoulder. "Totally wasn't ready for that. Scared me."

"They're okay," Hoolie called out. "Phoebe wants to play. Baby wants to lay down a few rules first."

"I'll give 'em some rules," Hank grumbled, discomfited by the loss of his dignity and his own confusion as to where it had gone.

Sally laughed again. "What are you, the Dog Whisperer?"

"I'm the alpha." He signaled Phoebe to stay put while the shepherd took a fallback position. "You got any other dogs around here?" he asked Sally.

"Baby's an only dog."

"That's her problem. We'll fix it, though. We'll teach her some manners. Won't we, Phoeb?" Hank patted the dog's silky head. "Scared you, huh?"

"It sure startled me." Sally twisted her arm for a look at her skinned elbow. "I didn't want to lose you over a dogfight. You've probably noticed I can be kind of a klutz sometimes. Two left feet." She gave a perfunctory smile. "Except when I dance."

"You stick to dancing and leave us to referee the dogs."

"Only if you'll dance with me, Henry." She was giving him that too cute look. "Do you know that song? You're supposed to say, *Okay, Baby.*"

Hank shook his head. "Nobody calls me Henry."

"That's your real name, isn't it?" She flashed a smile at Hoolie. "Henry's a fine name."

"*No*body calls me Henry."

"Ah, the soft underbelly. Our guardian is ticklish, Hoolie."

"I know the feeling," Hoolie said.

"I can handle a dogfight, but that name is a deal breaker."

"Duly noted." Sally slid a glance at Hoolie, who chuckled.

"Okay, now aren't you supposed to have some wild horses around here somewhere?"

"That's the rumor. But first, the tour." She gave an after-you gesture. "Please follow the silk thread."

Hank raised his brow and responded in kind. He knew her game. She was like his patients on the rodeo circuit—too stubborn to say they were hurt, so you didn't ask. You watched how they moved. *If* they'd let you.

"No go?" She grabbed his arm and coaxed him by her side. "All right, then, when you're ready to put your road-weary butt in a saddle, I'll show you horses, Henry. *Hank.*"

"You're askin' for it, woman."

"For what?" She met his loaded look with a coy smile. "Oh, no. I'm just hackin' on you. Make no mistake, when it comes to serious matters, I don't fool around." She glanced away. "Well, I do, but I don't ask. Do you?"

What he didn't do was answer foolish questions.

By the time he'd seen the outbuildings—shop, machine shed, barn, loafing shed, grain bins, bunkhouse—the suggestion of food held considerable appeal. He was impressed with what he'd seen so far. It was a nice layout, but the cattle operation was a shadow of what it had been in its heyday, two generations ago. According to Hank's tour guide, the Double D ran a small herd of cattle, partly to satisfy state requirements to claim agricultural status and partly for income. But the ranch's main enterprise was the wild-horse sanctuary, and it was decidedly nonprofit. An unusual concept for a third-generation rancher, but Sally Drexler was an unusual rancher. Hank looked forward to seeing the horses.

After his stomach stopped growling.

He hit the front steps heavily to cover the noise as he headed for the door behind Sally, but the twinkle in her eyes let him know she wasn't deaf. Embarrassing. He didn't like to give anything away unintentionally. Not even the fact that he hadn't taken time to eat anything before he left home.

Beset by the aroma of juicy beef, his stomach spoke up again as he followed her in the house while Phoebe protested having the door shut in her face.

"She can come in, as long as she's okay around cats," Sally said. "Sounds like she's hungry. We usually don't eat supper around here until pretty late, but we never keep the critters waiting."

"Something smells good." He stood like a maypole while Sally circled around him. "Enough to eat." He watched her let Phoebe in. "Right now."

She turned one of her bright-eyed smiles on him. "Right now?"

"Be glad to help you get it on."

"Would you?"

"On the table."

"I've always wanted to try that," she told him over her shoulder as she led the way through foodless territory. "But let's eat first."

Willing as he was, he didn't have to help much. He was a straight shooter, and she was a woman who loved to tease. She'd had supper simmering in a Crock-Pot, ready to dish up anytime. She put him to slicing bread and filling water glasses while she washed salad greens. Hoolie came in the back door all slicked down and washed up precisely at five-fifteen.

Pretty late, my ass.

Pretty tasty. Pretty entertaining. Pretty woman. Maybe he could get used to a little teasing.

"How much of the Double D can you reach on wheels?" Hank asked as he sipped his coffee. "You use ATVs?"

"Hell, no," Hoolie said. "Too damn noisy. This is a ranch, not a playground."

"I'm with you on that score." And he'd told his

brother as much last night when Greg had shown off a picture of the one he wanted. A kid's toy, Hank had said.

"We can cover a lot of ground in a pickup, but there's places we don't go except on horseback."

"We have some totally pristine grassland here," Sally said. "Some of it is pretty remote."

"I'll stow my gear in the bunkhouse, and then maybe we could all take a little pickup ride," Hank suggested. "Give me a feel for what's out there while it's still light."

"We can do that." Sally sounded hesitant. "But we have a room for you here in the house."

"I'm fine with the bunkhouse."

"We get kids out here sometimes helpin' out. Volunteers come and go. You'll be better off in the house." Hoolie shrugged. "I snore."

"We're hoping to add on to the bunkhouse to give Hoolie more privacy." Sally and Hoolie exchanged looks. "Definitely on the to-do list."

"Definitely," Hoolie said. "Sally's used to having Annie around. And Zach, too, since he come along. We don't want Sally rattlin' around here alone at night."

"She could get into trouble?" Hank set his cup down. "Hell, whatever works. I just figured…"

"It's a big house," Hoolie said. "And you're a guest more than anything. I'm the hired man."

Hank looked at Sally. He had something she wanted, and she'd decided it was hers for the taking. She'd try to tease it out of him, would she? He gave a suggestive smile. *Game on, woman. Your house, my play.*

"Do *you* snore?" he asked her.

"I've never had any complaints."

Hoolie took Sally's unspoken hint and begged off the after-supper tour. "I'll let you take my pickup." He offered Hank two keys and a metal Road Runner trinket on a key ring.

Ignoring the handoff, Hank nodded at Sally. "She's giving the tour."

"This thing he offers is a great honor," Sally quipped, B-movie style. "To refuse would be an insult."

"She's a 1968 C10," Hoolie boasted. "She's a great little go-fer pickup. Short box with a six-pony engine. Overhauled her myself."

"Classic," Hank said appreciatively. "My dad had one when I was a kid. Got her used, ran her into the ground. He was on the road a lot."

"Don't know how many times the odometer's turned over on this one, but she runs like a top. You gotta try 'er out."

"My pleasure."

Watching Hank handle the big steering wheel and palm the knob on the gearshift was Sally's pleasure. She'd stopped driving altogether after proving she really could hit the broad side of the barn. It was the first time she'd lost all feeling in her right leg, the one that gave her the most trouble. She'd been backing up to the barn with a load of mineral blocks when suddenly the leg was gone. Might as well have been lopped off at the hip. By the time she'd moved the dead weight by hand, her tailgate had smashed through the tack-room wall.

The damage to the barn had been easy to repair. Her pickup, like her pride, had become an early victim of her unpredictable body. But her independence had begun to erode that day, and with it went bits of confidence. Dealing with the disease wasn't as difficult as plugging up holes in her spirit. During bad times she'd start springing holes right and left, and she could feel herself draining away. She'd learned to take advantage of the very thing that made MS so cruel—its capricious nature. When the symptoms ebbed, she dammed up all her leaks and charged ahead, full speed, total Sally. She took pleasure in the little things, like the way it felt to get up and walk whenever the spirit moved her, the feel of water lapping against bare skin, the smell of a summer night and the look of a man's hands taking charge.

Phoebe was sitting pretty in the pickup box behind the back window, her blond ears flapping in the breeze. They plied the fence line at a leisurely pace, following tire tracks worn in the sod. Sally pointed out the "geriatric bachelor band" grazing in a shallow draw. They were too old for the adoption program, and some of them had spent years in holding facilities—essentially feedlot conditions—before finding a home at the Double D. Heads bobbed, ears perked at the sound of the engine, and they moved as one, like a school of fish.

"They have no use for us, especially this time of year," she said with a smile. "Which means we're doing something right." She nodded for a swing to the west, punched the glove-compartment button and felt around for the binoculars. "From the top of that hill we might get a look at some of the two-year-olds. There are some beauties in that bunch. Do you like Spanish Mustangs?"

He swung the big steering wheel. "I don't see too many."

"They don't come shoe shopping?"

"I work mostly rodeos, so I see a lot of quarter horses." The engine growled as he downshifted for the hill. "I did shoe a couple of mustangs at an endurance ride last fall. They had real pretty feet."

"We need to interest more people in adopting these horses. The BLM had an auction out in Wyoming last month and sold less than half the number they projected. If they don't find any more takers and we can't make room for them, some of them will end up…" She glimpsed movement below the hill and to the right, but she had to turn her head to see what it was. Her right eye was going out on her again. *Damn.* "Look!" She pushed the binoculars against his arm. "Stop! Hurry, before they get away."

"Look, stop, hurry?" He complied, chuckling. "How about hurry, stop, look? Or—"

"Shh!" She tapped him with the binoculars again, and he took them and focused. "How many? Can you tell?"

"Eight. Nine."

"See any you like?"

"Nice red roan. Three buckskins. Aw, man, would you look at that bay."

He offered her a turn with the binoculars, but she shook them off. "I can't use those things. But I know which one you mean. He looks just like his daddy. Fabulous Spanish Sulphur Mustang stallion we call Don Quixote." She nodded as he put the binoculars up to his face again. *Stop, take a look, really see.* "Give that boy another year, and you'd have yourself an endurance racer, a cutting horse, whatever your pleasure."

"You won't have any trouble finding him a good home." He glanced at her. "If you're having trouble with numbers, show me what's left after the next auction."

"We can usually place a few more with special programs. Police units, military, youth programs, even prisons."

"After all's said and done, show me what's left. Never met a horse I didn't like." He handed her the binoculars. "I'd sure like to see that bay up close."

"You will. They're getting cut this week."

"All of them?"

"Only the ones with balls. If you like the bay when you see him up close, he could be spared." She smiled at him as she snapped the glove compartment shut. "Which puts his balls in your court."

"Damn." He chuckled as he lifted his hand to the key in the ignition.

"He'd make a wonderful stud." She stayed his hand

with hers and slid to the middle of the bench seat. "This is my favorite time of day. Between sunset and dusk. Late meadowlarks, early crickets."

He said nothing. The enigmatic look in his eyes wasn't what she expected. Maybe she'd misread his signals. Maybe her receptors were on the blink. Life's ultimate joke. Just when she was getting the *go* light on all major systems except her troublesome right eye, which wasn't a major system at the moment.

She would not take this lying down.

Who was she kidding? She'd take him any way she could get him, but in a small pickup, lying down wasn't gonna happen.

Alternatives?

"Did you ever go parking in your father's C10?" she asked.

"He was dead and the pickup was gone by the time I started meetin' up with girls after sunset."

"Where did you meet them?"

"Down by the river. You're fifteen and you get a chance to be with a girl, you're not lookin' to take the high ground."

"Fifteen?"

"Late bloomer." He moved the seat back as far as it would go and put his arm around her. "I like this time of day, too, Sally."

He leaned over her slowly, fingers in her hair, thumb grazing her cheek, lips moistened and parted just enough to make hers quiver on the cusp of his kiss. He made her feel dear and delicate, and she was having none of it. She slipped her arm around his neck and answered his sweet approach with her spicy reception. She was no weak-kneed quiverer. She could match him slam for bam and thank you, man. She didn't need coddling, and she told him as much with a heat-seeking kiss.

The catch in his breath pleased her. The new-found need in his kiss thrilled her. She answered in kind, kissing him like there was no time like the present. Because there wasn't. Deep, caring kisses like his were rare. She drew a breath full of the salty taste and sexy scent of him and grazed his chest with her breasts. They drew taut within her clothing. She pushed her fingers through his hair, curled them and rubbed it against the center of her palm. She would fill her senses with him while she could, because she could. She slipped her free hand between them, found his belly, hard and flat as his belt buckle. She took the measure of both.

He nuzzled the side of her neck and groaned. "I'm not fifteen anymore," he whispered. "I can wait."

"Why would you? I'm not a girl."

He raised his head and smiled at her. "In this light you could be. Young and scared. A little confused, maybe."

She frowned. "But since I'm none of those things..."

"I don't know that." He caressed her face with the backs of his fingers. "Who said you could call all the shots?"

"Is there something wrong with me?" She swallowed hard. "I mean, something you don't like?"

"Uh-uh. Everything looks just right."

"Looks can deceive." She dragged her fingers from his belt to his zipper. "But this feels right."

"You don't wanna believe that guy." He moved his hips just enough to let her know that there was nothing wrong with him, either. "No matter what the question, he's only got one answer."

"He's honest," she whispered. "Stands up for what he believes in."

He kissed her again, so fully and thoroughly that the taste of his lips and the darting of his tongue, the strength of his arms and the sharp intake of his breath satisfied all her wishes. She had feeling in every part of her body. She didn't want it to go away, not one tingle, not one spark, and she reached around him and held him the way he held her. Maybe more so. Maybe harder and stronger and more desirous of him than he could possibly be of her, but she was honest. Her embrace was true to what she felt, and feeling was everything.

"Easy," he whispered, and she realized she had sounded some sort of alarm, made some desperate little noise. "You okay?"

She nodded. Laughed a little. God, she was such a *woman*. She was the one who was scaring him.

"Look at Phoebe," he said, and she turned toward the back window and laughed with him even though she couldn't really see anything. Her right eye had gone dark and her left was looking at the top of the seat. "I'm not hurtin' her, Phoeb. I swear."

The dog barked.

"Tell her," he whispered.

"I'm okay, Phoebe."

The dog jumped out of the box and up on the passenger's side door.

"Don't—"

Too late. Sally had already opened the door, and the dog was in her lap.

"Cut it out, Phoeb. I didn't break her. Down!"

Phoebe sat on the floor and laid her head on Sally's thigh.

Sally stroked her silky head. "The physician's assistant's assistant. We girls look after each other, don't we, Phoebe?"

"You can tell she's never been parking."

"It can be almost as much fun as skinny-dipping." Sally smiled into the big, round eyes looking up at her from her lap.

"And almost as risky," Hank said. But he still had his arm around her shoulders, and she loved the way it felt.

"I won't hurt him either, Phoebe. I swear."

Hoolie came out of the bunkhouse to meet them as soon as they parked his truck.

"You had a call from your favorite neighbor," he told Sally. "Claims a loose horse caused him to run into the ditch. I drove all the way up to his place and back, didn't see nothin'. No horse, no fence down, nothin'. Did you see anything?"

"We saw horses." Hank tossed Hoolie his keys. "Nice ride."

"They're right where they're supposed to be," Sally said.

"Except the high one Damn Tootin' rode in on. He said he reported *the incident* to the sheriff. You know what he's tryin' to do, don't you?"

"Drive me to commit murder?"

"Build some kind of a case. You know how he loves to sue people."

"Good. We'll kick his ass in court. That might be more fun than murder."

"Maybe he's trying to wear you down." Hoolie planted his hands on his indeterminate hips. "Keep you dancin' till you drop."

Sally sighed. "The trouble is he's got friends in high places."

"So do you," Hoolie said. "Maybe not so much around here, but there's high places all over the country, and they're full of horse lovers."

"Good point." Sally glanced at Hank. "The trouble is, sometimes those high places are too far off. All politics is local."

"A politician is your friend until he gets a better offer."

"*The trouble is* we don't have any more to offer."

"I didn't say *more*. I said better." Hoolie folded his arms. "Don't dance for him. You can put your energy to better use. Not to mention your considerable imagination."

"Another good point." She smiled. "Thank you for persisting in making it."

"No trouble." He stepped back. "I'll say good night, then."

Hank took his keys from his pocket, clicked the remote and whistled for Phoebe.

"Where are you going?" Instantly, Sally wished she could call back the question, or at least the anxious tone.

"Nowhere. Putting Phoebe to bed and getting my stuff."

"You're making her sleep in the pickup? Phoebe!" The dog perked her ears, but she stood her master's ground. "Oh, Hank, she can come in the house with you."

"You keep your dog in the house?" He sounded surprised. "We go by house rules."

"Baby has her own corner in the bunkhouse. We have a cat in the house, but she doesn't believe in dogs. She barely acknowledges people. I'll bet Phoebe's used to sleeping with you."

"The Lakota don't sleep with their dogs," he said. "Phoebe sleeps wherever I put her bed. Where do you want her?"

"I didn't mean to insult you. I just didn't want you to think you had to—"

He challenged her with a hard look and a harder stance. "What's the big damn deal about my sleeping arrangements?"

"It's no big damn deal. You do what you want. I just want Phoebe to be comfortable."

"Comfortable? Okay, she likes to sleep on the east

side of the house near an outside door and an open window on a feather bed."

"That can be arranged." She spun away and tripped.

He caught her. "What's wrong, Sally?"

"Defensive clumsiness. When I get rattled, I spaz out sometimes. Great way to ruin a dramatic gesture." She glowered. "What's your excuse?"

"Defensive gruffness."

"That's against house rules, but we'll call it even since it sounded like good ol'-fashioned sarcasm to me. I can hardly fault anybody for that." She signaled, "No penalty."

"You sure you want me to bring her bed in the house?"

"I'm sure this dog gets every vaccination and preventive treatment on any vet's list. So I want you to put her bed where the sun don't shine—" she smiled "—in the afternoon."

He hauled his duffel bag and Phoebe's denim pillow into the house and settled the dog down. He wasn't kidding about the outside door. Then he followed Sally through the living room, around the stairs, and down the hall, where they crossed paths with a calico cat, which scampered up the stairs.

"This is my room," Sally said of the first door in the hall. "It's also my office. Next is the main bath. I'll work around your shower schedule." She pushed the last door open and flipped the light on. "I'm putting you in this room because Zach and Annie have the upstairs. This used to be Grandma's room, which is why everything's purple. But now it's a guest room. I think you'll be comfortable. The trees shade the windows and keep it cool. There's a half bath through there. Say the word if you need anything. Help yourself in the kitchen anytime, anything you want. There's a TV in the den, just off the living room. And, um…" She looked up at him. "Thank you for doing this for us."

"No trouble."

"That I can't guarantee. Sleep well."

"You, too. I enjoyed the tour."

She gave a little nod, a wistful smile. She didn't quite know what to make of him, and he hadn't quite decided what to do with her.

It was going to be an interesting three weeks.

Chapter 4

"Kevin's back," Hoolie announced as he came thumping in the back door. "Add one for supper. Any coffee left?"

"It's cold, but you can nuke it. I'm brewing iced tea."

Sally laid aside the ice pack she'd been using on her right eye and filled the teakettle. Hoolie was still banging around in the mudroom, and she was only getting about half of what he was saying, but she'd catch up on the rerun. He had a habit of repeating himself, especially if one of the teens court-ordered to work at the sanctuary was giving him trouble.

"So I've got him ridin' fence along the highway," was the upshot as he clomped into the kitchen. "You know damn well there was no horse on the road, but that don't mean Tutan didn't put another hole in the fence to back up his story. We got some volunteers set to help cut hay this weekend. So Hank and me, we're gonna…" He noticed the ice pack. "You feelin' okay, big sister?"

"I'm not okay with that question." Cold packs were her standard first-line remedy, and they were helping. Loss of vision in one eye wasn't unusual with multiple sclerosis, but neither was remission. She'd had this problem before and regained a good measure of sight back. She'd do it again without losing ground anywhere else. Not for a good long while.

She closed the microwave door on his cold coffee and pressed the button. "My health is my business. I want nothing but positive health vibes. That wheelchair is staying in the basement. There's only one person around here who needs a cane."

"Crutch."

"This reprieve could last for months. Years, maybe."

"Trouble with your eye again?"

"A little, but I'm loading up on vitamins." She believed in vitamins. Exercise, meditation, hydrotherapy—she believed in believing. She popped the microwave open and handed Hoolie his coffee. "You and Hank are going to what?"

"Move the cows."

"You can't ride with that ankle."

"I'm not okay with that order." He pulled two chairs away from the kitchen table, sat in one and propped his foot with its dirtier-by-the-day cast on the other. "I'm taking this damn thing off. My foot itches. That means the mummy boot has been on long enough."

"What does Hank say?"

Hoolie questioned her with a look.

"He's a professional."

"You ask him about your eye, and I'll ask him about my ankle."

"No deal." She snatched the whistling kettle off the stove. "I know more about MS than most doctors. These symptoms come and go. Eventually, some of them come and stay, but I'm not on any fast track to eventually." She pointed to his ankle. "*That* is going to heal. Give it time, and it'll go the way of all your other previously broken bones."

"My health is my business," he echoed in an irritating falsetto.

"Not when all your stories end with *I got the scars to prove it.*"

"I tell it like I remember it. The truth is always in there somewhere." He sipped his coffee. "I said I'd look after you."

"Look all you want. Just don't talk about it." She laid a hand on his bony shoulder. "I'll ride with Hank. We'll move the cows, and then we'll ride out to Coyote Creek and see if we can get a look at the Don."

"If something happens, you tell him why. You wouldn't fall so much if you'd keep a cane handy when you get tired or—"

"Three weeks." She squeezed his shoulder. "That's all I'm asking."

* * *

Hank was finishing up the hooves on the saddle horses when Sally came looking for him in the barn. From the first, he'd had her figured for a night person. Seemed he was right. Their ships would be passing mid to late morning, which was fine by him. Hoolie had filled him up with a hearty breakfast while they planned a few things out. He met one of the helpers he kept hearing about—Indian kid named Kevin Thunder Shield, who showed up ready to ride. Hoolie hooked the kid up with a horse and gave him an assignment, but Hank couldn't let the gelding go without a hoof trimming. And he wasn't herding any cattle until the rest of the saddle horses got the same treatment.

"That looks great," Sally said of the third set of hooves he'd filed. "You are *good*."

"The trim's the important part. Right, girl?" He patted the black mare's rump. She'd behaved well. Hard to believe she'd ever been wild. "The shoes are icing on the cake. It's getting the right trim that makes the difference for most horses."

"We go easy on the icing around here."

"And that's fine. These horses don't have to hang out in stalls and watch their toenails grow. Except that one." He pointed to a big gray gelding. "Without shoeing that crack will keep growing."

Sally ran her hand down the horse's leg toward the hoof. "I didn't see that."

"I'll take care of it when we get back. Hoolie and me, we're gonna do some cowboyin'."

She straightened and faced him with folded arms. "You were going to let Hoolie ride with that cast on his foot?"

"I was gonna ride with Hoolie. Figured he could do what he wanted with his foot."

"Any objection to riding with me?"

He shrugged. "I'm here to help out."

"Weak," she warned.

"Let me try again. Objection? Hell, no. My pleasure."

"That's the spirit." She gave a tight smile. "I'm an excellent cowboy."

"I don't doubt it."

She sighed and put her arms around the big gray gelding's neck, nuzzling his thick black mane. "But I was hoping to ride Tank."

"Tank?" Hank chortled. "I'll have Tank retreaded for you by tomorrow." He started loading his files and nippers into his shoe box. "I thought I'd try a Double D mustang. Maybe Zach has some started. I'm a pretty good finisher."

"Me, too."

"Once they're green broke, I can put a nice handle on 'em."

"I'll bet." She raked her fingers through the gelding's mane. "Tank was my first adoption. When I picked him out ten years ago, he was as wild as they come. I was a stock contractor back then, but Tank really opened my eyes."

Hank eyed the horse. "He's no Spanish Mustang."

"Of course not. Like so many wild horses, he's

got a lot of draft blood in him. You know, a lot of them just sort of walked off into the sunset back in the days when farmers started going horseless. And during the Depression, when they were going home-less. Tank's forebears were equine hobos." She un-hooked one of the horse's cross-ties. "Can't you just see them running across a herd of mustangs in the Badlands? Freeee at last!" she whinnied, and Tank's ears snapped to attention.

Hank couldn't help smiling. "Until they got their farm-boy asses kicked."

"This big steel-drivin' man's gonna fix your hoof, Tank, so let's let that remark pass." She hooked a lead rope to the halter, scratched the horse's neck, and he lowered his head. "If he calls you farm boy, he's Henry," she said in the horse's ear.

"Nothin' wrong with Henry."

"I didn't say there was. Some of my best friends are named Henry."

"Hoolie?" he asked. She nodded. "Like I said, it's a good backup name. What's yours? Bet your mama didn't name you Sally."

"Ain't tellin'. It's a good name, but it doesn't fit me, so I don't use it." She pointed to a small buck-skin gelding. "I'm riding him. He fits me well. We call him Little Henry."

Hank cracked up.

They rode side by side, soaking in sights and sounds and smells of summer in South Dakota with-out talking much. It was enough to point out the circling hawk, the coyote on the hill, the hidden gopher hole and to keep riding, keep looking and listening to the birds in the air, the insects in the grass, the *thump-swish-thump* of their mounts. It all felt right to Hank, as though he, too, had found a fit. Be damned if he'd try to work up some discomfort over feeling comfortable, not while it was working for him. This feeling was sacred.

He'd gotten away from the traditional practices his parents' generation had struggled to take back from obscurity—ceremonies nobody wanted to explain and a language hardly anybody used—but he'd soaked up the stories. The People had emerged from the Black Hills. *Paha Sapa.* White Buffalo Calf Woman had given them the pipe, and the horse—*Sunka Wakan,* or sacred dog—had given them a leg up in a land only the Lakota truly understood and appreciated in its natural state. It was grassland. Pull the grass up by the roots, and the earth would fly away. Tell the river how to run, and you would pay a price that had less to do with money than with home. And home, for the Lakota, had less to do with a place to live than with a place to walk.

Preferably a dry one.

Hank loved the stories and honored the wisdom even if he'd taken up a different kind of medicine. Even if he'd let his family fall apart—the traditional Lakota's worst nightmare—he believed that all people were relatives. All things? Being equal—not in this lifetime. But being relative? Sure. Relative to family life, being alone sucked.

Relative to reservation life, the old ways were healthy and holy. Relative to urban life, the reservation wasn't half bad.

But relative to anyplace he'd ever been—and he'd been all over—the vicinity of the Black Hills felt right.

The Double D was southeast of the Hills, but Hank could see their silhouette looming at the edge of the grasslands like a hazy purple mirage, a distant village of ghost tipis. The sight was beyond beautiful. Its power worked his soul's compass like polar magnetism. His whole body knew what it was about. It had been years since he'd pushed cattle on horseback, and while the method hadn't changed, he realized the madness was gone. He was no longer the angry young man who resented the cattlemen who leased the Indian land its owners couldn't afford to use. It didn't matter that none of the animals belonged to him or that the land they were crossing was claimed by someone else. He was one with the horse, and the woman who rode abreast of him functioned easily as his partner. Cows moved willingly as long as their calves bleated regularly to check in. They must have known the grass was greener wherever they were headed. Maybe they trusted Sally not to let them down. They belonged to her, after all. They must have known something.

You've never had much luck with women, Night Horse. Maybe you should take it from her animals. Just go along with her. Nothing to worry about.

Either that or just take it. Take as much as she offers. Hell, the first few weeks are always the best.

Hank drew in a whole chestful of clean Black Hills air. He had a bad habit of thinking too deep and breathing too shallow. He was attracted to this woman, pure and simple. Thinking only complicated the matter.

Stop thinking, Night Horse. Enjoy the pure and simple. She's pure. You're simple.

Sally loved the way her world looked from the top of a horse. The way Little Henry's gait made her hips move, the way he smelled, the way he snorted and strutted and swished his tail and made her sit up a little straighter, feel just slightly bigger than life—she loved every heady detail. But put the joy of sitting her horse together with the pleasure of watching Hank sit his, and Sally was all sweet spot. Watching him swing down from the saddle and open a wire gate gave her goose bumps. Pushing the cattle through the gate gave a taste of success, and making it happen together rubbed her utterly the right way.

She watched him muscle the wire loop over the top of the gate post, admired his easy mount, lit up inside when he looked her way as if to say, *What can I do for you now?*

"Follow me," she called out. "Let's take a ride to the wild side."

Little Henry pricked his ears, and Sally shifted her weight and gave him his head. She bid her hat good riddance as the wind rushed through her hair. Hank could have flown past her if he wanted to—his mare was faster than her little gelding—but he gave his horse cues according to her pace. When they reached the creek, Little Henry splashed right in. The crossing required a few yards of swimming this time of year, but nothing major.

For Sally.

She *whooped* and the water *swooshed* as Little Henry bounded up on dry land. Wet to the hip, she was loving every drop of water, every ray of sunshine, every bit of breeze. She circled her mount and saw Hank eyeing the water warily from the opposite bank.

"Don't worry," she called out. "She's a good swimmer."

"I'm not."

"You don't have to be. I promise."

He looked up at her. He'd held on to his hat, but clearly he wasn't so sure about the value of her promise.

"I can go back and lead you across."

"Hell, no." He continued to stare at the water. "What's my horse's name?"

"Ribsy."

"What kind of a name is that for a horse?"

"It's from a book. My sister named her." What difference did it make? What the heck was in a horse's name? He wasn't moving. Wasn't looking at anything but the water. Needed a moment, maybe. "My sister, the teacher. It's a kid's book." No connection. "Ribsy's Henry's best friend." Still no movement. "Ribsy's a dog."

He looked up. "This horse is named after a dog?"

"Henry and Ribsy. Ribsy's a dog."

"Hoka Hey!" Hank called out as he nudged the mare with his boot heels.

She took the plunge. Hank kept his seat, and the big black easily ferried him across the water. He looked a little sallow, but his dignity was still intact.

"What did you call me?" Sally asked, grinning like a proud instructor. "Hooker something?"

"I said, *Hoka Hey!* It's a good day to die." He leaned forward and patted the mare's neck. *"Sunka Wakan."*

"That's right," she enthused. "It means *holy dog,* doesn't it? Well, there you go. Ribsy, Phoebe and me, we're your destiny. Stick with us, and your hydrophobia will be cured."

"What's that?" He glanced back at the murky water. "A monster with a bunch of arms?"

"I think that's a hydra."

"Yep. They're all down there." He looked up at her and smiled sheepishly as he joined her on the high ground. "Kind of embarrassing. I had a bad experience when I was a kid."

"Maybe you should try a different war cry."

They covered a lot of ground and saw a couple of eagles, a few deer and a few dozen mustangs before they found Don Quixote, a stout bay who'd surrounded himself with the prettiest mares on the Double D. There were roans and paints, mouse-brown grullos, buckskins and "blondies." After what had turned out to be a more tiring ride than she'd expected, Sally was energized simply by the sight of them, mainly courtesy of her left eye. But the vision of blue sky, green grass, striated hills and a motley band of mustangs was glorious. She didn't have to see Hank's excitement. She could feel it. His rapt interest was palpable.

"Let's get down for a while," he said quietly, as though speaking might disturb something.

She nodded. He must have sensed her weariness because he swung to the ground and came to her, and she dismounted with far less grace than she would have wished. He noticed. He didn't say anything, but he took her full weight in his arms, drew her up to him and recharged her with a deep, delicious kiss.

It wasn't until he took his lips from hers that she realized she couldn't feel her right leg. She had to hang on to him—not that she didn't want to, but not for this reason.

"You made the earth move under my feet," she said. "Either Night Horse or Charley horse, I'm not sure—ah!" The sound of sharp pain was an innocent lie, if there was such a thing. Everybody understood pain, at least to some extent. Numbness was harder to explain.

"Damn cousin Charley's beatin' my time." He supported her against his right side. "Can't let him get away with it." He brought the horses along on the left and found a little grass for everybody on the shady side of a clump of chokecherry bushes.

"Better already." Her butt welcomed contact with

good old terra firma, but she felt obliged to protest. "I'm okay now."

"Not so fast. I know how to—"

"Seriously, it's coming back."

"That's Charley for you. Right calf?" He massaged with practiced hands. She didn't feel much at first, but her nerves responded steadily to his gentle kneading. "This can be a sign of calcium deficiency."

"I'll load up on it tomorrow."

"I'm a big believer in truth and supplements for all."

"Good to know."

"Better?"

"Infinitely. Like your talents." Smiling, she grabbed his hand. "Wait. I think he's moving into my feet."

"Sorry, Charley," he quipped as he slid his hands down to her boot.

She stilled them with hers. "I'll take a rain check."

"Sounds good." He went to his saddle and brought back the canvas pack he'd tied behind the cantle. Squatting on his heels, he took out a bottle of water and cracked open the plastic cap. "It might be warm, but it's wet."

"You think of everything." She took a long drink.

"Second nature when you spend your life on the road."

"I'll bet you're starving. I do have supper waiting in the refrigerator. I almost brought something along, but then I thought, no, we'll be sweaty and dirty, and we'll appreciate it more after we get back, and it's nice and fresh and…" She handed him the bottle. "Annie would have packed a nice picnic. She's like you. She thinks of everything."

He took a drink from the bottle and laughed. "It's just water."

"I'm easy." She smiled. "Simple pleasures. I don't do this often enough. I used to ride out here all the time, but it's become…" She gazed at the bluffs in the distance. "I've become lazy. It's easier to hop in the pickup. And now that Zach's come on board…"

"You don't get out here in a pickup. It's too rough."

"And we don't want this area disturbed by anything motorized." She pointed west. "There's some public land beyond those hills. Very isolated. And there's tribal land adjoining that." She swung her hand in a northerly arc. "If…*when* we get those new leases, we'll almost double our carrying capacity. The Tribal Council has been very supportive of our program, but Dan Tutan's been leasing it forever, and he pays practically nothing for grazing permits on the public land. He has his own support from Pierre all the way to Washington."

"You're running publicly protected wild horses for the Bureau of Land Management, aren't you? You should get preference. Plus, if you've got the Tribal Council…"

"We have the majority. We're…pretty sure we do."

"You can never be too sure about those Indians."

"I'm not too sure about *you*." She smiled. "But I know what *assume* makes out of me." She lifted one shoulder. "And Tutan's been taking us all for granted for far too long. He knows how to work the system. Like anything involving property, it's all about location."

"Tell us about it." He glanced at the barren draw below. "I've got some beachfront reservation land for sale. Complete with a big bridge."

"I'll take it," she enthused. "Where do I sign?"

"I'll have my people draw up the treaty." He adjusted his hat by the brim, leaned back on his elbows and eyed her for a moment. "You've got a good thing goin' here. Why push it?"

"Because we can." She leaned closer. "Because the push needs to be made. More needs to be done, and we can do it. All we have to do is show that our program is viable, that we can handle more land, more stock, and we're in the catbird's seat. Tutan's free rein over the range will soon be over. For a considerable piece of these grasslands, it's back to nature."

"This part doesn't look like it's ever been away."

"My father never got much use out of this part of the ranch. He would have sold it, but back then there weren't any takers. But the takers are…" The look in his eyes set her back on her heels. *The takers are what? The takers are who?* "I don't want to take any more land. I want to set some aside, and I'm willing to pay for the privilege of standing aside." She smiled. "Pay with what? you may ask. My sister asks every other day. I have to get creative about getting more public support."

"I seem to recall some mention of a plan."

"Plan? What plan?" Mock innocence was one of her favorite shticks.

"It was on hold for the wedding. Then you had to get the honeymoon back on track. You are one smooth operator, Sally." He plucked a droopy-headed grass stem and stuck it in the corner of his mouth. "So, what's the plan, and how many days before you have it in place? You've got what? Twenty-one?"

"Give or take." She smiled. "Sam told the newlyweds to stay as long as they wanted."

"And Zach told me if I had any problems, he could be back in twenty-four hours."

"No worries, mate."

"If I were a worrier, the words *creative* and *plan* might give me pause."

"I'm glad you're not." Arms around her legs, she drew her knees up for a chin rest. "Because if I had a plan, I'd really want to tell you about it. I would *really* value your thoughts. You strike me as a practical man. And I'm a creative woman." She gave a slow, sensual smile. "Yin and yang."

"Hmm. If I were a thinking man, my first thought would be…" He winked. "Somebody's yin-yangin' my chain."

She groaned. "Is that what passes for humor where you come from?"

"Well, there's Indian humor, and there's edumacated Indian humor."

"Edumacated?"

"Half-assed educated, which is a dangerous thing."

"Zach says you're the best doc he knows."

"If they ain't broke, I can fix 'em up good enough for the next round. You can't take the cowboy out of the rodeo unless he's out cold. Then he can't argue." He tossed his chewed grass. "'Course, I'm not a doctor. Started out to be, got myself edumacated."

"Meaning?"

"Got married, had a kid, dropped out of school."

"Happens to a lot of us. Even without the marriage and kid part." She thought twice, but it wasn't enough to stop her. "What happened to your son?"

"He got hit by a car. He was in a coma for six months. By the time he died…" He drew a long, deep breath and sighed. "By the time we let him go, we had nothin' left." He lifted one shoulder as he scanned the hills. "Bottom line, I thought she was watchin' him, she thought I was watchin' him." He shook his head, gave a mirthless chuckle. "It's not the bottom line that kills you. It's all the garbage you have to wade through before you find it. And when you do, hell, there's no way to forgive if you can't even look at each other anymore."

Sally could not speak. Her throat burned, and she knew it would be a mistake to open her mouth. She knew hospitals. Technicians with their tests, nurses with their needles, doctors with no answers—she knew them all. She imagined them easily. She knew what it felt like to be poked and prodded and eye-balled. It could be painful. It was often scary. When it became part of life's routine, it was miserable, maddening, frustrating, and it hurt. Physically, when it was your own body, it hurt. Sometimes you thought, *if this kills me, that'll be it. Over and out.* She could imagine that part. Easily. What she could not imagine was sitting beside the bed rather than lying in it, watching over your child, losing your child piece by piece until finally the terrible word had to be said.

She reached for his hand. He flinched, but she caught him before he could draw away and kissed him, there on the backs of his healing fingers, rough knuckles, tough skin. She met his wary gaze. Her eyesight was a little hazy, but her heart was not. Whatever she was feeling, it wasn't pity. Wouldn't give it, couldn't take it.

He smiled, just enough to let her know he understood.

"So." He glanced away, withdrew his hand, gave a brief nod. "Back to the plan."

Hank thought it over on the ride back. She was pretty quiet—must've talked herself out—and he had time to watch the evening sky begin to change colors while he thought about the land, the horses, Sally and her big plan. She wanted to publicize the merits of the sanctuary and the appeal of owning a once-wild horse. She'd done some internet research and pitched the idea of a documentary, but only a couple of documentary producers had responded, and they'd said the story had been done. She needed a new angle.

"I have a killer idea that I haven't told anybody about except Hoolie. And now you." Her secret Henrys, she'd called them, but he couldn't see her keeping any secrets the way this one had tumbled out of her. She wanted to hold a competition for horse trainers. They would choose a horse from the best of the three- and four-year-olds, and they would commit to conditioning, gentling and training the horse to perform. She would bring in experienced judges, award *big, huge* cash prizes and auction off the horses. "It's got everything," she'd claimed. "History, romance, suspense, sports, gorgeous animals in trouble, beautiful people who care, and lots and lots of money."

Hank had enjoyed the sound of her enthusiasm so much, he hadn't asked whether the beautiful people cared about the animals or the money. He hadn't asked where the money would come from. Maybe Zach's brother, Sam, would sponsor the whole thing. He'd hit the jackpot, and he seemed like a good guy.

Covering the last mile between a job well done and supper, Hank knew one thing about the woman riding at his side: she lived for wild horses. She was the real Mustang Sally. She was serious about her dream, and no matter how big the undertaking, she would do what she had to do to make it come true. He was sure she had him figured into her doings somehow. It would be fascinating to watch the woman roll out the rest of her strategy. She'd already shown him she could get something out of him he never, *ever* gave.

Now it was his turn. She was keeping something close to the chest, some heavy weight that bore down on her. He'd seen it knock her over. He'd watched her get right back up. He wouldn't press her—she had enough pressure—but she was going to have to strip off more than her clothes. Whatever she was figuring him for, trust would be the price for Night Horse insurance.

They crossed paths with Hoolie on his way out the back door. The way he said *hope you two had a nice time* made it sound like he was mad about something—supper, maybe, although he said he and Kevin hadn't waited—and Hank questioned Sally with a look. She smiled, shrugged it off, said *we did* to the slamming door. "Grumpy old men," she stage-whispered.

"I got twenty-twenty hearing, big sister."

"I love you, too, ya big grump." She lowered her voice. "The older he gets, the more he sounds like a mother hen."

"Thirty-thirty," was the rejoinder from the yard.

"Shoot me, then," Sally called back, eyes sparkling. "Chicken sandwich anyone?" she whispered.

She wasn't kidding about the chicken. Hank was used to cold suppers, but not like this. Sally piled on the fruits and vegetables, fresh-picked garden greens, potato salad and whole-grain bread. At first glance, it struck him as a woman's kind of meal. At first bite, a man found himself taking his time. No rush to fill up when there was taste and talk on the table.

"I think your plan for a horse-training contest could work." He could tell he had her at *work,* but he added, "I'd compete."

"I was hoping you'd help me run it."

"That wouldn't play to my strong suit. I'm not much of a runner." He leaned back in his chair and eyed her thoughtfully. "Especially behind a friend's back. What do the newlyweds think about running a contest?"

"They're on their honeymoon, for which I thank you very much." Sally popped a green grape into her mouth. "Annie thinks we've already bitten off more than we can chew. She's very careful, very conservative."

"And she married a cowboy?"

"You toss *careful* and *conservative* out the door when you fall in love. At least, that's what I've heard." She went for another grape. "I don't have time for *conservative*. Or patience. I know it's a virtue, but time doesn't stand still while we take small bites and chew thoroughly. This land and these horses look tough, but they're vulnerable. They're right for each other—they *need* each other. We've come a long way getting them back together, and we can't backtrack. Every acre we add to our program is home for another horse." She lifted one shoulder. "Okay, a tenth of a horse, which is why we need more acres. They need space. Wide-open space. You can't have wild horses without wild places."

"I'm down with you on wildness, but I'm no organizer."

"I just need an able-bodied ally. Somebody who knows horses." She leaned toward him. "You wouldn't have to stick around. Just help me get started. Back me up."

"I'm not from this reservation," he reminded her.

"I can back you up, but you're always gonna have holdouts on the council."

"I know, but you're cousins, right?"

"We're all related."

"I'm not saying you all look alike to me. The Oglala and the Hunkpapa are like cousins, aren't they? And you're Hunkpapa."

"A woman who knows her Indians." He gave half a smile.

"Not *my* Indians. And I know cousins compete with each other, just like sisters do."

"When we say *all my relatives,* we mean you, too."

"But you don't include *Damn Tootin'.* He's all about Tutan, and nobody else."

"We won't let him in the circle or the contest," Hank assured her. "I'm here for you, Sally. For three weeks. What do you want me to do?"

"I've already written a proposal, and the BLM is sending someone out to look me over. Basically make sure I can do what I said I could do, which is set the thing up and make it happen."

"And your sister doesn't know about any of this?"

"I want to see if it's even feasible first. I need to pass muster with the bureaucrats so they'll let us use the horses this way. If the BLM approves, I know Annie and Zach will be thrilled. And won't that be some wedding present?" She reached across the table and laid her hand on his arm. "Just help me look good, okay? Me and the horses."

"You look fine, Sally. You and the horses."

"Thanks." She drew a deep breath. "My only other

worry is Tutan and his little shenanigans. Not to mention his connections."

"You know…" He turned his arm beneath her hand and drew it back until their palms slid together. "I don't like Tutan."

"He doesn't know his Indians." She smiled and pressed her hand around his. "Why didn't you tell him the Night Horse who worked for him was your father?"

"I'm not tellin' him anything." He lifted one shoulder. "He's probably checked me out, probably knows by now."

"What happened?" she asked gently.

"My father had some problems, but he wasn't afraid to work." He looked into her eyes, saw no prejudgment, no preemptive pity. Nothing but willingness to listen. "Jobs are hard to find on the reservation, so he'd go wherever the work was and do whatever he was asked to do. He used to hire on for Tutan, and he'd be gone for weeks at a time.

"Come deer season, Tutan liked to have weekend hunting parties for his friends—probably some of those important connections you're talking about—and he'd take one of his hired hands along to bird-dog for him. You know, beat the brush, flush out the game. Half those guys didn't know the butt from the barrel, but they knew how to party."

"Which resulted in the so-called hunting accident."

"Out there alone, got drunk, fell on his gun." He shook his head. "Tragic."

"How old were you?"

"Old enough to know that dog wouldn't hunt. Not unless he was on somebody's payroll." He shook his head. "He wouldn't take my brother and me hunting. Said he'd had enough of it when he was a kid. He didn't hunt for sport. He called and said he wasn't coming home that weekend because Mr. Tutan's friends wanted to do some hunting, and Dad was gonna make some extra cash.

"He'd been dead for weeks when they found him. Tutan had about as much to say as he did the other night. He thought John Night Horse had gone home after he'd drawn his last wages for the season. Tutan didn't post his land, so, sure, hunters came around all the time, but nobody had stopped in that weekend, friends or otherwise."

"So it could have been an accident."

"I didn't think so, but who listens to a twelve-year-old kid?"

"What about your mother?"

"People believe what they want to believe, she said. Indian blood is cheap. Accidents, suicide, murder—what's the difference? Dead is dead. And she proved that by dying when I was fifteen."

"What do you believe?" she asked softly.

"I believe life is life." He gave her hand a gentle squeeze. "From first breath to last, it's up to you to live it in a good way."

"I'll drink to that." She took up her water with her free hand, paused mid-toast and took a closer look at her glass. "What about blood? Are some kinds dearer than others?"

"You're lookin' at one Indian whose blood ain't cheap." He waited for her eyes to actually meet his. "O positive. Universal donor." He smiled. "Priceless."

Chapter 5

Sally was up early.

She'd checked her email—the honeymooners had landed safely and a group of church campers wanted to schedule a day trip to the sanctuary—and paid some bills online before leaving the room that had served variously as the "front" bedroom, the den, the office and now all three rolled up into Sally's lair. She refused to consider it her confines, but there were times when parts of her body wouldn't do much. For Annie's sake she came out for meals, but otherwise she worked long hours in the office. She profiled every animal on the place, recorded every piece of machinery, kept the books, researched everything from parasites to nonprofits and hatched plans. Her motto was: When the Moving Gets Tough, the Tough

Get Moving. One of these days she was going to stitch up the words into a little plaque.

Just as soon as she learned to stitch, which wasn't happening anytime soon. Not as long as the good times were walkin' instead of rollin'.

She helped herself to coffee, popped an English muffin in the toaster and glanced out the back window.

Here came Grumpy.

She couldn't get it through Hoolie's head that as long as she could get up and go, she was going. He knew as well as she did that her physical condition was predictably unpredictable. Most people didn't believe they could get seriously sick or hurt anytime. They *knew* it, but they didn't *believe* it. Sally remembered what that carefree, wasted-on-the-healthy frame of mind was like. She'd been there, BMS—before multiple sclerosis. MS had made a believer of her. Her body could turn on her anytime. Just a matter of time.

She'd had to admit that her eye had been bothering her. She was in the knowing-but-not-really-believing stage—was that the same as denial?—but Hoolie couldn't be denied. He was old and dear, and he knew better. Annie was young and dear, and she could be put off. So, yes, she'd been waking up some mornings—just *some*—feeling like she had something in her right eye. And sometimes—like the other night in the pickup with Hank—it would totally blur up as though she were crying Vaseline. Weird. These things often hit her when she was feeling stressed, which was hardly what she'd been feeling that night.

Hoolie mounted the back steps, crutch thumping, black shepherd in tow. He told the dog to stay outside, but she took off as soon as the door closed, presumably in search of somebody else to herd.

"Have you guys *edumacated* Phoebe and Baby yet?" The word was Hank's. She felt giddy about knowing it and saying it, like a girl with a crush. She laughed at the funny look Hoolie gave her. "Hank's teaching me to talk Indian. He got himself *edumacated.* I guess it's learning the hard way."

"Seems like a real smart fella. Zach says he's halfway to bein' a doctor and twice as good as most of them he knows. Guess he's met a few." He glanced down at his cast. "So, if I have any more trouble with this, I can probably…you know…"

"Ask him to take a look. I doubt if he'd charge you much." She pulled a chair out from the table and spun it around. "You know, you're supposed to use two crutches."

He ignored the comment, but he accepted the chair.

"I didn't mean to get testy last night. You were gone a long time, and it's been a while since you've been on a horse."

"It was wonderful." She positioned a second chair for his footstool. "It was just what the halfway doctor would have ordered. *If* orders were in order."

"What's he chargin' for fixing up Tank's hooves? He's out there now gettin' set to work on him. You might wanna go watch and learn."

"Like I've never seen horseshoeing done before."
She headed for the coffeepot.

"Not like this. Hank's firing up for a hot shoeing.
Got his portable forge out. Took his shirt off. Got a
nice set of tools all laid out." He nodded his thanks for
the coffee she handed him. "Sometimes they charge
extra for hot shoeing, but they say it's worth it."

She laughed. "If I didn't know you better, I'd say
you were playing a game that has everything to do
with firing up, nothing to do with horseshoes."

"Game? What game? I'm just sayin'…"

"I have a couple of volunteers coming in today,
and I thought we'd get them started on—"

"Mowing the ditches along the right-of-way and
putting up the new snow fence. I'm already on it."
He raised one unruly eyebrow. "In case you wanted
to take Hank something cold and wet, there's pop in
the fridge."

"I don't want to give him the wrong idea. I'll just
take him some ice water." *In a tall, sweaty glass.*

The smell of burning charcoal drifted through the
barn's side door, where Sally was greeted by wagging
tails and canine smiles. Phoebe and Baby were buds.
The Dog Whisperer had spoken.

Her ear followed the soft metallic *tap tap tap* to
the bright side of the barn where the big door stood
open, the big gray gelding was cross-tied and the
big bronze man wielded hammer over nail. Wearing
a short leather apron over his jeans, Hank bent to
the task supporting the horse's front leg on his knee,
lining hoof up with shoe and chewing on a nail. His

shoulders glistened, forearms flexed, hair curtained his face, sweat rolled down the side of his face. He looked magnificent.

He plucked the horseshoe nail from his mouth, lined it up, and spoke without sparing her a glance. "I had to score and burn the hoof a little bit above the crack. That's the key to keeping a quarter crack like this from reaching the corona. You keep shoes on him until the hoof grows out, he'll be fine. You say he's never been shod?" *Tap tap tap.*

"I didn't see that crack. I should've noticed."

"I'm not faulting you." He lowered the gelding's leg and straightened slowly. Maybe his back was stiff. More likely, he wanted to prolong the unfolding of his smooth, strapping, sweaty, dirt-streaked torso. He smiled. "I'm impressed with how cooperative he is."

"He's a good boy." She watched Hank out of the corner of her good eye as she patted the horse's flank. "Aren't you, Tanksy? You're still my boy. Henry isn't half as smooth as you are, so don't worry about being replaced."

"You have no idea." His hammer clanked into the wooden toolbox.

"I was talking about *Little* Henry. You thought I meant you? You've asked me not to call you that, so don't worry."

"Are you worried, Tank?" He scratched the horse's face. "Me, neither."

"I do love a smooth ride."

He nodded at her glass of water. "Is that for me?"

"You're welcome to it."

"Did you bring it for me?"

"Hoolie said you were out here in the hot, um…" She laughed and handed it to him. "I did. Hoolie suggested pop, but I thought water would be—"

"Thanks." In three long gulps he drained half the big tumbler.

Then he tipped his head back and let the water overflow the corners of his mouth, slide down his neck and over the hills and valleys of his chest. She watched his Adam's apple bobble once before he lifted the glass from his lips and dribbled the rest of the water over his face. A thin rivulet coursed quickly down the middle of his sleek torso and disappeared behind his belt buckle. She imagined it puddling in his belly button. Thank God she had perfectly clear vision in one eye.

Her gaze retraced its route slowly. She knew what she'd find when her train of thought reached the station. Dark-eyed male satisfaction. They loved it when a woman took the time to look, didn't mind letting it show that she liked what she saw.

"I could get you some more."

He gave a slow smile as he handed her the glass. "That hit the spot."

Touched off by his smile, her popgun laugh tickled her throat on its way out. Oh, she did like the way this man made her feel. She turned carefully—this was no time for an uneven keel—and froze halfway through her next step. And it was all his doing. His hand on her arm.

Instantly carefree, she reversed her turn and lifted

her face for the kiss she felt coming. She hooked her arm over his shoulder and pressed the cool glass against his back. She felt the shock of it—or of her—shimmy through him, felt his damp heat against her breasts, smelled the fire from his portable forge and horse sweat and barn dust and the heady scent of Hank at work. She pressed close and kissed back and gave a sound of raw need and deep delight.

"Pardon my sweat," he whispered.

"It hit the spot." She giggled. A mortifying sound, but there it was, like a bee in a jar—a bright, girlish buzz in her throat. "Different strokes for different spots."

"Mmm." He let go of her arm as he stepped back, glancing at the smudge he'd left. "I stroked you a new one."

"Put your mark on me, did you?" She checked her arm, nodded, felt deliciously, dementedly silly. "I didn't mean to interrupt."

"Yeah, you did."

"I did. My boy needed a break." She glanced at the horse. "Tanks!" The animal raised his head. "You're quite welcome."

Hank chuckled. "I love me some comic relief. Have a seat, Sally. The show gets better."

"I believe it. I don't think I've ever been kissed by a man wearing an apron." Or one who hauled an anvil around. She took in the array of long handles extending from his toolbox—tongs and nippers, hammers and rasps. A bucket of water stood near the small, conical forge. "Why are you hot shoeing him? Because of the crack?"

"I pulled a side clip out of the shoe for support behind the crack. You want the hoof to grow out right, you make the right shoe." He lifted another steel masterpiece at the end of his tongs for closer inspection. "And if the shoe fits…"

"Mustangs rarely have hoof problems."

"Not if they have room to run on ground that isn't plowed or paved over."

"Or chopped up into small pastures and overgrazed." Disagreement over Western land management had raged around her all her life, but she'd taken up the opposite side of the land-use argument since her days as a rodeo stock contractor. Wildlife, including horses, needed protection. "I don't know what my father would think of what we've done with his ranch. He was a cattleman."

"You don't worry about what your neighbor says, do you?"

"Tutan? No. I worry about what he does, or what he could do. He acts like we're the ones who don't belong here, like the horses are intruding on his God-given grazing rights. Where does he get off, thinking he's entitled to use a piece of land any way he wants just because it's there?"

"Where I come from, we ask that question a lot." He poked through the nails in the tray on top of the toolbox.

She grimaced. "Serious case of the pot calling the kettle black, huh?"

"Maybe." He came up smiling. "After that kiss, I gotta wonder what else you've got cookin'."

She laughed. "I'm an acquired taste. At least that's what I'm told."

"Sounds complicated."

"And you're a meat-and-potatoes man?"

"Some people like to cover it all up with sauce, but I prefer to know what's in the pot." He ducked under the cross-tie and took up the next hoof on the far side of the horse. "Tell you what, Tank, if the kiss was any indication, she's not as complicated as she thinks she is."

She took the hint and walked away laughing.

Right.

And Hank wasn't champing at the bit to haul her back in his arms and ram his tongue down her throat.

Sally was a woman, the creature conceived for the sole purpose of complicating a man's life. She was what she thought she was and then some. Her kiss was complex, compounding his interest, confounding his brain. What did she want from him? Besides sex. That he could do, *would* do in his own good time and to their mutual satisfaction. She'd piqued his interest in more ways than one. But beyond a man's two or three straightforward ways lay the mystifying maze of women's ways, where men could sure lose their way in a hurry.

Hank didn't care about the color of a pot so much as what it was made of and whether he could grab it by the handle without getting burned. Pretty damn hard to earn a living with blistered hands. He couldn't help wondering about that little hitch in her step as he watched her walk away.

Sashay away. Was that it? She was either flirting or hurting.

Or both. He couldn't help wondering.

He finished shoeing Tank, and then he trimmed Ribsy's hooves. He liked this work. He'd picked it up after Deborah left him. It was either fill his hands with tools or a bottle. He wouldn't want to do it full time—horseshoeing could be hard on the back—but what had started out as a therapeutic hobby had become a rewarding sideline, and working with his hands gave him time to clear his head.

Sally's interruption was like a paddle plunked in a pool. She'd stirred him up a little, but everything had cleared up when she went away.

Only she hadn't gone far. After he turned the horses out, he ran into her a few yards from the kitchen door. She was playing in real water, aiming a garden hose at a tiered planter with one hand, waving him down with the other.

"Come see the house that Zach built!"

"What house?" It looked like a huge green wedding cake with three metal scarecrows stuck into it.

"This strawberry planter. Sort of like a house."

Damn, that water looked good.

"The boys made this for us. They made these wonderful sculptures for us for Christmas. See, that's Zach with a bull." She pointed to a metal figure with a twist of sheet metal for a hat and contorted hayrake tines serving as bowed legs and handlebar horns. "And Hoolie. And Kevin."

He studied the pieces of implement parts and scrap metal welded together, recognizing a head here, a couple of arms there, maybe a dog or a horse, another...

"And Hank!"

She blasted his ass with the hose.

If she was hoping for noise, she wasn't getting any. He turned and walked into the onslaught without hesitation, letting the water cool his chest, drench the front of his jeans, turn the dust on his boots to mud. It felt fine. Even better when he tossed his hat toward the house, took the hose from her hand, leaned over and turned the water on the back of his head. He raked it through his hair and then slurped a drink while he zeroed in on his next move. With his free hand he spun her around and shoved the end of the hose into the back of her pants.

"Eeeyiiiii!"

She snatched at the hose, grabbed, yanked and failed. "I'm caught!"

"Just barely dropped my line." He reached for the hose. "Here, stand—"

But she went down as though he'd pulled a rug out from under her, landed flat on her face in the mud.

"You okay? What happened?"

"Nothing! I tripped."

"I'm sorry. Here, let me—" her arm was tucked behind her back like a chicken wing, grappling with the hose, which she was about to dislodge "—turn it off."

"No! Leave it on. Leave it!"

"You'll slip." He stopped in his tracks. She wanted to play? He jumped over the spray she shot at him, wrested the hose away and offered her a hand. "I'm not goin' down with you if that's what you're thinkin'."

"I can do it." She waved his hand off. "I'm fine. I can do it myself." Like a child with something to prove, she scrabbled to her feet. "See? Now…" She spread her arms wide. "Fire away. C'mon! With the hose."

"I just knocked you over with the hose."

"Bet you can't do it again." Hands on her hips, she stood firm. "Come on, hose me off."

A quick, cold shot bought Hank another round of music to his inner boy's ear. Her shrieks dissolved into laughter, at once sucking him in and drawing him out. She looked and sounded as fine as she claimed to be, and he had to laugh with her. She would have it no other way. The dogs got in on the act, and all four of them were soaked by the time Hank assumed the role of killjoy and turned off the water.

"Ah, that felt good," he admitted as they planted wet bottoms on the sun-warmed cement steps. "Now what? We go in and track up the floor, or we sit out here looking like two dogs left in the rain?"

"Speak for yourself." Sally puffed out her chest. Her wet white shirt had become a translucent third skin, her bra a silky second, and a hint of nipples the ultimate attraction. "I look like a cool cat."

"Am I your mirror?" He mussed her hair, and she countered with claw and yowl. "You do look cute."

She returned the hair mussing. "You do, too."

He nodded. "When are you gonna tell me what's goin' on with you?"

Her smile faded, and the light in her eyes dimmed. He felt as though he'd hit her. It wasn't like him to pry, but he'd seen too many missteps, and he had a gut feeling.

He glanced away. He wouldn't ask again.

"Zach made that, huh?" He braced his elbows on his knees, laced his fingers together and stared at the planter. "When do I get some strawberries?"

"You like strawberries?" To his relief, she had perked up. "Would you rather have them for dessert tonight or breakfast tomorrow?"

"I'll take them whenever they're ready. I don't think I've ever had homegrown strawberries."

"How about homemade ice cream?" She smiled. "I've got you now, haven't I? My sister's the cook in the family, but we've got this great little machine that makes the best ice cream. That's my summertime specialty. Do you like watermelon?"

He grimaced.

"How about sweet corn? We planted tons of it. Annie's the gardener around here, too, but I really took an interest this year. The weather's been great. It feels good to dig around in the dirt. Good therapy."

"For what?"

"Anything. You name it, Doc."

"You're an interesting case. Mind if I look for a few more clues?"

"Knock yourself out."

"I've tried that, and think I'll pass." He gave a humorless chuckle. "Actually, I've done that, too. Down and out. From what I was told, it ain't pretty."

"When you're as clumsy as I am, you learn how to catch yourself."

"That's not what I see. You've learned how to *protect* yourself."

"Same thing."

"Uh-uh. I'm not a doctor, Sally, but I've done some doctoring."

"And I've done some knocking my head against the wall. Nothing a little session with Mother Earth can't cure. Down and dirty." She gave him her saucy Sally look, the one that made him itch in places it wasn't polite to scratch. "Down *in,* not out. Down deep and inside and underneath." She laid her hand on his thigh. "And you, my flawlessly fit friend with the healing hands, even you've stumbled."

"A time or two, yeah."

"And what did you do? You picked yourself up, hosed yourself off, got back in the game. Right? The more time you spend thinking about it, talking about it, picking it apart, the harder it is to get back up and get moving again." She gave him a merciless little pat before she took her hand away. "A time or two? Is that all? You're quite a paragon, Mr. Night Horse."

"Yep."

"You dry?"

"I've been dry for a while." Seven years. Lucky seven. "I'll flip you for the shower." He pulled a quarter from his jeans. "What do you want?"

"Heads we go separate, tails we go in together."

Damn. "What do you want?"

"Ask me no questions, I'll tell you no lies." She had a half-scared look in her eyes that didn't match up with her smart mouth. "Figure it out."

She was pushing too hard, questioning herself, lying to herself, and he wasn't going there with her. He grabbed her shoulders and held her at forearm's length, willing her to give it up. Not her body. Her act. *Cut the crap, Sally.*

The look in her eyes was killing him. He covered her mouth with his and gave the kiss she had coming, the one that said *This is me, baby. Give me the real you.*

Her eyes were closed when he lifted his head. She opened them slowly, and for an instant she was his. But she promptly covered.

"That's a start," she tossed out, smiling too quickly. "There's nothing wrong with me that a little physical therapy can't put right."

"You're the damnedest woman I've ever met."

"That's what they all say."

"That won't work, either." He drew himself away. "I know people, Sally. I know when someone's been around the block a few times, and you haven't. We both have hurts, and yours didn't come from knocking yourself out. They're not of your own making." He flipped, slapped the coin on the back of his hand,

and challenged her. "You either come clean with me or we ain't comin', Sally. At least not together. Heads or tails?"

"Be my guest."

Sally escaped directly to the laundry room. Three weeks. Was it too much to ask? Three weeks of remission, three weeks with a man, *this* man, *the same damn three weeks*. Couldn't she have her wish, her way for three, just *three* short weeks? She pulled a load of fluffy towels from the dryer, satisfied her nose with the fresh scent, and folded each one carefully, telling herself to straighten up, put her house in order, stop acting like a female in heat. He was willing to kiss her. He was a good kisser. It was something. She needed *something*.

Her armload of towels was something he needed, and when she heard the water running she told herself she would just slip them inside the bathroom door if the one from her room was open. The towel stand was within no-peek reach. The tub-shower combination was on the adjoining wall. The door hinges were quiet. There would be no disturbance.

As long as the curtain was closed, which it wasn't. As long as she didn't look in the mirror on the opposite wall, which she did. She would have backed away if she could have. She would have been able to if his astonishing body had presented itself to her right eye instead of her left, her good eye. But the stars were aligned for full disclosure, and her good eye was thrilled. His head was tipped back, his eyes closed, his chest taking on water, one hand braced on the wall and the other pleasuring himself.

Damn him. Why wasn't he letting her do that?

Any man who preferred his hand to a woman's body was just plain...

...not interested in the woman. For whatever reason.

Maybe it was just him.

More likely it was her. Her imperfect body.

Hell, nobody was perfect. Surely he knew that. *No body was perfect.*

Except maybe his. Damn, he looked delicious, all warm and wet and hard as rock candy. Her heart pounded, her mouth watered, and her throat went dry.

Was this what he called *coming clean?*

She called it a terrible thing to waste. She called it the worst travesty of justice she'd yet to confront, and she'd confronted some doozies. What god had she offended? Which goddess had abandoned her?

What in hell was she doing wrong?

Well, for one thing, she was staring. She unloaded the towels, stepped back, pulled the door almost shut, and then she committed the losing error. She lifted her gaze from his hand to his eyes. They were open, of course, and they had her dead to rights.

He came into the kitchen carrying his duffel bag.

She was sitting on a tall kitchen stool concentrating on keeping her hands from shaking while she shelled peas into a glass bowl. "Are you leaving?" she asked softly.

"No. I gave my word. I'll be back after I find a place to stay."

"Hank, I'm…" She sighed. She couldn't say it. She was feeling a riot of emotion, but sorry simply wasn't part of it. "You're the damnedest man I've ever met."

"Then I'd say you've met a lot of boys who only looked like men."

"You had your free look. Now I've had mine."

"Fair enough." He took a step closer, offering her no quarter. "The next one's gonna cost us both. We drop the playacting and get real. No protection except a scrap of rubber."

"Get real? Haven't you had enough reality?"

"I don't know if I've had any."

"But that's what you're looking for?"

"If I'm looking for something, that would be it. I like your ass, Sally. Hell, I like your sass. What I don't like is the chip on your shoulder. I could knock it off, easy." He shook his head, lowered his voice. "But that wouldn't get us anywhere, would it?"

"Stay here, Hank." She pushed the bowl aside. "I really want you to stay here."

"What for?"

"For the sake of…" She lowered one leg, and her bare foot touched the floor, a cold shock. "For my sake. This chip is getting pretty heavy."

"Like I said…"

"I know, but it draws your attention, doesn't it?"

"A chip is a chip, honey. I've seen a lot of them. I know what they're about." The look in his eyes went from cold to kind. "Fear and pain."

"I'm not—"

"*I'm* not. I'm not your antidote." He waved his free hand as though sweeping cobwebs. "Let's clear the air, Sally."

She bristled. "Why? I like it steamy."

"I don't like feeling crowded. One minute we're getting to know each other, having a little fun, the next you're…" He scowled. "What do you want from me?"

"How does friendship with benefits strike you?"

"Like something out of a TV show." He gave half a smile, but the light went out of his eyes. "I can fly you to paradise on my benefits, but not for free. I'll babysit for free. You want peep shows? You want slap and tickle? That's extra."

"Wow." She clapped her hands. "Congratulations, cowboy. Way to slap my chip into next week."

"That's all it takes? You disappoint me."

"Sorry, but it's just not fair to talk about paradise when you're throwing me under the straight-talk express."

He glowered at her. She glared right back.

One corner of his mouth twitched.

She smiled, straight up.

"Okay." He wagged his head, gave a reluctant chuckle. "Look, Sally, I've had friendship with benefits. Sooner or later one messes up the other."

"Is three weeks your idea of sooner? Or later?"

He laughed. "It's my idea of eternity if we're gonna keep this up."

"We're not. We're even." Her voice dropped to

a notch above a whisper. "You took my chip, I take your point."

"I don't think so, but we'll see. Go take your shower." He tossed the duffel bag, and it slid across the floor until it hit the wall. "One of the benefits of my friendship: I'm one hell of a cook."

Chapter 6

When the call came from BLM Wild Horse Specialist Max Becker, Sally was filling out forms on the computer. Bureau forms begat Bureau calls, and Sally was not a fan of either. But Max was one of the good guys.

"So far, so good." His tone was heavy on *so far*. "Everybody I talk to likes your proposal for a trainers' competition. It falls right in line with some of our other incentive programs, and I know you'd do it up right. I'm a big Mustang Sally fan. But I just got another letter from somebody who isn't."

"Dan Tutan."

"Let's see. Yep. That would be him. Says you're letting the horses run wild." Max laughed. "Guess he's a comedian on the side. Anyway, he copied your congressional delegation and some lawyer, along with the Cattlemen's League and the governor of South Dakota."

"Threatening what? To sue me and the horse I rode in on?"

"To strike his magic match and hold some big feet to the flame until he gets me fired." He chuckled. "The horse I rode in on gets roasted over my coals."

"Are you scared?"

"Are you? This guy lives right down the road from you. Sounds like he's the kind who rams push into shove and takes credit for casualties."

"He's a dinosaur. They weren't green, were they? Tutan's not green. Kill, baby, kill. That's his motto."

"Well, I gotta tell you, Sally, there's a lotta people in the Bureau right now he can get to back his play. The district manager's going deaf from the miners and drillers screaming in one ear and the hunters and ranchers barking in the other. The rangeland management specialist rolls out his tricolored, multiple-use spreadsheet, and before I know it, all those little boxes are filled up with test drills and grazing permits. He's got a few deer and antelope playing around in the margins, but there's no place to put my horses. They say we have to gather up another five hundred by the end of the summer. And I say..." He sighed wearily. "I say, give Sally Drexler's proposal a shot. And they say, *Shot? Euth injection, or is she talking guns?*"

"Are you serious?"

"You know I'm serious, and you know where I stand, but the squeeze gets tighter every day. All options are on the table, and that includes the one no horse lover wants to hear."

"They're protected," she insisted, but she knew the Wild Free-Roaming Horses and Burros Act had been challenged continually since 1971. With so many horses confined to holding facilities, the *free-roaming* part was becoming a joke. Some in Congress were saying that *protection* was just another word for nothing left to waste money on. A welfare program for wild horses they called it, and the horse was not an endangered species. "Where's *your* spreadsheet, Max?"

"Under my pillow."

Sally groaned. "Who's the comedian now?"

"That's all I've got going for me at one of those damn meetings. Guess I'm gonna have to break down and call the Video Professor about one of those free computer-training programs."

"I'll send you one. What else do I have to do to get the go-ahead on this project?"

"It would help if your neighbor would back off."

"What else?"

"I'm willing to work with you, Sally. I can appraise trainer applications with you, and I can set up the adoption after the competition is over. I'll be down in your area in a couple of weeks. You need sponsors."

"I have them." *Almost.* Zach's brother was going to contribute to the sanctuary. She hadn't asked him to sponsor the contest yet.

"Do you have enough help out there? I hear Little Horsin' Annie got hitched to that rodeo cowboy you had working for you. That's one way to reduce the payroll."

"And Zach brought a friend on board. A farrier." Hank wasn't there at the moment. He'd left early yesterday for a rodeo not far from the Wyoming office Max was calling from, but he'd be back today. "A *volunteer* farrier."

"Now if we can just marry you off to a veterinarian," Max teased. "Your sanctuary is a little piece of horse heaven, Sally. I'm in your corner."

She felt so much better. Max Becker was in her corner. Damn Tootin' was calling in favors from his hunting buddies. And Hank Night Horse was on board with her for three weeks. Minus three days, and he was surely counting.

Maybe she could reason with Tutan. Compromise somehow. *Come on, Dan, let's share. Let's join forces and save the world.*

Not likely. Threatening him was more his speed. But with what? Letters, litigation, lawmakers. *It's who you know that counts.*

Sally was surrounded by people who counted. She was committed to a way of life, a legacy, a whole population of animals that counted. She was needed. *She* counted. Marrying her off to a veterinarian, doctor, lawyer or Indian chief would not make a difference in how much Sally Drexler contributed to the sanctuary.

She had work to do. Some of the horses would be tamed so that some could remain wild. *Wild.* Not kept alive in a holding pen. The sanctuary wasn't wilderness, and public land wasn't exactly open range, but it was a fair imitation of freedom. Sally had learned from the mustangs—you take your bliss where you find it, and you run with it when you can.

Tutan needed some tutoring on that particular point, but maybe Sally hadn't chosen the best way to go about it during their last meeting. She'd known the man all her life, and she'd never liked him. She'd been friends with his daughter, Mary, who had declared her freedom from her overbearing father by joining the army. She hadn't seen much of his shy, ever-cloistered wife since her friend left. Maybe Mary's mother could be recruited to her cause. Audrey Tutan was a gentle soul, and Sally knew she could gain her sympathy, which might count for something. Possibly a moratorium on complaints to the BLM. Maybe a purloining of letters.

Otherwise she would move to Plan B. She would build a threat bomb. The components were yet to be determined.

Hoolie had all volunteer hands on deck for haying, which made it a good time for Sally to pay a visit to the Tutan ranch, especially since Dan was probably out in the field, too. Fresh off the call from the BLM, Sally was itching to try her hand at woman-to-woman diplomacy.

Trying her hand at driving was another matter. It had been a couple of years since she'd driven, but she was feeling good today. Good and irritated. She was powered up, and her mission wouldn't take long. She scanned the array of keys hanging on hooks in the mudroom. She decided she could handle Hoolie's little go-fer pickup. She'd be back before anyone knew she was gone.

Sally hadn't missed driving as much as she'd thought she would. She'd never told anyone, but there had been times when she'd scared herself when she was behind the wheel, even before her nervous system had started going haywire. She took it slow, kept the dust wake to a minimum, and reached the highway without incident. And why shouldn't she? Her vision in her left eye was better than what a lot of people could claim in both eyes put together. Five slow and easy miles up the road she drove through Tutan's fancy wooden gate.

Audrey Tutan answered her front door tentatively, as though the sunlight was too strong or the air outside was too thick. She had always reminded Sally of a caged bird. Her hair had been white ever since Sally could remember, and she had always been fair in the face and thin everywhere—lips, hips, hands, voice. She looked confused as she peered from the shadows. "Dan isn't here right now."

Sally tipped her head to one side and smiled. *Remember me, Mrs. Tutan?* "I really came to see you."

"You did?" Audrey brightened as she drew the door back. "Well, that's very nice. Please come in, Sally. You're looking well. Dan said as much after he saw you at the wedding. I mean, when he stopped by the, um… He said Hoolie was the only one using a cane." Audrey caught herself. "I hope Hoolie's all right."

"He broke his ankle, but he'll be fine."

"Was it nice?" She closed the door. "Annie's wedding, I mean. Come sit with me. I'm all by myself today."

"It was lovely." Sally followed the tiny woman into the living room with its massive pine furniture and heavily draped windows. "Very small. Family, mostly."

"When you girls were all in school, we were like family." Audrey turned, took Sally's hand and drew her down beside her on the spruce-and-pinecone sofa. "I miss those days."

"I do, too. I miss Mary. Have you heard from her recently? We were emailing regularly, but so much has been happening…"

"She must be okay." Audrey glanced away. "I would've heard otherwise."

"Time gets away from us, doesn't it?" Sally gave the bony, loose-skinned hand a slight squeeze. "Audrey, I don't understand why Dan is so completely opposed to what we've done with the Double D."

"He says it's hard enough to make a living raising cattle these days without competing with animal rights fanat—" she pressed her lips tight "—folks. You know how he is."

"You know me better than that, Audrey. I'm no fanatic, but I've always loved horses. So does Mary. She used to come over all the time, and we'd ride fence and check cows. The sanctuary is a dream come true for me."

"Dan says there's plenty of horses in the world."

"How do you feel about it?"

"I'm staying out of it. He's getting older. The kids are gone. I've never been much help as far as the cattle operation goes." She shook her head slowly, a helpless gesture. "If Dan says the horses are a nuisance…"

"He's been complaining about us to the BLM. We're trying to expand the program, and he's been calling the district office in Wyoming and complaining about the people coming in and out, the horses, the fence, the way we manage just about everything."

Audrey withdrew her hand, twisted her head to the side and spoke into her shoulder. "He says you're moving in on his grass."

"It's not his grass," Sally said gently. "We're taking unadoptable horses out of crowded pens. We're giving older animals a place to live out their lives the way nature intended. Audrey, they used to slaughter them by the thousands."

"I remember."

"It could happen again." She lowered her voice. "There's talk of allowing them to be rounded up and sold for slaughter."

"I don't like to see animals suffer, but I don't know how I can help you, Sally. Dan doesn't talk to me about these things."

"I was hoping you might talk to him."

"It wouldn't matter what I said. Ranching is his life. He knows his business." Her eyes were empty. "The older we get, the less we talk."

Sally couldn't keep pressing. It was too much like throwing a stick for an old dog. For Audrey's sake, she was glad she had come, and she asked, *hoped* she would return the favor. But she knew it wouldn't happen.

Now she was eager to get home. Barreling down Tutan's gravel approach toward the highway, Sally thought about options for getting Damn Tootin' off her back. Call the law. Call Congress. Call the media. Call…what time would Hank be home? *Back.* What time would he be…

She was homing in on the gatepost on the left side, favoring the left side, her good side. She missed the movement on the right, the pickup turning onto the approach from the far lane, her fuzzy lane. There it was, left. Wheel hard right. Clutch, brake—leg? Leg! *Crunch.* Engine, killed. Gatepost? *Bull's-eye.*

Alive? *Check.* Conscious? *Must be.* Hurt? *Stay tuned.*

"What the hell are you trying to do?"

Tutan.

Rewind. Over and out.

"Are you all right?"

The last thing Sally wanted to see was that fat red face, but she carefully turned her head to the left anyway. Sure enough.

"I think so." She felt around the inside of the door for the handle.

"You better be sure. You wrecked your truck."

"Hoolie's truck."

"Did you break anything?"

"Hoolie's truck."

"I'd better call for help."

"Just let me…" She couldn't see much, but a roaring engine, screeching brakes and flying gravel were distinctive sounds. Had the two-lane highway become the scene of a demolition derby?

So was the voice calling for "Hoolie?"

Hank!

"It's not Hoolie," Tutan shouted. "I don't think she's hurt."

"Don't touch her. Sally?"

"This seat belt is a piece of crap." She hoped she sounded disgusted. She wasn't ready to look up and let him see the face of a rattled klutz.

"Take it easy. Do you hurt anywhere?" He reached through the side window and touched the side of her neck. "Your head?"

She closed her eyes and let relief wash over her. "I can't feel…anything…"

"Nothing? How about—"

"She's not even supposed to drive, for God's sake. Look what she's done." Red face, red voice. *Red filled her head.* "With her medical problems? I don't know what you people think you're doing, letting this girl get behind the wheel."

"Stay out of the way, Tutan." Hank opened the driver's side door. "Sit, Phoebe."

"Phoebe?" Sally whined. The dog answered in kind.

"She's okay, Phoeb. Tell her, Sally."

"I'm okay, Phoeb. Nothing hurts. I mean, I don't think I'm—"

"Is she bleeding? Anything broken? That's all you need on top of your MS, Sally. You almost hit me."

"*I will hit you* if you don't back off." Hank slid his arms under her legs and behind her back. "See if it hurts to put your arms around my neck. Slow and easy, okay? You tell me if you feel the slightest…"

"You were outta control, Sally. I don't know what you're doing over here, but you coulda just called. Your father was my friend." The red voice followed, but Sally kept her face tucked against Hank's shoulder. "How long is that thing gonna be sittin' here?" the red voice demanded from a faraway place.

"I'm taking care of her first," Hank said. "If that *thing* ain't here when I come back for it, I'll be looking for you."

"Look what she did to my gate!"

"Which way should we go?" Hank looked up and down the highway, but he was running a checklist in his mind. No blood, bruises, bumps, breaks. He was pretty sure she hadn't been injured, but *pretty* was the operative word.

"You know the way home," she said quietly.

"I don't know the way to your doctor. Did you hit your head? That's the main thing."

"I lost my head. I do that sometimes." She paused. "Sometimes I need a good thumping."

"Well, you got one." He laid two fingertips on the signal-light switch. He was feeling impatient. "If you're not gonna tell me where to find your doctor, I'll go with my best guess."

"Which one do you want? My GP? My neurologist? My—"

"North or south?" he clipped. "Let's start there."

"South," she said. She reached into the backseat, where she got a hand-licking from an ally. "Take me home. I think I'm okay, but if not, I trust you."

He stepped on the brake and turned to her, scowling. "I don't know whether you're lyin' to both of us or just me, but trust me on this. I'm not taking you anyplace that doesn't have an X-ray lab."

"North."

He pulled into the highway and stared straight ahead. Yes, he'd heard. Yes, he knew what MS was. Basically. Questions? Comments? Not without an invitation from Sally.

But for Sally, there was nothing more to say. She'd blown her chance at three weeks of let's pretend by acting stupidly for one day. She glanced at the dashboard clock. *One hour* out of one day. He probably would have guessed before her time was up, but it was too soon. If she hadn't pushed, she could have been normal for a while longer. She could have deluded herself almost completely during this remission. Maybe it was over. Maybe her body had beaten the disease or at least found a way to hold it in check. Maybe she would actually live the scene she'd imagined so many times—the one where she was surrounded by cheerful people wearing white, proclaiming miracles. People, not angels. *It could happen.*

No. What could have happened—up until an hour ago—was a lovely three-week affair with a man who didn't look at her and hear a voice in the back of his head saying, *Don't forget, she's incurable.*

Hank waited in a chair outside one of the small, rural clinic's three exam rooms. Phoebe lay at his feet.

MS. So that was it. He should have known. *Would have* known if he'd been halfway objective. *Damn Tootin'.* Damn Tutan for telling him. He'd wanted Sally to tell him. Trust him. *Come clean,* he'd said, as if whatever she was keeping from him was something dirty. *Dirty secrets.* What other kind would a person want to keep?

From the beginning, objectivity hadn't been an option with Sally. He'd stayed out of the water, but that didn't mean he hadn't gone under. He knew the signs. He'd been there before. The trick was not to fight it. If you let go, you were supposed to be able to float. So he'd heard. Now that they were on par with each other in the personal-history department, maybe they could explore the options she'd laid out on the table. She wanted a friend. She needed certain benefits.

He was her man.

When the door opened, he almost jumped to attention.

"Dr. Bergen says I'm fine."

"That isn't exactly what I said." The doctor adjusted her wire-framed glasses. "I don't see any injuries except a bump on the head and probably some back strain, although Sally says it's nothing. She tells me you're a PA. You'll be around for a while?"

"I'm helping out at the ranch."

"The sanctuary," Sally said. "Hank's taking a working vacation. He's sort of an experiment. If he gives us a good review, I'm going to offer that as a volunteer option on our website." She glanced at Hank. "I'm working on a website."

The gray-haired woman gave an appreciative nod. "I could go for something like that. I've always wanted to volunteer for Doctors Without Borders, but this place can't spare me for more than a few days at a time."

"Rural clinics are hurting for staff," Hank said.

"Hank just got back from a rodeo. He patches up cowboys for a living, so he can still—"

"Did you take any X-rays?" he asked.

"None indicated." Dr. Bergen eyed Sally as though she might have missed something. "You're not experiencing any numbness now, right? Other than the vision in your right eye, which you were having problems with before the accident." Back to Hank. "Any sign of concussion, bring her back right away. How long have you been a rodeo medic?"

"Seven years."

"Well, then, you've probably had almost as much experience with injuries like this as I have. Of course, multiple sclerosis complicates things a bit."

"I don't suppose you've run into too many cowboys with MS." Sally gave him her Sally-go-round-the-roses look.

"You're my first."

"Good." She smiled at the doctor. "We never forget our first."

"Make an appointment to see your neurologist as soon as you can get in. You're good to go." Dr. Bergen waved a business card she'd been palming all along. "This is where I'll find the Web site?"

"As soon as we launch it. If you know any veterinarians, we're always looking for volunteers."

Sally's limp was more noticeable as the three of them headed for the pickup, sitting there with the front tire kissing the curb and the back end a good three feet away. *Somebody* had sure been in a hurry.

"I like your style, Sally." He opened the door for her and offered her a hand, thinking his style wasn't too shabby, either. She questioned him with a look— like maybe she could read his mind about the way she walked—and she grabbed the door handle and hauled herself up onto the running board. "The business card, the volunteer comment. Opportunity comes knockin', you're not afraid to jump."

"Opportunity must be jumped while the jumping's good."

He laughed as he let Phoebe in back. He buckled himself in while Sally picked up where she'd left off.

"In my case, while the jumpers are in good jumping order."

"Ah, Sally." He shook his head, chuckling. "You are the damnedest… Did you think it would matter to me that you have MS?"

"Hmm, how should I answer this question? I hope it matters. Or…" She drew herself up and turned to him with a perfunctory smile. "I *knew* it would matter. It matters to everybody. When I'm using a cane, sometimes a wheelchair, that's the first thing people see." She raised an instructive finger. "Maybe it throws them off, maybe it doesn't, but that's who I become. And it's less than I am, and I get tired of waiting for them to catch up to me. When I'm having myself a nice little remission, why should I tell people? Especially people who won't be around that long."

Good question.

"Maybe because some people don't know what to make of all this jumping." He plugged the key into the ignition, shrugged, gave her a look that was probably more sheepish than he intended. "Some of us are scared spitless when it comes to jumping."

"Not you." Her eyes softened. "You were ready to jump when you thought I'd fallen in the lake."

"I wasn't thinking."

"But you've been thinking ever since. Thinking, *there's something wrong with this woman. Can't quite figure out what it is, but...*"

"Not wrong. Risky. I like to know what I'm getting into. The ol' look-before-you-leap routine."

"You already looked!"

"Yeah, I did. And I was goin' for it." He gave a mid-forehead salute. "I had the image fixed in my mind."

"You saw yourself swimming?"

"Hell, no." He smiled. *Honey, cut me some slack.* "I saw myself giving you mouth-to-mouth."

"Now you tell me. I would have thrashed around and swallowed some water for you. Right, Phoebe?

I've never had a water rescue." She returned his smile. "Your Damn Tootin' rescue was beautifully executed. Nice entry. Perfect timing. Thank you for that."

"It would've been sweet to put my fist through his face."

"I know." She dropped her head back on the head-rest and stared at the ceiling. "How much damage did I do to Hoolie's pickup? I wish I could get it fixed before he sees it." She smacked her forehead with the heel of her hand. "Stupid."

"Don't beat yourself up." He reached for her smacking hand. "You can't help being a woman driver."

She raised her brow and smiled sweetly. "I guess not. If you like, I can teach you how to parallel park."

Chapter 7

Hank had been the perfect gentleman. He had seen
her to her bedroom door, asked about a heating pad,
brought her cold packs and Sleepytime tea, and gone
to the front door to answer Hoolie's "Where the hell's
my pickup?" On his way out, he'd suggested a warm
bath, even offered to fill the tub. She'd thanked him,
said she'd take it from there knowing full well she was
doing no such thing. She was letting him answer for
her, and she was shamefully content to do so.

But she indulged herself with bath salts and a few
bubbles. Why not? It was what she did best. Overex-
tend, underperform. She wasn't hurting much—she'd
never claimed she was—but water was always wonderful. *Feel while the feelin's good.* She laid her head
back, closed her eyes and soaked it up.

Sally didn't need sight or sound—the door made no noise—when she was hooked into feeling. When the feeling was good, she felt change. New electricity, energy, presence. Manpower. She opened her eyes and smiled.

He wore black jeans. Nothing more. She hoped.

She drew a deep breath and sat up. Foam cascaded over her breasts, tickling her imagination. *Don't look now, but we are hot.* "I'm sorry you didn't catch me doing something more interesting."

"I'm not here to watch."

But he was. Something interesting was happening in the tub, and he was fascinated. He closed the door behind him without looking anywhere else.

"You came to play?"

"Brought you a bath toy." He plunged his hand in his pocket and pulled out a foil packet. "Rubber duck."

"Is that your bath toy of choice?"

"It's the one that's gonna float your boat."

She shrieked with delight as he stepped into the tub, jeans and all. Water sloshed onto the floor, bubble islands rocked back and forth. She drew her knees up to make room, but he took hold of her ankles, straightened her legs and wrapped them around his waist.

"I don't see how." She wiggled her bottom—a hen getting comfortable in a flooded nest—and stroked his beautiful, brawny shoulders.

"You'll figure something out." His smiling eyes plumbed the depths of hers, tempting a little, teasing a lot. "You wanna get into my jeans, woman, you're gonna work for it."

"While you—"

"—find out what you taste like." He ducked as he slipped his hands around her, thumbs tucked into her armpits, lifting her until her nipple touched his lips. He brushed her so slightly, made her wind up so tightly that she almost interfered. But she held on, and he made it worthwhile with his nibbling lips and the barest tip of his flickering tongue and the warm whisper of his breath. "Sweet cakes with foam." He smiled against her nipple. "Which has a bite to it." He suckled, and then chuckled as he teased with his nose. "Not the kind I was hoping for."

"Sorry," she whispered.

"I don't mind swallowing."

"My kind of man." She buried her fingers in his hair. "You'll come out…smelling like a rose."

He grew and stirred beneath her. "Only for you."

She used his hair to ease his head back until his lips were within reach of hers, and then she kissed him. His thumbs toyed with her breasts, and their tongues played tag. He trailed fingers down her side, over her belly, between her legs and teased her most sensitive flesh until she thought she would die for want of him inside her. But he permitted only the edge of madness and not the full measure. It was at once excruciating and exhilarating, too bright to keep and too fine to let go. She closed her eyes, sheltered them against his neck, and gave herself over.

"Not fair," she whispered when the shuddering subsided.

He turned his mouth to hers and kissed her kindly. He was big and hard beneath her, fit to bust his zipper. She tightened her seat and rolled her hips slowly, raising wants and making waves. His kiss turned hungry, and he tasted every part of her mouth, but he couldn't seem to get his fill. He groaned. "Not fair."

She reached for the soap bottle, pumped a dollop into her palm, rubbed her hands together and lathered him—shoulders, arms, chest. She laughed when her turnabout with his nipples had him sucking air through his teeth. She took the measure of his rib cage, his flat belly, belly button, jeans button. Beneath the bath water it came undone easily. She hoped he would not.

He stilled her hand, poised on the zipper tab. "If I get caught in the teeth, it's all over."

She slipped her hand into his pants, becoming his protection. The tip of his penis pushed against the heel of her soapy hand. She smiled. *This puppy wants out.* She inched the zipper down. "Lift up."

"We're at T minus ten, honey. Any more *up* and it's *liftoff.*"

"Hips, silly."

He braced his arms on the sides of the tub and lifted. And when she had his jeans down, she lowered her face into the water and took advantage of his precarious position, just for a moment. Just for a bit of pleasure he would not soon forget. The limited-time offer ended when the breath she could no longer hold became bubbles. He gave a pained laugh as she rose over him like Nessie, pushed her hair back and settled on his lap with an added bonus. It was hard to tell who was torturing whom as he opened the condom and she put it on him, but the pleasure that followed was mutual.

They stepped out of the tub into almost as much water as they left behind. They dried each other with thick bath sheets and traded more kisses and dove into her bed for more exploration and discovery. Every nerve in Sally's body was on high alert. None slept. None missed the smallest trick.

And, oh, from head to toe, she felt wonderful.

"Tell me how you feel." He braced up on his arm and rested his head on his hand. Moonlight streamed through the window with cool night air and cricket calls. He smoothed her hair back from her forehead, his fingertips barely brushing the bump above her eyebrow. Marble sized. Not a shooter, but not a peewee either. Big and hard enough to give him concern.

"Happy." Her eyes were closed. Her mouth formed a soft crescent. "Drained and dreamy."

"How 'bout a massage?"

"Mmm…later." She turned toward him, tucked her whole body into him. "How about a snuggle?"

"I'm not letting you go to sleep yet."

"Why not?"

"I'm not ready."

She looked up, eyes wide with mock shock. "What kind of a man are you?"

"You have to ask?"

"Oh, that's right." Her eyes drifted closed, and that sweet, satisfied smile returned. "The doctoring kind."

"I'm not a doctor."

"And it's a good thing. I really don't like doctors." She laid her hand on his chest. "Play doctors, yes. Real doctors, no."

"How's your head?"

"I told you. Drained and dreamy."

"If you fall asleep, I'll just have to wake you up." His thumb grazed the knot on her head. "Still the same size."

"I have other bumps you can play with." She claimed his hand, drew it down and held it against her breast. "When you touch them you make them feel much bigger."

He chuckled. "You're the damnedest woman I've ever met."

"I think so, too, sometimes. I get all tucked up inside, and I—"

"*Tucked* up?"

"That's what I said, Henry. Tucked up." Clutching his hand in both of hers, she turned to her back and scooted up against him, like a small creature seeking shelter from the wind or shade from the high-plains sun. "I sort of suck myself inward. I become a prune, and I imagine myself screaming, 'Come on, you demons, try to take a piece of me now.' But I don't. I stay quiet and still, and I focus on getting through the next breath. I think that's what it's like to be damned."

"Me, too. It's not burning. It's drowning."

"And it's not painful. You know you're damned when you don't feel anything."

"I don't know about that. I've seen—"

"I do," she insisted. And then softly, "I do know. When you can't feel, you'd take anything. A hot poker. A wrecking ball." She drew a deep breath, and then let it go quickly. "Oh, I shouldn't say *I know*. Only part of me doesn't feel sometimes, and it comes back. It always comes back. I don't claim to know what it's like not to feel anything at all." She pressed his hand tight to her breastbone, and he uncurled his fingers and felt her heartbeat in the hollow of his palm. "I'm not a drama queen. I promise."

"I promise to stop calling you the damnedest woman, and we'll leave it there."

"No, no, then I'd be just another damned woman. One of your many damned women. If I'm the damnedest one you know, I'm queen of something. Queen of the damned, that's me." She stretched, full body, like a cat. "I'm not giving up the damnedest title without a fight. The next damned woman comes along, you can't call her *damnedest* unless she can take the crown from my cold, dead hands."

He laughed. "God, you're beautiful."

"I love your hands. They feel cool."

"They do? Maybe that's why you feel so nice and warm."

"I always do. It's part of the package." She looked up at him. "So now—I've avoided it as long as I can—the dreaded question."

"What's that?"

"Did you have to tow Hoolie's pickup? What did he say when he saw it? Was he—I'm such a coward—did he think it could be fixed?"

"That's three dreaded questions." One mental sigh of relief after another. "Starting with number two—because this really says it all—he wanted to know about you. Where were you, how bad were you hurt, had you seen a doctor, and all like that. As for question number one, the pickup started right up, and we took off before the devil knew we were there. We got back, he wanted to know what you were doin' over there. I said, damned if I know. I was just goin' down the road and saw his C10. Damn good thing you stopped, he said, and I said amen to that."

"You sound just like him."

"Is that a bad thing?"

"There's only one Hoolie," she said firmly, as though he thought otherwise. "What about question number three?"

"I know it can be fixed, but if it'll keep you awake for a while, you can keep worrying."

She smiled big. "One Hoolie, one Hank. One Little Henry, one medium-size Henry, one big beautiful Henry. I'm blessed."

"So much for queen of the damned."

"Damned crown's giving me a headache, anyway."

"As long as it's not me." He kissed the bump on her forehead. "Got that? I don't wanna be anybody's headache."

"I don't either. Let's make a pact." She lifted her chin. "Let's kiss on it."

* * *

Sally turned Hank down for breakfast. All she wanted to do was sleep. He decided to give her a couple of hours before checking up on her one more time, and then he'd get after Tutan's damn gate. He'd have it fixed good as new, maybe better, and then he'd welcome the criticism, the complaints, hell, the lawsuit. Bring it on. Sooner or later he'd give Damn Tootin' the tuning up he deserved. He hadn't figured out just what form it would take, but there would be a suitable settlement. But for now, Tutan's property would be repaired.

Hank found Hoolie and Kevin in the machine shop, their heads under the hood of the C10, which they'd driven back from the scene of the accident without incident. Hank stationed himself on the third side of the male-bonding altar. A pickup engine was as good as a campfire.

Maybe better.

"Yep," Hoolie said, "she's gonna be good as new, soon as her replacement parts come." He patted the dented fender tenderly. "I've already found the head-lamp housing and this whole quarter panel on the internet."

Hank acknowledged the find with a raised brow.

"You search the internet much? Any tool you can think of for shoeing horses, you just put the words in the box…." Two bony index fingers proudly demonstrated on the air keyboard. "You want the good stuff, put the word *vintage* in there somewhere. Press

Enter, and here they come. Like cake, like pie. You ever play Scavenger Hunt?"

"Nope." Hank glanced across the man-bonding pit at Kevin. "You?"

Kevin shrugged. "Sounds like what I got arrested for last year."

"You gotta learn the rules of the game, boy. The tricks of the trade. You should see all my bookmarks. You scavenge around on the internet, you can buy and sell, you can trade, you can—"

"Snag yourself a rich widow," said Kevin. "Come on, Hoolie, I've seen you friending the women on Facebook."

Hoolie folded his arms. "No harm in exchanging emails with females."

"You want the good stuff, you leave out the word *vintage,*" Hank said.

"The best e-pal is a gal with a little age on her," Hoolie advised. "If she asks for pictures before the third message, one of us is swingin' on the wrong porch."

"How's Sally?" Kevin asked Hank.

"I kept her up all night, so she's sleeping in this morning. She hit her head. She's got a goose egg the size of your *pahsu.*"

"His what?"

"Nose," Kevin said. "And mine ain't that big, so it's no excuse to keep her from getting her rest."

"I see a lotta concussions. You let her go to sleep too soon, she might not wake up."

"Hank's halfways a doctor," Hoolie told Kevin. "Physician's practitioner, they call it."

"Physician's assistant," Hank amended.

"What was she doing over at Tutan's?" Hoolie asked. "Did she say?"

"We didn't get into it." Hank leaned his forearms on the fender and admired the old six-banger engine. "She feels real bad about the damage on this baby."

"She, uh…she's a terrible driver."

"I know she has MS." He said it quietly, without looking up. "Tutan was turning into the approach, and they nearly collided. She couldn't work the pedals. 'Course he pitied her for having MS and ripped into her for driving." He glanced across the engine at Hoolie. "She coulda told me herself."

"We don't talk about it unless she…you know. It's for her to decide. Lately she's been…you'd never know unless…"

"Unless somebody told you." Hank nodded. Pride. He knew what that was like. "The leases she's trying to get, the horse-training challenge, she's pretty determined."

"That's Sally for you."

For *him?*

Hell, it had nothing to do with him. Sally was determined to be Sally. She'd honed the edge on her defensive game long before he came along. Which was understandable. Nothing personal, which was good. Under the circumstances, friends with benefits probably made perfect sense, especially since he wouldn't be around long.

"What's it gonna take?" Hank straightened his back, braced his hands on the pickup fender. "More people, money, connections, what?"

"Yeah, all that and maybe a guardian angel. I don't think she oughta be takin' so much on. Zach and Annie don't know the half of it." Hoolie smiled. "Sally's the one who got the sanctuary started. I didn't think much of the idea at first. Now I can't imagine a better one."

"She's supposed to make an appointment with her neurologist. I'd like to be the one to take her."

"I'd offer you my pickup, but…"

"We'll take mine. I'll take the topper off and leave it in the shop if it won't be in the way. About everything I own is in it."

"No problem," Hoolie said.

"We might be gone overnight. You never know. Can you handle—"

"'Course we can." Hoolie eyed Hank anxiously. "She's okay, isn't she? She's just getting double-checked, right?"

"Yep. When you're special, you see a specialist." Hank rapped his knuckles on the fender. "Right now, I've got some repairs to make on Tutan's front gate."

"I'll go with you," Kevin said eagerly.

"I need you here." Hoolie had cold water for Kevin, heated advice for Hank. "Don't let him push you around. Sally had a good reason for goin' over there. Whatever it was."

"You think he'll try to push me?" He could only hope.

"No. He ain't that stupid."

"Unfortunately." Kevin was greatly disappointed.

Hank tried the Tutans' doorbell, but there was no sound. He knocked on the door. Either way, it was a formality. If there was anyone home, they'd seen him coming a mile away. He gave a full minute before turning to leave. The door whined softly, a tentative opening, slight shape in the shadows.

"I'm looking for Dan Tutan. The name's Hank Night Horse. I'm helping out over at the Double D."

"Night Horse?" It was a woman's voice.

"I'm a friend of Zach Beaudry's. I came to fix the front gate."

"Oh." The door opened, and a small, mostly gray lady emerged. She wore a blue shirt and tan pants, but everything else about her seemed gray. "Dan's out cutting hay. How's Sally? Is she home?" She hung on to the doorknob with one hand and the door frame with the other, but she seemed hesitant, like she was trying to decide whether she should try to block an end run or step aside and let him score. "I was going to call, but I didn't want to cause any upset."

"I took her to the clinic. No injury to speak of."

"Tell her I hope she's…" She dropped her gaze along with her left hand. She looked defeated. "Tell her I'm sorry."

"Sorry for…"

"Upsetting her. I know stress causes those spells sometimes, where she loses control over her legs or something. All she wanted me to do was talk to him."

"Talk to your husband?"

"He's got his side, too. Who's to say?" The thought of two sides seemed to buck her up some. "Tell you the truth, I wish he'd cut back on the cattle. We don't need a big operation anymore. He's got nobody to take over for him. Kids are gone. They've got their own lives. But…" She gave an open-handed gesture, a sigh. "Sally was my daughter Mary's best friend."

"Sally stopped by to visit with *you*, then."

"Hardly ever see her anymore. She's like me— doesn't get out much, especially in the winter."

"She's completely dedicated to the horses. She wants to get along. She was just hoping you'd put a good word in your husband's ear."

"It wouldn't make any difference. He doesn't want to give up those grazing permits, plus the Indian land. He has some influence with…important friends, I guess you could say."

"It doesn't hurt to have important friends."

"Or *any* friends. We all need friends." She frowned. "Dan didn't say anything about you coming to fix the gate."

"He said a little something *to me* about the gate. You can tell him I came by with materials and offered to fix it like it was."

"Are you…?" She gave him a quizzical look. "Did you know John Night Horse? He used to work for us." He stood uncomfortably for her scrutiny. It surprised and almost disappointed him when she shook her head. "No, that was a long time ago. You would have been a child."

"I would have been twelve."

"He was related to you, then." She gave him a moment to make his claim, and when he offered none, she looked relieved. "He was a good man. I don't think they ever really found out what happened. But he was a good man."

Hank nodded. Like some TV prosecutor, he almost said, *no more questions.* Mrs. Tutan probably took most people for good, even though she was mostly a sad woman. Pumping her for information was like kicking a wounded animal. She clearly lived her life on a need-to-know basis. She didn't know what had happened to John Night Horse, didn't want to know. She hadn't told Tutan why Sally had come over, and wouldn't tell Tutan about Hank's call unless she was asked for some reason. She wouldn't want to cause an upset.

Hank had missed lunch. Sally was trying hard not to miss him, telling herself that last night he'd given her something she'd never had before, and that was all she wanted to think about now. Not the whys or the wherefores or whether it would happen again.

Replay the experience, Sally. Everything he said and did, everything you felt and felt and felt. Keep it alive inside, where nothing can take it away and you can have it over and over again, no matter what.

But she couldn't help watching the road while she watered the garden, listening for his pickup when she turned off the faucet. He'd gone to the neighbors' on a peace-making mission, which—given he had no real duty to any part of the Double D—was so far above the call it was almost saintly.

Whys and wherefores be damned, she waited. She watched and listened, and when she saw the flash of white on the highway, heard the rumble of the engine and felt the promise of having him back, she was content with whatever he was up to, as long as she was part of it. And she knew she was.

There was no we're-a-couple-now kiss when he met her in the yard. She could have offered, but she was tuning in to his cues, which went against all her instincts. She wanted to jump his bones and plant one on him. She made do with returning his glad-to-see-you smile and telling him she'd saved him some lunch.

He closed the back door behind them, grabbed her arm, turned her and drew her to him. His kiss brought last night forward. It was still with him, too. She clung to him and celebrated, trading kiss for kiss with equal satisfaction.

"How's your head?" He pulled back so he could get a look.

"All better."

He smiled wistfully as he measured the lump on her forehead with his thumb. "Not quite, but you're still alive and kissing."

"You fixed Tutan's gate?"

"Not yet. He wasn't around, and his wife wouldn't give me the go-ahead. We tried, huh?"

She slipped her arm around his waist and walked

him into the kitchen. "I have an appointment in Rapid City tomorrow. Hoolie says you're taking me."

"Makes sense, doesn't it?"

"Not if you're doing it because you're, you know…"

He laughed. "A halfways doctor?"

"Hoolie's a kick, isn't he?" She slid away, went to the refrigerator and took out the sandwiches she'd made for him. "I know that's the real reason Zach talked you into staying." She took a plate from the cupboard. "I didn't care then—I just wanted them to go on a honeymoon, for heaven's sake—but I wasn't planning to con you into being my personal halfway doctor. I don't want you to…" She turned to him, her hands, braced on the counter, bracketing her hips. "You don't need to be involved in my medical issues."

"Okay."

"That's not one of the benefits."

"Is there a list somewhere? I know our arrangement was pretty vague, but you start talkin' benefits, seems like there should be some negotiation."

"I'm serious, Hank. You were absolutely right—you're not the cure for what ails me. And I'm not your patient." She gave a shy smile. "I want to be something you don't already have."

"That covers a lot of territory." He lifted one shoulder. "I have friends. One or two, anyway."

"Women?"

"I know some women." His smile was slow and lazy. "None like you."

"That's nice. I like that. And I appreciate your offer to drive me to Rapid City. I just don't want you to feel like you have to—" she drew a deep breath and sighed "—take care of me."

"I don't feel like I have to do anything. What time is your appointment?"

"Nine." She perked up some. "And there's something I want to show you afterward. It's a little bit out of the way, but I really think it's important for you to see it."

"Out of the way in what direction?"

"North and east."

"Perfect. You show me yours, and I'll show you mine." He loaned her an actual smile. "I've got a few things to take care of at home."

"Cool! We'll take the high road to the day horses and the low road to the Night Horses."

"What's the quickest way for me to get to that food behind you?"

She returned his smile with interest. "The toll road."

Chapter 8

"Mr. Night Horse?" The crisp voice jerked Hank out of his waiting-room-aquarium reverie. He blinked up at the red-haired, flour-paste-faced woman standing over him. "This way, please."

He followed the crepe-soled shoes and ample ass down a bright, narrow hallway. If she was taking him to a different part of the clinic, it probably wasn't a good sign. He imagined Sally "resting comfortably," tried to imagine what might have come up, what he could say or do to add to her comfort. Back to the friendship part of the bargain. He'd lied. He had more than one or two friends.

He'd told the truth. There was none like her.

The nurse rapped on the door before ushering him into a plush exam room. Specialists had it made.

This one was losing his dark hair a patch at a time, but he was letting the sides grow to compensate. He wore a crisp shirt and tie with his white coat, and he stood to glad-hand Hank. "Sally's all set, doing just fine. She was telling me you're a rodeo medic. I have a friend who works with the Justin Sportsmedicine Team. Rod Benoit from Billings. Wondered if you've run into him."

"Dr. Benoit. Sure." Hank held a flat hand five feet above the floor. "Little guy with big hair. Crazy mustache."

"That's Rod. If he hadn't gone into medicine, he would've been a cowboy. He loves rodeo. Been pushing helmets and safety vests on bull riders for years."

"He's made a lot of headway." Hank chuckled. "So to speak."

"It's a good program. I see a lot of sports injuries. I know cowboys don't like to take off their hats except to eat or pray, but I'm a big supporter of helmets."

"Yeah, me, too."

"I just wanted to meet you. When Sally said she had a rodeo medic sitting out there in the waiting room, I told my nurse, I said, bring him on back."

Hank only had eyes for Sally, who was sitting in the corner, curiously quiet.

"Oh, she's fine," the doctor said. "Far as I can tell, none of her marbles fell out."

"So there's nothing…"

"She looks a lot better than the last time she was in. Well, except for her vision in that right eye, but that—"

"That's why I'm not driving." Sally sprang from the chair as though her name had been called.

"No, that's not why. That's not what caused the accident. We all have our limitations, and you know yours. You can't deny the disease, Sally." The doctor turned to Hank. "Tell Benoit Tony Schmidt said hello." He snapped his fingers. "Almost forgot." Schmidt took a folded check from his pocket, snapped it open with his thumb and handed it to Sally. "On my account."

With the door closed behind them, Hank turned to Sally. "*He* pays *you?*"

"He supports the sanctuary. I told him about the Wild Horse Challenge, and he wrote out a check." She gestured eagerly toward an exit sign at the end of the hallway. "We can go out this way."

"That nurse came to get me, I didn't know what was goin' on."

"He just wanted to meet you."

"And how did that come about?"

"He wanted to know how I got here. So I told him all about you." She turned to him as she leaned on the push bar of a side door. "What did you *think* was going on?"

"Hell, I thought something was wrong." He reached past her to lend his hand to their escape. "The way the nurse said, 'This way, please.' And then Dr. Tony's quizzing me like he's checkin' out my credentials."

"He thinks what you do is pretty cool. He says it's become a highly specialized field since I was involved as a stock contractor. There aren't that many of you, and I'm monopolizing an important team member."

"He said that?"

"*I* said that." She was on the march to his pickup, and he noticed her limp was more pronounced. "He said the part about you being such a rarity, and I just said…" He clicked the remote to unlock the door while she stood with her back to him. "I didn't say anything. Do they think I'm a child? A helpless, hopeless…" She jerked on the door handle. "I hate being talked around."

Hank knew what she meant. Talked down to, talked around, ignored. It was no way to treat people. He laid his hand on her shoulder. "You're not the kind to put up with it, either."

She turned her head, scowling. "What's that supposed to mean?"

"It means we're both rarities. Some people don't know how to act around us." He reached for the door handle, but she hung on. "Let me show you how a cowboy treats a lady." She hung on still. "An *Indian* cowboy. Rare as hen's teeth."

Her scowl melted. Her hand gave way to his claim to the privilege of opening the door. He wanted to kiss her right out there in public, but he figured the way she was looking at him, the way he felt looking at her said it all without letting anyone else in.

"Hank," she said, just when he was ready to roll. "I also think what you do is pretty cool. It's way more important than repairing busted gates and driving me around."

"I just came back from an event in Wyoming. I call my own shots. I think you know that." He stopped at the street corner. *Yield, shift gears, move on.* "So, I'm calling on you to call our next turn. We're headed east on thirty-four? How far?"

Forty miles east of town, she showed him her second-worst nightmare. She asked him not to stop the pickup, but to slow down and take a good look at the two hundred "unadoptable" horses warehoused on a few acres of land owned by a private contractor. They had been rounded up by helicopter and removed from public land where they were supposed to be left to roam freely. One by one the unattractive, unhealthy, uncooperative and otherwise unlucky creatures that had passed their sell-by date turned sad eyes toward the road. These were some of the horses an expanded Double D sanctuary would accommodate.

"If all goes well," Sally said, more to the faces in the field than the man who had her back.

The edgy growl of the pickup's big engine echoed Hank's feeling. He'd heard about the holding facilities, but he hadn't seen one. "Why can't we stop?" This crawling along the shoulder of the road was not how he rolled. "Are we being watched? Through a rifle scope, maybe?"

"You have to admit, I add considerable excitement to your life."

"Hell, you're a walk in the park."

"Didn't you notice that sign back there?"

"Which one?" He was looking for a gate.

She turned to him, all cocky, giving him that *what-*

of-it? look. "I'm practically blind in one eye, but I'm pretty sure it said Stay in Your Car."

"Oh, *that* sign." And *that* Sally. The unsinkable one. "That was just the top line. The practically blind line. The twenty-twenty line said, Entering Sioux Indian Country."

"It did not."

"The next one will. Watch your picnic basket. If they smell food, you're in real trouble."

She smiled for him, her eyes gleaming, defying deficiency. "You keep the engine running while I open the gate."

He laughed. "I was thinkin' the same way."

"Which is why we can't stop." She turned to the window. "Hang in there," she told the watchers. "We'll be back." And to Hank, "Won't we?"

How had he missed it? It was always the eyes that got to him—somebody looking to him to toss her a bone or toss him in the air, to take away her trouble or take away his pain. The eyes had it, said it, got to him and stayed with him long after his were closed for the night. More each day he was finding himself lost in Sally's eyes, but somehow he'd missed her loss. It was physical, and he was all about *physical*. As long as he didn't see any medical problems, she didn't have any. Right? He was the doctor. *Halfway.*

But he could have sworn she saw him clearly. Whether she accepted what she saw as what she got was another matter, *her* matter.

So, what the hell was the matter with him? If this was a classic case of the blind leading the blind…

He put his foot down. The pickup leaped onto the blacktop, engine roaring on the front end, tires kicking gravel out the back.

"It's only one eye, you know," she said.

"What?"

"My right eye's been sucky lately, but I have X-ray vision on the driver's side. I can see the wheels turning in your head. What are we doing?"

"Damn if I know." Getting away from a gate he couldn't open, pain he couldn't touch, eyes he wouldn't forget. "Tutan has friends in high places. I've got relations in all kinds of places. You're gonna meet my sister-in law."

Sally had been sleeping. She hadn't meant to, but Hank had gone silent on her, and she'd dozed off. Her mouth had probably exposed still more of her less-than-appealing side by falling open. When she opened her eyes, she saw tall grass in myriad shades of green and tan carpeting mile after mile of rolling plains. Buffalo grass it was called, but it fed horses just as well. Cattle, too, but they were relative newcomers. Before the cattle and the cattlemen, all of it had been Indian Country. Hank pointed out a sign that did, indeed, declare that they were entering the small portion that was left. South Dakota buttes and badlands softened into hills and bluffs as they traveled north.

The Night Horse place was tucked into the hills. In a suburb it would have been called a tract house. Here it was a "scattered site"—a modest home without neighbors. Cattle and a few horses grazed the hill-sides. A few cottonwood trees, a small swing set, a couple of cars and a vegetable garden filled the yard.

A slightly shorter, somewhat heavier version of Hank without the cowboy hat emerged from the front door as Hank and Sally closed the pickup doors.

"Back so soon, brother?"

"I smelled frybread."

Sally inhaled deeply. Hot lard, sage smoke and tomato plants.

"Where's Phoebe?"

"She's hangin' with friends." Hank turned, winked at Sally as she approached. Either that or he was squinting into the sun. She chose the wink. "Sally, my little brother, Greg."

"Is this that Sally you were talking about?" Greg's eyes had a quicker sparkle than his brother's. Quick and sweet, as opposed to slow and killer. "Look at her smile. Yeah, he's been talking you up."

"You told your doctor about me, I told my big-mouth brother about you," Hank confessed. "I guess that means something, huh?"

"It means you're a fast worker when you put your mind to it." Greg punched his brother's shoulder. "We've got fresh fry bread and *wojapi.* Come and eat."

Kay Night Horse welcomed Sally to her kitchen with a glass of wild mint tea and a chair next to the counter. Golden-brown squares of bread were piled high in a cardboard box next to a huge iron skillet on the stove. Steeped mint and steamy fruit scents mingled with deep-fat frying and yeast.

Sally nodded toward the oil-stained box. "I can tell that's the fresh fry bread, but Greg mentioned canned something, and it smells like berries."

"Juneberries," Kay said. "Dried from last year. We're a couple of weeks away from fresh. Don't you pick juneberries?"

"I wouldn't know a juneberry from a june bug. My sister offers wild-plum jam to any of her students who'll bring her the plums. Annie's a wonderful cook."

"Sally's sister teaches at Winter Count Day School," Hank said. The men had taken chairs at the table. "Isn't that where you went to school, Kay?"

"For a year, but then I went to Pierre. How long has your sister been there?"

"Five years. She's younger."

"Sally and her sister turned their ranch into a home on the range for wild horses." Hank nodded as Kay set a glass of tea on the table in front of him. "Since there's already a Home on the Range for Boys, they call it the Double D Ranch."

Sally caught Greg looking doubtfully at her chest. "My father's name was Don Drexler. My *grand*father's name was Don Drexler." She laughed. "We do get some strange calls when we advertise for volunteers."

"What did this guy say?" Greg wanted to know. Hank whacked the back of his brother's head, and everyone laughed.

More animated than she'd yet seen him, Hank described the wild-horse sanctuary and the need to expand it. He had the air of a man on his home turf, but he kept Sally center stage. She was Mustang Sally, Snow White and St. Francis rolled up into one. And he was just the man to hook her up.

"Does the name Tutan ring a bell, little brother?"

Greg gave the name a moment's pause. "Was that the guy who owned the ranch where the old man was killed?"

Hank nodded. "He's Sally's neighbor. He's also her main opposition. There's some remote country west of Sally's place that should be part of that sanctuary. It's prime for mustangs. Nobody would ever bother them. Some of it's tribal land." He raised his voice toward the kitchen. "Do you still have relatives on the council down there, Kay?"

"I've got one who generally looks out for the land-owners, two who side with the Indian ranchers, and one who'll butt heads with anybody." Kay refilled Sally's glass. "Your neighbor leases Indian land?"

"Some." Sally held up her hand and whispered *thanks.* "If I can get those leases, I can get the graz-ing permits on the adjoining public land. We could accommodate twice as many mustangs."

Greg grinned. "What's in it for us?"

"Horses."

He laughed. "Looks like you've finally found a soul mate, brother. Did you show her your latest res-cues? My brother's a soft touch when it comes to horses."

"They become part of who you are," Sally said. "They can lift a person off the ground—body, mind and spirit. They've been such wonderful partners for us for so long that we forget they were once wild. Like dogs and cats, domestic horses should have wild relatives. We must make sure of it. Some roots must be preserved, some seeds, some…"

She glanced at the brown faces, the brown eyes turned her way, and she could feel herself turning red. She lowered her gaze, studied the glass of pale tea. Wild mint. The scent of wild berries filled her nose. "We bring some of the horses in for people to adopt, to keep and use so that some can be left alone."

"Do you think they know?" Hank asked. "The one who doesn't get away, does he say to himself, I'll stand in a corral the rest of my life so my relations can run free?"

"I think so," Sally said hopefully. "I really do. And that's what we get out of the deal. We get to be with the ones who sacrifice. Maybe they can teach us something."

"Sure. If we can figure out how to learn."

"People adopt horses for their own use, but they go to all kinds of programs as well." Sally leaned into the discussion. "They're amazing, these horses. They're incredibly sensitive, and lend that sensitivity to us, in our lives…" She lifted one shoulder. "They've helped me."

"One of my cousins got in on a horse-training program in the prison in Nevada. It changed his life." Kay brought a plate of frybread and a bowl of hot fruit pudding to the table. "See if you like this, Sally.

The missionaries taught us to make fry bread, but the *wojapi* is what makes it really good, and that's ours."

Sally savored the food. It was almost as good as Annie's blueberry pie, which was to die for. As was the generous and gentle man who shared his family with her. He believed in her cause, and this was proof.

"I have to go pick up the girls from basketball camp," Kay told the group after taking a phone call. "They missed the bus again."

Sally started gathering dishes off the table. "May I ride along with you?" She glanced at Hank, who nodded and smiled.

Once the dusty, white Chevy was rolling on smooth blacktop, Sally turned from her polite questions about Hank's athletic nieces—questions eliciting little more than a word or two in response—to her real concern. "I don't mean to put you on the spot with your relatives on the Tribal Council. I don't usually ask for favors five minutes after I meet someone."

Kay didn't miss a beat. "How much time did Hank get?"

"Funny you should ask. Within the first five minutes, I think I did him a favor." She chuckled. "Of course, I could be flattering myself."

"First he's singing for some cowboy's wedding— he tried that song out for us, and *jeez* that was pretty."

"It was wonderful."

"And then he's helping this cowboy out for a few weeks, and then it's all Mustang Sally and Kay, can you help us out? I don't know what you did for him, but I hope it lasted more than five minutes."

Sally stared. She gave it at least five seconds. And then she burst out laughing. She had met her no-bull match in Kay Night Horse. When she caught her breath, she told Kay the skinny-dipping story, and they shared a good laugh.

"I'll do what I can for your sanctuary because Hank wants me to," Kay said. "If he says it's a good thing, then it is. What you said about the wild horses goes for Hank, too. He's helped a lot of people. The kind who won't let just anyone get too close."

"I know."

"That's the kind he wants to be. Tries to be. Lift a person off the ground, brush him off and send him on his way. You do that day after day, you keep your guard up, you should be fine."

"My, um…this friend who's a doctor, he was eager to meet Hank. He says—"

"He took care of Greg after their mother died. Hank was fifteen. They stayed with relatives, but Hank looked after his little brother. When Hank got into the Indians in Medicine program at the university, Greg stayed with him. Stayed with him for a while after Hank got married."

"Was he there when Hank's son was killed?"

"Greg was with me by then." Kay glanced at her as she slowed for a turn at a T in the road. "Deborah—Hank's wife—she was pretty and everything, maybe not as smart as she thought she was, but smart enough. It turned out she couldn't do real life. When that little boy died and that woman left, Hank's world caved in on him. But he's a survivor. He's the kind who picks himself up and goes at it again, only twice as hard as he was before. He'll turn himself inside out for you if that's what you want."

It wasn't. And he wouldn't. Kay had it all wrong. "We haven't known each other very long."

"Like I said, the way you talked about the horses, you could have been talking about Hank."

"Amazing," Sally whispered, thought about it, turned to Kay and smiled. "Did I use the word *amazing?*"

"Amazing he let you get close to him so quick."

"Don't worry. His guard is secure. And I'm harmless."

The look Kay gave said *we'll see*. But she smiled. "At least you come with some horses."

Nothing had been said about how long they would be staying or where they would be sleeping, but Hank and Sally sat outside on kitchen chairs as dusk fell and traded stories with Greg and Kay. Stars appeared and so did the guitars. In the old days, Hank said as he strummed, he and his little brother had often sung together for their supper. But those days were gone, Greg crooned as he tightened his E string. Now dessert would do nicely.

Sally was charmed by the music, mesmerized by the stars glittering against the black-velvet sky. When she saw flashes of color, she thought her bad eye was playing a good trick on her. Her senses were, after all, weirdly wired. Maybe she was hearing in color.

She closed one eye at a time, and the stars danced for her, but the colors vanished.

Kay touched her arm and pointed. There it was again, a bit brighter, a little braver. Hank looked up, strummed a final chord, and grabbed Sally's hand. "Grand finale," he said as he pulled her out of the chair. "You guys comin'?"

"Can't." Greg hit a low note. "Kids."

Hank's pickup roared to the top of the steep hill behind the house. He cut the engine, and all seemed suddenly quiet. Cut the lights, and all was dark. He grabbed a couple of blankets out of the back, spread one over the crisp grass, and with a sweeping gesture offered Sally the best seat in the universe. A soft breeze rustled the grass, a few crickets held a pow-wow in the draw below, and a brigade of ghostly rainbows jostled in the northern sky.

"Northern lights," Sally whispered. "I haven't seen them since I was a girl."

"You're still a girl." He stretched out on his back and tucked his arms beneath his head.

"Oh, no, I'm not." She lay down beside him. "You need a woman."

"We used to come up here at night when we were boys. No girls. But you're right. We thought about women. Each of us got to pick one to bring up here. If we couldn't get that one, we'd be out of luck."

"Who did you pick?"

"Natalie Wood. I'd've had her for sure if she wasn't dead. Greg was gonna get Madonna. He wanted to see what was under those cones. I told him a woman

who shows that much skin in public can't be trusted."
He chuckled. "We were boys."

"Natalie Wood," she mused. She wondered what
Deborah looked like. She wouldn't ask. *Natalie Wood*
she could say aloud, but not *Deborah*. Deborah was
not harmless.

He sat up. She woke up from her musing, looked
up and followed his lead. One by one the lights were
turning on—a battalion of vertical rainbows bobbing
shoulder to shoulder to shoulder across the night sky.
The colors were vivid, the palette complete. So vast
was the sky, so enormous the display that it was im-
possible to be separate from it. Sally's vision cleared.
Her body melted. She became blue-green. She ebbed
and flowed with the swells of refracted light. She
was beautiful.

She was flawless.

She touched Hank's arm, just to be sure he was
still there. He put his hand on her thigh. So cool. She
could feel it right through her jeans. Deliciously brac-
ing, like springwater. Wherever the lights took them,
they were going there together.

"Lie back," he told her when the lights began to re-
cede. He unbuttoned her jeans, unzipped, unleashed
his mouth and all its unsettling skills on her belly. He
lowered her clothing, nibbled and tickled and tongued
until all the colors of the rainbow rushed ahead of his
painstaking advance on her sentient core. She could
neither keep still nor silent. "Keep your eyes on the
skies," he whispered. "Still there?"

"Yes." It was all she could manage. A single word for infinity fading too fast.

"Don't close your eyes yet." He kissed her high inside her thigh and low between her thighs. "Still?"

"Yes, but..."

"Close your eyes and open your legs for me," he whispered, his breath soft and stimulating. She could hardly move, and so he helped her. The lights were still there, and his tongue charged them up, more brilliant than before. Brighter than icy morning, more dazzling than sun through rain.

He caught her colorful thrills and delicate spills on his lips and delivered them to hers, let her taste her essence, which only made her crave his. They peeled each other bare and touched, tasted, breathed each other in until they blended so perfectly that her leading him to her and his going inside was inevitable.

They made their own rainbow.

Chapter 9

The brown-and-white sedan with the word *Sheriff* emblazoned on the sides was the second most unwelcome traveler on the three-mile stretch of gravel between the highway and the Drexler house. Not that Sally had anything against Cal Jenner—she'd voted for him three times—but the news he brought almost always had something to do with the owner of the *most* unwelcome vehicle.

"You've got horses on the road again, Sally," Cal announced as he closed the door with the letters *S-h-e* behind him and hitched up his brown pants. "I don't see a gate open, don't see any fence down, but they're getting out somewhere."

"Kevin!" Hank beckoned with a gesture. The boy took the rubber ball from Phoebe's mouth, tossed it up and hit a pop fly into the shelter belt, sending both dogs on a tear before he dropped the bat and headed for home. "How far south?" Hank asked the lawman.

"They're actually about four miles north of here."

"I've been gone for a couple of days, just drove down that road not thirty minutes ago," Sally protested. "Somebody's messing with our fences."

"Probably some of your volunteers. Have you taken on any new recruits lately?"

"No, but even if we had they wouldn't be cutting our fences."

"I didn't see any sign of anything like that goin' on," Cal said. "You got any better ideas?"

"Well, let me think." Sally tapped her chin and rolled her eyes skyward.

Cal shook his head. "Dan hasn't complained to me in—I don't know—couple weeks at least. Now, I have heard from the BLM out there in Wyoming. They want to know how you're doing. I say, *how they're doing what?* And they say, how you're doing with the community. Which is a loaded question, and I'm trained to duck and cover."

Sally wasn't amused. "Are you getting reports on us from anyone else?"

"Nope."

"Then why are you ducking?"

"I admire what you're doing, Sally. You know that. I want to see the Sheriff's Posse go completely Spanish Mustang." Cal turned to Hank. "We've got braggin' rights to six adopted mustangs on the drill team now. I'll take them over any other horse in the bunch.

The spirit of the old West lives in those horses. I'm all for—"

"You don't get any other complaints," Hank affirmed.

"An anonymous call once in a while. Horses on the highway. Usually there's nothing to it, but I always check it out."

"You mention that to the BLM?"

"If they ask."

Hank laid his hand on Kevin's shoulder. "There's some horses out on the right of way, a few miles north. Saddle up and run 'em across the road and through the west gate. Make sure that side's secure."

"In with the cattle?" Kevin asked.

"For now." Hank turned to Sally. "I'll have a look on the east side."

She nodded. "We keep our fence in good repair. You know that, Cal."

"Yours is better than most."

"Riding fence is everybody's favorite assignment around here." She glanced at Kevin, who was beating a path back to the barn, eager to carry out Hank's order.

"On the other hand," Cal added, "if horses are the spirit, cattle are the lifeblood of this part of the country."

"We have cattle, too. The Drexlers have been here longer than the Tutans. We've changed our focus." Sally divided her smile between the two men. "It used to be disappointing not to make any money ranching. These days we're *purposely* not making a profit."

"Somebody has to make enough profit to pay some taxes, or the county's got no way to gas up my squad car." Turning to Hank, Cal adjusted his tan Stetson by the brim. "If you see any new breaks in the fence or something doesn't look right, you give me a call."

Two days later Hank found an opening in a cross-fence between the Drexlers' land and Tutan's. No breaks. No cuts. This time, the fence had been taken down from the posts. It could easily be put back up, and no one would be the wiser. Was that the plan?

He swung down from Ribsy's saddle for a closer look when a distant rifle shot nearly caused him a long walk back to the house.

"Easy, girl."

He'd nearly calmed her down before another shot was fired and he opted for an awkward running re-mount over losing the reins. He loped the mustang in a tight circle to distract her from taking off across the flat, which was what her one-track mind was set on. He started to head back the way he had come—no way would the mare go along with any human-brained investigation—when he noticed a small carcass. Prairie dog. *Dogs.* He counted five. He'd ridden into their little town and found carnage.

Another distant gunshot.

"Easy, Ribs."

Who in hell would be shooting prairie dogs in a wildlife sanctuary?

Damn Tootin'. Who the hell else? Hank wondered

how many hands he hired to keep his ranch going while he ran around playing games.

He had a pretty good idea where the shots were coming from. He'd taken a ride out this way, noticed a couple of dog towns and thought he'd come back sometime with a pair of binoculars and watch the big birds make meat. He could watch hawks and eagles all day long. But little men with big shotguns? Not so much.

Hank headed for high ground, following the fence line. The scrub brush on the bluffs hid him from the rider of an ATV pushing through the draw below with a discordant whine that set Hank's teeth on edge. Then he saw the rider's game. He was running horses. He was terrorizing a band of four mares, three foals and a stud. And the stud was Don Quixote. A shot rang out, and the horses flew past. Hank looked down and saw the rifle barrel and a green baseball cap at least a hundred yards below.

With a little backtracking he was able to circle behind the shooter without being seen or heard. Leaving Ribsy ground-tied a few yards behind enemy lines, Hank was able to get close enough to count coup or cause a coronary. With luck, both.

"Going hunting, Mr. Tutan?"

Hank gave himself a moment to enjoy the look of a man who'd just heard a ghost. His brother favored their father in looks and build, but Hank had the voice. Not that John Night Horse had been much of a talker, but whenever he showed up in church, he always sang his heart out. Tutan's eyes bulged in a ruddy face gone pasty as he looked right and left, searching for the voice's owner.

"What's in season this time of year?" Hank stepped out from behind a scraggly clutch of choke-cherry bushes.

"It's you." Tutan clapped his hand over his eyes. The color drained from his lips, and Hank had to wonder whose luck was in play. If the man keeled over, Hank might have to find a new profession. "Damn, you scared me," Tutan gasped.

"Did you take me for someone else, Mr. Tutan?" He said the name the way he'd heard it long ago, with his father's distinctive inflection.

"Night Horse," Tutan said carefully. "What was he to you?"

"I'll tell you what he wasn't." Hank raised his chin. "He wasn't a hunter. Had no patience for it. Didn't own a gun. Said he'd eaten enough deer meat growing up to last him a lifetime."

Tutan's eyes narrowed. "You don't look much like him."

"What happened to him?"

"Sounds like you know more about him than I do."

"Maybe." Hank nodded toward the draw. "That's quite a horse, isn't it?"

"Which one?"

"The one you're gunnin' for."

"They're protected. They're good for nothin' but making trouble, but the law says you gotta leave 'em alone. Even when they run right through your fence." Tutan hefted his rifle as though he'd just remembered he had it with him. He wore a loaded hunter's vest over his white T-shirt. "What's not protected is those damn prairie dogs. It's open season on those sons-abitches."

"You're running those horses."

"I don't know who that is on the four-wheeler. Figured it must be one of Sally's people. Or Annie's. Or yours, maybe." He turned his head and spat. "I'm shooting prairie dogs."

"You're on the wrong side of the fence."

"They're the ones on the wrong side of the fence." He shouldered his rifle and pointed it toward the foot of the hill. "Look down there. See? I hit one, two, three. Oops. Still twitching." He aimed and fired. "That's four. They're pests. They destroy good pasture. A cow, a horse, she steps in one of those holes and *snap* goes the leg. She's all done." He turned and squinted up at Hank. "Fence is down again. Bet you've got horses scattered from here to Texas." He nodded toward the low ground. "Those prairie dogs don't give a rat's ass whose side of the fence they dig up. Horses don't care about fences. Why should I?"

"Because you're claiming to be the injured party."

"*That's* an injured party." Tutan waved his rifle at the dead prairie dogs and laughed. "Tell the Drexler girls they don't have to thank me. It's something I like to do in my spare time."

"Anything happens to that horse, I'm comin' after you."

Tutan tucked the butt of his rifle into his armpit, pointing the barrel at the ground. He gave a cold smile. "I'll leave the light on for you."

Nothing riled Hank more than a mean-spirited smile.

Sally stared at her stick. She hadn't used it in two and a half months—*months*—but she could've used it today. After getting her fingers tied up in tack and caught once in a drawer, once in a cupboard door, she'd pronounced herself "all thumbs" and turned the job of straightening out the tack room over to a volunteer. She'd tripped over her own feet on the way back to the house, and she'd cursed the words and the placement of a rail fence four feet out of reach.

All thumbs. Numb thumbs would have been more accurate. But who would get it besides somebody like her? *Tripped over her own feet.* Normal people did that all the time. But normal people had no trouble getting back up.

A few more days. Was that too much to ask? Couldn't she be an ordinary, active, fully functional woman for just a few more days? A few more days living in a whole woman's body with the whole, healthy man whose boots were bringing him to her right now, across the wood floor in the foyer, into the hallway. She knew the measure of his stride, the sound of his boot heels, the feel of his presence in the house.

She hadn't wasted any time using her senses while the disease was sleeping. Maybe they'd given her more of him than she would want to be left with in his absence, but she wasn't about to back down. She turned, saw him standing there in her doorway, and willed herself—for the hundredth time since she'd last picked herself up when no one was looking, which meant it didn't count—to hold out just *a few more days*.

"Guess what." Springing from her desk chair like an eager schoolgirl was a private test. Publicly passing, she smiled accordingly. "I just had a call from a guy named Logan Wolf Track. He's on the Tribal Council, and he's related to Kay Night Horse." She put her arms around him and gave a full-press squeeze, another personal best. "She already put in a good word for us."

"'Course she did. What did he say?"

"They'll be voting at their next meeting. He says he's looked at our application, and he's quite familiar with the sanctuary. He's been up on the back roads, and he says he really likes the stallion, and that's a nice band of mares he's got running with him and all like that. So, I know he's on the horses' side, which is good. And I don't think he likes Tutan."

"Why not?"

"He didn't say it in so many words. It was kind of an oh-yeah-*that*-guy response. Maybe it was just a tone, but I got the distinct impression he's on our side." She laid her fingertip on his square chin. "So, thank you."

"Thank my sister-in-law."

"I did. I will again. And I won't pop any corks until after the vote is taken, but I'm feeling good about it."

"Yeah. That's…" Hands on her shoulders, he drew himself from her arms. She dropped them quickly to her sides and started her own withdrawal, but he caught her hand before it was complete. "The honeymooners should be back soon, huh?"

"In another week. But that doesn't mean…" She squeezed his hand despite her inclination to pull away. "You're free to go anytime you need to. Or want to."

"We still have to separate out those horses Kevin ran in off the road. We'll take care of that this morning." He rubbed his thumb over the back of her hand. He was trying to tell her something, but he was *all thumbs*. "But Kevin got them in without any help."

"Kevin's come a long way."

He met her gaze. "I just had a run-in with Tutan."

"The fence was down?"

"Yeah, but that's not the half of it. He was shooting prairie dogs."

"No law against that."

"On your property."

"Double D property?"

"Your side of the fence, where all those dog towns are."

"They've gotten out of control in that area on both sides of the fence. I haven't decided what to do about it."

"Is letting Tutan have at 'em one of the options?"

"Well, no, but I don't want you to—"

"Because whatever he's up to, it's about horses, not prairie dogs. Some young guy was runnin' your Spanish stud and his band up and down that draw, and Tutan's all gun happy. Then I come along, and he starts shootin' off his mouth."

"Oh, Hank. You two are fuse meets powder keg."

"No, we're not. He's nothing. No fire, no fire-power, *nothing*. But I'm not goin' anywhere until Zach gets back."

"Are you supposed to be somewhere else?"

"Doesn't matter."

"Are you scheduled for a rodeo this weekend?"

"I'm not goin' anywhere, and I'm not callin' any-body. I don't want you to, either. Let them take all the time they want. I'm just checking."

"They haven't changed their plans," she said qui-etly. "One more week. We'll call the sheriff, Hank. We'll be fine. You do what you need to do."

"I need to stay. I made Zach a promise. Hell, I made Tutan a promise. I need to be here until Zach comes back."

The weekend passed without incident. Not that there weren't happenings. Feel-good happenings—the kind Sally craved above all else—and concern-ing happenings, which she covered pretty well, she thought, keeping her concerns to herself. She would not bring the cane out until Hank left. He knew about it, but not firsthand. If she played her cards just right, she could preserve her dignity.

The feel-goods—or the good feels—were happen-ing with delightful regularity. She pitted Little Henry against big Ribsy in a cutting contest, separating wild horses from a herd of watchful bovine mothers. Lit-

tle Henry lost only because Sally lost her stirrups—
actually lost her feet for a little while there, but the
two of them were the only ones who knew. Under
the circumstances, not losing her seat was a major,
if private, victory. Cutting was a tricky feat for any
rider, with her horse changing direction at the drop
of a hat, stopping on a dime. Both mustangs had improved their cutting skills under Zach's hand in testa-
ment to Sally's claim that mustangs could be trained
for almost anything.

Her aching butt was a glorious feeling. She hadn't
put a horse through any real paces in a long time. Better to have ached and lost than never to have ached at
all. But it was the moaning and groaning every time
she sat down that brought her the best reward. Hank
took her to his room, stripped her down, buttered her
up with lotion, kneaded her muscles into putty, and
made slow, sumptuous love to her until every nerve
in her body grabbed a part in her physical version of
the *Hallelujah Chorus*.

"I'm going to miss this," she told him as she lay
in his arms, languidly stroking his hard, lean hip.

"That's not the part you'll miss. Come on."

"It's not the only part, but it's *part* of the part.
They're bolted together." She stroked him, back to
front. "Without the bolt, you'd lose your screw."

"Naughty girl." He grabbed hold of her bottom
and pressed her against him. "Without the bolt, *you'd*
lose *your* screw."

"And I would definitely miss that." She looked up
at him in the dark. "I'm going to miss all of you. Es-

pecially your hands." She kissed his shoulder. "I love the way they feel on me. Anywhere, anytime. Your hands touching me makes me feel special."

"You are."

"A cool connection. A warm kinship."

He kissed her hair, the bump on her forehead, her nearly blind eye. Her heart fell. He had her deficiencies all mapped out. Except the hair. She had good hair. Knowing Hank, the hair kiss was a diversionary tactic. He knew her legs were about to start giving her real trouble again. Not so special. Very undignified.

"I hope we hear from the BLM about the training contest this week."

"I hope you do, too. I hope it works out."

"Thank you." That wasn't what she wanted to hear. "You don't have to… You know, you could just enter the contest. If you had the time." He tossed off a chuckle. "But I know you have places to go and people to see."

"I don't have a place to be, or people to see. What I have is a job. I have things to do. That's something you never run out of—never runs out on you. There's always something to do."

"Of course. I know exactly what you mean."

"If you need any help with your mustangs… You probably don't need much shoeing, but maybe with the contest…"

"If they approve."

"If they approve."

"Max Becker probably thinks I have a screw loose, just proposing such a thing."

"Your screws are none of Max Becker's goddamn business." He braced up on one elbow and cupped her face in his other hand. "Not as long as I'm here."

Hoolie and Sally met the newlyweds at the Rapid City Airport. They came off the plane holding hands, still looking like they weren't about to come down from the clouds anytime soon.

"Getting from Sydney to New York was the easy part," Zach said. He looked tired, but at least part of the bleariness was clearly deliriousness. It was contagious. Sally felt a little dizzy herself.

"New York to South Dakota is the real stretch," Zach was saying. "But I could get used to that first-class treatment. They just keep pourin' on the bubbly."

"*That* explains it." Sally laughed. "And I thought you were still—"

"Except the Denver to Rapid City leg. That twenty-passenger egg crate, that's your reality check."

"The reality is, you're still married."

"Oh, yeah. It's official." Zach threw an arm around Hoolie's shoulders as they headed for baggage. "How's ol' Hank been makin' out?"

Hoolie nearly choked on his cherry Slurpee.

"You'll have to ask him," Sally said. "After I look up the directions for turning myself into a fly on the wall."

Zach gave his wife the high brow. "I'm thinkin' things went well."

"I'm thinking you don't know my sister."

On the way home, the women sat in the backseat of Zach's beloved pickup, Zelda Blue, and the men sat in the front, South Dakota style. Zach fondled Zelda's steering wheel, and Annie teased him about his separation anxiety every time they'd ridden in a foreign vehicle. Hoolie wanted to know if they'd seen any Australian "Brumbies" like the horses in *The Man From Snowy River,* and Zach turned up the country music and sang along with Willie and Waylon and the boys.

Annie took pointed notice of her sister's cane. "How are you feeling?" she asked quietly.

It was the wrong question. Sally was neither ready nor willing to make up an answer.

Hank hated goodbyes. If he had anything to say about it, it wouldn't be the forever kind—he was planning on seeing Sally again, one way or another—but he didn't want to say goodbye to the time they'd shared. Even with the same woman, a guy never knew who he might be saying hello to the next time around.

He decided to be gone when the family got back. Let them tell their stories back and forth, show pictures, give out souvenirs. He'd give Sally a call tonight and explain. He just didn't want his last three weeks getting thrown into the mix with somebody else's honeymoon.

Before he headed for the Denver Stock Show, he had one stop to make. He wanted to make an indelible impression on Tutan, make sure the man knew exactly who he was dealing with and that it wasn't time for counting because the dealing wasn't done.

Tutan was just toolin' into his yard on a familiar-looking ATV. Hank purposely parked in the man's road to let him know he was there for a powwow and got out of the pickup. A man with decent manners would have done the same, met in the middle and given his visitor a courteous ear. Not Damn Tootin'.

"Zach and Annie are coming home today," Hank shouted over the infernal small-engine racket.

"So?"

He nodded toward the yard light. "I saw your light on."

"It's always on," Tutan bellowed. "What's on your mind?"

"Shut this thing off and I'll tell you!"

Tutan complied, folded his arms across his barrel chest, and kept his seat.

"You got the news about the tribal leases?"

"I did. You can be damn sure it's not the final word. I've had those leases since—"

"It's the final word, Mr. Tutan. Indians love horses. There's no gettin' around that fact."

"So, you went to the tribe and said something about John Night Horse. Am I right? But he wasn't from this reservation, and neither are you. You got no right coming down here and making trouble over something that happened years ago."

Hank's blood ran cold, which kept him cool while he stared steely eyed through a red haze and spoke carefully measured words. "What *exactly* happened?"

"Nobody knows." Tutan gave an insolent shrug. "He'd been dead for who knows how long by the time they found him. Been drinking. Looked like he might've been hunting. Might've fallen on his gun. Might've…" He stared straight at Hank's face. "Who the hell knows?"

"And no one was with him."

"Might've been. Nobody ever came forward, so there's no way to find out, is there? It happened a long time ago." Tutan's eyes narrowed. "What was he to you?"

"He was my father."

"I figured as much. You should've told me right away. I know it's a little late, but you have my condolences."

Unable to look at the man any longer, Hank stared across Tutan's alfalfa field at the hills bolstering the blue horizon. He had what he wanted for now. Back to nature for Lakota land, open spaces for a few more wild horses.

"You still hold some Indian lease land," Hank reminded Tutan.

"That's right. And the way I heard it, I still have some support on the council."

"You could lose the rest of your leases," Hank warned. "I'm not from this reservation, but we're all related. You mess with those mustangs, you'll regret it."

"I don't have time for horses."

"I do," Hank said quietly. "Not only that, I have time to make your life a living hell in ways you haven't thought of yet. You cause Sally Drexler trouble, I'll cause you trouble. I'll match you, and then I'll go you one worse. You've got friends? I've got friends. Plus I've got cause." He took a step back. "I don't know who killed my father, but you do. One way or another you'll take his death with you to your grave. *Sooner.* Or later. That's your problem."

"The hell you say." Tutan laughed. "I'm not superstitious."

"Neither am I." Hank's smile was cool and calculated. "You keep trying to kill Sally's sanctuary, you'll pay in *this* life, *Mr.* Tutan. And you'll pay dearly."

Hank watched the man and his little scooter shrink in his rearview mirror as he drove away. Regrets all around, he thought. He was already regretting his decision to leave.

But, hell, he had a job to do.

He jammed a CD into the slot in his dashboard and sang along with another Hank.

He was so lonesome he could cry.

Chapter 10

Within a few months the new lease on tribal land would become the bridge between the Double D and the more isolated public land Sally hoped to add to the sanctuary. Tutan's leases were paid through October. After that, he was *outta there*.

Sally had it all now. Everything she and Hank had talked about—a place to be, people to see, a ton of work to do. Most of the work she had to do could be done on her place, and that was a good thing. She wasn't quite as limber as she had been when she'd last seen Hank about a month ago. *Exactly* a month ago if the month were February, which was what it felt like. Cold, barren, desolate—a feeling Sally kept bottled up while she served as a smiling maypole for the newlyweds to chase around she couldn't have dampened

Annie's and Zach's spirits even if she'd wanted to. And before Hank, she might have wanted to.

Before Hank, she might have retreated to her room and let them have the rest of the house, knowing full well that they would wonder and worry, at least a little. She always said she didn't want that. Now she meant it. She wanted what she had—a place to be, work to do and people to see. One in particular.

She glanced over Little Henry's rump and past the corral fence. The road was long and empty, but the place—*her* place—was shaping up the way she'd long dreamed. She was working on it. The round pen and the new bigger, better outdoor arena were already half finished. She worked on her people—volunteers were coming out of the woodwork since the training competition had been advertised.

She worked when she relaxed, if currying her new favorite mustang could be considered work. Little Henry loved attention, and she loved the way he smelled, the way he snuffled, the way his ears twitched, but mainly the way his hide felt against her palms. She liked the feel of feel. It made her feel alive.

She couldn't stand for hours on end anymore, and she'd stopped pushing it. Pretty much. Her cane stood ready to get her back to the house if a bout of no-feel threatened. Heat brought it on sometimes, but she loved the feel of the sun on her face. Stress could do it to her, but she hadn't heard from Damn Tootin' in more than a week.

Loneliness was a killer. Not literally, of course. She wasn't about to die from MS, and she could live without Hank Night Horse. He'd kept his promise, and he'd given her the best three weeks she'd had in years. She didn't blame him for taking off before she and Hoolie pulled in with the bride and groom. Who needed to ooh and aah over a thousand pictures of kangaroos and Australian ranches and horseback riding in the outback? Hank, too, had places to be and people to see. Not to mention work to do. *Two* jobs. He was a busy man.

He'd called that night, said he'd just pulled into Denver.

"Hope I didn't wake you up," he said quietly. "I figured you'd all be up gabbing, but you sound... distant."

"I am distant. How far is it from here to Denver? I haven't been there in years."

"The Stock Show starts in a couple of days."

"A couple of days?"

"A guy called me—another PA—asked me to fill in for him. I owe him one."

"When did he call?" When he didn't answer, she felt foolish. She laughed a little. "I mean...I didn't know you'd be leaving so soon."

"It felt like the right time. You're back to a full house now."

"I wouldn't say that. It's a big house." *Say no more, Sally. You might look pathetic sometimes, but you never have to sound pathetic.* Jack up that voice. "But, hey, your work here is done."

"Yeah. Back to earning a paycheck."

"We didn't keep you from—"

"No. You didn't. I was…glad to help out."

She knew he was. Hank was an honest man. She loved that about him. Among other things. "If you ever feel like donating more time to a worthy cause…"

"You mean the horses?"

"All charity work here is tax deductible." She put on a happy face and gave a good ol' Sally laugh.

"Yeah." This was straight-shooter Hank she was talking to. No laughing matter. "I want to see you again."

"You know where to find me. The days of going down the road are pretty much over for me."

"You're in a good place, Sally. Doing good work."

"I know. I truly appreciate everything you did, Hank." She drew a deep breath. "Stop by whenever you can."

And that was that. She'd said she'd see him whenever. *See you when I see you.* And she meant it. She'd missed a lot of things in recent years. The rodeo was one of those things. Dancing, driving, getting from here to there without embarrassing herself were a few more things. Seeing clearly out of her right eye would have been nice. A man? Sure. Why not. Add Hank Night Horse to the list. When he came back through her corner of the world, maybe they could pick up where they left off for a day or two. If she felt like it.

If he came back.

Please come back.

She felt tired when she put the grooming bucket back in the tack room. She was glad she had her cane handy. She felt a few months of wheelchair rides coming on, but not, she hoped, before fall. Her right foot wanted to turn on her as she limped back to the corral with a feed pan full of oats for Little Henry. She should have used a bucket with a handle. It wouldn't be the first time she'd ended up facedown in a pan of oats.

Nor the last. She called to the horse and laughed aloud when he came trotting toward her. She'd heard recently that several good belly laughs a day could make a huge improvement in a person's overall health, and her good ol' Sally laugh was always at the ready. She was all about improvement.

"Are you feeding my namesake?"

He startled her, but she kept her cool. No tripping over her own feet, no face in the oats. She turned, and her heart rate redoubled when she saw his handsome face.

"Can I help?" Hank asked.

"Thanks. I've got it." She hoped her smile wasn't coming off all shaky. "You're sneaky, Hank Night Horse."

"I've got a reputation to protect."

"I'll spread the word."

He glanced at the horse inside the corral. "Doesn't look like he's been ridden."

"I've gotten lazy."

"Can't have that." He took the pan from her hand. "Little Henry should have to earn this."

"I'm really not up to—" She was nearly up to Hank's shoulders, swept off her feet by two strong arms. Like *that* would ever happen. "What are you doing, you crazy man?"

"We're going for a ride." He carried her to the fence. "Get the gate, will ya? I've got my arms full."

"I can't." But she did. She opened the gate. "I mean I shouldn't. Not—" He lifted her onto the horse's back like a sack of feed. "I'm gonna ride with a halter and lead rope?"

"Can you throw your leg over before you slide off and I have to lift you back up there?"

"You see, that's part of the prob—" He lifted her leg by the boot heel and gave her a leg over. She grabbed a handful of mane and scooted toward the withers while he made a rein from the lead. "Okay. But what's this *we* stuff?"

"Which is your good eye? Oh, yeah, the left. Watch over your left shoulder. You don't wanna miss this."

He took a step back and vaulted over Little Hank's rump almost faultlessly. There was one small *oomph.*

"Impressive performance," she allowed as he rested his chin on her left shoulder. "Of course, we named him *Little* Henry for a reason."

"And big Henry only does that trick once in a blue moon for a reason." He kissed her left cheek and whispered in her left ear. "There will be no second performance of any kind tonight."

She laughed. Hell, she was a woman. What did she know? Besides the fact that he had to be kidding.

"Just for that, I'm withholding the reach-around I was about to give you, too." But he did reach for the reins, and he pushed the open gate and nudged Little Henry with his boot heel. "I might as well tell you right up front—"

"I think you're riding what the drovers call drag."

"—that I'm crazy about you."

That shut her up. Briefly. "How do you know this?"

"I've been crazy before. Wasn't planning on goin' there again, but there it is." He slipped his free arm around her, sneaked his hand under the bottom of her T-shirt and spread his fingers over her bare skin. "Here's what I know. I truly appreciated everything *we* did. I appreciated falling asleep with you at night and sitting down to the table with you in the morning."

"Oh, come on. What about the part *before* the falling asleep?"

"That goes without saying." He chuckled. "I will say I appreciate your appreciation on that score."

"I did, didn't I?" She shivered as his little finger invaded her waistband. "You weren't easy, but I managed to score."

"I'm not easy with being crazy about somebody. Scares the hell out of me."

"So…how does this work, exactly?"

"Crazy doesn't really work. It just is." He tightened his arms around her as he guided Little Henry around the house that Zach built. "But if I work, and if you work, with any luck we can make crazy work. I can't just stop by. I want to be with you, Sally. All or nothing." She heard him swallow. Hard. "Of course, the feeling has to be mutual," he added softly.

"Oh, Hank." She let her head fall back and rest on his shoulder. "I have a disease—"

"I know."

"—that isn't going away."

"You're telling this to a halfways doctor?"

"You couldn't even tell."

"That's the half I'm missing."

"Sometimes…sometimes I look like a drunk staggering around because…"

"This is supposed to bother me?"

"Because I can't control what I can't feel, Hank!"

"What can't you feel, Sally?"

"My feet, my legs, my fingers sometimes. I told you, it's as unpredictable as…"

"You're unpredictable, with or without MS. And I'm as predictable as sunrise. I'm tellin' ya, it can work." He turned his lips to her temple. "I can't control what I *can* feel. And what I feel for you isn't going away. *Ever*."

She closed her eyes. Her left one—the *good* one—leaked a damn tear.

And a pair of full, sweet lips kissed it away.

"Can you feel this?" he asked. And she turned her mouth to take the kiss she felt coming.

"You know what, Sally?"

"What?"

"Neither one of us is watching where we're going." She opened her eyes and drank the smile from his as he whispered, "This little mustang is one hell of a horse."

* * * * *

COWBOY, TAKE ME AWAY

For my wonderful editors,
Leslie Wainger and Charles Griemsman.

Chapter 1

Skyler Quinn's viewfinder served as both protection and pretext for her hungry eye. Naked, her eye was never more than mildly interested. Behind the camera, it was appreciative of all things bright and beautiful. The viewfinder found and framed views she had schooled herself to ignore, like the rear view of five fine-looking cowboys hooked over a fence. She would call the shot *Five Perfect Pairs of Jeans*.

And then there were four.

Skyler lowered the camera. The best pair of jeans was getting away. Up one side of the fence and down the other, the cowboy on the far left had spoiled the symmetry of her shot. She climbed a set of wooden steps and took a position on the first landing of the outdoor grandstand, where an audience would later gather to watch professional rodeo cowboys ride, rope and race for cash prizes. For now, the place belonged to cowboys, critters and one unobtrusive camera.

Skyler watched the runaway piece of her picture stride purposefully across the dusty arena toward one of several ropers who were warming up to compete in the afternoon "slack" for overflow timed-event contestants. The roper responded to a quick gesture as though he'd been summoned by the coach.

Skyler zoomed in as the two men changed places. She knew horses, and the blazed-face sorrel hadn't been working for his rider, but the animal collected himself immediately with a new man in the saddle. The camera committed the subtleties of change to its memory card. Eyes, ears, carriage, gait—the animal transformed from ordinary to outstanding before Skyler's hidden eye.

Now, that's what I'm talking about.

Or *would* talk about when she got around to putting a story together. The centaur lived, she would claim. He was no freak of nature, anything but barbaric, and beyond comparison with a mere horse master. He was a partner. He shared his brainpower with the horse and the horse gave him legs. It was a pleasing blend of assets, particularly when both partners were beautifully supplied. Not only would her pictures tell the story, but they could sell the story. Most horse magazines were bought and read by women, and here was a man who would stop any girl's thumb-through dead in its tracks. Long, lean, lithe and leggy, he was made to ride. The square chin and chiseled jaw were promising, but she wished he would push his hat back a little so she could see more of his face.

Skyler kept her distance as she followed the cowboy through his ride. She supposed he was giving a demonstration—teaching, selling, maybe considering a purchase. A cowboy with a good roping horse often "mounted" other ropers for a share of their winnings, but the sorrel didn't fit the bill. She wondered what the cowboy said to the original rider after his smooth dismount. Deal, no deal, or a word of advice? She'd be interested in the man's advice. Lately she'd been learning the difference between horse master— that would be Skyler—and master trainer, which she was not. *Yet.*

At the moment she was interested in taking pictures. She clambered down the grandstand steps and strolled toward the exit, eyeing a long shot down an alley where two palominos were visiting across a portable panel fence. The rodeo wasn't Skyler's favorite venue, but horses and horsemen were among her favorite subjects for her second-favorite hobby. And it was high time she turned at least one of her hobbies into an income-earning proposition.

"Business or pleasure?"

Skyler turned to the sound of a deep, smooth voice and looked directly into engaging gold-brown eyes. Unexpected, unshielded, up close and personal. *There you are,* said her heart. "I beg your pardon?" said her mouth.

"You were taking pictures of me." His eyes hinted

at some amusement, but no uncertainty. "Are you a professional or a fan?"

Skyler's brain cartwheeled over her other body parts and took charge.

"I don't know you, but I know horse sense when I see it, and I like to take pictures." She smiled. His face complemented his body—long, slender, neatly groomed, ready for a close-up. "I wouldn't mind getting paid to do it, but at the moment, it's merely my pleasure."

"Taking pictures of...horse sense."

She turned the camera on, pressed a button and turned the display his way. "Would you like to see?"

He clicked through her pictures. "You've got a powerful zoom there. Look at that." He stepped closer and shared a peek. "You can see where I nicked myself shaving this morning."

"I don't see anything."

"Luckily, it's just my face. No harm done to the horse sense."

"It's a valuable asset." She nodded toward the picture on the camera display. *Commanding Cowboy on a Collected Mount.* "Do you have an interest in this horse?"

"I might buy him." He studied the picture, considering. "If the price is right. This guy's trying to take him in the wrong direction. He's not a roping horse. He's small and he's quick." Their fingers touched as he handed the camera back. She bit back an apology and a cliché about cold hands. His warmth reached his eyes. "Make a nice cuttin' horse."

"You're a trainer?" *Obviously.*

"I'm a bronc rider. Got no sense at all." He tucked his thumbs into the front pockets of his jeans. "You coming to the show tonight?"

"I haven't decided." She was committed to watching the ropers in the afternoon slack, which moments ago had seemed like enough rodeo for one day.

"You'd get some good pictures."

"I'm not your *Rodeo Sports News* kind of photographer. And I'm really not interested in the kind of ride that only lasts eight seconds."

"Only?" He laughed. "That's eight *real* seconds. You know you're alive when every second really means something. How many seconds like that can you stand, one right after another?"

"I feel very much alive on the back of a horse. I could go all day."

He took her point with a nod, eyes dancing. "They say when you meet your match, time stands still. You believe that?"

"I think your idea of the perfect match is different from mine."

"What do you look for?"

"A great ride."

"Same here. You say *girth* and I say *cinch,* but, hell, we're both horse people. If you're thirsty, I know a good watering hole that's probably pretty quiet this time of day. First round's on me."

"That's very tempting, but I have to…" Not really. There was nothing she had to do in Sheridan, Wyoming. If she'd come on her own, she could watch the afternoon calf roping and go home, where she always had things to do. "Are you competing in the rodeo tonight?" He nodded. "Which event?"

"Bareback." He pushed his right hand deep into his jeans pocket. "I've got an extra ticket. One is all I've got, so if you're with somebody…"

"No, I'm…" But she took the ticket he handed her and inspected it as though she hadn't seen one before. "I mean, I haven't decided. I wouldn't want this to go to waste."

She looked up to find him grinning as he backed away. "You should see my horse sense in a pair of chaps. Bring your camera."

She met his grin with a smile. "You cowboys are all alike."

"I won't ask how many you know. You can tell me tonight when you come by the chutes to wish me luck."

"I don't even know your name."

"It'll be on the program." Safely out of returning-the-ticket distance, he paused. "You gonna tell me yours?"

"I haven't decided. And I'm not on the program."

Trace wasn't holding his breath. The woman was as intriguing as she was beautiful, and her showing up behind the chutes or even in the stands was a long shot, which was what made the bet interesting. Surprise was the spice of Trace Wolf Track's life.

He hadn't always seen it that way, but he'd lived and he'd learned. Life was full of surprises, people were totally unpredictable and a guy could either try to buck the system or enjoy the ride. Sure, he searched the crowd for that pretty face once or twice, and he turned his head to the sound of a female voice just before he lowered himself into the chute and took hold of his bareback rigging.

And then he cursed himself for losing his concentration when he should have been calling for the gate. He'd drawn a chute fighter. *No screwing around, cowboy. I'm outta here, with or without you.*

Trace made the whistle, but his signature dismount turned ugly in the face of a flying hoof. He didn't mind getting clipped in the head, but mentally he took points off his score for stumbling and losing his hat. Winning a go-round wasn't everything. He scanned the bleachers as he acknowledged the applause with a wave of the errant hat. He had no idea where to look for the seat he'd given her, but did a double take at the sight of a pretty woman in the front row jumping to her feet.

He had to laugh at himself when the woman reached across the aisle and took a toddler from somebody's arms. Not his ticket holder. The hair was too yellow, the hips were too broad and the kid appeared to be hers. He'd been thinking about his green-eyed photographer with the reddish-blond hair all afternoon, recalling her sweet scent, guessing her name and making up her story. It didn't include kids.

Trace unbuckled his chaps as he ambled back to the chutes. He wiped his head with his shirtsleeve. Sure enough, the hoof had drawn blood, which he didn't mind getting on his shirt, but he hated like hell messing up the sponsor's patch on the sleeve. He'd sold his right arm to promote cigarettes. Took the money and quit smoking, thanks to the bloody patch.

He put his hat back on for a dignified departure. Exiting the arena on the heels of a good score required cowboy reserve. Win or lose, the slight swagger in his step came from years of forking a horse nearly every day. Ordinarily he would have been mentally downshifting now that his workday was over—one man's eight seconds was another's eight hours—and it was time to celebrate, whether he felt like it or not.

"Nice ride," said saddle bronc rider Larry Mossbrucker as he caught up with Trace on the way to the medic's van. "Where's the party tonight?"

"Haven't heard."

"It's your call, man. First round's on the winner." Larry clapped a beefy hand on Trace's shoulder. "Bob's? You don't wanna miss BOGO Burger Night."

The only thing worse than one of Bob's Bronc Buster burgers would be a second Bronc Buster burger, but the place would be packed to the gills on Bob's stuffed-and-mounted trophy trout.

"Think I'll pass on the gut busters. Busted enough for one day. But I'll stop in and pony up after I clean up and get something to eat." Trace glanced at Larry, who looked disappointed. "Something that won't bite back."

"How's the head?"

"I'm keepin' it under my hat."

"Aw, man, don't let a fresh wound go to waste.

That's good for unlimited female sympathy. A rare treat. Tender." Larry grinned. "Juicy."

"Mmm. I can taste it already. But that kind of meal don't come cheap and they don't give a free one on top of it." Trace eased his hat off. The sweatband was killing him. "'Course you don't need it when the first one's that good."

"Yeah, well, you gotta do a few shots between burgers at Bob's."

"Should be good for unlimited sympathy all around."

"They started burger night after they had to quit Ladies' Night." Larry was keeping pace with Trace, who wasn't in the mood for much conversation, which meant he wasn't in the mood for Larry.

But Larry was a talker.

"Some tourist said it wasn't right to charge men more than women. Discrimination, he called it. Maybe they've got a big supply of women where he comes from, but out here the good ones are scarce, and no shortage of demand. No shortage of bars or beer, either, so which law should we go by? Supply and demand, or whatever it is that outlaws discrimination?"

Trace chuckled. "My guess, it's that ol' killjoy, the U.S. Constitution."

"The only woman willing to go to Bob's for a free burger would have to be another tourist."

"With an iron gut. Hell, Bob's not hurtin' for business and we ain't hurtin' for women."

Larry snorted. "Speak for yourself."

He *was*.

Another twenty yards and Trace would be speaking to the rodeo medic about whether he needed stitches, and he wouldn't be expressing any more interest than he was feeling when he asked, "Angie kicked you out again?"

"Hell, no. She's letting me sleep on the sofa." Larry gave an unconvincing chuckle. "Hell, when I first met her, she was all about being with a cowboy. Now she wants me to quit riding."

"Gotta quit sometime." While you're ahead. *While your head is ahead.*

"Not me, boy. Not till I'm damn good and ready." They'd reached the "Cowboy Clinic" van and Larry was dragging his heels like a pouty kid. "Hell, I don't know what else I'd do."

"This is where I get off, Larry. Maybe I'll catch up with you at Bob's."

Larry nodded, but he wasn't moving.

"Where are you staying?" The question was out before Trace could stop himself. He knew the answer. Larry hadn't scored in the money, and he was nobody's favorite road warrior, so he had to be sleeping single in his pickup.

"Put it this way, there's no running water," Larry said.

"Come on over to the Sheridan Inn. I got myself a room this time out."

"I wouldn't wanna put you out, Trace. That's a fancy place."

"I know. All I'm offering is soap and water." Trace

tapped the big man's chest with the back of his hand. "You don't wanna out-reek Bob's burgers."

Trace topped off his steak by washing down a few aspirin and left the hotel dining room hoping Larry hadn't left the bathroom in a mess. Trace didn't mind sharing—he'd been raised to share—but he'd also been taught to clean up after himself, especially when he was sharing a room or a bed. Growing up he'd shared a low-end range of small quarters and smaller beds with his younger brother, Ethan, who'd never done well with rules. Cleaning up after Ethan had taught Trace a corollary to the cleanup rule. People should do it for themselves. Otherwise, each mess was a little harder to deal with than the last. Leaving a mess in the bathroom had become a deal breaker for sharing a room with Trace. But he'd still make an exception for his brother. All Ethan had to do was show up.

Or the camera lady. She could drop her towel on Trace's bathroom floor anytime. He hadn't expected her to use the ticket, but he knew damn well she'd given it some thought. No matter what her circumstances, he knew he'd caught more than her eye. And she'd sure stimulated his imagination. If a woman like her went out on the town, where would he find her? Provided he felt like looking for a woman who smelled like an orange tree standing in the middle of a horse barn. Pretty risky for a horse-barn kind of a guy.

He was on his way to the hotel bar and a shot of

218 Cowboy, Take Me Away

pain reliever when he ran into calf roper Mike Quinn, who said he was buying. He could have sworn Mike wasn't old enough to get served, but his driver's license said he was legal. Barely. Trace had just finished turning up Mike's roping horse, a sideline that was becoming increasingly profitable.

"I owe you one," Mike said as he smacked his cash down on the bar as though he had a point to make. "Eleven-two, man, that's the fastest run I've made all summer. You put a hell of a handle on that horse."

"That's what you paid me for."

Trace stepped aside for a lady looking for a barstool. He wouldn't be riding one of those tonight. With a rodeo in town, one drink in a fancy hotel bar was all he was good for. If he could get past his headache, he'd find the party down at the low end of Main Street on the other side of the tracks.

"I know what you're thinking," Mike said quietly. He'd suddenly gone shy. "The horse did his part, but the roper's a little slow on the ground."

Trace lifted one shoulder. "You drew a big calf."

"Caught him, too, but *damn* them doggies're getting heavy. Now that you've got my horse lined out, I'm gonna have to get myself a personal trainer. I don't suppose you'd…"

"I only work with horses. Cowboys can be temperamental." But they didn't call calves *doggies* anymore. Mike needed to put some new tunes on his iPod.

"Not this cowboy. Win or lose, I celebrate." Mike was pushing it, laying his novice hand on Trace's proven shoulder. The kid had a lot to learn before he could rightly call himself a cowboy. "Whatever you're drinking tonight, it's on me. Frank Taggert's here and Earl Kessler. You know Earl?"

"I don't."

"Earl has a big spread over on the Powder River. I belong to a team-penning club that meets at his place. You should check us out. We've got guys coming from as far away as Casper."

"I haven't played team sports since high school." And he damn sure wasn't interested in driving a hundred miles or more to play cowboy. Not that he had anything against the popularity of team penning. He'd trained a couple of cutting horses for penning club members.

"Earl's place is kinda central, easy to get to, he doesn't charge us to use his stock, and he always fires up the grill and ices down the beer. I fixed him up for dinner tonight." Mike laughed. "With my mother. You believe that?"

Trace glanced up from his drink, ready for some weird punch line. Mike had a weird sense of humor.

The kid shrugged. "My dad's been dead a year now and it's time she moved on. So to speak."

Trace remembered a time when he'd hoped for a new dad. Not that he'd missed the old one, whoever he was, but at the age of ten he'd imagined his mother doing a better job of mothering if she hooked up with a man who'd stick around. He couldn't have asked for better than Logan Wolf Track, who'd stuck by Trace and his brother even after their mother had walked out on all of them. So Mike had just earned a few points in Trace's book for looking after his lonely mother.

Glancing past Trace's shoulder, Mike frowned. "Speak of the devil…"

Trace suddenly felt a little buzzed and he knew the whiskey wasn't *that* potent. He turned slowly. She was a willowy silhouette standing in the doorway, backlit by the bright lobby. He suddenly got all tingly. Strangest, most god-awful giddy sensation he could imagine, partly because he knew who she was, knew she was surprised to see him even though he couldn't quite make out her face.

"That's your *mother?*"

"Stepmother," Mike said quietly as they watched her approach them at the bar, at once purposeful and unhurried. "But I don't like that term. Sounds cold, y'know?"

"Cold as the devil." Trace nodded, inadvertently lifting his hand to touch a hat brim that wasn't there. "Mrs. Quinn."

"Trace Wolf Track," she said, eyes alight. "Your name was on the program."

"You were there?"

"How else was I going to get a program?" She smiled. "You were magnificent."

"Thanks." *Magnificent.* Damn.

"For eight whole seconds."

"Just a sample. Imagine eight whole hours."

Her quick laugh was throaty and rich. "You're all alike."

Trace raised one eyebrow and challenged her with a look. *Try me.*

"Looks like we can skip the introductions," Mike said.

"Only if your mother likes to be called Mrs. Quinn." But Mike could skip town now for all Trace cared. He only had eyes and ears for...

"Skyler."

"This is the guy who trained Bit-o-Honey," Mike supplied. "You wrote the check. Remember?"

Trace glanced down at the glass in his hand. He'd hardly looked at the check. Counted the zeros, copied them onto the deposit slip. Why did it feel funny knowing that she'd been the one who'd paid him?

"I'm the bookkeeper." She gave a honeyed laugh. "Names might escape me, but I never forget an expense category."

"You remembered mine from the program."

"I had a face to put with it." She turned to her son. *Step*son. "I was taking pictures at the arena this afternoon, and Trace and I...crossed paths."

Trace slid her a smile.

"What happened to Earl?" Mike demanded, glancing toward the lobby.

Skyler stabbed Mike's arm with a small but forceful forefinger. "The question is, what happened to you?"

"I told you guys to go ahead and get supper. I'm toasting my trainer here."

"Were you invited to Mike's party, too?" she asked Trace.

"I was offered a drink." He lifted his half-full glass. "I'm a long way from getting toasted."

She claimed Trace's drink and mirrored his gesture. "Here's to Mike and his trainer."

Down the hatch.

She set the empty glass aside and took number two from Mike's hand, flashing an enticing glance at Trace as she raised the glass. "And to Trace Wolf Track and his impressive horse sense."

Down the hatch.

Glass on wood, she called out, "Bartender! Another round for these two cowboys."

"Okay, she's mad now," Mike told Trace.

"Not anymore." Skyler gave Mike a perfunctory smile. "If you aren't having dinner with Earl, you might want to tell him he's excused."

"I was coming back."

"You were on your way back, but you ran into a couple of buddies, and one drink led to another." She shifted from script reader to instructor. "Earl doesn't interest me. Nothing about Earl interests me. I had a wonderful time at the rodeo, Mike. You interest me because you're my son. Trace interests me because he's…interesting." She spared Trace a pointed glance. "Earl does not interest me."

"But he's got—"

"I don't care what he's got. You don't have to worry about me. Okay?" She shrugged dismissively. "And if this is a celebration, I'm not feeling it."

"One more oughta do it." Mike gave a nod for the

two drinks the bartender was just setting down near his elbow.

"You know what?" Trace pulled a couple of bills from his pocket and tossed them on the bar. "In the interest of mutual interest—" he turned to Skyler and smiled "—why don't we hold off and take a walk?"

"What about Earl?" Mike demanded.

Trace laid a friendly hand on Mike's beefy shoulder. "I'd say Earl is your problem, son."

"Son?"

"You make a date, it's yours to keep, yours to break."

"Impressive," Skyler said. "Who trained the trainer?"

"My dad. Logan Wolf Track is the best there is." He gestured toward the exit with a flourish. *After you.* "What's your pleasure tonight, Mrs. Quinn?"

"Do you dance?"

"Hell, yeah, like nobody's watching. You know any cowboys who don't?" He offered his arm. "Mrs. Quinn?"

"Mrs. Quinn doesn't remember how to dance like nobody's watching." She slipped her hand into the crook of his elbow and smile up at him. "But let's see if Skyler does."

Chapter 2

There was a sweet sensuality about the way Trace held her when they danced—not hard, not tight, but close enough to feel the power in his thighs and the heat in his belly and the cool in his carriage. Her body moved with his, riding double on a silky new song. New for Skyler, anyway. She hadn't danced in ages, which was not a measure of time, but a chunk of life. She felt lighter on her feet than she had in ages, lighter in heart and head. Giddy-light, something a man like Trace would know nothing about. She felt so new she was afraid if she opened her mouth she'd squeal with delight or babble some kind of gibberish and he'd have no interest in a translation. So she kept quiet and rode her senses, her thighs glancing off his, her nose sneaking up on his neck, her ears tuning in to the drums and the steel guitar.

Given the kind of erotic thoughts she'd been having lately, it was probably pretty risky for her to let a man who smelled this good get this close, but she was sure she had the upper hand. She was a woman, after all. She knew how to smell the flowers. Or, in this case, the alfalfa. She knew how to lose herself on a little detour, soak up some unexpected warmth and inhale the greener grass.

Close your eyes and take a long, slow breath. Let the picture draw itself in your mind. Pure, natural manhood.

Now that she knew why Mike had insisted on her coming to Sheridan to watch him put his newly trained calf roping horse to the test, she had to admit, he wasn't totally off base. It felt good to "meet somebody." Not Mike's choice of somebody. Not an internet site's choice or the choice of a friend worried about her widowhood, but her own out-of-the-blue discovery. Somebody who tapped into her own senses and jangled nerves she'd tried and failed to forget she had. Not that she didn't like the feeling, but she wasn't sure she could rein it in if she gave it any slack.

"It was nice of Mrs. Quinn to let me take Skyler dancing." He leaned back and smiled at her. "Tell her for me next time you see her."

"Tell her yourself." She looked up, but not, she realized, as far up as she'd expected to. The way he carried himself made him seem taller than he was.

"Truthfully, I don't see her. Everyone else does, but I don't."

"You're like that comedian on TV, huh? He doesn't see skin color, including his own?" He chuckled. "How do you know what everyone else sees?"

"Maybe not you. Who do you see?"

"Right now, I see a woman who's enjoying herself."

"Good eye, cowboy." Wolf eyes. Tawny and teasing, they twinkled with every charming line he spoke. "Would you have fixed me up with Earl Kessler?"

"Absolutely not. And I don't know Earl Kessler." He shook his head. "I don't know what Mike was thinking. He should have fixed you up with me."

"He shouldn't be trying to fix me up at all."

"If he hadn't, would we be dancing right now?" He raised his wounded brow. "Would Mrs. Quinn have let Skyler come out to play?"

"Mrs. Quinn might have gone out with you herself. You wouldn't have been able to dance this close, but otherwise you wouldn't know the difference."

"Ah, so you *do* know her."

"I don't see her, but she was fifteen years in the making, so I know her."

He smiled again. "I only dance as close as my partner wants me to. Sometimes it's like this. Sometimes it's even closer. But I always know the difference."

"Instinctively?"

"My instincts are pretty good. I've got good ears, too."

"And you've got a good lump on your head." The

knot on the right side of his temple was decorated with Steri-Strips. Without thinking, she touched the outer edge of the goose egg. "Does it hurt?"

"Only when I touch it." He laughed when she jerked her hand away. "Do that again. Your fingers feel cool."

She put her hand back in its proper place on his shoulder. "I've fallen off a horse a few times, but I've never been kicked."

"I didn't fall."

"You were unloaded."

"I made the whistle. That's what counts."

She welcomed the excuse to touch his head again. "This counts."

"That's what I've heard," he said, grinning. "I know it draws sharks, but I didn't realize blood was a chick magnet."

She laughed. "Hardly."

"Hardly attracted?"

"Hardly a chick."

"You're right. My bad." He flashed that infectious grin again. "You like 'filly bait' any better?"

"Give it up, cowboy. I like you, okay? No blood-shed necessary. Extra points for not calling me a mother hen."

Trace guided her to the corner booth they'd claimed at the Mane and Tail Tavern, one of Sheridan's quieter nightspots. Rodeo cowboys preferred Bob's Place and rodeo fans followed rodeo cowboys. His hand on the small of her back was their only contact point, but she felt him covering her back, head to heels.

"I like you, too," he said as she took herself from him, only to slide around the vinyl curve of the seat and meet him at the back of the booth. "So let's get this out on the table. I'm not a kid. I'm not sure I ever was. I was raised by my stepfather, and he was younger than my mother. Still is if she's alive."

"You don't know?"

"I like to think she isn't." He toyed with his watered-down whiskey, spreading its sweat ring in an ever-widening circle. "I made up a story about how she was trying to get back to us when she got hit by a train. That's the only reason we never heard from her again." He sipped his drink before eyeing her. "How's that for bloodthirsty? Do I lose points?"

"She just disappeared?"

"She told us she was gonna look for a better place for us. I knew she wasn't coming back. Logan had adopted us first thing after he married her. He told her he wasn't goin' anywhere, and for a while he thought she'd come back." He smiled wistfully. "He was so damn young." His eyes suddenly gleamed. "But he was a good father, and he will be again. He just re-married. Took him a while, but, hell, when that man makes up his mind, he doesn't waste any time. I hope this one works out better for him."

"Is this one older, too?"

"Older than Logan?" He shook his head. "She's probably not much older than me. Funny. I don't remember ever running into her, but turns out she didn't live too far away. Two different worlds, I guess. Small, side by side and different."

"Where are they?"

"South Dakota. Logan—my dad—he's Sioux. Lakota Sioux."

"You're not?"

"In name only. He offered his name when he adopted us, and we jumped on it. Who wouldn't? Wolf Track." He punctuated a tight-lipped growl with a fisted gesture. "Powerful name."

"So he's your true father."

"Oh, yeah. Taught me everything I know about horses. Not everything he knows, but everything I know."

"Is he a rodeo cowboy, too?"

"No. He's smarter than that. Logan's a tribal councilman, and he's also a horse trainer. He wrote a book about it and everything."

"You did a wonderful job with Bit-o-Honey. I can't believe he's the same horse." Skyler lifted her shoulder. "Of course, Mike's still the same rider."

"It's a good hobby for a rancher."

"He told you he was a rancher?"

Trace nodded.

"Good to know," she said offhandedly. "He tells *me* he's a calf roper."

"He's young. He can still be a lot of things."

"He'd better decide which is the hobby pretty soon, or the choice won't be there for him."

"What time is it?" Trace slid his hand over the

back of hers and turned her wrist for a peek at her watch. "Almost tomorrow. Big day tomorrow."

"Bigger than today? You won your go-round today. What's happening tomorrow?"

His fingers skimmed her palm. "Our first kiss."

"Really?"

"Yeah. First thing." He winked at her. "So tell me when it's midnight."

"I'm nobody's timekeeper, Trace. Trying not to be." She gave her head a quick shake as she echoed her admonishment to him. "Give it up, Skyler."

"We're talking past each other here. Look at me." He waited for her full attention, which she granted. "Right here, right now, you and me. One kiss to start the day. It's my birthday."

"Oh." She smiled. "Well, that's different."

"*I'm* different. Give me a day to prove it."

"Why?"

"Because…" He glanced at her watch. "It's midnight."

"Happy birthday." She tipped her head and leaned close to bestow a friendly kiss.

He slid his arm around her and met her halfway, raising the ante on her gift by making it interactive, taking her breath away. Her kiss became theirs as she slid her arm around him and smoothed the back of his shirt with her eager hand. She felt trembly inside when he lifted his head and looked at her with a twinkle in his eyes that said *gotcha*.

"Spend the day with me," he entreated, and she

had to glance away from those glittering eyes to keep from jumping all over the suggestion.

"What's holding you back?" He raised an eyebrow. "Tell me, and I'll get it out of your way."

"I have things to do at home."

"I'll help you. Give me one day and I'll give one back." She hesitated, and he laughed. He knew he had her, but he offered, "*Two.* I'll trade you two days for one, and I'm a damn good hand."

"Now, that's tempting." A crazy idea was taking shape in her head. Lately they'd been popping up like soap bubbles. Crazy notions pushing for bubbleheaded moves. She'd made one or two, just to get herself off dead center, and she was about to make another one.

She smiled. "What can I get out of you on those days?"

"What do you need?"

"Mostly horse sense."

"Well, then, I'm mostly your man."

"I own horses, condition them, ride them, school them. I'm a natural, really. And I've had some spirited horses." She leaned into her story, trusting him with the girlish enthusiasm that was generally reserved for her horses. "So I thought, why shouldn't I be able to turn a mustang into a mild-mannered saddle horse? We could learn from each other. Wouldn't that be interesting?"

"For me?"

"For me. I entered a training competition. But I might have bitten off more than I can chew." She lowered her gaze to his smirking lips. She could still taste them. "How are your teeth?"

"I'm not missing any, but you'll have to take the deal before I let you count 'em."

She laughed. She liked this man. She truly did. "After two days, can I have an option to hire?"

"Nope." He leaned back, challenging her with a playful look as he reached toward his glass. "Free agency after three days. Then we renegotiate."

"Sounds fair."

"It's more than sound." He gestured, glass in hand. "You're getting a twofer."

"Can't pass that up, can I?" She slapped the table. "Okay, I need to rest up for the big day."

"Oh, no. Today is my day." He drained his drink and then set the glass aside. "I get to call the shots. You play Hearts?"

"The card game?"

"We're gonna shoot the moon, Skyler Quinn," he promised with a charming wink. "We're gonna make room for sunrise and then watch it together."

The image made her smile. The image and the challenge. She remembered that shooting the moon meant collecting all the hearts in play, and this man clearly had the knack. But if there was one heart that wasn't going down on the table, it was hers.

So call your shots, cowboy. The night's as young as you are, and I'm game.

He lifted a strand of hair from her shoulder and rubbed it between his thumb and forefinger. "What do you call this color?"

"I think the bottle said strawberry."

"I don't see strawberries. I don't see a bottle. But I *have* seen this color somewhere." He abandoned her hair and took her hand, drawing her out of the booth. "It'll come to me."

"Where are we going?"

"To find some slow and easy holding-you-in-my-arms music. I just danced out of my twenties and I wanna dance into my thirties." He squeezed her hand. "You with me?"

"Yes, I am." She squeezed back. She was getting that giddy feeling again, and she was beginning to like it. "I like your style, cowboy."

"Skill takes you to the whistle, but it's style that wins the buckle."

Trace turned off the highway and followed a familiar dirt road to a spot overlooking the Powder River with a long view to the east. He'd found it back in his rookie days, and it was still a favorite place to pull off the highway and catch a little sleep knowing the sun would roust him in plenty of time to get to Casper to make the afternoon show and then head for Denver or Boise. He slept just fine in the cab of his pickup as long as there were no headlights coming at him, no 18-wheelers whooshing past him in the night.

Skyler was asleep. At his suggestion, she'd cranked her seat back and drifted off in the middle of her own sentence. Something about not being able to sleep on the road. He wasn't going to let her sleep much longer. He'd flipped the center console upright and made way for a close encounter. With the moon on the run, it was the darkest part of a night that would soon be cracked by daylight. If he'd picked the right spot, they were in for a spectacular moment. But in the dark he couldn't be sure the landscape hadn't been sullied since his last visit. Miners and drillers were tearing into the Powder River country like some Biblical plague. He wanted this sunrise—his sunrise—to reveal nothing but pristine Wyoming.

But watching the woman sleep was nice, too. He was trying to decide how to wake her—whether to say her name or touch her bare shoulder, maybe her cheek—when she stirred, edging closer, giving faint voice to her soft sigh. He touched his lips briefly to hers and felt the sweet beginnings of a smile. He lifted his head and watched her lashes unveil her eyes, a gradual dawning. The smile vanished momentarily, but then it returned. It was too dark to see it in her eyes, but he knew it was there. He could feel the connection when she recognized him.

"Are we there yet?" she asked sleepily.

"No, but we're here. I promised you sunrise."

Her smile broadened as she closed her eyes. "I've seen it before."

"Not this one." The horizon was beginning to lighten. He released her seat belt and patted the empty leather space between them. "Come on over," he whispered, and he drew her under his arm as soon as she gave him the chance. She snuggled against him as though he were her favorite pillow. "Tell me about your mustang," he said. "How long have you had him?"

"Three weeks. I've managed to halter him, but that's about all."

"What do you want him to do for you?"

"Take me places."

"Where do you want to go?"

"I haven't decided. Maybe just down the road." She tipped her head back without lifting it from his shoulder. Out of the corner of his eye he saw her smile, and he felt favored and strangely honored by her ease with him. "Isn't that what you're doing, cowboy? Goin' down the road?"

He nodded. He wasn't feeling the *hell, yeah* he would have given with gusto back...when? A few months ago? A year? The rush that came with the ride was still good, but the road between rushes was getting longer. And something else, something that was beginning to wear on him more than sore muscles and aching joints. He wasn't ready to name it. Naming it would give it power, and he didn't feel like putting up a fight, not while this woman's head was resting on his shoulder. Which felt dangerously sweet.

"Here it comes." He laid his free hand on the top of the steering wheel and pointed a finger toward a burst of gold spearing through the pinks and purples washing over the jagged horizon. It was a common sight of incomparable beauty. "There it is, Skyler. On the edge of that cloud. I knew I'd seen that color before." He lifted a curl from her shoulder. "You have the morning sky in your hair."

"And you…" She sat up and looked him in the eye, laughing. "No, I won't say you have a silver tongue."

"I won't say don't knock it." He drew her close and she met his kiss fully, paying him back with interest, forcing him to be the reluctant quitter. "Mmm. That was a knockout."

"It surely was," she said dreamily. He liked the sound.

"And it's only day one."

"Between us we could cause a lot of damage in three days."

"Damage," he said as he touched her hair, "is not my style."

She gave him a quick *good boy* kiss and then turned her attention to the buoyant sun. "It's beautiful here," she said. But what he heard was *moving right along...* "This is the kind of place I want that mustang to take me."

"You picked the right trainer, then." He drew his arm over her head, effectively taking his pillow back. He was still thinking about those kisses. The first one was great. The second one rubbed him the wrong way. He knew what she was thinking.

Hell, he knew about a lot of things.

"Are you signed up with the Double D Wild Horse Sanctuary competition?"

"Mustang Sally's Makeover Challenge," she recited. He nodded, giving her pause. "You're not already in it, are you?"

"No, but my father is, and my brother was trying to

get into it, too." He shrugged. *I'm way ahead of you, lady.* "I hear there's a big prize at stake."

A moment passed before she spoke again. "We have a deal, don't we?" From her tone, the shoe that had changed feet was a little tight. "The clock's already ticking on it."

He was a little surprised. He'd wanted her company, pure and simple, but he could have sworn her side of the deal was born of a whim. He didn't mind that her whim affected her need for his skill. She had already seen him make a difference with a horse and she'd soon realize there was more where that came from. Maybe there was more to this arrangement than he'd thought. Maybe there was more to this little dance of theirs, and maybe what had felt like a kiss-off was just a sweet little kiss.

And maybe she was a little more high maintenance than he was used to, but, damn, he wasn't about to quit now.

He offered a smile. "Trust me, Skyler, I'm a man of my word."

"Trust *me,* cowboy, *trust me* is a line with a definite sell-by date." She raked her fingers through the hair he'd touched tenderly. "It expired for me a long time ago."

Don't ask, Wolf Track.

"Mike gave me the impression your husband was a good man."

That's asking, you idiot.

"He was." She sighed. "He was."

"If you don't wanna go back there, I sure don't

mind moving ahead. It's a new day." *Right. Good luck with that.*

"The perfect beginning for a three-day event," she quipped. "You won't be competing against your family. I just need a little help getting over the first hump."

He made the catch, grinning and grateful. "Like I said, I'm your man."

"Briefly," she amended with a straight face, and he acknowledged with a shrug and a smile. "So let's make the most of it. I took this on thinking a horse is a horse."

"Of course."

"Of course!" Her laughter sounded girlish, and her eyes glittered in the morning sun like bits of green-and-brown bottle glass. "But he's a wild horse, and he wanted absolutely no part of that halter."

"Yeah, but he wants a part of you," Trace said as he pulled the pickup keys out of the cup holder and plugged one into the ignition. "So he'll take the halter, the bit, the saddle, the whole crazy outfit," he continued as he put the pickup in gear. "Just give him free rein when you hit that next hump, and you'll go—" he made the jump with his hand, arching from gearshift to steering wheel "—up and over."

"Free rein," she echoed as she turned to him, her enthusiasm mounting as the pickup bumped and rattled over red clay ruts. "I saw a news clip about the competition and how they're trying to drum up support for the wild-horse sanctuary in South Dakota that those two sisters have devoted themselves to, put everything they have into it, and I just thought, this is important. I've trained horses. *I can do this.*" Her tone took a contemplative turn. "The wild ones are different, though. You wonder…"

"They're horses," he assured her.

"But they seem more sensitive. I swear, that horse can read my mind."

"That's a two-way street, isn't it?"

"Right now he isn't thinking *free rein.* He's thinking *no rein.*"

"He can't imagine a rein, so go easy and try to stay one step ahead of him. You're just as sensitive as he is. You're a woman."

"Of course." She smiled playfully. "I know how to stay a step ahead without letting it show."

"There you go."

"Maybe I don't even need you."

"Maybe you don't, but you're curious about me." He returned her smile in kind. "It shows."

Curious didn't begin to describe where Skyler's head was. She was charmed, but she hoped it didn't show too much. She was as keyed up as a kid on her way to a carnival, but when he reminded her they'd be taking in the WYO Fair after he rode in his event, she tried to beg off, saying she didn't "do dizzy."

Trace was having none of it. No foot dragging today, he had said. It was a gorgeous midsummer day, and there was a program to get with, a crowd to entertain, a good time to be had. Skyler found herself eager to keep up with him, but something told her she'd better slow down, stay cool, be the grown-up. Childhood was, after all, much overrated.

Skyler had chosen to marry a man twice her age, and she'd worked hard to shed inconvenient youth in favor of sophistication. She'd achieved a certain dignity as Tony Quinn's wife for fifteen years and his widow for one. Dignity was about all she had left. She was too old to be a buckle bunny, too young to be a cougar and too smart to get herself stuffed, mounted and labeled with a trophy plaque. There wasn't a man in the big, wide world worth playing the fool for, not one.

Especially not one who regularly risked his fool neck bucking out rough stock. Skyler couldn't breathe watching Trace tether himself to a snorting sorrel bronc and call for the gate, but she couldn't close her eyes to the thrill of the horse's first jump and the skill of the man in making the jump his own. Trace rode the action more than the animal. He leaned back and became less the rider than the ride itself. He defined *going with the flow,* and it was breathtaking.

When the buzzer sounded, he bailed off the hurricane deck and landed on his feet. He waved his hat to the cheering crowd and then turned to where he'd left her, standing behind a chin-high fence under a Wrangler Jeans sign adjacent to the bucking chutes. Hat back in place, he dodged the pickup man, who was herding the high-stepping bronc toward the exit gate. Trace scaled the fence and swung over the top, but rather than drop to the ground, he eased himself rail by rail—giving her time to notice how nicely the fringed chaps framed the cowboy ass, Skyler supposed.

He turned and reached for her, and she stepped under his extended arm, slid her arms around his waist and gave him the kiss he deserved. Somebody sitting atop the chutes shouted, "Woo-hoo," and somebody else added, "Way to go, Trace!" He finished off the kiss with a little extra smooch and then gave the boys up top a wave with his free arm while he wheeled Skyler in the other direction, muttering something about his damn joints.

She tightened her hold on his side. "Are you okay?"

"Yeah, yeah. Just my trick knee." The smooth rowels on his spurs jingled as they rounded a fence corner and took refuge in an alley among the maze of stock pens. He flicked the chaps buckles loose at the back of his thighs, unbuckled the front and peeled them off.

"Can I help?"

"Thanks." He handed her the chaps, grabbed a rail with one hand and his knee with the other and "Sheee—" *Crack!* "—zam!" He straightened slowly. "Gotta start letting the pickup man do his job." He offered a sheepish grin. "Swear to God, that was my last flying dismount."

"It was magnificent," she enthused. "Can you walk?"

"Oh, yeah." He laid his arm around her shoulder and favored his knee as they walked. "All in an eight-second day's work."

"Won't it swell?"

"Not much. It's prewrapped. Did you get any good pictures?"

"I… No, I didn't. I forgot about the camera." She lifted the chaps she'd been clutching against her side. Yes, she still had her shoulder bag. "Oh my God, I forgot about the camera."

"You left it somewhere?"

"No, I have it. I was watching. I wasn't thinking about anything else." He relieved her of the chaps and she smiled. "Pretty amazing."

"That watching can take your full attention?"

"That you can make a crazy ride like that look easy. The rest of those guys are working overtime, but you looked like you were quite comfortable. Like you were actually having fun."

"It's a helluvalot of fun when I'm on a roll. It's been a good season. Haven't broken anything in months."

"Ninety is a wonderful score. Do you think you'll win?"

"Can't lose." Grinning, he flipped the chaps over his shoulder. "It's my birthday."

"Let me take you out for dinner."

"You're on. I want a corn dog and a snow cone."

"I want to take you someplace nice."

"Exactly. The WYO Fair." He gave her a playful squeeze. "It's my *birthday,* woman! You take me to the corn-dog stand and I'll take you up on the Ferris wheel."

Skyler looked up. The wheel looked huge up close. The red seats rocked gently like the storied cradle in the treetops and the lights on the spokes were gaining on the dimming sky. She hadn't faced one of these things since Mike had last dragged her to a line like the one she was standing in now and handed off two tickets. She remembered being surprised that the top of his cowboy hat reached her nose, and he was barely eight.

She lowered her gaze and watched the cars dip, drag and rise. A starry-eyed young couple. Mom with kids. Dad with kids. Kids with kids. Lots of kids. Beautiful, beautiful kids. They all looked fairly secure, pretty happy. Begging off would have her looking like a stick-in-the-mud. It wasn't a roller coaster, after all. One Ferris wheel ride couldn't hurt.

"You wanna eat first?"

Skyler looked up at the handsome face below the brim of the cowboy hat. "Why don't we do this before we tackle the corn dogs?"

Going up was fine. Uploading. Uplifting. Upstanding. It was all good. At the top of the arc, she looked up at the sky, darkening from the top down as though an angel had bumped a bottle of blue ink. It washed over the remains of crimson and gold as the stars popped open one by one and hovered playfully just out of reach. Better than good, she thought.

"You won't find any prettier country than this," Trace said.

Skyler nodded. Her stomach signaled the shift from ascent to descent and her smile stiffened. She gripped the lap bar.

"You see that?" He laughed. "Guy just flew off

the mechanical bull, landed on his head. Back to the bucking barrel for you, boy." He lifted his arm over her head and laid it across the back of the seat, glanced at her and then did a double take. "You okay?"

She nodded again. "Taller than I thought."

"Who, me?"

"The *thing*. The wheel. We're really high."

"Both of us? I was afraid it was just me. Gettin' hooked on a…" He paused, gave a look of concern and a blessed break. "Heights bother you?"

"A little."

"If you want me to, I can give the operator a distress signal when we hit bottom."

She shook her head. "No distress. Felt funny just because it was the first time around." She offered a tight smile. "You?"

"Yeah, a little." He snugged her up and she scooted a little closer as they slid across home plate and started back up. "Okay?"

"Talk to me. I don't want to be a wimp." But that was home. *Total ground control. Wimp city was a secure no-fly zone.* "My head says I'm fine, but some of my parts see it differently. I mean, my eyes are in my head, right? So how do my legs know how high up we are? And what's with my stomach?"

"It's probably talking to your legs, saying *get us off this thing.* How serious is it? What does your gut tell you? Because if it's saying—"

"It isn't. No rebellion in the making. It's just acting silly." She was looking up and out and feeling some improvement. But then came the lurch and the slow rocking, and she buried her face in his shirt. "Oh my God, we're stopping."

"Somebody's ride is over. We get down, yours will be, too."

"No, no, I have to do this." Head up, shoulders back. *Jennifer Grey in* Dirty Dancing. "I have to make the whistle."

"Nobody's scoring you, honey. You should've told me you don't like—"

"But I do. I mean, I *want* to. There's so much to see from here. I like this spot right here. As long as I keep my chin up, there's only up. Right?"

"Right. You want a score? Lean back, hang on to me. But not with this arm." He took her right hand from his shoulder and lifted it toward the sky. "That's your free arm. Can't touch this with that arm."

"Can't touch what?"

"Any of this." He referred to himself, hat to boots, with a sweep of his free hand. "You gotta control yourself in the face of the uncontrollable."

"Is this a twelve-step challenge?"

"Cowboy two-step, honey. We don't count much higher than that. Lean back and hang on."

She laughed.

"Not that we can't, but why bother? It doesn't get any better than two."

"Yes, it does. Two is just a start. Three is holy."

"Four is sacred."

"Seven is lucky."

"You are beautiful." He touched her chin and she tipped her head to receive his kiss. A cool breeze lifted her hair while his warm kiss turned her sinking feeling into a rising one. "Feels like we're moving," she whispered against his lips.

"It does." He brushed her nose with his. "But we're not."

"Let's try again." She paid his kiss back, thinking to improve on it with his help. His fingers teasing her nape helped. His distracting tongue, his soothing breath, the pleasured sound coming from deep in his throat. "You're right," she said at last. "Two is just a start."

"If we count down from ten, I think we'll get liftoff." Another mechanical groan set the wheels in motion. She stiffened. He cuddled her close. "Hold me, Skyler."

"You'll deduct points."

"New rule," he said. "The more you touch, the better your score."

She laughed. "*You'll* get liftoff, and I'll be left hanging."

"I'm not goin' anywhere without you. Damn. We're moving."

"Distract me again."

She didn't have to ask twice. They kissed like teenagers who'd held off until the third date. She didn't care about numbers anymore—how many times around, how many birthdays, how many seconds, points, days, dollars or debts—she was deliriously distracted, disappointed when the ride slowed down and started unloading passengers.

"Mmm," she crooned. "I think we made it."

"Not even close." He winked at her as they came to their final stop. "But we will."

The ride operator—a clean-cut kid who might have been earning tuition money—grinned as Trace lifted his loop over Skyler's head. "I was about to apologize for the delay, but looks like you did okay with it."

"What delay?" she asked.

"Right after you guys got on we had to stop for a puking rider. You were probably stuck up top for a while, huh?"

Skyler looked at Trace. "Were we?"

He shrugged dramatically.

"You can keep going if you want. Otherwise—" the kid offered tickets "—next ride's on me."

"Thanks, but we're good. We're heading for the carousel." Trace waved the offer off. "We're horse people."

Chapter 3

"I was kidding about the snow cone."

But that was where they were heading. Skyler had the carnival midway's feedlot in her sights, and she was bearing down on a row of stands marked with painted fairgoer favorites, like an apple wearing a caramel coat and bananas splashing around in a vat of chocolate.

"I was actually looking forward to the corn dog," she said merrily as she turned and let him catch up. "A rare treat, as it should be but still…" She folded her arms and took a Mama stance, but the look in her eyes was all about big flavor, little nutrition. "Perfect for a kid's birthday party."

"You kiddin' me, woman? What kid?" Without pausing he hooked his arm around her and swept her along, zeroing in on a fading picture of two dancing corn dogs. "Do I kiss like a kid?"

"Uh-uh."

"Uh-uh. And I'm not the one who wimped out on the Ferris wheel. Sure, I like playing games, but my game pays pretty well." He lined them up for supper on a stick. "When I'm on my game. 'Course, as of today, I'm past my prime. Over the hill." He flashed the ponytailed man in the window a two-fingered order. "Are you a mustard or ketchup girl?"

"I like mine unsauced." She took the deep-fried dog in hand and flashed him a *yum-yum* smile. "Clean and sober."

"Hold mine, then." He chuckled as he pumped mustard from a gallon jug into a small paper cup. "Down and dirty."

They finished their main course in silence, eyeing pictures of their follow-up options as they strolled amid parents catering to children and couples caught up in each other. It was a good time to be part of a pair. Trace didn't always feel that way, but tonight was different. It was his birthday and he was with somebody. Not just hanging out, but being together and actually looking forward to another day of the same.

Without the birthday, of course. So maybe not quite the same. Or maybe better. He damn sure wanted to find out whether he'd like her even more tomorrow.

"Last I heard, the hill was forty. Not that I've been there myself." She gave him the over-to-you eye as they tossed their wooden sticks in a red trash bin.

"What?" He wasn't going there either.

"Go ahead and ask."

"I was raised by a gentleman." To prove it he offered his arm. She smiled, tucked her hand in the crook of his elbow and they walked on. "Let me ask you this—how old was Mike when you married his dad?"

"He was seven. I took a summer job as his nanny. I was—" she glanced up at him, her eyes teasing "—in college. I didn't finish." She lifted one shoulder. "Unfortunately."

"Me neither. The only subject I was interested in at the time was college rodeo. But I don't say it was unfortunate. I say, fortunately I can go back when I'm ready." He tuned in to the distant echo of the rodeo announcer talking up the final event. Bull riding. Unless a buddy was entered up, Trace didn't care to stick around for the grand finale. "I was ten when Logan came along," he went on. "It's never too late for good fortune."

"Or snow cones," Skyler said cheerfully as she dragged her boot heels to a halt. He followed her gaze to the top of a tiny stand. Big Bad Ice.

"You want one?" Matching her delight, his cool was blown.

"No." She went from straight face to sassy smile. "But I'll have some cotton candy."

He let her taste his purple snow cone and she fed him wisps of spun pink sugar. They shared a deep-fried funnel cake and a crisp cone full of frozen custard. She sang "Happy Birthday" to him over the cake and he smiled at the way her tongue stormed that tower of custard, her green eyes flashing as she left no surface unlicked. He pointed to the drip at the point of the cone and she caught it before it escaped and then sucked noisily for good measure.

She caught him staring.

"Your turn." She lifted the tongue-marked treat close to his mouth. "Sorry, but it's melting so fast and it's the kind that needs licking."

"I know the feeling."

"Well, we've already exchanged..." she said, as Trace plunged the tip of his tongue into custard, curled it and scooped out a substantial niche. "Oh."

"Don't give me that look. It was my turn." He licked his lips as he scanned new midway territory. "You like to play games, too, don't you?"

"That's what birthdays are all about. Fun and games." She handed him the rest of the ice cream, lighting up as she pointed at a new attraction. "Ring-toss! Now we're talking." And she was walking off on him again. She had the prettiest, most purposeful stride he'd seen on a woman, and her jeans loved her for it.

But his knee didn't. He did a little hop-step as he followed her to a stand that housed an arrangement of bottles and an array of stuffed toys.

"Slow down, honey, you've got an injured man here."

She turned in front of the stand, smiling and giving him the come-on as if nobody was hurting. "I'm gonna win you a birthday present."

"It's your birthday?" the burly huckster asked as

he spread three plastic rings on the counter. "First toss is on the house, then. Happy birthday, cowboy."

"Getting older *and* better," Skyler reported as she reached into her purse. "He gave a fearless performance a while ago."

"Let me guess," the man said. "Bronc rider."

"That, too," she quipped. Trace laughed, elbowing her as he slapped some cash on the counter. She snatched it up ahead of the ringtoss man and tucked it under the flap of his Western-style shirt pocket. "Pick your prize, and it's yours."

He smiled into her eyes. "I only see one thing I want, and I'll have to win that myself."

"The sky's the limit."

"Then I'm all in."

"And I'm all ears, waitin' to hear who's payin'," said the huckster. "Sounds like the lady's landed her share of rings."

Trace warned the man with a look—the lady was in no way his business—and then glanced at the next booth. "How are you at knocking down milk bottles?"

"This is *my* game. Really. It doesn't pay well, but I'm very good at lots of things that don't pay well." She traded cash for plastic rings and then she sized up the targets. "What should I go for?"

"A rabbit's foot." He gave a nod. "That pink one."

"That's too easy. Pick a top-row prize." She pointed to the big stuffed bunny.

"I'd look pretty silly carrying around a pink rabbit. All I want is the foot."

"Come on, cowboy. I like a challenge as much as the next person."

"Good to know." He gave her a little smile. "I've got two more days to come up with one that isn't rigged."

"Hey, this game ain't—"

Huckster took the hint. He folded his arms over his man boobs and watched his pints and quarts.

Skyler hit one of each, and Trace gave an appreciative whistle.

"It doesn't matter whether it's rigged," she told him as she lined up her next shot. "It's all in the wrist."

Skyler won the rabbit's foot in three tosses. "Three ringers, zero misses. The big three-o." She held her hand out for the chosen prize, which the huckster quickly turned over. She slid it into Trace's shirt pocket with his money. "Very lucky, indeed."

He lifted his pocket flap and eyed his present. "Not according to a certain pink rabbit hopping around somewhere on three legs."

Trace didn't want his day to end, but it was almost midnight. The lights of Sheridan glimmered beyond the last intimate stretch of darkness. They'd traveled a long, quiet road, and he'd taken it slow and easy.

"You must be tired," she said, breaking a remarkably comfortable silence. "You have to ride again tomorrow night, don't you?"

"One more go-round. I'm sittin' first right now, so, yeah, I should catch a little sleep." He glanced at her and smiled. "But I'm sorry to see the day end."

"You had a good birthday?"

"The best. I was gonna let it come and go like I usually do, but you came along and changed things. Change is good."

"Not always."

"It was good for me." The headlights illuminated a city-limits sign, and he eased up on the gas. "I'll make it good for you, too. You've got two days coming."

"Wow. I might have to rethink my plan."

"You do that." He nodded. "And then I'll do what I do best."

"Your end of the bargain starts *after* the rodeo." She chuckled. "Do you realize how many times eight seconds goes into two days?"

"I'm only signed up for one timed event. Everything else is off the clock."

"So my two days won't start until—"

"Not until I can give you my undivided attention. One more ride." He patted his shirt pocket. "Try out my new rabbit's foot. Oh, and I have tickets for you. Best seats in the house. You and Mike."

"Mike is going home today. At least, he said he would. Right after the slack events. He has work to do. We have a hired man who needs to be kept busy."

"Must be hard. Losing his father is bad enough, but picking up the slack on the ranch, young as he is…" Another sign appeared in the headlights. They were back at the hotel. Trace slowed the pickup. The turn signal sounded like a grandfather clock echoing down a long hallway. "The man of the house, he said. Sounded like a line from a movie."

"He said that?" Skyler laughed. "A line from a movie describes it perfectly. But the only place it's playing is in Mike's head."

"So…no other kids?"

"No other kids. Michael is all he…all *we* had."

"Why does he call you by your first name?"

She lifted one shoulder. "I asked him if he wanted to call me Mom, and his only answer was to keep calling me Skyler. He's never had any problem letting me take care of him, but I was never quite Mom."

"He said you were his mother." Trace raised his brow, giving his recollection a second thought. "Then he said *step*mother."

"And that's *correct,* isn't it? Technically. *Legally,* even though I'm the one who's been there. Maybe he thought his father made all the decisions for both of us because for a long time he did. The big ones, anyway. But we never talked about adoption." She gave a perfunctory smile. "It doesn't matter what he calls me. He's my son."

"He's a nice guy." Trace turned off the motor. He'd passed several parking spaces close to the front entrance and chose one at the far end of the lot before he turned to her.

Here it comes, she thought. *The big move.*

"He'll grow into those boots," Trace said.

Meaning he wasn't ready, either. Or maybe he wasn't as interested as she'd thought. Assumed. *Hoped?*

She'd been mentally vacillating among possible responses to probable approaches like *How about a drink?* And *My room or yours?* Unoriginal propositions—he was a cowboy, after all—could be refused easily enough if she wasn't, for some foolish reason, hoping for something. But what? Something quick and easy that would move her off dead center? This night couldn't amount to much more than that. Not with a rodeo cowboy.

"Mike got interested in rodeo when he was in high school," she told him, surprised at how easy it was to kick an expectation aside, especially when it was open-ended. "About the time his father's health started to decline. Tony had always been a pretty good roper, but he gave it up after his first stroke. Mike got him into team penning, which was good for both of them. And Tony's outlook improved when Mike tried calf roping."

She glanced through the windshield, into the night. "Then Tony had another stroke, and he just couldn't… get back in the saddle, you might say. It was hard for Mike to watch his father break down, piece by piece."

"Must have been hard on you."

"Hard on me?" She shrugged. "I did what I had to do. Mike never had to do much, so he watched. Until he couldn't anymore and then he found more and more reasons to stay away."

"You're a strong woman."

"He was my husband. And Mike is…" She gave him a smile. Wistful. *Grateful.* "Michael is Michael."

"Well, he picked himself a decent prospect. Got himself a hell of a trainer, so now he has a fine horse under him, and he just needs to throw that rope every chance he gets and pick up his groundwork." He nodded. "Mike made a good catch yesterday. A few like that could start the fire in his belly."

"Is that what makes you do it? Fire in the belly?"

"A guy's gotta eat."

"I've seen how you eat. The fire in your belly might be from junk food."

"I've seen how *you* eat," he teased. "Watching you go after that ice cream was…stimulating."

"That was no ice cream, cowboy. It was frozen custard. Soft serve."

"For you, maybe." He gave her one of those cocky winks of his and let himself out of the pickup.

Skyler followed suit. *Was that it?* Granted, she hadn't thought about the dating game in years, wasn't even sure what they called it these days, but had she lost her knack for reading the opposite sex? Trace was going to bed, where he meant to sleep.

"I'm gonna take another look at that horse I tried out when you were taking pictures," he said when he came around to her side of the pickup. "I'd like to get your opinion."

"You would?"

"Yeah. You put him through his paces and tell me what you think." He pushed his hat back and briefly rubbed the bandage on his forehead. "After we eat. A good meal this time. Birthday party's over."

"I really enjoyed it, Trace. You've got the right idea. For one whole day, just say yes." She glanced up, offered a *poor baby* look. "How's the head?"

"Hat's a little tight. When's *your* birthday?"

"Not telling."

"Come on. I'll bring all the junk food." He took her shoulders in his hands. "Call me when you're ready for breakfast. We'll pick up where we left off."

"Which was?"

"Here." He lowered his head for a kiss, and they made it the kind they both regretted leaving off.

By midmorning, the hotel lobby was quiet except for the woman arguing over her bill with the desk clerk while her husband shushed the two young children who wanted food. The boy was also trying to talk his little sister out of a stuffed alligator exactly like one Skyler had seen at the ringtoss booth, but the girl had a choke hold on the gator and was having none of her brother's pathetic offers. Her pigtails bobbled each time she shook her head. She laughed when he made a face at her, which prompted him to repeat his woeful claim that he was starving and his sister to chime in with "Me, too, me, too, me, too."

One child would be enough, Skyler told herself as she closed the horse magazine she'd been thumbing through. Girl or boy. She'd feed her on time, and she wouldn't have her stand there watching her mother argue about two phone calls and a bag of peanuts. The boy was probably about seven or eight. They could be a handful at that age. Boys could be a handful at any age. *Maybe a girl,* Skyler thought. *A daughter.* It was just a *what-if,* she reminded herself as the child glanced at her suddenly. Sensitive little beings, weren't they? Skyler smiled, and the little girl smiled back.

"Hey, Skyler, where were you yesterday?"

Skyler turned to the sound of Mike's voice as he emerged from the dim first-floor hallway.

"Were you looking for me?"

"I thought maybe you'd caught a ride back home. Tried calling, but…" He took the leather-bound chair kitty-corner from hers and leaned in to offer his most endearing smile. "You still mad?"

"About what?" If she were, they both knew it wouldn't last long. That boyish look of his always got to her.

"You know. Setting you up with Earl."

"Is that all you did?" She shook her head. "I know you meant well, Mike, but don't. Okay? Just don't."

"You've been hangin' back long enough. I know you're not ready to jump off the high dive, so I thought we'd ease you into the shallow end, you know?"

"Poor Earl. The stationary horse on the dating merry-go-round."

She slid a furtive glance toward the restaurant. If she was getting stood up, she probably deserved it, considering poor Earl. Rather than call and wake him up, she'd left a message telling Trace she'd gone downstairs for coffee. As if she had her own agenda, but she'd made room for him if he was still interested.

"That's cold," Mike was saying.

"So is the shallow end of the pool, Mike. It's cold and it's boring. I'm only interested in strong swimmers, and you don't find many of those at three feet."

"Of course not. You gotta go six, at least. Dad was over six feet."

"The answer is no, I'm not mad at you." She let his six-foot illusion pass. She remembered a time when she'd shared it. She hadn't been much older than Mike was now and Tony Quinn was the man in charge.

"Good," he said. "What time do you want to take off?"

"I think I'm staying for the rodeo tonight."

"Even better! I just talked to Grady. He wants to knock that alfalfa down a little earlier than we planned so we can get ahead of the weevils. But one or two more days won't… Wait a minute." His delight turned to disbelief. *"Trace Wolf Track?"*

"What?"

"You're with Trace?"

"The high dive is out of the question, Michael. I'm afraid of heights." Skyler failed to suppress a smile. "Last I rode the Ferris wheel."

"You mean you…you and Trace?" He looked like a kid who'd just realized that his mama *did* dance.

"I mean I *rode a Ferris wheel.* We went to Casper."

"For the rodeo," he filled in.

"And the fair. Corn dogs, cotton candy, frozen custard, ringtoss. I won a prize." She patted Mike's knee. "So I want you to go home and get ahead of the weevils. Trace is going to take me home and he's going to help me with the mustang."

"You were pissed when I gave you his bill for training Bit-o-Honey."

"We're trading services." She spread her hand over

the picture of *The Quarter Horse* on her lap. "I've been taking lots of pictures and most of them are actually pretty good. Trace says he'll get me closer to the action tonight. I know how to get those human-interest moments behind the scenes, but I want to work on getting good action shots, especially outdoors, even under the lights. That's where it gets tricky. Trace won't be riding under the lights, but by the time they get around to saddle bronc…"

His eyes glazed over. "I don't know, Skyler. Rodeo photography is kinda specialized."

"I'm exploring," she said. "I know I can sell more pictures. I just need to broaden my horizons. Function the way the horse does. Diversify."

"I think it's great, you getting out there, but you wanna watch out for those—"

"Hey, Mike." Skyler looked up to find Trace towering over her behind her chair. He met her startled glance with *you and me* in his eyes as he touched her shoulder and mouthed *morning* before turning back to Mike. "How'd you do yesterday?"

"I, uh…didn't qualify for the final round, but Bit-o-Honey sure did his job." Mike stood up, and Skyler followed in the next heartbeat. "How 'bout you? Hear you went down to Casper."

"I made the whistle."

"He won," Skyler reported happily. "And I realized—you know, from a photographer's perspective—there's so much that goes into that eight-second ride that you don't see unless you…" The amusement in Trace's eyes didn't escape her. She smiled back at him. *That's right. I forgot about the camera.* "Well, unless you're up close and personal."

"You mean, like the woman trying to knock the cowboy's teeth out with her microphone?" Mike substituted his fist in a mock interview. "Talk about how it feels, Trace."

Skyler dropped her voice and added a twang. "Feels like hell, but it smells like victory."

"There's none of that kind of coverage in Casper." Trace nodded at Skyler. "I don't sound like that, but it's a great line. Mind if I use it?"

"It's all yours."

"So…" Mike shifted and shuffled, but nobody was looking. "I guess I'll be heading back to do some honest work. Nothing like finishing out of the money to take the cowboy out of the cattleman."

"From what I hear, not too many cattlemen are finishing in the money these days, either," Trace said.

"Skyler says we gotta diversify."

"Sounds like good advice for all of us."

"But you've got nothing to worry about, Trace," Mike said. "You always find your way to the pay window."

"Not always. Show me a cowboy with nothing to worry about, I'll show you a man with a backup plan."

"Hell, what cowboy do you know has a Plan B?" Mike laughed. "Unless *B* is for buckle."

"No, that's Plan A," Trace said. "You go home and study your letters, boy. You get down to *C,* that's when you cowboy up."

"And then *D*-versify," Skyler said. She was enjoying this. Mike didn't quite know what to think of the fact that his friend was suddenly her friend.

"It's good to see you having some fun," he said to Skyler.

"I have no idea what he's talking about," Skyler said as she watched Mike push through the glass entrance doors. "I'm always having fun. Even when I'm working I'm having fun." She turned to find Trace smiling at her, as though he got a kick out of watching her protest too much. "But not this much fun."

"How much?"

"Enough to make me change my plans and stay another day. That's huge."

"Were you planning something huge?"

"I was planning to stick with the plan I made before I ran into you," she told him as they headed for the hotel restaurant. "It's the *change* that's huge. Anything else has yet to be seen."

"Honey, the fun has just begun."

Two hours later, Trace watched Skyler ride the sorrel roping horse he'd tried out two days ago under the watchful eye of her camera lens. Only two days? He'd been thinking about the woman so much, he'd almost forgotten about the horse. But watching the gelding move beneath Skyler—who made every move look as though it was all the horse's idea—made him want both.

He didn't want Skyler watching him dicker with the horse's owner over a price—couldn't afford to have her cramping his horse-trading style—so he signaled her for another turn around the arena while he closed the deal. He didn't mind taking advantage of the fact that the owner wanted to unload the horse so he could buy a better one. This time next year Trace would be considering the "better" one. A horse would only do so much for a rider who was all muscle and no finesse.

Trace knew the makings of a profit when he saw it, but that wasn't the side of his business he liked to display. Not to someone like Skyler. He wanted to show her what a horse would do for Trace Wolf Track, and he wanted to show her how he got there, from start to finish.

With the deal in his pocket and the sorrel fed and watered, Trace took Skyler behind the chutes and introduced her to some of his competitors. No one refused her request for pictures, and she offered printed cards to direct them to her online photo display and promised to send them prints of anything they liked. Then she stepped back and quietly snapped pictures of riders with wives, girlfriends, kids and other cowboys while Trace made sure his gear was in order, his body loosened up and his mind tightly focused.

Some cowboys donned parade chaps for the Grand Entry, but bareback was first on the program, so Trace didn't have to participate in the preliminaries. Like all athletes, he had his pregame rituals, but hanging over the chutes and tensing up wasn't one of them. It was Trace's custom to get ready, get set and then let go. He wasn't going to count down the minutes or worry about the darkening sky.

He tore Skyler away from the rodeo's staging area, found her a vantage point above the chutes where they could watch the stock handlers sort out the bareback horses and move them through the gates.

"That's my ride, that sleepy-looking dun over there." He pointed out the calmest horse in the first bunch. "Look at him, pretending he doesn't care what's going down. We've got a history, Vegas and me."

"Doesn't look like you'd be taking much of a gamble on him."

"He's a sure bet if you can stick him. That sleepy look is a con. They call him Vegas because he's a high roller. Comes alive as soon as the gate opens. Jumps up real pretty when he's in the mood. Snakier'n hell when he's not. Either way, he's a good draw." He allowed himself one quick look skyward. "Just hope it don't rain."

"Oh, but think of the pictures." She tucked her arm around his elbow. "I'd love a good splatter shot."

"And I thought you were my friend."

"I am. I'll gladly take on a share of the mud if you'll get me inside."

"Inside?"

"The arena. Can't I get inside the fence?"

"You got a card?"

She questioned him with a frown.

"I can get you behind the chutes, but you gotta be a card-carryin' Professional Rodeo Cowboy Association photographer to get inside the arena." He wagged a finger against whatever retort was about to come from those pretty lips. "For good reason. The rider has no control over the animal. You're on your own and so is everybody on the ground."

"I have a good zoom, but I like to be able to maneuver."

"So does Vegas." He wiped a drop of rain off her cheek with his forefinger. "Looks like you'll get your splatter shot."

"Or maybe you'll get rained out."

"This ain't no baseball game, honey. I don't get paid unless I ride."

But the sky wasn't fooling. Scattered drops turned into a deluge just as they reached Trace's pickup parked in the contestants' lot near the stock pens. Trace jerked the passenger door open and ducked inside the cab behind Skyler, both of them laughing.

"What happens now?"

She was looking up at him, all wide-eyed and eager, as though he had a hat full of magic. He had to take it off and check. He chuckled as he tossed it on the backseat. A bloodstain on the brow band didn't count.

"Now we watch it rain," he said with a sigh. "And maybe we talk and I start thinking about my last ride in a muddy arena."

"What happened?"

He lifted his arm over her head and put it around her shoulders. "Or we make out like two horny teenagers who don't have a care in the world except getting pregnant." He lifted her chin and kissed her softly. "Which means we enjoy the hell out of first and second bases."

She smiled, her eyes all dewy. "This ain't no base-ball game, honey."

"And we're not teenagers."

"We're responsible adults," she whispered.

"Careful what you pitch me, woman. I can read your signals." He slid his fingers across her back. "Must be a clasp here somewhere."

"You talk too much, cowboy." She buried her fingers in his hair and pulled his head down for a base-stealing kiss.

A five-minute rain led them into temptation, and foggy windows delivered them from gawkers. She opened herself to him—her arms, her mouth, her sensitivity to every shift or sound or silent supplication—and it was all he could do to contain himself.

"Bareback riders, report to the chutes," called the announcer.

Damn those wimpy rain clouds.

Back-to-back, she fiddled with her camera while he fooled with his rigging. Maybe Trace carried the momentum from one kind of rush to the next, but Skyler needed a little Zen stillness to move her from the *life* side of the mirror to the *art* side. *Inhale slowly. Exhale. Steady, Skyler, he's only a man.*

But he was focused. The line *He spoke not a word, but went straight to his work* came to mind as she claimed the vantage he'd suggested—halfway up the fence adjacent to the bucking chutes. From there she photographed his every preparatory move—checking the cinch, taking his seat, taking his grip, pounding his gloved hand to set the rosin on the rigging grip and finally grabbing a piece of sky with his free hand and calling for the gate.

Skyler's heart pogoed into her throat, but she would not miss those action shots this time. The bronc sprang free of the chute like a flying reindeer. Trace marked his horse out—spurs above the shoulders—and took the first jump in classic bareback-rider style—back-to-back and spurs to shoulders. The front hooves' first landing gave Skyler the coveted splatter shot. His chaps flapped like fringed bat wings as he racked up the points by spurring high, wide and handsome. Skyler tried to forget who he was so she could remember to keep him centered in her viewfinder. She wondered how much punishment his riding arm could take. Without bit, reins or saddle, the only part of the ride he could control was his body. He had the strength and skill of a gymnast or a trapeze artist, except that his apparatus had muscle and a mind of its own.

Four Mississippi, five Mississippi... She wasn't breathing. She wondered whether he was. *...six ride him, cowboy, seven one more second... Bzzzz!*

He made the whistle, but he missed the pickup rider and down he went.

Skyler froze.

A clown and a cowboy wearing an official Justin Sportsmedicine Team vest pulled Trace out of the mud while the second pickup man released Vegas's flank strap, and the high-headed horse cantered toward the exit as if to say, *Step aside, boys. My work here is done.*

Trace was on his feet, but only one leg was steady. Between clown and cowboy medic he left the arena through the gate instead of the preferred over-the-fence exit. But the crowd cheered him—first for his plucky wave and then for his high score. The open gate gave Skyler several clear camera shots.

"Comin' through," the clown barked, and Trace didn't look at her. A tall Indian cowboy took over for the clown, who scowled at Skyler as he passed on his way back to the arena. Clearly, she'd committed some offense.

She shoved her camera into her bag and followed Trace and his human crutches to the medical tent, where she was able to talk herself inside. He was the evening's first casualty, so he had the no-nonsense medical team's full attention. A big, tail-wagging yellow dog was part of the reception crew.

"Who're you?" a woman in a pink shirt demanded. She had the Sportsmedicine patch on her sleeve. She was official.

"Skyler," Trace called out. "She's with me."

Somebody piped up behind her. "You trust her with your hat, Trace?"

"Damn straight." He acknowledged her with a glance and a nod, but he was concentrating on keeping upright while the aides peeled off his muddy chaps. They hoisted him up on an exam table. "How'd you do?" he asked Skyler.

"How did *I* do?" Somebody tapped her arm from

behind and "trusted" her with a muddy cowboy hat as she edged closer. Absently fingering the brim, she watched the medical team handle their charge with care. "Is it your knee?" she asked.

"Ankle. Mostly." Trace was looking up at one of the men who'd brought him this far—tall, attractive, vaguely familiar Indian cowboy, who she now noticed wore the red-and-black Justin Sportsmedicine patch on the sleeve of his crisp white, once clean Western shirt.

Where had she seen him before?

"Did you get your pictures this time?" Trace was asking.

"I think so." She watched the medic bend to the task of removing Trace's boot. "How bad is it?" she asked gently.

"Ahh!" Trace gripped the edge of the exam table. The dog nosed his hand until he relaxed it and petted her big shiny head. "Just cut it off, Hank."

"Aw, c'mon, it can't be *that* swollen yet. These boots look barely broke in. Hang on, it's comin'."

"Ah!" The boot came off in the medic's strong hands followed by a brown sock. "Damn, that smarts. It ain't broke. Look, I can—ahh! But I can move it just fine." The dog whimpered and licked Trace's toes.

"He's okay, Phoebe," the medic said. "Can you feel that?"

"Yeah." Trace braced himself on his arms and leaned back. "Wet, warm and gentle."

"Best nurse around." The medic rolled up the bottom of Trace's jeans. "What about the knee?"

"No problem. Skyler was just takin' a wild guess." He flashed a tight smile over the medic's head. "Skyler, you know Hank Night Horse?"

"I don't... You look familiar." The man spared her a glance and a chance, but his name wasn't ringing any bells. "Skyler Quinn," she offered. "How bad is it?"

"If Trace says it ain't broke, there's nothing to fix." He took Trace's ankle in hand.

"What do *you* say?" she asked.

"Nothing yet. He just got here." The medic was intent on his examination. "You want an X-ray, Trace?"

"No."

"Good, 'cause I left my Superman cape back at the Double D. I can send you to the ER, but..." He pressed gently while he slowly rotated Trace's foot. "Wiggle your pigs."

Trace moved his toes. "I can do that all the way home."

"As long as you're not driving. It's swellin' up pretty good, but I don't think anything's broken. You'll know soon enough if you've got a fracture. Short of that, you know what to do. Gen, could you get us some—" the woman in the pink shirt plunked a plastic bundle in the medic's outstretched hand "—cushion?"

"Right." She snatched a vinyl-covered cushion off an empty exam table. "You were thinking ice, Hank." She turned away muttering, "Best nurse around, he says."

"You want Gen to shave you, Trace? She needs a job."

"Hell, no. Use the underwrap," Trace said.

"Keep your ol' leg hair, then," Gen said and Trace laughed.

Skyler was thinking Double D, the wild horse sanctuary, the competition. "That's where I saw you," she told the medic. "You're the farrier."

"Feet are my specialty." He had Trace's propped up, and he was applying the ice. "Lie back and take it easy," he told Trace. "You've won yourself a roll of tape."

"Better be more than that." Trace finally gave in and lay back. "Heard you got hitched, Doc."

"Sure did. Your dad and me, both. Where the hell were you?"

"On the road." Trace laughed. "Hell, if I'd known it was you and Logan, I wouldn't've missed it. Must've been a pretty sight. Who carried the flowers?"

"Sally and Mary did, you smart-ass. You wouldn't wanna piss me off while you're on my table, Wolf Track."

"Not Sally *Drexler*," Skyler said.

"Not anymore," Hank said with a proud smile. "She goes by Sally Night Horse now."

"I love what she's doing with her ranch, turning it into a home where the wild horse roams," Skyler said. "I entered the mustang training competition."

Hank nodded. "How's the horse coming along?"

"Slowly. Trace was going to give me a few pointers. But now…"

"He can still point." Hank pulled out a length of stretchy white tape and started a figure-eight wrapping. "Baby him for twenty-four hours or so, and then make him start putting some weight on it. If he can't, he gets it x-rayed."

"Hey," Trace said. "It's my ankle."

"What, you're not gonna milk it?" Hank cut the tape, tossed it in a box and took out a roll of green tape and another of red.

"Trace Wolf Track in here?" The cowboy clown stuck his head in the tent door, looked around and snapped one of his red suspenders when he located his target. "Hey, man, you took first in bareback. They want me to get you out there for the announcement."

"They love a wounded winner," Hank said. "Load him up on the go-cart and let him take his bow."

"I'll take my check," Trace muttered as he sat up.

"I'll get him a walking cast boot," Gen said. "Stay out of the mud with it, though."

"I ain't finished with him, so don't let him out of the cart." Hank smiled at Skyler. "Like they say, the show must go on."

Chapter 4

Armed with crutches, ice pack and pills, Trace turned his keys over to Skyler and climbed into the passenger's side of his pickup. From the swelling and the kind of pain Trace was experiencing, Hank had suspected at least a second-stage sprain and loaded him down with warnings. The crowd's adulation had cheered him, and collecting his check had taken that up a notch, but Skyler had a feeling the man would crash soon and she didn't feel like driving a hundred miles tonight.

She started the pickup and turned to him. "Let's get you to bed."

"You say that like you think you're gonna tuck me in and kiss me good-night." He slid down in the seat and offered a slow, sexy grin. "Take another look and think again."

She had no idea what that was supposed to mean. The party was over. The less damaged cowboys would be heading for the next rodeo. "You heard the man. He said *elevate*."

"Hell, I got no problem elevating. I am…" True to his name, his hazel eyes glittered. "Let's get *you* to bed."

"At least I don't have to ask what kind of drugs you're on."

"El-ev-ate! El-ev-ate!" he sang as she turned the pickup onto a hill.

She had to laugh. "I'm glad you're feeling no pain. Once we get you down, you will be out."

"That's why I ain't goin' down, darlin'. I already checked out."

"I did, too, but we can check back in. You're—"

"Win or lose, I ain't payin' for another night. I told you I was leaving after the rodeo, and you said you were going with me."

"There's been a slight change in the plan, cowboy."

"Another change? Damn, that came easy."

"We've already agreed. Change is good."

He dropped his head back and smiled at the ceiling. "Yeah, but this one won't be slight."

"We'd have to go back to the rodeo grounds and find your trailer. You did bring a horse trailer."

"Never leave home without it."

"I'd have to hitch it up. I'd have to load your new horse." She glanced at him. So far he wasn't taking exception. "And since my place is on the way to yours, you'd have to lay over for a while."

He turned his silly smile on her. "Lay over who?"

"You're incorrigible."

"Ha! You love it."

"And you're all alike."

"All who?" He waved her answer off. "Nah, forget it. Just tell me when I'm like nobody else. Whisper it in my ear. *You're different, Trace. I've never met anyone like you, Trace.*" His smile mellowed. "Because you're already there, Skyler. You're like nobody else."

"You hardly know me."

"You're hard to know. Mmm, but you're so very easy to look at."

"Thank you."

They'd reached the hotel. She parked close to the side entrance, got out of the pickup, went around to the passenger's side and opened the door.

He didn't move. "What are we doing here?"

"They're holding my bag at the desk."

"Oh, yeah, let me get that for you." He sat up, grabbed the door and swung himself onto the pavement, one leg jacked up like a flamingo.

"It's on wheels. What do you need out of the back?"

"Nothing." He patted the front pocket of his jeans. "Got my spare foot right here. The pink one."

"Besides ice pack, crutches—" she opened the back door of the crew cab and found the first two items "—toothbrush, pajamas."

"*Pajamas!* Good luck with that, woman."

She positioned his crutches and he flapped his wings. "Good luck with that, cowboy. I'd let you lean on me, but you seem a little buzzed. I'm afraid we'd both go down."

He moved one crutch and hopped a couple of inches. "These damn sticks don't fit me."

They really weren't a bad fit, but he gave her such a befuddled look that she wasn't going to argue. Back into the backseat went the crutches. She drew his arm around her shoulders and told him it wasn't far. "You stayed on that crazy horse, and now you're gonna let a pair of crutches throw you?"

"Nope. I'm stayin' off 'em. You ever ride a stick horse?"

"Probably."

"Neither did I. Never had one. I wanted one, but I never got it."

"Step up," she told him at the door. She noticed he didn't put any extra weight on her when he hopped up the single step. *Big faker.* But it took them a while to get to the lobby, which was quiet. She breathed a sigh of relief when they reached a chair.

"I'm a lightweight when it comes to painkillers."

"I wouldn't say that. Sit. Take a load off both of us." She bent to lift his bandaged foot and place it on the coffee table. She glanced up when he thanked her. He smiled dreamily.

She came back with her wheeled bag in tow and offered him a hand. "We're on the first floor. No stairs."

"I never stay in town once the rodeo's over."

"But there's only one bed."

He took her hand. "Like I said, it sure would be nice to lie down and elevate."

It was an old hotel, and the room was small but nicely appointed with a brass bed, a highboy and a vanity. Trace said he was too dirty to sit on the bed, so she helped him to the low-back wooden chair, stood back and took a look at him in the soft light.

"You need food," she determined.

"I need a shower more than anything." He glanced around the room. "*Almost* anything. I could use a shot of Jack Daniel's."

"*Food*. I'll order something, and then I'll get your stuff from the pickup." She glanced at his booted foot. "Where would I find you some clothes?"

"There's a duffel bag in the back and a pair of Ariats on the floor. My favorite boots. They lace up."

"Perfect," she said, genuinely cheered by that news. But then she considered the taped foot. "I don't know how you'll manage in the shower."

"I don't, either. Probably need some help."

"Does it still hurt?"

"Like a sonuvabitch." She gave him a doubtful look and he smiled. "You wouldn't know it, though, would you? I'm toughin' it out."

"I'm impressed." Back to the bandaged foot. "You can't get that wet."

"You think?"

"So I don't know how you'll manage." She shook her head sadly. "Keep on toughin', I guess."

He burst out laughing.

"What do you want to eat?"

"Not much." He started up from the chair, and she went to his side. "I'm good," he told her. "Plenty of wall to hang on to."

"And a safety rail in the shower."

"Yeah, they think of everything these days."

"Still, there's that bandage…"

He slipped his arm over her shoulder. "Truth is, that bandage ain't goin' nowhere. Hank's a master taper and a little water won't hurt. I'll take whatever they've got between two pieces of bread. And I'll tell you what else." He touched her cheek with the backs of his fingers.

The look in his eyes made her throat go dry. "What else?"

"For taking such good care of me you've got at least a week comin'."

"A week…"

He nodded. "Comin'. Yeah. And don't think I can't do just as good on one leg as I can on two."

"I wouldn't… You don't have to. I mean, this changes—"

"Nothing." He gave her a quick kiss. "I hate crutches. I'll be off them in no time."

She patted his flat, hard stomach. "I'll be back in no time."

"Sure you don't wanna throw me in the shower first?"

"Whatever you need."

"The list is short, but the need…" He kissed her again. "You'd better get going while you can."

"I'll drop you off in the bathroom on my way to the door."

He laughed. "Hell of a date."

Moonlight brightened the parking lot. Skyler had the keys in her hand, and she was going to gather some of his stuff from his pickup. He'd trusted her with his hat and now his pickup. She eyed the sleek topper that covered the pickup bed. The contents of a cowboy's pickup probably revealed a lot about him, she thought. Not that she would ever snoop, but she had to wonder what Trace carried with him on the road. What would it hurt if she took a peek?

Maybe she'd find a few books or magazines, and she'd learn more about his interests. Maybe he kept clippings, and she could learn more about his career. He didn't brag himself up—old-fashioned cowboy modesty was rare these days—but it would be fun to see what he'd done, what sportswriters had said about him. It would have to be fun. He was a fun guy.

Or maybe she'd find pictures of some of the horses he'd trained. Maybe family pictures. Maybe girlfriends. She was just curious, wanted to find out what he liked and who and why. She could ask him, of course. She could be nosy without being downright sneaky.

Or she could act her age, as her mother used to say. She could mind her own business and take him his boots and his duffel bag and just…get hold of herself. Because she had plans. Some of them might work out, some might not, but she had to make her own way and she was beginning to see her way. *Her* way. Trace Wolf Track was a distraction, and maybe the mustang was, too. Lovely distractions—*necessary* distractions from the widow's box she'd built for herself—but they were just passing through, crossing her path.

And Skyler was moving out of the box. She was going to start getting real very soon now, start making it on her own. She really did have a life to live. Not as a princess or a caretaker or a guardian—and certainly not as a snoop.

She'd almost majored in journalism years ago, but even when she'd dropped the academic plan by the wayside, she'd kept up with her photography. She didn't enjoy bookkeeping or ranch management, but she'd taken them on out of necessity, and she could actually see herself setting those roles aside. The ZQ Ranch. With the fall would come the time for selling calves and maybe everything else unless Mike decided to get with the program. Skyler would lay out a program. Do or die, she would say. And then she would call for the gate.

She smiled to herself as she located the boots and the bag exactly where Trace had said they would be. She locked the pickup, gave the topper one last glance and headed back inside.

"Food's here."

Skyler stowed the boots and the duffel bag next to her rolling suitcase in the corner of the room and set the take-out bag near Trace's foot, propped on

the edge of the bed. He was sitting in the room's
only chair, back to the door. She'd noticed his jeans
on the bathroom floor along with a rumpled towel,
noticed his powerful shoulders, all buff and bare as
she'd walked past him.

"Oh, good," she said, staring at the purpling skin
that disappeared beneath layers of taping on his foot.
"You're icing."

"It's okay to turn around." She heard the amusement in his voice. "I'm RICE-ing. Rest, ice, compression, elevate."

"You've done this before." She turned, sat on the
bed, looked up and smiled.

"Many times." He closed his eyes and dropped
his chin to his chest, his arms resting on the wooden
arms of the chair. His hair fell over his forehead in
dark, wet tendrils. "More than I can count."

She gave herself a moment to take in the sight of
him, during which her only thought was, *Man, oh,
man.* But what she said was, "Boxer briefs. It's true.
We do wonder." They were black. Sexy. She glanced
up and found him smiling. Reading her mind. So
much for the humble cowboy. "How's the swelling?"

"Alive and well."

"Well, I have something for you."

She patted his "ol' hairy leg" in parting, moved behind him, laid her hands on his shoulders and pressed
her fingers into knotted muscles. He groaned, a blend
of protest and pleasure. She had done this before,
more times than she could count, and she was good
at it. She pushed hard with the heels of her hands, dug

deep with her thumbs until his muscles gave a little and a little more until finally his shoulder sagged and his head fell back and rested on her stomach with a great sigh. She pressed her thumbs into his nape and tunneled her fingers into his hair, massaging his scalp, drawing heavy thoughts up, up and away. He gave a soft, throaty sound. Pure pleasure.

"Something smells good," he said long moments later. "Besides you."

"Comfort food." She took a foam box from the bag and made a presentation of it with a cloth napkin and tableware—she'd firmly nixed paper and plastic. "Meat loaf and mashed potatoes."

"I'm not real..." He glanced up and quickly changed his tune. "Perfect."

"Nobody is," she said with a smile. "But physically—well, except for the ankle and the knee... Otherwise, I have to say, you're pretty damn close."

"I clean up pretty good, but perfect is a tall order." He stabbed his fork into the potatoes, took a taste and then dug in ravenously. He'd eaten half his food before he came up for air and took notice of her takeout box. "What've you got?"

"Chicken with wild rice. Here. Taste." She reached across the divide and held a forkful to his lips. He approved the sample with a nod. "Trade?" He shook his head, still chewing. "This late, these were the choices."

"It's good. Try this." He gave her meat loaf dipped in potatoes. "Hmm?"

"Mine's better."

He shrugged. "We'll get started early. I don't like to hang around on the last night. On a good night, you collect your winnings and hit the road. Bad nights, you just hit the road." He spared his ankle a glance as he raked his potatoes with his fork. "But I won't be pushing anything with this foot, not for a few days at least. I don't think I tore much. Maybe a little something, not much." He stabbed the meat loaf. "Ten days until Cheyenne. I never miss that one."

"What's special about that one?"

"It's Cheyenne. You ever been?"

"I've been to Cheyenne."

"You live in Wyoming, and you haven't been to the Cheyenne Frontier Days?" He shook his head, frowning, couldn't fathom such an oversight. "I'll take you with me. You'll see what's special. It's one of the granddaddies."

"You owe me two days."

"Starting tomorrow," he reminded her around a bite of meat loaf. "And like I said, I can do better on my end of the deal."

"Tomorrow you'll still be RICE-ing."

"Mmm. You were right. I didn't think about food."

"Because, there's no *F* in RICE, and you're following doctor's orders to the letter."

"How about we add a little therapy that starts with *S*? RICES. End the day on a high note with a little—"

"*Elevate* is high."

"So am I." He leered. "You could take advantage of me so easy."

"No, the *I* is for *ice*," she said as she closed the lid on her supper. "My home court. I'm the ice queen."

"No problem. I come equipped with an ice pick."

"I have one, too. Mine has my name engraved on it." She stood and moved to the highboy, where she unloaded the box. "I was Winter Carnival Queen. Also Miss Northern Lights, Princess Kay of the Milky Way, Miss Harmon County, Lake Festival Princess, Miss Potato—" she smiled to herself, touched his shoulder on her way back to the bed "—Head."

He gave an appreciative whistle. "That's a lot of... Potato Head?"

"I got a complete makeover out of that one. New nose, eyes, lips, big funny ears." She'd wiped the smile off her face, but it was still in her eyes. "They all came in a box."

"Are you gonna crown me if I laugh?"

"Maybe."

"Talk about perfect, that's you." He set his empty box on the floor beside his chair, and then his gaze claimed hers. "Seriously, you could be queen of the world. Mine, anyway."

Cowboy flattery. Next he'd be calling her Miss Skyler. Or worse, ma'am.

"There's always some kind of scholarship attached," she explained. "That's how I paid for a year of college. I dropped out when I married one of the judges." She gave a perfunctory smile. "I was only first runner-up in that contest. I didn't marry him right away."

"He was married?"

"He was a widower. He hired me as a nanny for the summer." She shook off the memory and scooped his empty box off the floor. "What's the *R* for? *Rest? Time to rest.*"

"I don't take too well to nannying."

"That was my nursing voice." She unzipped the side pocket of her bag and took out her toiletry case. "My nanny voice is more like, *I'm going to count to three. One. I know one of your feet hurts. Use the other one. Two.*"

"I'm *going.*" He flicked the ice pack out of the way and groaned pitifully as he lifted his foot off the bed.

"You want your toothbrush?"

"You're cold, woman. I might as well be sleepin' with an ice pack."

"Only twenty minutes at a time."

"That's not what I meant."

"It's what I meant." She took her toothpaste and night cream out and sat down on the toilet to pull her boots off. "Nursing voice again."

"Will that be the one bringing me my toothbrush? Most nurses I know are warm and tender."

"You trust me to rummage around in your personal stuff?"

"I'm *dying* to have you rummage around in my personal stuff."

She smiled at herself in the mirror. She'd forgotten how much fun this game could be.

He was in bed when she brought him the water and toothbrush. He laughed and shook his head and said this was "damned humiliating," but he complied with her directions in return for her agreement to stop fussing around.

He patted the empty side of the bed. "You lie down beside me."

"Will you be a good boy?"

"No. But I'll be a good man." He pulled the covers back on what would be her side of the bed and smoothed his hand over the stiff white sheet. "Come here. I'll show you." She hesitated. "Are you afraid of me, Skyler?"

"No," she said, and then she glanced at the ceiling. "A little. Or maybe it's me." She laughed nervously. She'd been a dutiful wife for fifteen years, but she hadn't been pleasured by anyone but herself in… She couldn't remember the last time. "Maybe you should be afraid."

"Maybe I should. I don't know much about royalty."

"Why did I tell you that?" She shook her head.

"Come here. We've only got this one bed, honey, so I guess we'll just have to make the best of it. And, hell, I'm…" He made a sweeping gesture toward the foot of the bed. "So make yourself comfortable. I'm harmless. Do you generally sleep in your jeans?"

"I'll take a shower and, um…I'll show you what I sleep in."

"Mmm. I love surprises."

Her Joe Boxer pajamas were hardly sexy. Long pink-and-blue-striped pants and a jersey tank with an aptly placed pink heart weren't what she would have chosen if she'd planned to spend the night with a man. She wasn't sure what she would have worn. If she'd planned it, she would have shopped Victoria's Secret catalog.

But she wouldn't have planned it. Dreamed it, maybe, but never planned it. Her best-laid plans would not have led her to a bed nearly filled with an injured rodeo cowboy. They would have led her back to the bed she felt safe in, the one that was hers alone. Had been ever since Tony had—over Skyler's objections—banished her to another bedroom.

He'd been a proud man, and it was hard to watch him go down with that particular ship. The SS *Pride*. But Skyler had stood her ground when he'd asked her to hire a nurse. They couldn't afford it, but she hadn't told him that. She'd said she wanted to take care of him herself, which, to her abiding shame, hadn't been completely true. Not every day. There were days when she'd imagine him getting better and others when she'd wish it would all be over.

Damn the memory. Why couldn't she just do what she wanted to do for a change? She'd once been a princess. Where was her crown when she needed it?

She spritzed herself with the scent of cherry blossoms, turned to the mirror and lifted her damp hair away from her face with splayed fingers. The hair dryer had cleared the steam away and she watched her hair fall bit by silky bit. She looked fine. Once she got over herself, she would feel fine, and she would remember what it meant to be a whole woman.

When she returned to the bedroom, his face was turned away and he had kicked the makeshift prop off the end of the bed. He was asleep. She took a seat cushion from a chair and made a wider shelf for his bandaged foot, arranging pillows until they formed the perfect mound. She moved his leg gently and covered him. He hardly moved when she stretched out beside him between crisp sheets chilled by the air-conditioning he'd asked her to jack up. He had all the pillows.

The vapor light from the parking lot streamed through the space between the blackout curtains and cast a white glow across his handsome face. His arm folded behind his head was like an open invitation to tuck in close to his side within a hairbreadth of touching him. His body was a radiator. He smelled tangy, like oranges and clove. Without opening his eyes he lowered his arm, and she lifted her head and found a pillow in the pocket of his shoulder.

Trace woke to a soft gray light, a hard ache and a killer throbbing all wrapped up in a thick analgesic haze. He could either try to sort it all out, or lie still and hope some part of it would go away. He tried the second option first, but something moved, and it wasn't him. He turned his muzzy head and ran into a pile of pale hair the color of the morning sky. He breathed its scent and imagined a tree full of flowers.

She lifted her face as though he'd spoken her name. Her lips parted, and he greeted her with a kiss. She turned herself to him, pressed her whole sweet body tight against his. He gave another kiss and another as he shifted to take her in his arms and keep her from slipping away. She felt real, but he didn't trust anything he was feeling. He'd wished the pain away, but if she was part of the reason for it, he'd take the wish back. *Throb on.*

He buried his fingers in her soft hair to keep them from tearing into her clothes. He knew who she was, but not really. He remembered how they'd come to this moment, but not really. *Leave it at that,* he told himself. *Leave it and take it. Pain comes with pleasure, and this feels like the best of both.*

She had the advantage. She was lying on his arm. While she explored his chest with her upper hand and teased his belly with the back of her lower one, he made his advances with one arm tied behind her back and his other hand tangled in her hair. He was riding without reins. She discovered his nipple and sissified it with a kindly cruel fingernail, dragging an unmanly sound out of him, as if he was down and defenseless and didn't mind at all. He was about to even things up, but she suddenly slipped her hand into his Jockey shorts. For a second, he didn't know where his next breath was coming from.

She hardly moved. He didn't dare move. They were poised on a glittering runway. *Take off or turn around?*

He held her head in his hand and she held his. Thinking was not an option.

His kiss was his invitation. His tongue showed her what he wanted to do with her, what he would give her, what he hoped for in return.

But have it your way, Skyler. Whatever you want, have it now. Have it all.

Her hand closed around his throttle and moved down over him at the end of the runway and drew him up, up, up. His pain gave him pause. A modicum of control. Enough to allow him to withdraw his hand—carefully, carefully, no pain for her—and slide it over her hip, bring those silly pants of hers down, down, down and seek smooth, soft skin and springy hair and parting thighs and a lovely damp place. His thumb brought out the best in her, the wetness that would ease his entrance. But he would take his time, discover her a little at a time, feel the heat inside her and listen to her growing pleasure and make it crest and wash over her. He could do this for her without backing off, without turning around.

It was her turn to sound the need in her, a wordless, throaty plea that drove him to take her hand from him. He wanted her in the worst way but he wasn't prepared. She needed him in the best way, and he would do his best for her and hope for the same in return. She took him inside her before he could think what that was—his best, his hope, the possibility of some return on his investment.

Thinking was not an option.

They were in the air now. She was a high roller and he was a long rider. This was win-win, he thought. His pain intensified his pleasure, but he wanted to keep that to himself. He could not know whether there was pain for the woman who took him inside her, but if there was, he wanted to ease it. He wanted her to feel him fully and know him tenderly. He meant to give all pleasure, no pain. And no consequences.

He truly meant to.

Chapter 5

They lay side by side. He hadn't said a word, but she could hear his mind galloping over a washboard. Up, down, up, down. She felt the words in his heartbeat. *What now, what now, what now.* No narcotic fog killed his good conscience. He was that kind of man.

She was almost sure of it.

It was about the only thing she was sure of right now, except that she felt wonderful, and she didn't want any part of that feeling taken away. *Give me this euphoric feeling for five more minutes. I deserve that much.*

She laid her hand on his beautiful chest—a little soft hair, a lot of hard muscle—and felt his heart beating against her palm. She lifted her head and kissed the near side of his chest. Then she rested her chin

on the kiss and blew softly on his nipple until it behaved the same way its brother had.

He groaned.

"How's your ankle?" she whispered.

"What ankle?"

She kissed him again, same spot, near the bump
she had silently whistled to attention.

"Once more, and I'm all over you," he said. "Third
time's the charm."

"The other one didn't need three." She glanced up
smiling. "But they're both charming."

His eyes were closed. He lay still and quiet for
what started out as an easy moment, but it stretched
and stretched until it began to smack of misgiving,
the sour-tasting answer to *What now?*

Keep it to yourself, then, she thought. The morning had begun with a kiss and that was hers to keep.
As for intercourse, she'd made the call. If there was
one thing she did not want to hear it was an apology.

"I'll do better next time," he said at last.

"Better?"

"Much better." He tucked his free arm beneath
his head and looked her in the eye. "All over you."

"I'm going to hold you to that."

"Me, too." He frowned slightly. "Do you have anything against condoms?"

"I don't know."

"You're kidding."

She shook her head. "It's never been an issue
for me."

"Damn." He drew a deep breath. "It's…kind of an issue for everybody, don't you think?"

She nodded. "But I'm just getting back in the game."

His eyes were too keen, too perceptive. She wished she could say something sharp and sassy, but he'd just turned her fear of being diminished somehow on its head, and nothing she could say would hide that from him. She felt good. No regrets, no remorse, no guilt. She'd wanted him, and that was that.

Better next time.

She turned her cheek to his chest, closed her eyes and wondered how much better it could be.

Another time—maybe next time—she could say such a thing, but not now. She wanted to keep *now* just as it was. The end of a long, lonely drought.

The promise of more rain.

The pickup lurched as the ball hitch coupled with the horse trailer. Trace was ready to disembark. "Relax," Skyler ordered. "I've got this."

"You sure?" He settled back into his seat. "The doors can be tricky. Call me if you need me, and I'll hop right out." She gave him a parting thumbs-up, and he added, "His name is Jack."

"Jack loads like a dream," she reported as she buckled herself behind the wheel.

"Figured he would. He likes you." He slid his seat back as soon as she started the pickup. "His registered name is Ball in the Jack. When I first heard that, I thought, what were they thinking? Then I saw

it written out on paper. Not exactly what I pictured."
He chuckled. "Still doesn't make much sense."

She smiled. "It's an old dance."

"You know how to do it?"

"Really old dance, like early 1900s. I don't go back
quite that far, but I do know how to do it. I took dance
lessons growing up." She signaled in advance of the
on-ramp. "There's a song, too."

"Really? How does it go?"

"I've forgotten."

"No, you haven't. Come on. A few bars." He
reached across the center console and tapped her arm.
"How 'bout if I take you to a few bars? You'd be singin' after how many stops? Two? Three?" When he
couldn't get more than a tight smile out of her, he
drew back and settled in for the long haul. "What is
it, a game? Something girls play, I'll bet. Totally innocent. Ball in the jack."

"It was a railroad term." She hadn't intended to
pull out the trivia file, but with a hundred empty
miles ahead, might as well fill them from what Tony
liked to call her store of apropos-of-nothing facts. "It
was a signal to go faster, and it wasn't ball *in*. It was
ballin' the jack, spelled just the way you thought. The
jack was the locomotive—the jackass that pulled the
load—and the highball signal meant *go fast.* So the
dance…" She lifted one shoulder. "It's actually kind
of cute."

"When do I get to see it?"

"Let's see." She glanced left and right. Herefords
grazed on one side and a rocky red bluff flanked the

other. "Where's a Redbox when you need one? *For Me and My Gal*. Gene Kelly and Judy Garland. Early 1940s, I think. I'll have to check the date."

"I believe you. I'm partial to old Westerns, but I couldn't quote you any dates. Maybe a line or two. 'If God didn't want them sheared, he wouldn't have made them sheep.'" He grinned at her, gave her about three seconds and then whistled a dozen notes from "The Theme from the Magnificent Seven."

He was a good whistler.

"So you like trains?"

"My husband was interested in trains. I have lots of books about trains." She thought for a moment. "Go fast. Go all out," she mused. "It's a good name for a horse."

"If he doesn't mind the jackass part." He shifted his legs and pushed a seat button, but it wasn't getting him anywhere. He was as far back as he was going to get. "Speed isn't Jack's strong suit. He's quick and he's agile. Put some cow sense on him, and he's a cuttin' horse. He'll double my investment."

"Do you have cattle?"

"I keep a few head around for working horses."

"Around where?" She shook her head. "I don't even know where you live."

"You wrote the check."

"And handed it to Michael. Along with a few words about the amount and what it was for. Not the who or the where. Just the what. So tell me where."

"A few miles outside of Newcastle."

"I love that Black Hills country. Do you…"

"Yep." Lips pressed firmly he nodded slowly. "I live alone."

"Good to know."

"I'll bet." He turned to her, eyes smiling. "You carnival queens are all alike. Kiss the clown first, ask questions later."

"Touché."

"Just kidding. Some things you just know about a person. You don't have to take an application." He slapped the console for emphasis. "Right? Like if he's a cowboy, he's always goin' down the road. Big ego, little brain."

"Not always. They have their modest moments." She slid him a smile. "If she's a stepmother, she's mean and ugly."

"Not always. Not after she washes up and gets her face on." He tapped her arm with a loose fist. "Wait till you meet my new stepmother. Did I tell you she's a soldier? Logan did real good this time."

For a moment he was quiet. He took his hat off and tossed it onto the backseat, shifted his long legs. He was uncomfortable. She was pushing the speed limit, but she wished she could go all out, *ballin' the jack,* fly low and get him down the road.

"I've never met a dairy princess," he said. "Is that how you learned your way around an ice-cream cone?"

"Frozen custard." She flashed him a smile. "If she's a dairy princess, she must be a butterball."

"I met a pork queen once. We were both riding in a

parade. Fourth of July. She was a firecracker. Bright, wild, funny as hell."

"Sounds like a corker."

"And she was no porker." He wanted a laugh for that, and she obliged. "She was looking for scholarship money, too. She's probably a bank president or a rocket scientist by now."

"Or the mother of a couple of kids and the wife of a—"

"—rich pig farmer." He chuckled. "A lot of people look at life as a ladder, and that's kind of the way I've tried to go. More up the road than down. But lately..." He leaned back and rested his head. "Logan says it's a circle. I tell him I'm not interested in chasing my tail or following behind anybody else's. He says it's not like that. Doesn't have to be, anyway." He made a high-level gesture. "So here I am, standing on the top of Hill Number Thirty, and I'm thinkin', he's right. There's always a lineup for the ladder and then somebody on every rung. You make a circle, you're not lookin' at a bunch of tails." He rolled his head in her direction. "Is this what happens when you get a little age on you? Ego switches places with brain?"

"You're asking *me?*"

"I'm not asking unless that's what it takes. You want me to ask?"

"I don't see what difference it makes."

He chuckled. "Neither do I, but you've been chokin' on it, honey, so spit it out."

"I'll be forty," she chirped and gave a *dare you* look. "In three years."

"Damn, you're well preserved." He winked at her, and her stony stare melted away. "I figure I'm at least that in cowboy years. You start countin' the miles I've put on this carcass and all the repair work they've had to do on it, hell, I'm old enough to be your…" He smiled. "Whatever you need right now."

"You're right. It feels good to get it out. That and the beauty-queen thing. I don't know why." She glanced at his knees. "Is it bothering you much?"

"It never bothered me at all."

"Your *ankle*."

"Oh, yeah, that bothers me. It would feel good to get it up."

"I could help you with that."

"I know. Let's pull over."

"Do you want to stop now, or wait till we get to the ranch? We're fifteen miles out."

"It's throbbing pretty good."

"Your call," she said.

"I've waited my whole life to hear those words. I'm gonna call backseat. I can't wait fifteen miles."

She pulled off the road and helped him get situated on the narrow club cab seat with his taped foot braced against the side window.

"You should have been back here all along," she told him as she tucked his duffel bag behind his shoulders.

"We wouldn't've talked. I wouldn't've known what *ballin' the jack* means or how old you are. How old did you say you were when the song first came out?" She swatted his shoulder. "Watch it, woman. My hours on the injured list number in the single digits. And then I'm comin' for you."

"Thanks for the warning," she said as she climbed behind the wheel. "That's an eight seconds I won't want to miss."

"You know what, Skyler?" he called out from the backseat. "You're not just another pretty face."

"Nice little place you've got here." Trace grabbed the front seat and the back door and gingerly levered himself to the ground. She'd parked the pickup and horse trailer next to a corral with a loafing shed, which were only the beginning of a series of pens and outbuildings. He reached into the passenger seat for his hat, put it on and surveyed the rest of the setup while he adjusted the brim against the afternoon sun. The two-story rock and milled-log house was big enough for a good-size family, but it was the smaller house partnered with its own rickety barn that caught Trace's eye.

"Who lives in the other house? Ranch foreman?"

"The foreman would be me. I'm everything but the owner and the hired help."

"You don't own it, and you work for free?"

"I don't own the ranch, but the main house has my name on it. Mine and the bank's," she announced with a sweeping gesture. She nodded toward the smaller one. "That's the original house, the home place. That's Mike's, along with the land and the livestock."

"You aren't partners in the ranching business?

That's what he said when he handed me that check. 'My partner handles the finances.'"

"It's complicated." She motioned for him to follow her.

He stood his ground. He wasn't one to tag along on the heels of a shutdown.

She reversed her direction along with her tone. "I don't know how else to explain it," she said as she pulled his arm over her shoulder and slipped hers around his waist. "Come on, just a few steps. He's right around the corner."

"It's none of my business."

"I mean the horse."

He could've limped along by himself, but what fun would that be? He wasn't leaning on her. Now that she was coaxing rather than bossing, he was enjoying her attention.

"Trace Wolf Track, meet Wild Thing."

The sorrel-faced "flea-bitten" gray stood on the shady side of the loafing shed. He wanted shade, but there was no way he was going inside that three-sided trap all by his lonesome. He was more than the sum of his handsome parts—sleek and sturdy, regal head, beautifully appointed with black mane, tail and legs, and the generous application of red specks to a gray coat that tagged him "flea-bitten."

Trace grimaced. "Wild Thing?"

Skyler only had eyes for the horse.

"I read about the competition, and I thought I'd go over there and take some pictures, maybe work up a photo essay or even a video. From the first moment I saw him, I thought we had some kind of connection. I felt like I was supposed to take him home, like we could learn something from each other. There were a couple of other people there picking out horses for the competition, but he wanted nothing to do with them. He seemed to choose me."

The leap from *hard to explain* to *easy to believe* sent gravity packing, changing Skyler's whole demeanor. Trace smiled. "Don't tell me he made your heart sing."

"How did you know?" Without taking her eyes from the horse, she smiled wistfully. "I felt like Snow White, beloved of wild creatures. We got along really well at first, that initial waltz in the forest, and then we hit the castle wall."

"What happened, princess? You whistled and he wouldn't come?"

She tipped her head and squinted against the sun. "You like the way I set that up for you?"

"Beautiful." A breeze toyed with her blush-colored hair, and she lifted her hand to catch it or salute him or shade one eye. She might have been trying to wink at him and couldn't remember how it was done. God, he wanted to kiss her. "Are you afraid of each other?"

She lifted one shoulder. "I'm very comfortable on a horse. You saw that yourself."

"Yeah, but this guy really is a wild thing. Maybe he does connect with you on a gut level, but he doesn't choose to carry you on his back. Far as he knows, anything that jumps on his back is out to kill him."

"I've been all about showing him that I come in peace. I've managed to halter him. That's huge."

"It is. Then what?"

"I tried to longe him, but I think it was too soon. Either that or I did something that scared him off. I don't know what. I've taken it slow and easy, and he's even taken food from my hand."

"So he's like a pet."

"Absolutely not. Once I have him under saddle, I'm not going to ask him to be anything but a horse. I don't want to break his spirit. I like a horse with spirit."

"Are you out to win this thing? You could've adopted a mustang. You didn't have to sign on for the training contest."

"It isn't just a contest. It's a cause. And it's a personal challenge. Horses have always been an important part of my life—maybe the best part—but starting a horse from square one is something I've never done. I went to the Double D thinking I would take some pictures and talk to some people, and I found a story I wanted to be part of. I've had some ups and downs, but that's all part of the story."

"You don't care about winning?"

She folded her arms over the corral rail, rested her chin on her sleeve and considered the mustang. "I wouldn't *mind* winning. If that helps any."

"Does that help you any, big guy?" Trace called out to the horse. "Don't worry about being all you can be. Good enough is good enough."

"I stopped taking contests too seriously a long time

ago," Skyler said. "Trophies collect dust. It's all about how you play the game. I really believe that."

"I like to play hungry." He scanned the empty corrals. "What else have you got here? Since we're just past square one, any chance of a round pen?"

She grinned. "There's an *almost* square one. It's pretty small."

"Show me."

"Why don't we turn Jack out with my wild child here? Wouldn't that give us—"

Trace laughed. "You really don't have a name for him, do you?"

"It hasn't come to me."

"Guess he must be holding back on you, huh? Connection interrupted." He turned and leaned back against the corral. "Now, my dad would want him to have a good name. But Logan's an Indian, and I'm just a cowboy. I don't think that horse cares what you call him as much as *how* you call him. Wild or tame, he's not your baby." He shook his head, grinning. "I gotta say *thing* and *child* don't work for me, but the horse doesn't care what word you use."

She turned away from him and said quietly, "I want a copy of your father's book. Can I buy it online?"

"I'll hook you up with a copy."

"No, I'll order it."

"Suit yourself. I buy them by the case. Don't tell Logan that. I've given a bunch of them away."

"It's too bad your father isn't aware of the compliment you're paying him. You're a good man."

"I'm doing it for the horses." He leaned his shoulder against the corral and faced her. "Okay, for Logan because he put a lot of work into it, but he speaks for the horse. Maybe that sounds hokey, but it's true."

"I can't wait to read it," she said quickly, suddenly a little girl, eager to please. "What do you think? Put Jack in with…" She turned to the horse. "I don't have the heart to name him when I have to give him up at the end of the competition. I'm just a foster mother."

Trace laughed. "He doesn't need a mother, and if he did, he wouldn't *choose* you."

She waved his words away. "Forget I said that choosing part."

"And he'd take Jack's company over yours any day, which is why we're not putting them together. Not yet."

She couldn't let go. "I guess it sounded silly when I said he chose me. Or *hokey.* Some people would think that, but I know we had a moment. It was like he recognized me. *Hey, Skyler, I'm over here.*"

"A dog will choose you over his own kind, but not a horse." He wanted off this ride. Considering what he was feeling for her and what she wanted from him, the whole mystical connection was a tight fit at the moment. He wanted to take it off and start over.

He reached for her hand. "Did we decide that I was gonna lay over for a while? Because I'd like to lay my head down and put my foot up."

"I'm sorry." She slipped her arm around his waist. "Here I stand yakking and I should be taking care of my guest."

"Just point me to a piece of floor and maybe a chair, and I'll take care of the rest."

Trace allowed the woman to hold the back door open for him since he'd surrendered the use of his arms to the damn crutches. He promised himself he'd be off them tomorrow. He'd get his legs under him, get his head on straight, help Skyler and the mustang negotiate their wall, enjoy their company for a day or two and then head on down the road. He'd keep in touch, sure. She was one hell of a woman, but a couple of days and he was already in pretty deep. He knew how to rehab an ankle, but his heart was the last part of himself he'd lay on the line. He wasn't ready.

Mike walked into the kitchen eating a sandwich. The look in his eyes said he'd been expecting playmates and here came the cat. But he recovered quickly.

"Hey, Skyler, looks like you brought one of them hard-luck cowboys home with you. Need any help?"

"No, thanks." Trace claimed the closest kitchen chair. "Speak for yourself, kid. A hard-luck cowboy isn't the guy who takes first in his event."

"Way to go." Mike took a glass down from a cupboard. "Must've been the buckle-bunny stampede afterward that took you down."

"It was a bad landing. Second one in less than a week."

"Plus your birthday. Maybe the gods are trying to tell you something, Trace."

"As long as I keep winning, we're good. That's a message I can take to the bank."

"How's the hay coming, Mike?" Skyler asked, and then she turned to Trace. "Can I get you something?" He shook his head, bemused. *Two men, two questions, one breath.*

"Grady wanted to finish knocking that grass down on the west side," Mike reported as he pulled a jug of milk from the refrigerator. "I figured I'd ride along the creek up to the north fence line and take a head count, but the morning got away from me, and now it's too hot."

"Grady's still out there cutting hay," Skyler pointed out.

"In an air-conditioned cab. 'Course, he's an old man. He deserves all the amenities."

"Grady doesn't use the AC in the tractor. He says it's a waste of gas."

"So, Trace." Mike glanced past the glass he was filling. "What do you think of Skyler's latest project? She had it going on pretty good, and then she kinda got frustrated. Thought she might throw in the towel." He slapped the plastic cap on the jug with a flat hand. "Since horse trainers don't figure into the budget."

"I like him," Trace said. "We'll see if I can help get things going again."

Mike took a drink. "How long are you staying?"

Skyler snatched the abandoned milk jug off the counter and spared her stepson a cutting glance on her way to the refrigerator. "How long have you been rude?"

"I didn't mean…" Mike flashed an empty palm. "Hell, Trace, you're welcome to stay as long as you want. Especially with…" He turned surrender into sympathy with a gesture toward Trace's ankle. "You gotta stay off your feet. You need some ice or something?"

"I'm good, thanks. I just need to get down and get the foot up. Let the air out of the balloon."

"Let's find you a pillow and a prop," Skyler said as she stowed the milk. She patted Mike's arm. "How long can *you* stay?"

"I can stay for supper, but I'm going out after that."

Mike's delivery struck Trace as a little too straight for a joke, which meant they would be three for supper. Disappointed, he followed Skyler into the living room and dropped his crutches beside a big leather chair with an ottoman.

"Right here is fine."

She spun on her heel. "I can do better than this."

"I'm sure you can, but I don't want to put anyone out." He sat down and swung his feet up to the cushy footrest. "Ahh, elevation."

"This is my house. I get to say who's welcome to stay and for how long." She knelt beside him and eased the loosely laced boot off his bum foot. He started to tell her he could do it, but the words wouldn't come. "I hope you'll stay as long as you can, and I don't want you to worry about the horse."

"Do I look worried?"

"No, but I have a feeling worry doesn't show on you."

"It shows on you." She gave him a curious look— part pouty, part puzzled—and he smiled. "It doesn't look bad. It just looks like something you don't need. Something a man wants to take away from you." He laid his head back and closed his eyes. "You should catch yourself in the mirror when you're having fun. Makes my heart sing."

"I'd groan, but I don't want to seem ungracious."

"That, and you started it."

Skyler returned to the kitchen and to Mike, who had finished his first sandwich and was building a second.

"I thought you liked Trace," she said quietly.

"I do. But don't you think he's a little young for you?"

"I don't think I need to think about it. I just met him."

"I just don't want you to get hurt by some…" Skyler shot him a *shut up* look, and he lowered his voice. "I know we're not doin' too well financially, and I don't want some guy to come along and add insult to injury."

"I don't know what to say. I don't even see a connection," she said absently, her mind switching to meal planning. But she stopped, backtracked. "Didn't you just break up with a woman who was a few years older than you?"

"She broke up with me."

She offered a token nod. "If I'd felt a need to make a case, I could rest it right there."

"Whatever that means."

"I was giving you the benefit of the doubt, but it

really doesn't matter. We don't have to protect each other. We're grown-ups."

"You're not the type to have a fling, Skyler, but you're easy pickin's right now," he said quietly.

"Eas—"

"I don't mean—"

"Keep your voice down." She lowered hers to his level. "We're not having this conversation. It isn't happening. You're going to ride fence, and I'm going to try to figure out how we can keep Grady on through the summer. And my guest is off-limits to you until you cut the crap." She nodded toward the sandwich on its way to his mouth. "So I hope your refrigerator has something in it besides beer."

"I'm just sayin'."

Have it. The last word is yours.

But her pointed glance at the back door was the last say.

And Trace—who hadn't heard everything, but he'd heard enough—bottled up the last laugh.

Chapter 6

"Keep him moving, Skyler. Keep talking to him. We want him to go easy, and he's not there yet." Trace let the camera run in video mode while he tested buttons. "How do you make this thing pull out? From close in to—" *Zoop, zip.* "Never mind. I got it."

Skyler was patient, and he had all the time in the world for watching the two of them play off each other. If this was her way of stepping away from her worries, it had to be working for her because she wasn't trying to rush the groundwork the way most people did. He'd told her to forget about the latest traveling trainer and his expensive two-day clinic or two-hour private consultation and horse tune-up. Throw away the video that promised a five-day miracle. There was no substitute for time and patience, and Skyler seemed willing to commit to both. He liked that about her.

Along with just about everything else. He wouldn't mind hanging around for a couple of days—time to help her out and let her come to terms with what she liked about him—but Trace could easily run out of time and patience if Mike wanted to be a pain in the ass. Trace's place was about two hours' drive, which put Skyler in his territory. This was Wyoming. Not too many places had fewer women per square mile.

He sat on the roof of his pickup using his bent knee as a tripod. She'd set the camera for the soft sunlight of late afternoon, and he'd set her up with a coil of double-braided marine rope and a few instructions.

"He's going easy now, Trace. I can feel it. You're groovin', aren't you, big boy?"

He smiled behind the camera, partly for the pleasure of seeing the beautiful dappled horse canter in a circle with Skyler at the center. They were both "going easy." She swung the end of the rope to keep him moving. He was unfettered, and she was undaunted. But his smile was mostly for the way she said his name, the way her voice shined it up somehow. *Going easy* described the feel of moving through the day as though they'd been together through many days and nights.

"Groovin'?" Trace chuckled. "Sounds like I found myself a hippie."

"Child of a hippie." She flipped a few feet of rope through the air and made it dance behind the horse to keep him moving. "That's good," she told him quietly, and then lifted her voice to Trace. "There's hip-pie blood on my father's side."

"I can tell. Better yet, the horse can tell. You've got that peaceful, easy feelin'."

"Yes, well, my father didn't believe in *bending another to your will.* Isn't that what I'm doing now?"

"If we open the gate, the horse *will* take off."

"So would Jack. A horse is a horse."

"That's right. We bend the will a little so we don't have to break the spirit. Now, drop your arms, turn your shoulder to him, walk away slowly and let's draw him to you."

She executed the draw perfectly, and the horse lowered his head and followed her lead.

"Sweeet," Trace crooned behind the camera.

"Do you think he'd take a treat?"

"What've you got?"

"Nothing." She took a serpentine turn around the pen, and the horse continued to follow. "I just won-dered. He should get a reward for this."

"He's not a kid, and he's not a pet, so don't kid yourself. The best treat you can give him is that grass out there."

"And the company of another horse or two. Pref-erably a herd."

"We'll bring that in later. Right now, you're all he's got. He wants a leader." She stopped, and the horse lowered his muzzle to the ground and sniffed the dirt. "See there? The lead mare chooses the grass. She picks her spot, and everybody else gathers around.

Maybe he smells your hippie blood. Take him away from this place and lead him to pastures of plenty."

"I can't keep him in?"

"You have a son who has a well-trained horse. They can get him back in."

She opened the gate to the adjacent small pasture and kept the lead until she had grass underfoot. The horse dashed well past her and celebrated his release by kicking up his heels. Trace kept the camera running, half expecting Skyler—coming to him all bright-eyed and beaming—to do her own little happy dance. He slid down the pickup windshield and met her at the edge of the hood, where he sat, legs dangling.

She put her hands on his thighs and stepped in close. "How're you doing?"

"I'm going easy." He handed her the camera. "I'd take a treat from you."

"What kind would you like?" She smiled up at him. She'd done well and she felt good. "I'm a pretty fair cook."

"I'm easy that way, too. I'm a lousy cook, so anything good is a treat. But I'm guessin' we won't be dining alone."

"We will if I say we will. I decide who grazes where."

"I should be checking in at home." He slid to the ground and claimed the crutches he'd left leaning against the pickup door. "My neighbor watches the place when I'm gone, but I don't like to take advantage."

"Food first." She watched him get himself lined up with the sticks, as though she'd taught him the way he'd taught her. "You said you'd take a treat from me, and I'm going to cook one up. I hope you're hungry."

"Always hungry." But he wasn't going first. The part of him that enjoyed having her hover over him needed to get over it. She was going free and joyful one minute and supervising every move the next, and he really liked her free and joyful. He was on his feet now. He wanted her walking beside him. No leading, no herding. Two people, side by side.

Soon he sat across the kitchen counter from her and took his turn following directions. He sliced an onion, shredded cooked chicken and grated cheese while she put the raw materials to use in the pans on her cooktop. She had a white sauce in the works. She shook a spice bottle over it and cried, "Oh!" She tapped his chopping arm with the bottle. "Watch this."

And he did. Another shake landed red powder in white liquid. The red flecks scattered quickly.

"What does that look like?"

He smiled. Two imaginations, one image. "Your flea-bitten mustang. Is that hot stuff?"

"It's cayenne. A little goes a long way." Her eyes widened. "Cayenne!"

He repeated the word. "Rolls off the tongue pretty good."

"Cayenne. Hot and spicy."

"Just the way I like it." He nodded thoughtfully. "It fits him all the way around, but I'd try it out for a day or two, see how it feels."

"Good idea." She moved the sauce off the burner. "You like salad?"

"I like everything."

Except the way she worried about whether he would like everything. Anybody who knew him would tell her he was low maintenance. When he sat down to the table, he was open to almost anything. She'd been taking meals with somebody who was less so, and he didn't want her confusing him with that somebody. Or any other body, and maybe that in itself was a big want for a guy who wanted for very little. But there it was. He wanted his voice to sound as special to her as hers did to him.

Which was a pretty unsettling thought. A little scary, in fact.

"Oh my gosh."

He looked up as he took his second bite of enchilada and he questioned her *gosh* with a look.

"Too much cayenne."

He lifted one shoulder as he chewed. "Just a little hair of the pony that, uh…" Warm. Hot. *Fire.* He grabbed his glass of water and chugged. "Creeps up on you," he admitted on the tail of a gasp.

"I'm sorry. I got carried away with the whole… peppery…picture." She reached for his plate. "Let me get you something else."

"No, this is great." He waved her off with his fork en route to his greens. "Especially with this, uh…"

"Salad."

"Salad, yeah. It's got a little fruit in it. Nice touch." He took another bite of enchilada. "Mmm. Could you pass the bread?" He made a stab toward the enchilada with his fork. "Looks real plain and quiet, but it's got a kick to it. Kinda like that dun horse."

"You mean Vegas?"

"Vegas. It's like they say, surprise is the spice of life."

"Variety."

"That, too. See, I wouldn't have tried a green salad that had oranges in it."

"Unless your mouth was burning up. It isn't supposed to be quite this hot." She apologized with a sympathetic look. "I gave it that one extra shake when I noticed how pretty it looked."

"You're an artist." He braved another mouthful of enchilada. The flame had burned down to a nice hot coal. The fact that he could smile was a good sign. "You're also a good cook, Doris."

"Doris?"

"Something my dad used to say. My brother, Ethan, he's a hell of a cook. Which was funny because he is kind of a hell-raiser, big strapping guy. I'm older, but he's taller, built to take on the world." The image of his little brother turned his smile wistful. His charge, his personal safekeeping until Logan had come along. The woman in their lives had not been the withstanding kind. He stabbed at his salad. "There's no Doris. That's just Logan. He missed the twentieth century." He shrugged. "Maybe it was just because we were three guys bachin' it. You know, if you're good in the kitchen, you're Doris."

"I usually do better than this. Please let me—"

He put his hand up as a stop sign. "Don't try to get between a man and his food." Then he raised his brow. "You know what would be great for dessert?"

"Ice cream?"

"Yeah." He winked at her. "Unless there's a frozen-custard stand in town. How far is it from here?"

"Twenty-three miles to Gillette," she said offhandedly. "Where's your brother?"

"South Dakota. He works with horses, too." He started to elaborate, but, no… "He's getting paid for it now, too."

"That's my dream. Getting paid to do what I love."

"Which is not cattle ranching."

"You noticed," she said quietly, as though she was confessing. "Not the way we've been doing it here. Mmm." She'd thought of something to replace the something she didn't want to think about. "Let's download the video from today. Would you like to see what I took at the wild-horse sanctuary? I've edited it, so it's pretty good. It's not very long. Or maybe just a few pictures. I'm putting a portfolio together." She leaned in, smiling. *"Horses."*

"And horse sense." His knowing smile matched hers.

"I've only just started with your kind of horse sense," she said. "Rodeo scenes and tight-fitting jeans."

"I don't wear tight jeans."

"I took a lot of pictures of a lot of jeans, and I have to say, you wear yours well."

"Guess I'd better stay off the ice cream. Now that

I'm standing on the top of that first hill, I see how the ass-scape starts spreadin' out." He pointed his fork at her. "Not yours. You're kind of a tight-ass."

She scowled. "How can you say that?"

"Call 'em like I see 'em, and I like what I see. Especially the part where you let your guard down just for me."

"You're sure of that?" She couldn't keep the corners of her mouth still.

"I'm sure. And I want to know you more. Everything about you."

But he had no smile for her now, and he'd just killed hers. Completely unintended. He'd meant to blow her away with his easy cowboy charm, but he'd missed breezy by a mile. He laid his fork down, glanced at the clock high on the wall behind her and shook his head.

"I just tipped my hand. I've never played this hungry, and I'm not real comfortable with it."

"If there's a game going on, I need to know what the rules are," she told him quietly.

"I've already broken the rules." He looked her in the eye. "I'm a stand-up guy. I generally don't let my wants get ahead of my wits."

"Well, your wits were under the weather."

"No. I wanted to be with you in every possible way, and my wits were right there with my wants." He pushed his plate aside. "It won't happen again. Not like that. You said it wasn't an issue with you. What does that mean exactly?"

"There's nothing to worry about, Trace. Really."

She reached across the table, laid her hand within his reach. "I wanted to be with you, too. You're right. I'm basically a tight-ass, but being with you…" Her fingers stirred, betraying her uneasiness, telling him she was not easy, not free for the taking. She cleared her throat. "That was my first time in a very long time. And before you, there was never anyone but my husband, who had been sick for a long time."

"Oh, jeez." He stared at her hand, but he wasn't sure he should touch it with his big… "You were like a virgin."

She laughed. "Okay, now you've gone over the edge. I like the cowboy chivalry, but that's pushing it." She drew her hand back and shifted into high gear. "We're just being honest with each other. You want to know all about me, that's another bit of information. Facts are facts. You tell me you've been with X number of women, it's…probably more like an estimate, which isn't exactly a fact, but it's more like—"

"I'm not with anyone now, and that's a fact. Never been married, and that's a fact. Don't have sex without a condom, and that's a fact. Or *was*. I screwed up on that score, but apologizing seems kinda lame."

"You're a good man," she said softly, "and that's a fact."

"You hardly know me."

"Sometimes facts get in the way of the truth. Let X remain a variable. I know what I know. And you're the first man I've ever said this to." She pushed her chair back and pinned him to his with a paralyzing green-eyed stare. "I really want to show you my pictures."

He wanted to laugh, but she was half-serious, and it was the serious half that was demanding its due. "I'll look at anything you want me to see."

Neither of them had finished eating, but he'd done better than she had. He figured it might be a while before he could taste anything again. He followed her lead, taking his plate with him. "I'll help you clean up. What do you use? Machine or man power?"

"I'll take care of it later." She took his plate and clattered them both into the sink. "Would you like a drink? A shot of caffeine or alcohol to get you through my picture show?"

"You wanna rephrase that so I can say yes?"

She laughed. "All of the above it is."

She called the room her office, but Trace didn't see much of her in it except a few pictures. Everything else was dark green and dull brown. The desk had taken refuge in an alcove bounded by shelves on two sides and a big window in the middle. He pictured Skyler sitting down to the computer, turning her back on a stuffed ram's head and a pair of rainbow trout, mounted separately but hung face-to-face. There was a heavy-duty leather love seat and another chair, more bookshelves, thick carpeting the color of Wyoming mud. This had once been a man's room, and Skyler had kept it that way.

She put a pillow on a footstool, and before she could do the rest for him—she was going there, and he enjoyed the view when she bent down and her top opened up for him—he showed her he could lift his leg just fine. His boot hovered above the pillow.

"I can take it or leave it, honey. The pillow, I mean. The boot's a keeper for now."

"Wouldn't you feel better without…"

"I'd feel better without a lot of things, including the swelling that's gonna happen when I take off that boot."

She went to the bookcase and opened a drop-down shelf. Trace was a whiskey drinker, but since his choice wasn't offered, he sipped the brandy she'd poured and handed to him as though it was some big deal. Okay, so the stuff was pretty smooth. But it didn't suit him.

Skyler's portfolios were a different story. There were horses, sure, and she showed him some shots she'd been hired to take for breeders and show people—beautifully groomed and all squared up with their ears standing at attention. The horses, not the horse people, who were a different breed of animal altogether. She seemed particularly proud of the kid pictures. If there was a kid on the place, she took the kid with a horse as a bonus.

"Look at this one." She slid the book from her knees to his and pointed to a little girl in big glasses, hair in pigtails, decked out in jeans and pink cowboy boots. The mare was twenty years old if she was a day and the string of trophy ribbons hanging from her halter was mostly pink and green. Not a blue one in the bunch. "Her name is Edie. She doesn't see well, but, boy, can she ride. She told me in confidence that the picture wasn't for her. It was a surprise for her grandmother, who loved pictures and had really good eyesight for an elderly person." She grinned. "That's what she said. *Elderly person.* She's six."

"Cute kid." He nodded. "Great picture."

She studied him briefly, as though she was looking for some kind of implication in one comment or the other. Maybe *great* didn't quite cut it.

She closed the book and put it aside. "This isn't what I want to do with my photography, but so far it pays more than the journalism."

"You can do both, can't you?"

"I am. I'm getting more calls from breeders and stud owners for portraits. But every story I sell is one more publishing credit for my résumé. I haven't made a professional-grade video yet, but I will."

"Go on YouTube. I'm on YouTube." He leaned back and sipped his brandy. "So they tell me."

"You haven't looked?"

"I'm not hooked up. I tried it through the phone, but it seemed like more trouble than it was worth." He touched her shoulder just for the feel of her sleeve. She'd showered, put on a silky orange shirt, and she smelled like a flower. "I guess I'm on the thing a few times, but the one people watch the most wasn't my finest hour."

"A bad spill?"

"Spill." He smiled. "That's when you get a little beer on your shirt."

"You don't get kicked around that often, do you? I mean, you're doing very well." She shrugged, cute little apology in her eyes. "I checked online."

"Damn. Yeah, I've won some serious money this

year. I'da bragged myself up, but you didn't seem that interested in the standings."

"It's like having your calf-sale check posted. They should just publish the scores."

"Nope. Rodeo isn't like other professional sports. You've gotta earn your pay ride by ride." He drained his glass. "I don't mind. I competed in roping and rough stock for a few years. Decided I wasn't gonna win the all-around, so I decided to go full-bore on my best event. I'm lookin' to take the bareback buckle this year."

"And you're looking good," she said cheerfully as she stood up and took the glass from his hand. "But I won't be looking you up on YouTube. I don't like spills. They can be messy."

"Yeah, but that's part of the draw."

"It can be hard on the horse, too."

"Nobody loves horses more than cowboys." Hearing the words made him laugh. "Correction. *Everybody* loves horses more than cowboys. A champion cowboy rides the most horses. A champion horse bucks off the most cowboys. Put the two together, it's win-win. And I'll tell you what." He raised an instructive finger. "Nobody wants to see that horse get hurt. The cowboy? Nothing like a train wreck to get the crowd's attention." He grinned. "So let's be ballin' the jack, boys."

She glanced at his propped-up foot. "Are you going to sleep in those?"

He nodded. "Gonna die in 'em, too." She turned

away laughing. "Where are you going? Hell, I'll take 'em off if—"

"You stay elevated. I'm going to get you another treat."

He laid his head back and closed his eyes. Had to admit, the sofa was more comfortable than anything he had at his place. Maybe he'd buy a new one with some of those winnings she'd found attached to his name. Leather on the furniture was classy. Stuffed animals? Logan had taught him to hunt only for food and to use up every part of anything he killed. He didn't know whether people hunted bighorn sheep for meat. Maybe some lucky cat had chowed down on that pair of kissing trout. Bottom line, he didn't much like hanging out in the late Mr. Quinn's museum.

"Trace?"

He nearly jumped out of his skin. Skyler was standing over him with two frothy drinks. "I'm sorry. Were you asleep?"

"You walkin' on cat feet?" He glanced down as he reached to meet the glass in her hand halfway. Beautiful bare toes.

"I'm tired of boots." She set her glass on a side table. "Isn't it time you took yours off?"

"I'm afraid to." He was eyeing the drink. It looked like Dairy Queen, but it smelled like booze. Contamination! He glanced up. The anticipation dancing in her eyes mowed down all resistance.

"Well?" she asked hard on the heels of his first taste.

"This isn't something I'd order in public, so it's a treat for sure." He sipped again. "Wow."

"Is that enough kick?"

He chuckled. "I don't think I have to worry about it fillin' out my back pockets. It's going straight to my head."

"Have you been taking those pills?"

"I took one after we ate. Figured the fire would burn up the buzz."

"And the swelling?"

"Seriously, I'll know when I take the boots off. I hope that's over. I wanna be ready for Cheyenne. Can't miss that one." He patted the space beside him on the sofa. "Neither can you. You've gotta keep taking pictures. Get hooked up with the right kind of media, you'll get your credentials. You gotta prove yourself. That's the way we roll in the PRCA. We don't have tryouts or drafts. You get an amateur permit and you fill it with money. Rodeo's a real sport. No unions, no benefits. Thank God for the Justin Sportsmedicine Teams."

He was talking a mile a minute without missing a move—the way she drew her legs up and tucked them to one side under her bottom without spilling a drop from her full glass. The way she sipped and made herself a little mustache then pressed her lips together and got most of it. But not all. Man, that little sliver of foam would taste good.

He laid his hand on her knee. She was wearing smooth-fitting pants that ended just below where his hand was. Two inches to Skyler skin. He drank deep.

"Yep. Gotta make it to Cheyenne."

"What's so special about Cheyenne?"

"It's a great show. Nice purse. Hometown crowd." He didn't want to sound overly eager, but he felt a crazy itch, worse than skin trapped in a cast. "I want you to be there, Sky. I'm asking you for a date."

She smiled from behind her glass. The foam above her lip taunted him. "Do they have a Ferris wheel?"

"You don't have to ride it. You don't have to ride anything you don't want to."

"I know that. But I want to ride again. I feel safe with you."

"I want you to be safe with me. But not untouched." He leaned over to kiss that sassy bit of foam away, and he bumped into her glass. "Damn." He glanced down. The spill painted a translucent teardrop on her sweet-looking pale orange shirt, smack-dab over her left breast. His eyes lingered—a glance and then some. "Can't talk smooth and make a move at the same time."

"It's washable."

"Let's see." He set his glass aside and leaned over the spill. "Nice top. Kind of a melon color, huh? Or just peachy." He circled the spot with the tip of his nose, tip of his tongue, slippery side of his lip. He took a bit of the cloth between his teeth, sucked on it while he slid his hand from her waist to the underside of her breast. "I'm gonna peel it. Taste the fruit."

She turned to him, straddled him, dropped her head back, lifted her arms as though she'd been cued by some exotic music. He skinned her top over her head, turning it inside out and then tossing it over-head. It opened like a parachute promising a lift, but he had a different conveyance in mind. Her bra gave way easily and flew the way of the parachute. He took full visual measure of her lovely pink-and-white breasts while he shifted beneath her, feeling the plea-sure of her weight and her heat and her energy bear-ing down on his flight deck. He cupped her breasts in his hands and teased her nipples with his thumbs while they kissed hungrily. When he had her nipples standing up hard and tight the way she was doing his penis, he ducked to suckle her, savor her, tease and torture her.

She returned the favor, but all she had to do was ride.

"Ah! You're killin' me, Sky."

She scooted down and unsnapped his jeans. "Lie back and let me finish you off." His zipper gave way to her invading hand. "Inside me."

"No, let me…get…" His hand started for his pocket, but his head knew better. He was unarmored.

And she was hot. Judgment was climbing into the backseat looking for air.

"There's nothing to worry about, Trace," she whis-pered as he undid her the way she'd undone him. No pausing, no peeking. She was going after his shirt buttons like the thing was on fire.

"You sure?"

"I'm sure."

"I'm a straight shooter, honey, but I don't shoot blanks." And he didn't mind firing off target. *Hardly* minded. Pulling out wasn't his first choice, but he'd do it. He could ask, or he could just do it.

She brushed his bare chest with her breasts and whispered, "How do you know?"

"I'm a cowboy." *Having a cowboy-up moment.* "We're all alike, remember?"

"You're the only cowboy I know. The only one I want to know." She nibbled his nipple while she cosseted his penis between her strong thighs. "Let me know you."

Or he could take her at her word.

She struggled for breath when he found his way inside her. He struggled for control. But he was bent on taking her breath away, and she was determined to claim control. And so the fight was on. He sank into her deeply, and she drew on him thoroughly, and the contest gratified both sides. It was win-win.

They ended up naked and sweaty and basking in wonder. He looked up at the ram's head and smiled. He was something of a leather expert, and he knew for a fact he was making his permanent mark in sweat on the couch. The museum had a new display.

"Does this mean you'll sleep with me?" he asked lazily.

"I already have."

"Not by choice. There was only one bed."

"I knew that going in." She shifted in his arms. "We have several beds here."

"Okay." He combed her hair with his fingers. "Point me to the one you want me in. Given the choice, I'll take a bed over the floor."

"You can take Mike's old room, which is now the guest room, or you can come to bed with me. I sleep in the old guest room. It's free of ghosts."

"Given the choice, I'll take a room that's not haunted."

"You might get more rest if you stay away from me for a while."

He laughed. "What about you?"

"I want to sleep with you. But given the choice, I might not sleep." And neither of them had chosen to make a move yet.

"Is every choice gonna be complicated with you? Because if it is, we can narrow it down to two. Yes or no."

"Yes." She kissed his chin. "I'll go to bed with you."

"Let's get at it." He sat up, taking her with him. "Lead me. Turn your shoulder to me and I'll follow." She tried to turn the tables by slipping her arm around him, but he warned, "Don't try to complicate it."

"I was going to say, *lean on me.*"

"You've heard the term *cowboy up?* That's what I'm doing. I've gotta start putting weight on this thing."

But he was soon limping along, and he thought, *What the hell? Nothing to worry about. Suck up a little sympathy and then suck it up.* "How much farther?"

"Last door on the right."

He put his arm around her. "I'm ready to lean."

"Sometimes a little *cowboy up* goes a long way."

She patted his bare stomach, and it occurred to him that it was a long way to that last door and that the only stitch of covering between them was elastic bandaging and that he was almost sober and that it was all good. Incredibly, ridiculously, unbelievably good.

"How about a shower?" she suggested.

"Sure, I'm game."

"So let's take care of that."

And together they did. They soaped and stroked, kissed and caressed, and if he'd been steady on his feet he would have made love to her under falling water. They toweled each other off and climbed into bed together where he pulled her back against his front and stroked her until she came crying out and quivering and crashing in his hand. She would sleep now, he thought, and he would hold her and breathe her fragrance and listen to her heartbeat.

He would sleep now, she thought.

And she would try to shut her mind down. She'd said he was a good man, which was the kind of observation you could make pretty easily after a day or two, toss it out as a nice thing to say when saying something nice was in order. And they'd had good sex—*really* good sex—between two good people, which probably didn't happen as often as it should. One was bound to be better than the other. Less selfish. More honest. But with Trace, all things were pretty much equal. Two good people. Whatever came of good sex between two good people would have to be a good thing.

But she knew damn well she'd slipped a couple of notches on the goodness meter. He *could* sleep now. She'd told him there was nothing to worry about. And there wasn't. She wasn't worried. He wasn't worried. Hey, she'd told the truth.

But she hadn't been honest. She couldn't sleep.

And he knew it.

"Skyler?"

"Hmm?"

"What's going on?"

"I'm trying to let you sleep."

"I can feel how hard you're trying." He braced his head in his hand and tried to see what was in her eyes, because they were usually so good at telling tales on her. But not tonight. "What's going on? You don't want to sleep with me?"

"I'm very comfortable with you." She touched his chin with one finger, and then she sighed. "Just not so comfortable with myself."

"I'm listening."

"Well," she said after seemingly endless, ominous silence, "to be honest, I'm not on any kind of birth control."

"Well, uh…neither am I."

"I haven't used any since I got married." Her voice went soft. "I had a miscarriage early on."

The word sounded sad. He knew what it was, but it was way beyond the realm of his experience, and he had no idea what it really meant.

"I'm still listening," he said finally.

"That's it. Those are the simple facts."

"Okay. Now move on to the complicated part." He gave her a good thirty seconds. "That's where I come in."

"I don't want to use birth control. I mean...I wasn't planning for this to happen between us, but it is happening, and it's good, and it feels right." But he felt her stiffen, and that didn't feel right. "I want a baby. I only have half the necessary ingredients."

"Damn." He felt numb. Confused. Broadsided. "What the hell, Skyler? You know, you can buy the other half. I hear you can have it professionally installed."

"I don't like that idea."

He lay back and stared at the ceiling, where moonlight challenged shadows. "You like this one better?"

She came crawling up the side of his chest. "I like *you,* Trace. It feels right to let nature take its course. But you wouldn't have to worry about..."

Another loaded silence.

"About what?"

"Anything. It probably sounds crazy to you. It sounds a little crazy to me, too, and I wasn't trying to trick you. I've never used birth control."

"Never *before,* maybe, but now is *after.* You're lookin' at a new partner here. I figured maybe you were allergic to latex. Or you couldn't get pregnant, and it was hard for you to come out and say it. But I thought that was what you were telling me."

"I don't know for sure. I've had tests. I should be...able."

"Able?" He gave a humorless chuckle. "So you're

looking for ready and willing. A proven breeder would be a bonus."

"That sounds bad. Not crazy. *Bad.* But if we didn't know each other, and you were just donating, it would be fine."

"With who?" He shook her off as he jacked himself up on his elbows. "Maybe I don't believe in donating like you don't believe in birth control. When the time comes, yeah, I want kids. Right now I want sex."

"I do, too." Her voice sounded so small, so tragic he almost wanted to take her in his arms.

"This is the damnedest conversation." He carefully swung his legs off the side of the bed, turning his back on her.

"Sometimes I think too much. This wasn't one of those times." She sat up in the middle of the bed and talked to his back. "It's been a long time since I thought about it at all, really. But here we are, and this is a chance. A small chance. If it happened, how would that be a bad thing?"

He turned to her, incredulous. "You didn't ask me."

"But it happens all the time without asking."

"Not to me." He peered at her through the shadows. She was all tousled hair and big eyes. "Look, I don't know anything about my biological father. Isn't that what you call a human breeder? A biological father? Or do you call him a stud? I don't know what else my *biological father* produced. You can't have a proven breeder unless you keep records."

"Oh, Trace, that's not—"

"I don't have a pedigree. I hear you can get some-

thing like that when you go to the sperm bank, but
me, hell, what you see is what you get." He leaned
closer, nose to nose. "Which is why any kid of mine
will get to *see* me. Every day, if that's what he wants.
Good times, hard times, I'm there. That's what I'm
holdin' out for." He lowered his voice. "It's called
fatherhood. I know how it works. I learned from the
best."

"Is there a chance your father—I mean your biological father—doesn't know about you?"

"Damn good chance. But he didn't stick around
to find out, and that's a fact." He grabbed a corner of
the bedsheet and pulled it across his lap.

"I wouldn't want you to go away," she said quietly.

"Yeah, but I do go away. A lot."

"I wouldn't ask you for anything, either."

"How about asking me for my kid?"

"Okay."

"What do you mean, *okay?*"

"I mean…okay, can we start over?"

"How do you propose we do that? You haven't
been honest with me."

"I am now. I'm being honest with both of us now.
Two good people. In the back of my mind, I—"

"You can't push stuff like that into the back of
your mind. Like I said, I know how it's supposed to
be done. I go by the name my father gave me. Logan
had a big ceremony, put on a feed, adopted us the
traditional Indian way. Not too long after my mother
skipped out on us. He'd already gone through the
court, but after she was gone he had this big fam-

ily thing, so we'd know we were home now. He even gave us Indian names. Two motherless white boys. Well, I guess Ethan's dad was part Indian. Who the hell knows where I came from?"

"Does it matter?"

"Everybody wants to know where they came from, Skyler. You want to know who, and…and why. That's the big one. *Why?*"

He drew a deep breath. He should've been out the door by now, but he realized he was crazy about this woman. He was thinking crazy, feeling crazy. And she was talking crazy to a guy who loved to blow the lid off crazy, but only for eight seconds a pop.

"You should meet him," he said quietly. "Logan. You need to meet my father."

"I know I'd like him."

"Yeah, well, I'm not sure…"

"Not sure he'd like me?"

"What's not to like? You're a woman who knows what she wants, and what she wants is not a bad thing. But I'm not…" He glanced toward the door. He wasn't sure where he should be right now. He knew his wits hadn't been serving him too well in the face of his wants. "What are my other choices again? The ghost's bed or the floor?"

"You stay here," she said as she scrambled toward the edge of the bed. "I know my way around."

"Not around me." She was a slender silhouette standing beside the bed, a shadowy beauty reflected in the mirror on the back of the door, and his hands ached to touch her.

But he shook his head. "You don't know your way around me."

Chapter 7

Trace looked up from the magazine he was perusing on the kitchen table. "You always sleep this late?"

"No."

Skyler adjusted her wraparound terry-cloth robe. She hadn't expected to be seen in it since nothing had seemed to be stirring. The only sound she'd heard was the regular predawn *coo-OO-oo-woo-woo-woooo* from her resident mourning dove calling his mate. She'd lain in bed listening, imagining Mrs. Dove's tiny heart ticking wildly as she fluffed up the nest. Even if he'd been out all night, who could resist that sweet, plaintive love call? *You always sleep this late?* didn't quite compare, but then Skyler hadn't fluffed or fixed anything, and her tatty robe was no feather dress. She wasn't expecting a love call. She didn't deserve one.

"I mean, it isn't that late, but, yes, it took me a little more time than usual this morning." More explanation than she'd intended, but a simple *no* seemed lonely.

Trace was hat-to-boots dressed, and he'd made his own coffee. Another missed opportunity for a feather. *Damn, he was good-looking.*

"You're leaving?" Of course. Why wouldn't he?

"We're leaving." He closed the magazine. "You're driving."

"How will I get back?"

"You'll figure something out."

"Mike can drive you, and I'll follow."

"Uh-uh. It's over two hours to my place. That's at least an hour and a half longer than I want to spend with your stepson." He sipped his coffee and then gestured with it. "No offense, but he's not that interesting."

"You'd rather spend two hours with me?"

"You're interesting. We haven't had a dull moment yet."

"That's true." He didn't question her willingness to go with him—obviously knew he didn't have to. She wasn't ready to go back to dull moments slowly adding up to dull hours dripping onto the squares of the calendar to form dull days.

"I'll call Mike and tell him to—"

"Forget Mike. Either he'll get his act together here,

or he won't, but you can't do it for him." He stood. "I made coffee."

"I see that. I'll get dressed and make breakfast."

"Make it quick. Goin' down the road, I like to get an early start."

"But I don't want you to have to worry about—"

"I know you don't, Skyler. And now that you've had your come-to-Jesus moment, nobody has to worry. You want a fresh start? You got it. I'll drop you off here on the way back from Cheyenne." He gave her a loaded look. "We have a date for Cheyenne."

She scowled. "That's almost two weeks away."

"I don't know what you think you're gonna do with that horse, but if we take him to my place, I can have you in the saddle by the time we hit the road for Cheyenne." He stepped closer. "I have a spare bedroom. I don't get many guests."

She could hardly breathe. She wanted to go with him, and it scared her. She wasn't afraid of him—he was a little gruff this morning, but he had his reasons, and they were more than halfway reasonable—but the leaving scared her. She might not want to come back, and it would be so easy to, as Trace said, let her wants get ahead of her wits. And then who would she be?

"You know how this is going to play out," she said quietly.

"No, I don't. But I'm into you now, honey, and I'm interested in finding out." He took her shoulders in his hands and looked into her eyes long enough and hard enough to make her tremble inside. "Maybe I'll give you what you want."

"Maybe you already have."

"I doubt it. These things take time." His slight smile did nothing to soften the look in his eyes. "You take the mare to the stud, where he's in his element and he's at his best. And you're right about natural cover. Definitely the way to go, as long as the mare isn't a kicker."

"Trace…"

"And if she is a kicker, a good stud knows how to handle her."

She lifted her hand to push his hat back and touch his four-day-old head wound. "You don't need any more of these."

Four days since they'd met. *Four days.* How could she know anything about him by now?

He smiled, and this time a spark flashed in his eyes. "I've got a hard head."

She could believe that, among other things. When he looked at her with that gleam in his eyes, there were things she knew, and they were sure things, true for the duration of that gleam. True for now, for today. All she wanted was today. They'd agreed to three days, and it was the beginning of day five. She wouldn't think about five rolling into six and seven. Maybe by day nine he would have a gleam in his eye for someone else. The French had it right: c'est la vie.

"You should wear protection," she told him.

"Right." He gave a dry chuckle. "None of that stuff is foolproof."

"There's always a risk, isn't there." Her fingertips disappeared in his hair as she laid her palm against his cheek. "Besides, it takes more than a hat to make a cowboy."

"You believe that or did you get it off a T-shirt?"

She shook her head, laughing. "I don't know what made me think you were all alike."

"Old movies, maybe. Are you gonna get your stuff, or should we just take off before the buzz wears off?"

"Who's buzzed?"

"Come on, woman, we both are. This isn't your first rodeo and it sure as hell ain't mine. Let's see if we can make the whistle."

She took his face in her hands and pulled his head down for a hard and fast kiss. "What's eight seconds in the grand scheme of things?" she proposed.

"Don't knock it. You've seen what I can do in eight seconds."

She grinned. "What about breakfast?"

"We'll stop on the way. Did I tell you I saw a ghost after you left the room last night? She was wearing a crown. Pretty scary. I thought ghosts were white, but this one was yellow. Turned out she was lonely. She asked me for a kiss, so I..." He tucked her hair behind her ear, leaned down and nibbled her neck. "Tasted like sweet creamery butter."

Skyler had always wondered what it would feel like to act on impulse. Her father had been impulsive, but her mother had planned every day of every life being lived under her roof. Tony had been impulsive, but for a long time she'd called it spontaneity because he was in charge. And then he wasn't. And then she realized he hadn't been, not for a long time. She was saddled with his unkept promises, unpaid debts and his undisclosed loose ends.

There was a bank account she knew nothing about, a woman from Tony's complicated past, a secret gambling history, who knew what else? But now that he was gone, she didn't want to think about it. She didn't want to blame him for it. She'd finished grieving and she might be able to tie up most of the loose ends, but the promises were not hers to keep. And the debts? Michael would have to deal with those if he wanted to keep the business. She loved Michael. She'd raised him—or at least she'd done the part of the job Tony had left for her to do. And while she couldn't undo the spoiled part—couldn't stop him from overestimating the gifts his daddy gave him—she wanted to put what there was in some kind of order and then move on. She wanted to *be ready* to move on.

But for now, she would claim a few days to fill with her own dreams. She grabbed her cameras and a few other necessities and found Trace cleaning up the kitchen from the night before. She'd forgotten about the dishes she'd left in the sink, but he'd rolled up his sleeves and pitched in. She told herself she had nothing to be embarrassed about, but it didn't take.

And he knew it. He turned, drying his hands on a dish towel, his cowboy hat pushed back from his face, his smile way too cocky for a dishwasher.

"You need to stay off that ankle," she said. "At least until—"

"You're welcome. It was no trouble."

"I forgot about the dishes. Thank you." She gave a tight-lipped smile. "Do you know how adorable you look?"

"Yep."

"May I take a picture?"

"Nope."

"Ooh, with an apron. I actually have one with…"

She started toward a drawer, but he caught her in one damp arm. "That *would* be trouble. You got your stuff together?" She nodded. "Then I'm taking you home with me."

"But I'm driving."

"*This* time."

"And I'm bringing groceries."

"I've got…" He frowned. "I don't know what I've got."

"I know what I've got, and we're taking some along." She nodded toward the pantry. "Fill up a sack with anything that looks good, and I'll get the cooler and unload the fridge."

Trace hesitated. "How about we stop at a store?"

"I *am* a store. Just ask Mike."

He winked at her. "Leave him the enchiladas."

They loaded the pickup and then drove to the corral, where they loaded the horse trailer. Jack went in first. The mustang gave them some trouble, but Trace had a few tricks tucked into his rolled sleeves, and the newly christened Cayenne mellowed out, at least for the moment.

Skyler plugged her cell phone into the dash and punched in a number.

"Hey. I'm taking Trace home."

"In his pickup?" Mike asked sleepily. "You want me to follow you?"

"I want you to take care of things here. Trace has a better setup for getting this horse started, and we really think he's a good prospect. So I might be gone for a few days."

"A few days?"

"That's right. Maybe even longer. I've gotten some good video, and I believe I'm on to something I can develop as a project." No response. "Help yourself in the kitchen." Still no response. "Leftover enchiladas."

With his hat pulled over his eyes, Trace's face was a nose and a smile.

"What kind?"

"Chicken."

"I like beef better."

"Next time. Speaking of beef, we need that head count. Can you get it done today?"

He groaned. "You'll be gone. What difference does it make, today or tomorrow?"

"None. It's up to you, Mike. If you're going to stay in this business, it's time for you to start dealing with…" She glanced at Trace again. He was tilting his seat back, settling in, otherwise occupied. *He'll either get his act together, or he won't.* "You're right. Today, tomorrow, next week, as long as you keep track of the ear tags and figure out what's missing."

"It's not just *my* business. We'll get that all straightened out, Skyler. It should all be fifty-fifty."

"I'm not worried about that right now. Call my cell if you need anything."

She ended the call and started the pickup.

"I have total cell-signal protection at my place," said the voice under the hat. "But Mike's got my phone number." He thumbed his hat back and gave her a knowing look. "If he needs anything."

"Gotcha." She slowed at the gate, and the pickup rumbled over the cattle guard. "Any day now it's going to sink in that things have changed, and when it does, it's going to hit him hard."

"Maybe it's time for you to stand back and let that particular signal get through."

"He should have his turn at the ZQ wheel." She glanced over her shoulder at the sign as they pulled onto the highway. ZQ Ranch. A. R. Quinn. "Maybe he can make it pay. His grandparents built the place, and his father did well with it for a long time. They say ranching is in the blood."

"They say that about everything. The big question is, is that what he wants?"

"It's what he inherited." She shrugged. "He really thinks he's kept things going and somehow it hasn't been all that tough. I've tried to get him to pay attention to the bottom line, but he just can't find his way down there. He likes clouds." Out of habit she kept an eye on the fence line and what could be seen of the pasture from the road. "And the ZQ is earthbound."

"How about you? You like clouds?"

"Who doesn't? They make pictures in the sky. I love making pictures." At the moment the eastern sky was clear, and the air was cool. "When you're a kid you try to get the window seat on a flight so you can look down at them, and you imagine getting out and playing on them, like they do in cartoons." She turned a quick smile on her copilot. "I haven't always been afraid of heights."

"I don't fly," he said. "Too risky."

"So you're earthbound." She frowned. "But you don't ride with a helmet."

"Hell, no. That's for bull riders. I ride broncs. I'm a *real* cowboy. You pay your money, you choose your limb." He chuckled. "On the tree of life."

"I guess so." But she couldn't let it go completely. "You really should wear a protective vest."

"You really should take another look at your protection priorities." He gestured, a two-handed holdup. "Okay, full disclosure. I have a vest, but I don't always wear it. Gets in the way sometimes."

"Full disclosure?" She couldn't help smiling.

"You like that one?"

"Not really, but I appreciate the effort."

"Close but no cigar?" He grinned.

"You did *not* say that."

"Hell, I don't even know what it means. Something bad?" He shifted in her direction, his eyes full of mischief. "Close to what?"

"I think it has something to do with—"

"Damn if she doesn't have an answer. Trains?"

"Games."

"That makes sense. Games of chance, right?"

"Carnival games."

The kind she was good at. Give it the right spin and take home a prize. This verbal roller coaster was something he was proving to be good at, and she risked her dignity by going along for the ride. But he was worth it.

"Where do they have you playing for cigars?"

"They used to, back in the day. Swing the hammer, ring the bell, win a cigar. But you never quite reach the bell, so the carny shouts—"

"Close, but no cigar," he barked theatrically. "How do you know these things?"

"I've been to a lot of fairs."

"Yeah, but princesses don't swing hammers."

"Princesses do what they're told. You might as well study up and do *whatever* better than the next girl."

"Close, but no cigar," he said quietly.

Always thinking. Nothing cliché about this cowboy. She could hear the gears whirring inside his head. Cigars were a joke. They were also a gift, a celebration, a recognition and a tradition. They were all over the map, and so was Skyler. And she knew it. He'd said he was into her—whatever that meant— so he might as well know it, too. She was a perfectly serviceable instrument slightly out of tune.

"I like my pink rabbit's foot," he said. And then he drifted off.

She attended to the road signs and the mile markers. Newcastle wasn't far from the South Dakota state line, but she wasn't sure how far Trace's place was from Newcastle. She waited as long as she could, but eventually she had to wake him up to find out.

"We're gonna turn left up here," he said, leaning forward in his seat as though he were pouring on the gas. "Say goodbye to the beaten path."

Beaten was right. They'd gone from interstate to battered two-lane county asphalt. A stretch of gravel parted the grassland down the middle and pointed the way toward pine-covered foothills. Another turn led to a hill, a sweeping valley and two log structures that looked as though they'd been planted rather than built amid the pines.

The house was small but brawny-looking with its dark, rough-hewn cedar bones and its white chinking. The big barn with its gambrel roof was surrounded by weathered corrals. Nothing was painted, but it didn't have to be. The materials had been borrowed from the surroundings and had stood the test of considerable time, but they made no sore thumbprint. One day the earth would welcome them back.

Skyler pulled up to the corral gate as wordlessly instructed. She watched Trace in the towing mirror and followed his hand signals precisely. She recognized an immediate *whoa* when she saw one, and an O with three finger feathers read like a gold star. The trailer was set, and the two horses were soon racing the length of a narrow paddock while Trace pumped water into a metal tank.

"You're a helluva driver, J.J."

"J.J.? What happened to *Sky?*"

"Have I called you Sky?" He looked up, adjusting his hat against the sun. "Skyler's a pretty name. I've never met one before."

"Who's J.J.?"

"Burt Reynolds in *Smokey and the Bandit,* one of Logan's favorite movies. A good cook is Doris, and a good driver is J.J."

"What about a bronc rider?"

"That was a J.W. until I saw *J. W. Coop.* That's another one Logan had in his video collection, but he'd forgotten about the cowboy's crazy mother. Said all he remembered was the bronc riding. But he let that particular handle go by the wayside, and now an up-and-coming bronc rider is another Trace Wolf Track—" he slipped his arm around her shoulders "—who likes to call for the gate and reach for the Sky."

She smiled and pressed her fist against his shoulder. "Now I know how you work those arms in the off-hours."

"Soon as we get electricity out here I'll probably lose my edge." He saw her surprise and laughed. "Did you think you were getting a free stay at some gentrified dude ranch?"

"I thought..." She pointed to a power pole. "Isn't that electricity?"

"Hell, that's a yard ornament." He nodded toward the far side of the outbuildings. "That's the round pen, there. I built that myself." It was made of cedar boards. Other than repairs, it was the only recent construction on the place. "That's the beginning of my training facility. I'm a year or so out from an indoor arena."

"How far from indoor plumbing?"

He looked into her eyes, shook his head and laughed again.

She had no idea what was so funny. "I'm not complaining, mind you. Just asking. How long have you been here?"

"I found this place two years ago. Been vacant for quite a while, so I got it pretty cheap. It's hard to find a piece of land in this state that isn't being tapped for oil or fracked for gas. I like my well water straight up." He tucked his thumbs into the front pockets of his jeans. "The house has its rough edges. It's pretty old, but it's solid. Worth saving."

"And it all fits together. What do you use for heat?"

He jacked up one eyebrow. "Love."

"Oh, good," she quipped. "Too bad it's summer."

"I'm countin' on global warming." He pointed past the round pen toward a grassy slope. "Buck-and-pole fence. You like that?"

"Love that," she said of the rustic wood fence that ran up and over the hill.

"See, that's how it works. All you need is love."

"Nobody loves a big tease."

"Who told you that? Your mama?"

"Probably." *Remember, Skyler, the girl who teases never pleases.* "I can't always tell when you're putting me on."

"That's what makes it fun. You've had a little fun with me, too." He gave her a firm squeeze. "Come on, admit it."

"I'm only a little bit of a tease."

"Which leaves the door open, doesn't it?" He winked at her.

"This much." She measured an inch between thumb and forefinger. "Seriously."

"That's enough to keep me from ever knowing for sure. Which makes things interesting." His arm slid away from her, and the playfulness faded from his eyes as he turned his attention to the weathered pine poles that lined up end to end and meandered through green needlegrass and blue grama dappled with clumps of silvery sage. "A couple of spans need replacing on the east side. I ran out of poles and strung up some wire, but that's temporary. I'm always working on something."

"It never ends," she said, feeling strangely bereft. "But think of the pictures we'll get here."

"You think about the pictures. I'm thinking about training a horse."

She helped him unload groceries in the sunny, farmhouse-style kitchen, which was as tidy as she should have imagined after he'd shown his true colors by cleaning up her dishes. It was also plumbed and wired. The appliances and the tile floor were new, the pine cabinets rustic and the countertop was faded Formica. There was a pine table with chairs at both ends and benches along the sides—furniture that might have come with the house.

He noticed her taking stock, and he smiled. "We never did stop for breakfast, did we?"

"I didn't want to wake you up." She nodded toward the cooler sitting in the middle of the floor. "I brought eggs and milk. Do you like French toast?"

"I like everything."

She smiled. "You'll have to show me how to turn on the love light for the stove."

"You want me to bring your bag in first?"

"I want you to take your boots off and put your feet up."

"I want you to forget about my feet. They're not my best feature." He set the cooler on the counter next to the refrigerator. "And you don't need to be cookin' all the time, Doris. Just relax and be Skyler."

"I like to cook." She laughed as he slid her a squint-eyed glance, unconvinced. "Don't worry. The only Cayenne I brought is the horse."

"Make yourself comfortable. I'll get the rest of your stuff."

The fieldstone fireplace took up a whole wall in the living room, which was sparely furnished with couch and one easy chair. A braided rug covered much of the pine floor, and the heavily chinked log walls were undecorated. The view from the large window was all the decor a cowboy probably needed. Beauty abounded here. Trace's land was surrounded by well-dressed mountains.

"It needs a lot of work."

"You can't improve on that," she said of the views. She hadn't heard him coming up behind her. "And I love the house. You can't get this kind of character in new construction. I know that from experience."

"You have a nice house."

She looked up as he came to stand at her shoulder, and then back to the mountain. Trace had better mountains. This was the back side of the Black Hills. "It was supposedly built for me, but I didn't get much input. He'd always been planning to build a bigger house, and he never said as much, but I think Mike's mother was in on the planning."

"What would you change?" He laid his hand high on her back. "Besides one of the bedrooms."

"There wasn't much furniture when I came along. Within the first few years I managed to make the place at least half mine."

"Not the half with the dead heads on the walls, I'm guessing."

She feigned surprise. "You wouldn't take me for a hunter?"

"I'll take you for who you are, woman. I say *woman*. You could be a hunter, sure. But you didn't..." He looked down at her quizzically. "Are you?"

"I've hunted." *Squeeze, don't pull. Take the shot. Now, Skyler, take the shot.* "I've never hit anything."

He nodded thoughtfully. "Did you want to?"

"I was hunting. Of course I wanted to hit something." One of the somethings appeared in her mind. Her closest call. "But I didn't want to kill her. Or injure her. So I just scared her."

"What happens when you shoot at a target? The red-and-white kind."

She looked up grinning. "Bull's-eye."

"That's what I figured. I've hunted, too, and I'm

not a bad shot. Ethan could shoot the pink eye out of a white rabbit half a mile away during a blizzard."

"Eww."

"But Logan was the one who brought home the meat." He lifted one shoulder. "We gotta eat, right? But we don't have to hang the leftovers on the wall."

"You have your trophies," she reminded him indignantly.

"Yeah, I know. Question is, where are they?" He made a pretense of looking around. "So, what would you change about ZQ Ranch if you ever got around to it?"

"The feel of the place, I guess. I should clear out all the leftovers. The arsenal, the toy trains, the fishing tackle, the trophies. Mine, too. I've never wanted them on display, but my husband was big on displays."

"I didn't see anything with your name on it." She gave him a questioning glance. "Yeah, I looked."

"You don't believe I was ever Princess Kay of the Milky Way?"

"I figured you were putting me on with that one. Just a little tease. Is that a real title?"

"It certainly is. My parents had a very small dairy farm in Minnesota. My mother had much bigger dreams."

"And your father?"

"My father had a very small dairy farm in Minnesota."

"Are they still—"

"No. They went under." Under the influence, under the weather and finally under the gun. She shook her head quickly. "I had no trouble giving away clothing. My husband was a collector of hats and boots, and Mike had no use for them, so we gave them away. Boxes of brand-new hats and boots. A thrill for Goodwill, let me tell you."

"Hey, if Mike wants to keep the trains..."

"They really weren't Mike's trains. Mike never cared for them. I should've taken you downstairs and showed you the train room. It's out of the way, and I wouldn't know how to begin to take it apart." She smiled, remembering. "He hired a master carpenter to build the foundation and brought in a hobbyist from Denver to help lay the track and set up all the miniatures."

"Must've been an expensive proposition."

"I'm sure it was. That was before he got sick. Before I took over the bookkeeping." She turned back to the window. "He loved his trains."

"And you loved..."

"Horses. I've had some *beautiful* horses. I have trophies for those, too."

"Where are they?"

"In boxes. I sold all my horses." She looked up at him. "Is there a secondary market for trophies with other people's names on them?"

"Probably," he said with a smile. "If the name is Elvis or Princess Diana."

"Wrong princess."

"Not my type." He squeezed her shoulder. "I have a couple of nice saddle horses. Care to go for a ride?"

"Not as long as you're still limping."

"I won't be limping. I won't be walking. That's what the horse is for." He stepped away. "You don't have to take care of me, woman. I'm a grown-up."

"Why do you call me *woman?*"

"Let me think. Why do I…" He folded his arms. "Let me look at you while I think. Oh, man. Man, oh, man." He thought for a moment and shook his head. "Nope, that doesn't work for me. *Woman, oh, woman.*" He grinned. "You make my heart sing."

He directed her to his tack room in the barn, offered her Jack with a nod and told her to saddle up. She met him at the gate. He was riding a beautiful dark bay Arab mare bareback.

"I could have done that, too," she informed him.

"Any way you want it, baby."

"I prefer *woman.*"

"See there? I knew that. I was just testing." He kept his seat while he leaned way over the horse's side to close the gate behind them. "I'm not showboating. Can't handle the stirrup right now. When we get back home I'm gonna break out the wobble board I scored from a physical therapist the last time around and see how much it hurts to wobble."

"That doesn't sound like the best idea, b—"

"Don't say it. We just put *baby* on the censorship list." He clucked for an easy trot. "Along with *boy* and… What else? *Bitch.* And *bitchin'.* Hate that one."

"I was going to say *but.* With one *t. But* I'm sure you know what you're doing, having injured many of your best features."

"No, I haven't. Not the one with the two *t*'s. That's prime cut."

"For now. Wait till you're looking at the next ten-year hill."

"Here's lookin' at you looking at the next hill." He saluted her. "You wanna crawl up the side or take it head-on?"

She dug in her heels and cried, "Ballin' the jack!"

And she took off like a shot. There was nothing better than a good race. But her head start was for naught. She heard the Arab closing in, felt them breeze past and take the hill, and admired their ascent to the top. She remembered reading that the bareback event required the greatest athleticism of all rodeo events, and seeing Trace ride effortlessly bore out that claim.

"Told you Jack wasn't born to run," he called out triumphantly as she topped the hill on the losing horse.

The mare had barely broken a sweat. "What's her name?"

"Teabiscuit." She laughed, and he added, "Seriously."

"Oh, man." She shook her head as the horses fell into a walk, side by side. "For a good time, call Trace Wolf Track."

"I don't give out my number. I like to make the calls myself. I'm old-fashioned that way."

"Will I get one?"

He reached for her hand. "You'll get more than that if you play your cards right."

"Play yours right and I might answer." She gave a sassy smile. "I have caller ID."

"I'm unlisted." He winked at her. "Two savvy players make an interesting game."

"You're more fun than a county fair." She was pretty sure she'd never held hands with another rider, but she could get used to it, she decided. The wink, too.

"Is that a good thing?"

"A very good thing." She drew on his hand, and he leaned offside again, clearly feeling another good thing coming. And that was her kiss.

Chapter 8

Cayenne took to the round pen like salt to a wound at first. He burned it up. But he quickly settled into the notion that Skyler was playing with him and the longe line they were attaching for the first time to one of Trace's hand-tied rope halters was one of her toys. He liked the circle better than the square, and Skyler soon shared his preference. She felt the connection she'd known from the beginning with this horse, but now it traveled back and forth along a smooth braided rope.

"You have to win him over by winning," Trace cautioned her. "But you want him to enjoy the game. He loves to move. Teach him to move on your terms."

"Do you really think I'll be able to back him before we go to Cheyenne?"

"You'll back him before we saddle him," he told her. "You'll know when it's time."

Supper was a simple soup-and-sandwich fare, and afterward they made a production of unveiling Trace's ankle. The mottled bruising was proclaimed a work of art. He put a CD into his living room sound system and tested his range of motion on the exercise disc, rotating slowly, rocking gingerly, wincing generously, cowboying up without much cussing. He obviously had more than a nodding acquaintance with a therapeutic wobble board.

"I always start with Willie Nelson," he confided when she offered her shoulder as a stabilizer. "He takes care of all the whining for me. If I was alone, I'd whine along with him."

"Please don't let me put a crimp in any part of your therapy."

"No, I'm doing fine. I don't feel sorry for myself." With his hands resting on Skyler's shoulders, Trace rolled the ball underfoot, alternating weight on, weight off for short intervals. Standing still, she felt like the reluctant partner in the dance couple. He smiled. "I've got your full attention."

When he'd had all the exercise he could take, he asked her to help him rewrap his ankle. Again, he knew what he was doing. He gave Logan credit for turning him on to the witch hazel he used on his bruises, and he praised his friend Hank Night Horse for teaching him the varieties and the wonders of elastic-bandage wrap. She learned all about figure eights and stirrups that had nothing to do with horses, about compression bandaging and basket weaving and how to work with all kinds of elastic and adhesive and tape that wasn't really tape. And after he pronounced it a job well-done, he offered "spirits for the spirited."

"I don't have any brandy," he said. "Or ice cream. But I remember you like your whiskey straight up."

"I don't like whiskey at all." She smiled, recalling the two drinks she'd knocked back within moments of meeting him that first night. "That was for show."

"Well, that was impressive." He braced his hands on his knees, ready to try out his new footwear—the bandage and a white tube sock constituting a pair. "I'd suggest a walk in the moonlight, but there's no moon, and my stride is way off. We could play cards for real. Or checkers. Or we could make out here on the sofa."

"What about TV?" She glanced at the shelving unit, where a small one was tucked in with the music system.

"You've got two channels to pick from on a good night, but that could be the lead-in to making out on the sofa." He squinted menacingly. "And don't try anything funny. I have a box of condoms in every room."

"You must entertain a lot."

"Not here. This is my sanctuary." He leaned back, stretching out his wings along the top of the backrest. "While you were cleaning up in the kitchen I went around spreadin' the love just for you."

"We're safe, then. All the bases are covered."

He stared at her for a moment, finally shook his

head. "Why do I feel guilty? Like I'm holding out on you or something."

"You really know how to spoil the mood. I thought cowboys were supposed to be sort of love 'em and leave 'em."

He kept staring, as though he was considering options that could set a definitive course. He moved suddenly, knelt in front of the side table, opened a drawer and pulled out a box. "Come on. Let's go."

"Where?"

"Kitchen table. That's what I always use."

"Oh. I thought you said…"

"You got a better idea?"

"I don't want to, um…"

"You don't wanna play with me anymore? I'm not the cowboy you thought I was? Cut the crap, Skyler." He tossed the box on the pine coffee table.

Bicycle.

"And cut the cards. I'm pullin' out all the stops, woman. I'll beat you every hand."

"I think I'll take that whiskey," she said, nonplussed.

He limped into the kitchen and came back with a bottle and two short glasses.

"What are we playing for?" She started to move so he could have the sofa.

"Well, let's see. *No, sit.* Do you smoke?" He sat on the floor across from her and poured two drinks. "You can't win, but you get close enough, I might let you have the prize. Horseshoe rules."

"Horseshoe?"

"Close," he said. "Close counts in horseshoes. Try to keep up, Sky. The stakes are high."

He won the first three hands of whist, but she took the next two. She would never know whether he threw the two after that, nor would she care. She loved winning. It made her feel flush and fierce. But all the posturing went by the wayside when he finished his drink, got up without a word and disappeared down the dark hall. She waited for a sound or a sign, but she heard nothing except cricket music outside the open window.

She hadn't paid much attention to anything but the bathroom when he'd first shown her down the hall. "I'll put your bag in here," he'd said, and she'd noted that *here* was the door across the hall from the one she was looking for. She skipped that door now. All four doors along the narrow passage stood open to darkness. She chose the one at the end and whispered his name as she entered.

He came to her, took her face in his hands and took possession of her mouth with a resolute, probing kiss. She clutched him to her, spreading her hands wide on his back and taking the measure of its size and shape and might. She kept her hands tight and took the tapered path to the small of his back, where she found more of the same—smooth skin over solid muscle.

Her discovery made him groan with pleasure. The sound of his name was all he needed to hear. He wanted her with him in the same sweet way—uncovered and unfettered—and he had to steady himself in the face of the wildness that threatened to overtake him. He took care in peeling away her clothing, unbuttoning and unzipping even as he saw himself tearing the stuff off and kicking it away. When it was gone he lifted her in his arms and kissed her breasts. She wrapped her legs around his waist and he felt the intimate touch of hair and moist folds of flesh and welcome and trust, all pressed against his stomach and ripe for the taking.

There would be no falling to the floor, no making do with the sofa, no repurposing the kitchen table. He wanted her in his bed—*his* bed—and he wanted her now, and then again, and long into the night, and slow and easy in the morning.

She rode him hot and hard, and he held her hips in his hands and bucked up to meet her as she drove down, moved as slow and deep as she could take, would take, stroking her inside and out until she quivered, cried out for him, called his name, screamed his name, whispered his name as she sank down, down, down into his arms and shed warm tears against his chest.

He didn't ask her why, but he asked himself why he would have joined her if tears were part of his nature. Maybe it was for the coupling of their bodies, the sheer power of one against one and one with one. Maybe it was for the way it happened, the beauty, the hazard of it, or for the small coupling that would not happen inside her and away from him. Not tonight. He wasn't kidding about the box of condoms in every room.

She probably wept for her confusion and for his.

He had little experience with a woman's tears. But, then, he'd had no experience with a woman like Skyler.

"Tell me something about your husband," he said quietly when they lay side by side in the cool night air.

"What?"

"Something that'll tell me who he was. I feel like I came into your life at the wrong time. Like you're still with somebody else."

"I'm not with anyone else." The first words were raspy. She cleared her throat and added, "I'm on my own."

He was nothing if not persistent. "Tell me *one thing* about your husband." Patient, but persistent.

"I'm here with you, Trace. We're making—"

"One telling thing."

He felt no resistance in her silence. She was trying to come up with the right thing to say. The honest and honorable thing.

"He was a good man." Her chuckle sounded humorless, and he thought it might be the effect of the darkness or the cool air. "That's what they all say, isn't it?"

"All who?"

"Eulogists." She paused. "But he *was* a good man. He was *take-charge Tony.*"

"Was that his name?" Of course it was. The sound of it chilled him, and he drew the bedsheet around his shoulders. "Logan doesn't name the dead. He's very traditional." He listened to the steady sound of her breathing. He wasn't ready for her to go to sleep. "But I don't have a problem with it. Do you?"

"It's only been a year."

"In my father's house, that's when you put on a feed in their honor and wipe the tears away. The Lakota have a ceremony for everything."

"And you—"

"Tell me something else, Skyler. Help me know him."

"Why?"

"Because I'm…" He found her hand lying between them, and he took it in his. "Don't think too much. Just tell me." *Tell me what I'm up against.*

"We had two marriages."

"You mean *he* had two marriages."

"I'm not thinking too much, so I said what I meant." She drew his hand to her lips and kissed him as if to reassure him or thank him. Quiet him, maybe. "You're playing the grief counselor, right? At first I liked playing May to his September. But I moved on to June, July, August, and he still wanted May. He wanted the girl who looked up to him and smiled prettily and never doubted." She sighed. "Logan's right. I shouldn't talk about him now."

"You're not talking about him. You're talking about you."

"Well, then, that's fair, isn't it? He's not here."

"Yeah, he is."

"Maybe you're right. A year isn't enough."

"I didn't say that." He groaned. "Hell, what do I know?"

"Good question." She shifted toward him. "Tell me something about your mother."

Damn. The woman knew how to aim. "She's dead to me."

"What do you remember?"

He was thinking, trying to remember what the woman even looked like. It was a strange thing to do, given the effort he'd spent in forgetting. Long ago he'd stopped wanting her around him, so why call up memories of her and run the risk of speculation, which was a ticket that had *frustration* printed right across the middle.

"What's her name?" Skyler asked softly.

"Tonya. Her name was Tonya. And what I remember is she left us."

"And you never heard from her."

"Yeah, we did." And, yeah, it was coming back. As if he needed this. But to be fair, he'd started it. "She called a few times and made promises. I told her I wasn't goin' with her. No way. I was done with her kind of life."

"It wasn't the first time?"

"Hell, no. She left Ethan and me alone for three days once. I think it was three days. Maybe it only seemed like…" He drew a deep breath, wishing he could tell it without calling it all back up in his head. "I know it was two nights. Two really long nights."

"How old were you?"

"Old enough to make baloney sandwiches and keep the door locked. We were living in, uh…" Which crappy shoe box? Which windowless pit? "Down south someplace. Alabama, or Texas, maybe. It was hot. I remember that." He tried to think of something funny about those years. Something tasty and easy to swallow. "I used to have an accent when I was a kid."

"You still do. A little bit."

"Nah, this haint nuthin'. I had a real drawl back then. Got rid of it purdy damn quick when I moved to Indian country. They like to tease the daylights out of you."

"That's where you learned it."

"Had to. Glad I did. It's funnern' hell. You think I'm any good at it?"

"Oh, yes. If they gave teaser trophies, you'd be a sure winner."

"I'd put it front and center, too. Set it in the middle of the table and fill it with flowers. Logan would love that." And Trace was breathing easy again.

"I feel as though I know him. You've drawn me a picture of a wonderful man. Why can't I do that? You know, for Tony."

"He left you alone, and you're mad at him for it."

"He died," she insisted. "He didn't run off."

"He left you alone. You took care of him, tried to keep him around, but he left anyway."

"He *died*." The word seemed to bounce around in the dark. They listened to it ping-pong, loath to pile on another troublesome word until that one settled. "It was almost…a relief."

"I know. Not to have to worry anymore, wondering what's gonna happen tomorrow. All at once you're free. You're alone, still not sure what's gonna happen, but you feel like the worst must be over. There's peace in the valley."

"It's not the same, Trace."

"Maybe not. But I know what it's like to feel a little guilty over that relief."

"Does it go away?"

"Yeah. It does." He stroked the back of her hand with his thumb. "And like you said, your husband died. No choice about leaving, and he can't come back. When I say my mother's dead to me, it's not because I'm angry. It's because I've let it go, and I don't want her back."

"And you're not alone. In your life, I mean."

"I'm not?" He chuckled. "No buffalo roaming around here, but I've got the deer and the antelope."

"You searched long and hard for a place like this."

"Yes, I did."

And he wanted to share it with someone. Someday. Once he'd followed the road to the pot of gold, made his mark in a young man's game before it took a crippling toll on his body. He wanted it all, and he wasn't going to let one dream step on the other. He'd told Skyler his wants had gotten ahead of his wits, and maybe that was even truer than he'd realized. His heart had gotten in on the act before he was ready. But the heart—the way it worked hard if not tirelessly and kept on working from start to finish— maybe the heart was always ready. *Ready when you are, slowpoke.*

"I'll say this—somebody's depending on you, you

gotta be there. That's the way I was raised. By my father."

"Not all mothers…"

"I know that, Skyler. Like you, for example. You took on a motherless kid, and you stuck by him."

"I married his father."

"Yeah. I hear that can work."

"*Work* is the operative word," she said. "Two willing partners. Maybe one more willing than the other at times, but it turns out there are so many more considerations than you anticipate when you take those lovely vows. The considerations are right there in the words, and you say them, but you have to live with them for a while before you know what they mean."

"Which is why kids shouldn't get married."

"I wasn't a kid."

"I didn't mean you. I meant the guy who played with the toy trains."

She laughed. "You're jealous!"

"I am not. I just wish I'd found you first."

"Let's see, you would've been about…"

"Don't you dare go there." It was his turn to laugh. "Look, it's a stupid way to feel, but guys aren't the brightest bulbs on the planet. I'm not supposed to say that out loud, but we all know it's true.

"I've got this image of you tied to the tracks and me coming to the rescue." He let go of her hand so he could draw her a picture overhead. He used both hands, big dusky shadows in the starlit room. "Little tiny you, little tiny me, little tiny train on the table some carpenter built." He spread his hands wide.

"Big man runnin' the transformer, setting the dial for ballin' the jack."

They laughed together, and he realized how very funny laughter sounded in the dark, and how it fed on itself and bred more laughter.

And when it died down and the silence rushed in to fill the space, the thoughts came back, which gave rise to words made weighty by darkness.

"Life seems so disjointed sometimes," she said. "Just when you think you know where you're going, you come to another unmarked crossroads. I don't know where I'm going now, but I know I'm going to be a mother. A good one. My baby will be the light of my life. I promise you that."

"My kid will have a father," he said. "I promise him that."

They worked Cayenne together for most of the next morning. When they came in for lunch, Skyler fell asleep on the sofa. She woke up staring at a rough-hewn beam in an unfamiliar ceiling. It took a moment to climb out of her sleep hole, the place she fell into whenever she slept during the day. It was an unsettling place to find herself in. She wasn't a nap-taker, and she didn't *fall* asleep as a rule. She *went* to sleep.

Trace's place. Ah, yes, she was in a good place.

She padded to the kitchen in her stockinged feet and called his name, but there was no answer. She heard a breeze swishing through the junipers outside and a woodpecker making its mark, but no trace of Trace except the sandwich he'd left on a plate and an apple on a note.

> *Sky—*
> *I took the pickup. If you feel like it, mount up and follow the fence over the hill. You might catch me working.*
> *Trace*

She ate the sandwich because he'd made it for her, and she took the apple and her camera bag to the bench by the back door, where she sat down, put on her boots and surveyed the tidy kitchen. *Plate.* She washed and dried her plate, and then she hurried to the corral to find that he'd brought Jack in from the pasture and had him waiting to do her bidding.

She was busy hauling up on the cinch, glanced over Jack's back and saw Cayenne checking them out from the other side of the fence. He was communing more with Jack than with her, but he knew she was there. She could feel his awareness of her. Not as wary as he once was, but still uncertain of her makeup. She slipped her camera out of the bag she'd hooked over the saddle horn and snapped a picture of gentle and wild, nose to nose. Jack, the blazed-face sorrel, and Cayenne, the red-faced, red-peppered gray, were as close as they appeared to be, and they knew it. Take away the fences, Trace had reminded her, and they would fly away and never look back.

Trace reminded her of a lot of things. Winning and losing, beginning and ending, hurting and healing came to mind. Something was different about the last pair. She'd have to think about it when she got around to thinking again. For now, she was doing what came naturally. She mounted up.

The buck-and-pole trail led her to the top of the hill, and from there she saw a most glorious sight—a working man. He was beautifully buff and bare to the waist, his chambray shirt flapping in the breeze from the top of the A-frame buck that had lost its poles.

She took a few pictures, put the camera away and started down the hill. Trace hadn't seen her yet. The pickup tailgate was down, and she saw a couple of new twelve-foot poles, a chain saw and a big wooden box like the one her father had kept in the barn. Nails, bolts, tools, the increasingly present pint. "Sippin' whiskey," he'd called it. And she'd shrugged off her sinking feeling and saddled her horse.

Trace wielded a mallet over the junction of span and brace, striking his target with every swing. His shoulders glistened in the sun. Skyler was going to descend on him like a thing with feathers. She nudged Jack's flanks with her boot heels and imagined herself flying down the slope. The best way to fly was on horseback, the wind filling her hair like a sail. He snatched his hat off and waved at her. Waved her off? Did he think she was going to—

Whoa!

Jack went down on his knees, scrambled back up and took a couple of stumbling sidesteps. Skyler dismounted as soon as the horse had his footing. Wild-eyed, snorting, he pranced in place, tethered by her hold on the reins. He was calmed by her voice, but he balked at her attempt to check his legs. She waited, apologizing and reassuring until the horse accepted her hand on his neck. He was okay.

"You must've been born in the saddle," Trace said quietly.

She turned, startled, which seemed a little crazy, considering the surprise she'd just had. Then she realized she was quaking inside. Aftershock.

Trace was tucking his leather work gloves into his back pockets. "I've never seen a tighter seat. By all rights you should've sailed over his head."

"By all rights he should've thrown me. But he kept us both…" She drew a slow, tremulous breath. "What was it? A trench?"

"Tried to warn you. Prairie-dog holes. Weren't there last time I was up here. Got some huntin' to do." He kicked at the loosened dirt surrounding another trap. "You okay? Scared me spitless."

"Us, too." Her voice had gone squeaky, but she managed a shaky smile. "Stupid move."

He stepped up and took her in his arms. "Is this what you were looking for?"

His skin was warm and damp, his arms blessedly powerful. Why *blessedly* she couldn't say. Her legs were just as damn powerful as his arms were. But her insides took the *settle down* cue from the rock-solid feel of him.

"You wanna buck one out in Cheyenne?"

"No, thanks."

"Let you wear my vest," he offered.

That wouldn't do it. Not if she was pregnant. And she could be, just might possibly be. The beginning of the very thing she wanted most might have been here and gone inside of a few days, and she'd have nothing to show for it other than a little blood.

She held Trace tighter.

"Hey." He leaned back and looked down at her. "Are you hurt?"

Damn her silly nerves, she was *crying*. She shook her head furiously.

"Just a little delayed heebie-jeebies?"

She nodded and pressed her forehead to his shoulder. "My car almost got hit by a train once. Felt like a bullet whizzed past my head."

"Damn trains."

She took a swipe at her hot tears with the back of her wrist. She was still holding one end of the split rein, which meant she wasn't a total failure. "I'm being silly again. Jack's the one who…"

"He's fine. Look at him. Steady as a rock."

Trace got her to take notice of the horse, already looking for grass. *If we're just gonna stand here, I might as well be eating.* She sniff-giggled like a six-year-old who'd fallen off a swing.

"Jack, you're a keeper," Trace called out to the horse. Jack was nosing around, picking over the possibilities. "That's the way I'll advertise him," he confided. "Did you hit pretty hard?"

She swallowed. "I think I bit my tongue." And she grimaced. "I taste blood."

"Open your mouth."

He ducked, peered, nodded. "It's a gusher. You want me to kiss it better?"

"Would you?"

He lowered his head and applied several soft, gentle kisses to her lips. Her tongue didn't get into the action, but she had the feeling he would not have recoiled no matter what shape it was in. This cowboy was a keeper, but Skyler would keep that to herself.

"How's your foot?"

"It's giving me passable understanding." He bent to pick up the loose rein and hand it to her. "Long as I don't stand on it too long."

"What can I do to help?" she asked as she took care of securing Jack to the fence.

"Almost got it licked. Can you hold a pole for me?"

"Just hold it?"

"That's all I need." He laid his hand on her arm before he put on his second glove. "You sure you're okay? You still seem a little shaky."

"I thought that was the idea." She offered a tentative smile. "Isn't that... I pride myself on my pole work." The surprise in his eyes bucked her up. "I took lessons."

He laughed. "I can function with a bum leg, but if I slip and smash a finger, it's all over. It all starts with the hands."

"I know. So please be careful."

"Let's see..." Trace made a production of eyeballing Skyler's height and the fallen end fence rail for placement on the buck. "What's the best way for you to do this? You could get underneath, but I'm not

sure you can bear the weight. And you're a strad-
dler, aren't you?"

She smiled a little more. "I like to ride."

"Well, throw your leg over and get behind me. This
baby's gonna get nailed good this time."

Skyler held the pole while Trace pounded the
spike. "Hey, guess what," she shouted at his back.
"We're riding the rail!"

Trace lay on his back in the grass with his legs
propped up on the A-frame buck, bad ankle crossed
over the good one. He'd put his shirt back on, but he'd
left it open because it was hot out, and he was hot, and
he'd noticed her taking notice of him, so he thought
he'd keep her options open. He knew what he had
going for him, and he figured he might as well use it.

He'd covered his eyes with his hat, balanced the
front of the sweatband on the bridge of his nose so he
could see her sitting up there on the rail they'd hung
together. She was wearing a battered straw hat, but he
was pretty sure her face and her arms and her chest,
even the top part of her breasts, were going to be red
tonight. And he was pretty sure witch hazel—generously applied by hand—would go a long way in
soothing the burn.

If she wanted to stay with him for a while, he'd
take good care of her. He wondered how she would
take to his caretaking. He could be as good at it as
she was. When he'd seen the horse go down with her,
his heart had rocketed into his throat.

But then she'd stuck the horse like a pro, and Trace's heart had come down singing.

"How's my pole holdin' up?" he asked her.

"Solid," she said. "You're an excellent nailer."

"Jack-of-all-trades, master of none."

"Is bronc riding a trade?" She lowered herself off the rail and sat down on the patch of grass beside him. "Because if it is..."

"I'd call cowboying a trade and rodeo a profession. Cowboys have to be skilled at damn near everything that comes up on a ranch. I can buck out a bronc, easy, but I'm still workin' on being a real cowboy."

"Interesting." She was quiet for a moment. He stole a peek from beneath his hat and saw her giving Jack some love, rubbing his velvety nose. "What happens to a ranch that doesn't have its own cowboy?"

"It gets tagged a *farm*."

She laughed.

"You have a hired man," Trace recalled.

"He's a retired teacher."

"Well, hell, you've got a professional and a tradesman rolled into one."

"Grady grew up on a farm. He lives with his wife in Gillette. She keeps saying if the winters here get any worse she's moving to Arizona. I don't know what we'll do without him."

"*We?* Isn't that Mike's problem?"

"I write the checks," she reminded him.

"And Mike swipes the credit card."

She bristled. "He doesn't have to *swipe*. He has his own."

"Swipes on the machine," he clarified. "I would never suggest that Mike would take advantage. He has his own account?"

"Well…" She sighed. "I write all the checks."

He braced up on his elbow, pushed his hat back and looked her in the eye. "Why do you want another kid? You've got one big one, probably eats enough to feed two or three small ones."

She glared at him. And then she glanced away. Finally she burst out laughing. "You're all alike," she said merrily. "Not cowboys. *Men.*"

"Oh, no, honey, that's just wrong." She was still chuckling, but he'd just thought up a way to sober her up. "Come live with me. I'll show you what you've been missing."

She thought he was kidding. He could tell by the way she was looking at him.

"You know what?" he continued. "You come into this world alone, and you go out alone, but you don't have to go it alone in between."

She tipped her head to one side as she went from point A to point B—amused to bemused.

"You're right—I'm not totally alone. I've got my brother, my father, a bunch of guys I can go down the road with whenever I need to save on gas. I've had some girlfriends." He swung his legs down and sat up, facing her. "But I've never found myself wanting to be with anyone day in, day out before. I want to be with you. I want to take you with me."

"Where?" She frowned and spoke guardedly. "For how long?"

"I don't know. As long as I can make you happy, I guess. Or until I break my fool neck. Like they say, I ain't asking you to back a horse that's only good for glue. But be with me now. Go down the road with me. Come back home with me."

"Trace, we hardly know—"

"We know we're good together, and we're learning each other. I want to keep it going." He lifted one shoulder. "It just feels right."

"I have…responsibilities."

"When are you going to stop letting them crowd out your dreams?"

"Most people have both. At this point in my life I have to be honest with myself about realities and possibilities."

"That's what I'm talkin' about. Sounds like a good plan." He backed off with a nod. "You oughta get to work on it."

She glanced at the fence. He had no clue what she was thinking, but he knew one thing. If she was going to let him down, she'd to it gently. She was that kind of woman. The kind he wanted to be with.

"Are we finished?" she asked quietly.

"We're finished here, but we still have a few promises to keep elsewhere." He offered her a hand up. "Cayenne for one. Cheyenne for two." He smiled, mostly to himself. "When the time comes for traveling music, I'm gonna write us a little ditty about Jack and Cayenne."

Chapter 9

"We're going to Sinte," he told her the next morning.

Skyler turned away from the stove to get the rest of the announcement head-on. She'd gotten up in time to watch the sunrise and cook breakfast in the hope that the door to Trace's room was closed because he was getting needed sleep and he'd wake up and smell the coffee and come out of his corner smiling. It could happen, even though they'd slept in separate beds last night. An unspoken agreement, but she was chalking it up to her choice, which meant she had to do something to make up for it. In her experience, these things generally worked that way.

Oddly enough, he wasn't going for coffee first

thing. A kiss on her neck came first, just under her earlobe. It tickled.

"It's a town over on the other side of the Black Hills. My hometown." He helped himself to a strip of bacon, fresh from the skillet. "Ouch! Mmm. It's real close to the Double D, where you got Cayenne. We can stop there, too, if you want to."

"I'd like that, but I think we should call first."

"Call who?"

"We can't just drop in on people."

"Why not?" He took another piece of bacon and moved away. "Did you get coffee?"

"Not yet." She ran the spatula across the bottom of the skillet, through the scrambled eggs. "Because they won't be expecting us."

"I just got off the phone with Logan."

"Is something wrong?"

He laid one hand on her nape and set a cup of black coffee within her reach. "My father wants to meet you."

"Why? What did you tell him?" She watched him brace his butt against the edge of the counter adjacent to the stove. He was giving her that dancing-eyes bit as he sipped his coffee. *What?*

"I told him you used to be a princess, but you weren't the kind to let it go to your head too much." He shrugged. "Told him you were trying to get us pregnant." She scowled. *Truth or consequences?* "Isn't that the way it is nowadays? Not *she's* pregnant, but *we're* pregnant?" He chuckled. "Yeah, I'm kidding."

"It's not funny. You didn't say any of that, did you?"

"I told him I met a woman, and he said, 'Bring her home. And the horse she rode in on.'"

She scraped up the eggs again. Too much heat, too little focus. "He's probably more interested in the horse."

"He's seen the horse. He remembers it. We agree, you made the right choice."

"I do know something about horses." She started loading up two plates.

"I thought you wanted to meet him," he said as he took breakfast in hand.

"I do. And I want to show Sally some of the pictures we've taken." She took up her plate and headed for the table. "I thought we were going to work with Cayenne today."

"We will." He was shoveling his eggs down and hadn't moved from the space beside the stove. "Work off some energy before we load him."

"Would you come sit down, please?" she said quietly.

"Oh, yeah." He picked up his coffee and ambled over to the table. "Habit, I guess. Kinda nice, eating off a plate."

"And this is a great table." She'd claimed the end of the bench and left the chair for him.

"Came with the house. You sit down by yourself and look way down to the end, you know how that guy on TV felt when his wife left and took the eight kids."

"*Jon* left," she said. "It's Kate who got the eight kids, the house and the show, and I can't believe you watch that."

"You stay in a hotel once in a while, you get a peek at cable TV. All I know is, these two get on TV because they have eight little kids, and then they split up." He lifted one shoulder. "That, and there was that long table."

"That's it in a television nutshell. Life unscripted." She smiled. "On with our own reality. The road awaits."

"Look, you wanna nitpick, could you pull in the claws?" He laid his fork down. "I'm not draggin' you anywhere." He reached under the table, found her hand and drew it into the open as he slid his chair back. He examined her manicured nails. "Damn. If you ever have a kid, you're gonna have to cut these."

"They're not that long."

"They're sharp." He released her hand, took up his dishes and gave her an odd look. "I'll call him back and tell him it's not a good time."

She closed her eyes and sighed. "I'm sorry. I don't know what's wrong with me."

"Hey," he said softly, touching her shoulder. "He just wants to meet you. He doesn't do interviews."

"I hope not."

"Yeah, we're not TV people." He smiled. "He's an author, and I'm a top hand in the PRCA, but we're like regular folks."

They cleaned up the kitchen together quietly. *We're good together.* What exactly did that mean? They

worked well together. Everything they'd done together seemed to turn out well. He picked up where
she left off and vice versa. Maybe they should do
things together without talking, Skyler thought. Telling a man what you really wanted could be dicey. He
might say, "Fine, honey," and let it ride. He might ignore you. Or he might treat you like a child and claim
you didn't know what was good for you. Trace's atti-
tude didn't seem to fall into any of those categories.
He wasn't on board, but she wasn't feeling rejected,
either.

How did he do that?

"I'll call and let Mike know where I'll be," Skyler
said as she headed down the hall to pack her little bag.

"You do that."

Meaning what? She wanted to march back down
the hall and point out to him that checking in was a
good thing, and that anyone she lived with could de-
pend on her to do just that. If she disappeared, she
wanted to tell him, call out the bloodhounds. She
probably *was* dead.

But she kept those thoughts to herself. If she had to
tell him, he hadn't come far enough. Really and truly,
they hardly knew each other. Being good together
and learning each other sounded like something her
father might have said. And her mother might have
gone along with it because Dad was good with everybody, and he would gladly have spent his whole life
learning people. It was a lovely idea—Dad had lots
of lovely ideas—but it had nothing to do with responsibilities. He'd taken on the little things—patched up

small holes, grew beautiful tomatoes, made fabulous vegetable soup—but he'd hated milking cows, which was a fatal flaw for a dairy farmer. He'd gone under. Drowned in milk and whiskey.

Trace was young, she told herself. He had plenty of time to get himself all set up while he was figuring people out, finding the right one for his one and only and making the pieces fit. She, on the other hand, had responsibilities. She wasn't set up, but she had a few things figured out, and one of them was that on any given day, body parts were easy to put together. But bodies were not the same from one day to the next. They aged or they became ill or the fit changed. And that little fact could be a big dream killer. She'd taken all the right steps and made careful choices, but *right* and *careful* had betrayed her.

Being dependable was all she knew. She had dependability to spare. Her sense of responsibility would easily cover for two people—mother and father—and that was where she'd decided to put her eggs—into the parenthood basket. She wasn't interested in following a man around the way her mother had done before she'd talked Dad into going back home and taking over his father's farm. It was a mistake to try to make a man over. And she was no longer interested in being beautiful and dutiful. She wanted to love and be loved for herself. Her below the skin and down to the core plain ol' reliable self.

But couldn't she afford to enjoy the good fit she'd found with Trace for a little while longer? Maybe the fit only went bad when you started trying to force it.

Fresh start, he'd said, and while she wasn't sure such a thing was possible for the long haul, it seemed doable right now. She was trying to turn a corner in her life, and maybe she'd turned too fast, too sharp, too hard, but he was still willing to take a ride with her at the wheel. He was, without a doubt, a good man, and she wanted to meet the man who'd raised him.

She also wanted to meet the man who'd taught Trace everything he knew about horses, considering how much he knew. She was taking a break that nobody had to give her, and nobody was going to put any limits on it. She wasn't looking for a small break. She was looking for something worth taking a risk for, and risking big.

The drive to Sinte was over three hours' worth of scenic beauty and heavy silence. Trace wasn't surprised by the silence. He'd known all along that he was dealing with a complicated woman. What he hoped to gain with the trip was time. They'd had some good times. They needed some real time. And there was no more telling reality than the first time a guy took a woman home to meet the family. Especially when the family was Logan Wolf Track.

They stopped on the way to check in with Sally Drexler Night Horse, for whom Mustang Sally's Wild Horse Makeover Challenge was named. The side door opened on the barn and out came Sally—the small but never meek—leaning heavily on her cane. She waved when she saw them. Multiple sclerosis never appeared to dampen Sally's enthusiasm.

"What to my wondering eyes appears." Sally gave her visitors a bright-eyed once-over that was the adult version of *Skyler and Trace, sittin' in a tree...* Then she acknowledged Trace's flamingo stance. "I heard about your injury, cowboy. How're you doing? You gonna make it to Cheyenne?"

"As long as I can swing a leg over a bronc, I'm good for another go-round."

"Is he?" she asked Skyler.

"If he says so."

Sally glanced back and forth between the two of them and winked. "I tell you what, this contest was the best idea I ever had."

"You're bringin' out the best," Trace said. "Is Hank around?"

"No, but Logan was here this morning. He said you were bringing a new girlfriend home for his approval. I asked him if that was a Lakota rule, and he said the Lakota don't have rules. They have *ways*. So I never really got an answer." Sally adjusted her sunglasses. "Except he did say you hadn't brought a girl around to meet him since you were in high school."

"You're not helping, Sally." Trace glanced at Skyler. Big, dark glasses, tight lips. *Go easy, Wolf Track. Bring her on home.* "I keep telling her, she's not meeting the chief of the Great Sioux Nation." He smiled. "He should be, but there isn't one."

Sally rubbernecked for a look at the horse trailer. "You're not bringing that horse back, are you?"

"Oh, no. We're out to win this thing." Skyler

looked at Trace and he gave her an *attagirl* wink. "I have a proposition for you, Sally."

"You can't keep the horse." Sally waved off the idea prematurely. "We're selling them after the contest is over. This is a fund-raiser." She turned to Trace. "Logan already took his wife's mustang out of the running. He adopted it for her, lovesick bridegroom that he is. But I can't let any more go." Back to Skyler. "Logan helped us get more lease land from the tribe. And Mary's my best friend." Sally shrugged. "So sue me."

"Who would dare?" Trace said. "No, Skyler wants to help you out, too. And she's a hell of a photographer."

"Photographer?"

"I've taken some still shots and quite a bit of video," Skyler said.

"She's a real pro."

"Well, not..." Skyler touched Trace's shirtsleeve. *Thank you.* "But I'm getting there. If you have time, I'd like to show you some of it."

"Time for pictures of my babies? You damn betcha."

"Because I have this idea." With encouragement from all sides, Skyler stepped closer. "About making a sort of a documentary video. Has anyone else approached you?"

"You're the first."

"Well, I'm sure I won't be the last, and I'm sure you'll be hearing from some *real* pros, but I just thought I'd—" Skyler punctuated her determination with a fist to the palm "—just *do* it. I'm just doing it." She shrugged. "And we'll see."

"How can I help?" Sally wanted to know.

"I'm focusing on Cayenne, and so far I have a video diary."

"Cayenne? Like the spice?" Sally grinned. "I like that."

"I'd like to set up some interviews, starting with you. Whenever you have time."

"Time to talk? I can always find time to talk." Sally nodded toward the corrals. "Turn Cayenne out in that empty pen over there, and let's have a look at your pictures. What do you want me to talk about? Have you ever seen that movie *Free Willy?* I love that movie." Skyler and Trace went about the business of unloading a wary mustang while Sally went right on brainstorming. "We can't call it *Free Cayenne* because we're gonna auction him off. But we could still have a scene where we turn some horses loose, and they take off, tails flying, and we all cheer. *Yay! Run free!*" She waved her hat. "It's okay if you show me in the wheelchair. Being all inspirational, of course. I always say, if you've got it, flaunt it." She grinned. "Schmaltz sells."

Sally's enthusiasm was a confidence builder. Skyler saw her pictures with new eyes. Video from the day she'd picked out her horse, from the work she'd done on her own and more recent video with Trace's voice behind the camera—all of it showed promise. *We could show this. We could add more of that.* The ideas poured in from all three sides, and nobody was more excited about them than Skyler was.

Trace begged off the offer of a meal. Logan was expecting them. It was Trace's turn to stare out the pickup's side window quietly as the fence posts and ditch grass flew past. They passed a sign that said Welcome to the Lakota Nation and another at the top of a hill marking five more miles to the town of Sinte.

From a distance it looked like most prairie communities—a collection of boxes all but lost in a sea of grass. As they drew closer, Skyler started framing shots mentally. Embraced by stalwart hills and overarching sky, there were community buildings of some substance, but the clusters of homes tended toward the ramshackle. Splendor and shabbiness in the same frame. Life.

Logan Wolf Track lived in a log house facing the highway. There was a round pen out back, much like the one Trace had built, but Logan's pole barn was made of metal and his paddock was smaller. A beautiful claybank mustang pricked his ears and monitored their approach from his vantage in the adjacent pasture.

Tall, lanky and darkly handsome, Logan met them at the door, ushered them in and shook hands with Trace first and then with Skyler as she was introduced simply by her first name.

Skyler launched what she considered to be protocol.

"I understand congratulations are in order. You just got married?"

"Thanks. I did. I'm a lucky man."

"Surprised the hell out of me." Trace nodded toward the kitchen table, and Skyler took a seat. "I didn't even get an invitation," he called out to his father, who was pouring coffee on the other side of the island divider.

"You got a call." Logan set cups on the table in front of each of his guests. "Kind of a shotgun affair. My wife's in the army."

"Who was holding the shotgun?" Skyler asked.

"The army," Logan said with a laugh. "Mary was home on leave and she had to get back to her post. But she's getting out soon. She's…" He took a seat at the table, folded his hands, fingers laced, and announced almost reverently, "We're having a baby."

"The hell," said Trace.

"Congratulations again," Skyler said, glancing at Trace. *Poor man. He thought his father's place would give him respite from any kind of baby talk.*

He shook his head in amazement. "Damn, you work fast."

"So Trace's gonna have a baby brother or sister in a few months." Logan was beaming. "What do you think of that?" he asked his son.

"I think it's fine." Trace sipped his coffee. He took another moment and then lifted one shoulder. "Hell, I think it's great. Have you told Ethan?"

"Haven't told anyone yet. Mary told her mother. You're my first." He grinned. "And it feels chest-swellin' good."

"So she's getting out of the army. Retiring?"

"She's not old enough to retire." Logan turned to Skyler. "My wife's a few years younger than I am. And I'm not old enough to retire." He chuckled. "Never will be. But Mary's been in the army more than ten years, and she's done more than her share in the Middle East, so she's taking a discharge. She's a dog handler."

"And Logan's on the Tribal Council." Trace glanced out the window. "I see you've got your mustang out back."

"You brought yours?"

"I always do what you tell me. You know that."

"How's the foot? You gonna be ready for Cheyenne?"

"Oh, yeah. You coming?"

"Wouldn't miss it."

"So what do you say we double-team Skyler?" Trace proposed. "She started the horse, and she's been doing the groundwork herself."

"I do what you tell me to do," she said. She wasn't sure she'd appreciate instructions from two Wolf Tracks at the same time.

"Ohan." Logan's tone said *aha.* "How's that workin' for you?" He caught her glancing at Trace. "Not for *him.* For you."

"I think it's going very well," she said. "But he gives you full credit. Oh, and I have a copy of your book, which backs him up on that. Will you sign it for me?"

"I like this woman." Logan's smile made Skyler

feel chosen. "You don't be waiting on him if he's act-ing *unsica* over a little sprain."

"That's *pitiful,*" Trace explained, "which I'm not."

"No, you're not." Logan tapped the table with a flat hand. "Let's see what your mustang can do. What're you calling him?"

"Cayenne." The look on Trace's face read, *Don't blame me.*

"Cayenne? What's that, some newly recognized Indian tribe?"

"Close," Trace said. "It's red pepper. Sneaks up on you and burns like the devil."

Logan laughed. "I'll bet it's good for the heart."

They turned the mustang out into the round pen, and Skyler went through her beginning ground rou-tine. Then she returned to the side of the ring, where Trace was holding the next piece of equipment—the longe line.

"Lookin' good," Logan told her.

"You think he'll take her on his back?" Trace asked.

"Damnedest thing," Logan said. "I can't get on our mustang yet, but Mary rode him already. Horses and women have a natural connection."

Trace looked at Skyler. She didn't say the words, but *What did I tell you?* was written all over her face.

"Yeah, let's put her up there today."

Skyler beamed.

Trace rode the fence beside his father while Skyler longed the horse. Logan had been his sounding board ever since he'd brought the family home. He seldom offered unsolicited advice, but unlike his brother, Trace wasn't shy about soliciting.

"Have you heard anything from my mother?"

Logan's brow furrowed. "Not since the divorce was final and I got the papers she signed." He didn't take his eyes off Skyler and Cayenne. "Why? Have you heard from her?"

"Not since she called and said she'd be coming to get us, but not for a while." He gave the idea a tongue clucking. "I didn't say anything. If she came, I wasn't going."

"You'd like to know what happened to her."

"Not really." It was a lie. He knew it, and he knew Logan knew it. "But I thought if anybody did…"

"I'd tell you if I did."

Trace watched the mustang canter at the end of Skyler's line. Life on the line. Two beautiful creatures. Maybe a third. It could happen. He was beginning to like the idea.

"You think she's dead?" he asked quietly.

"I don't think about her much anymore."

"But you married her," Trace said. "I never understood that."

"It seemed like a good idea at the time, and it brought me you two boys."

"You wanted kids?"

"I wanted your mother," Logan said. "She happened to have two kids. Some people say things happen for a reason. I say, things happen, and you take hold of the line and don't let yourself get run over.

Down the road, maybe you can say things happen for a reason." He adjusted his hat—the cowboy's way of adjusting his thinking. "I wanted to do what was right, and it turned out pretty damn good."

"You were the best thing that could've happened to Ethan and me. I don't know if I've ever told you that, but it's true."

Logan nodded. It was the kind of acknowledgment he wouldn't take lightly. For Logan, words were pretty lightweight in the scheme of things.

"You wanna hear something crazy?" He gave a chin jerk toward the horse in the pasture. "That horse—we call him Adobe—he knew Mary was pregnant before she did."

Trace chuckled. "Did he slip you a note? Scratch out the word in the dirt?"

"Smart-ass. You're good, but you haven't come quite far enough. You understand their nature, but you don't respect the mystery. *Sunka Wakan.* Spirit dog." Logan nodded. "That horse came to her, stood right up next to her—that wild horse—and he lowered his head right next to her belly." He looked at Trace. "Have you ever seen anything like that? It wasn't long after that we found out."

"When did she ride him?"

"Before she found out. His first time, too. Had nothing on his back before that. He took care of her like she was family." Logan lifted one shoulder. "'Course, if we'd known…"

"Trace, could you help me?" Skyler called. "I'm ready. Cayenne's ready. Boost me up?"

Trace hadn't noticed that Skyler had stopped working the longe line. She had the rope coiled, and she was rubbing Cayenne's neck. Trace quickly lowered himself down the fence and dropped into the pen on his good foot. Logan was right. Trace had the utmost respect for his father, but he didn't trust mysteries.

There was no way Skyler was getting on that horse.

Chapter 10

In the days that followed, Trace stuck to his guns. Skyler was in charge of the groundwork, but nobody was going to ride Cayenne except him. He didn't want the horse to acquire any bad habits from the get-go. Skyler stopped objecting when she realized what his problem was. Whenever she thought about telling him she wasn't pregnant just to take him off the hook, the lie wouldn't come. She understood that she wasn't alone in the possibility-of-parenthood basket. Her eggs would just sit there without his input. And Trace wasn't about to deny his input.

When it came time to pack up for Cheyenne, her body gave her its answer. *Not this time.* She gave him the news in three simple words, uttered as tonelessly as she could manage. He said nothing. He put his hand behind her head, drew her to him and kissed her forehead. She tried to discern his thoughts from the look in his eyes, but she couldn't be sure whether it was *Thank you, Jesus* or *You have my sympathy, Skyler.* What she knew for certain was that this man would be a good father someday.

He asked her to share a room with him in Cheyenne. He had a camper that he could load onto the back of his pickup, but he also had a hotel reservation. One room. Everything else was booked. They could take the camper and she could have the room, or...

She told him to leave the camper at home.

He still favored his injured ankle when he wasn't thinking about it, or when he'd been on his feet a while. Skyler welcomed the opportunity to drive the pickup. He didn't need to put any stress on that ankle. And she needed to be needed just now, and not by the boy she'd raised, but by the man she...

...*loved.* There, she'd formed the word. Not aloud, but in her mind. It felt true.

He emerged from the hotel bathroom wearing brand-new blue jeans and a bright pink shirt. *Pink.* All she could say was, "Wow."

"You like it?"

"I'd wear it myself."

He grinned. "It goes with my lucky rabbit's foot. I need all the luck I can get today."

"Well, take it off and let me iron it," she said. "You bought it off the shelf."

"I know how to iron." He reached for his hat.

"I know you do, but it would be my pleasure to iron your shirt for you."

He put the hat back, set up the ironing board for her and caught her gaze while he unsnapped his pink shirt. He could read her mind. She didn't know which part he was reading, but the look in his eyes told her he was picking up serious vibes.

When they reached the arena, she saw another pink shirt. She snapped a picture. Behind the chutes there were more pink shirts.

"Did you boys call each other about this? *Hey, guys, what color should we wear today?*" Skyler laughed. "Or did the Cat in the Hat visit the locker room?"

"We don't have a locker room." Trace pointed to the sign on the crow's nest. Tough Enough to Wear Pink, it said, and the loop of a breast-cancer-awareness ribbon explained it all. "It's been going on for a few years. Big fund-raiser for the PRCA." He smiled. "In some ways, I guess cowboys *are* all alike."

Skyler snapped a picture of the banner and a few more of cowboys doing their stretching routines and getting their equipment in order. She took pictures of the human ribbon the survivors and their families formed in the arena, and all the while she thought about Trace and his father and what kind of men they were. They were tough enough to be gentle. Tough enough to give all they had without worrying about what it might cost them. Tough enough to do the right thing.

For Trace, the right thing meant holding off on commitments he wasn't ready to make. Being with Skyler was one thing. Fatherhood was something else.

Which meant that Skyler had to get tough, as well.

Trace had the second-highest score in the first go-round, but he won the second, and he took first in bareback. It was a huge win. With a few more rodeos like this one he was a shoo-in for the National Finals and a good bet to take the championship. He had to keep "going down the road."

And he wanted her to go with him.

"I can't do this, Trace," Skyler told him on the drive back to Gillette, to her house, her responsibilities, her life. "I'm not a rodeo groupie or—what do you call those girls—a buckle bunny."

"I never took you for one. I wouldn't have been interested." He glanced over at the passenger's seat. "What can't you do? Go with me? Be with me?"

"I have to go home."

"To what?"

"What I know. Where I'm safe. Your road is a high place, and I need to be safe on the ground. I need to be necessary."

"You're becoming necessary," he said. "I'm not gonna say I can't live without you, but I will say I don't want to."

"And I'm not saying we can't be together. I want to see you as much as I can. As often as I can."

"Every day," he insisted. "Every day works for me."

"But not for me. I have to go home and help Mike

figure out what to do with his cattle operation." She sighed. "Okay, it's for him to figure out. But I have to help get things in order. I have to—"

"You do what you have to do, then."

Little was said after that. He pulled into the yard at the ZQ, parked, shut off the motor, draped his wrists over the top of the steering wheel and sighed. "I guess this is where you get off."

"Is that it?"

"No. I'll call you."

"Okay."

"I'll stop back when you're ready to take Cayenne out under saddle."

"Okay."

He turned to her, hooked his arm around her neck and drew her to him for a fierce and hungry kiss. "I'm not letting you go," he said.

"Okay. I…" She wouldn't say it. He hadn't said it, and she refused to say it. "I can call you, too, can't I?"

"You damn well better."

There had been no calls in the weeks that passed between Cheyenne and the approaching deadline for the wild-horse-training competition. Skyler was riding Cayenne every day, and she was proud of the progress she'd made with him. He probably wouldn't win any prizes, but he was saleable, and she had done much of the work herself.

She could do more of it. More horses, more training for a purpose other than her own. She could help get them ready for someone else. She could help Trace build toward the time when he would turn his corner. When he called, she would offer. Three *ifs* about that call. It would come.

And when it did, she would have much to tell him. She was Mike's mother, but she was no longer his nanny. She'd decided to think of herself as his employee. She had given him notice, but it wasn't the two weeks' kind. It was more like a presidential adviser letting the big guy know that she was getting close to burnout on this job. She would lay out his options the way she saw them, but he would have to sit down with her and pay serious attention. Otherwise, she'd have the two weeks' notice on his desk by the following day.

There was real work to be done before the ZQ calf sale. Mike had decided to sell half the cows. He'd recognized that it was the only way to pay the bills. With only half the breeding stock left, the future of the ranch was in jeopardy, and she was pretty sure he recognized that, too. She thought it was salvageable, but saving it would take hard work and determination. It was time for her son to decide what he really wanted to do. She told him about her father. It was a story she'd kept to herself for a long time, protecting it from harsh lights and harsher judgments. Mike seemed to understand what telling the story meant to her, and he thanked her for it.

Skyler's video was another story. It was going to be a masterpiece. Or close to it.

It would stand up in any light, withstand all judgment because the subject was as big as the West, a vital part of its heritage, and she had a knack for finding and framing the right images. She had the patience to wait for them and the eye that could pick them out from the piles and piles of pixels she'd recorded. She wasn't sure how she was going to get it out there, but between her and Sally Night Horse, *the way forward* would be more than just a catchphrase.

She was listening to an interview she'd done with the wild-horse manager in Worland, where the Bureau of Land Management regional office was located, when she looked up through the office window and saw a familiar pickup headed for the house.

She was a mess. Hair stuck up in a ponytail, ratty T-shirt, bare feet. But she ran to the door, tore it open and struggled to collect herself at the sight of her cowboy standing there on her porch. No smile. No salutation.

"I'm here to help out," he told her. It sounded like an open-ended offer, and the look in his eyes said he was ready to fend off any objections, reject any exceptions.

She had none. All she really wanted to do was feast her eyes, but instinctively she launched into a report.

"Cayenne is taking a bit, changing leads quite nicely, learning to—"

He caught her in his arms and shut her up with a kiss, hard and fast at first—much like a rodeo event—but when she gave as good as she got, he slowed down and kissed gently, greeting her tongue with his, dropping back and then kissing again. And again.

"Not with the horse, unless that's what you need,"

he said finally. "I'll be your handyman. Your jack-of-all-trades. I don't know what you're gonna do with this place, but, hell, I'll help you cut your kid's steak for him if that's what it's gonna take. I want to help with whatever you need. So you can be with me."

"Be where?"

"Anywhere. I don't care. Like I said, it's not that I can't live without. It's just that I'd rather not."

"Me, too." She put her arms around him and hugged him hard. "I don't care either. I'll ride the rails with you if that's what you want."

"It isn't." In his eyes relief displaced the readiness to play defense, and he took her face in his hands. "I'm in love with you, Skyler. That's why I'm here. I want to marry you and train horses and play games and make babies and pictures." He laughed, probably because she was laughing, which was one of the many things that made them good together. "And baby pictures."

"I don't want to wait," she said. "And not because I can't wait. I can if I have to, but I don't want to. I want to get on with loving you, and I want our babies to come from loving each other. But—" she drew the breath she needed, the one that gave her pause to consider him "—we can work that out. I mean…I'm not the one wearing the condom."

He laughed so hard she was afraid he was going to fall down on the porch, so she pulled him inside, closed the door, pressed her forehead against his chest and gave him a playful punch in his quivering gut. "But I want the pants," she said.

"After I get yours."

"Would you believe me if I told you I had an allergy to latex?"

"Nope." He put his arms around her. "You think I *like* wearing the damn thing?"

"I think…" She looked up at him. "I think you're a good man. After we get the fall work done, I want you to take me away from here," she said. "Where can we go?"

"To the National Finals for starters," he told her. "And then we'll make a home together."

"Where?"

"Together. This is your house, right?" She nodded. "Is it the home you want?" She shook her head. "So we'll work that out, too, and we'll be together as much as we can while we're workin' it—" he charmed her with a sweet smile, teased her with a cocky wink "—baby. What do you say?"

"I'm ready, cowboy." She held him close again and whispered, "I'm so ready."

* * * * *

We hope you enjoyed reading this
special collection from Harlequin®.

If you liked reading these stories,
then you will love
Harlequin® Special Edition books!

You know that romance is for life.
Harlequin Special Edition stories show
that every chapter in a relationship has its
challenges and delights and that love can be
renewed with each turn of the page.

Enjoy six new stories from
Harlequin Special Edition every month!

Available wherever books and
ebooks are sold.

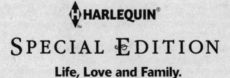

HARLEQUIN®

SPECIAL EDITION

Life, Love and Family.

www.Harlequin.com

COMING NEXT MONTH FROM

HARLEQUIN®

SPECIAL EDITION

Available April 21, 2015

#2401 NOT QUITE MARRIED
The Bravos of Justice Creek • by Christine Rimmer
After a fling with Dalton Ames on an idyllic island, Clara Bravo wound up pregnant.
She never told Dalton the truth, since the recently divorced hunk insisted he
wasn't interested in a relationship. But when Dalton discovers Clara's secret, he's
determined to create a forever-after with the Bravo beauty and their baby...no
matter how much she protests!

#2402 MY FAIR FORTUNE
The Fortunes of Texas: Cowboy Country
by Nancy Robards Thompson
On the outside, PR guru Brodie Fortune Hayes is the perfect British gentleman. But
on the inside, he's not as polished as he seems. When Brodie is hired to fix up the
image of Horseback Hollow's Cowboy Country theme park, one lovely Texan—his
former fling Caitlyn Moore—might just be the woman who can open his heart after all!

#2403 A FOREVER KIND OF FAMILY
Those Engaging Garretts! • by Brenda Harlen
Daddy. That's one role Ryan Garrett never thought he'd occupy...until his friend's
death left him with custody of a fourteen-month-old. He definitely didn't count on
gorgeous Harper Ross stepping in to help with little Oliver. As they butt heads and
sparks fly, another Garrett bachelor finds the love of a lifetime!

#2404 FOLLOWING DOCTOR'S ORDERS
Texas Rescue • by Caro Carson
Dr. Brooke Brown has devoted her entire life to her career—but that doesn't mean
she isn't susceptible to playboy firefighter Zach Bishop's smoldering good looks.
A fling soon turns into so much more, but Brooke's tragic past and Zach's newly
discovered future might stand in the way of the family they've always wanted.

#2405 FROM BEST FRIEND TO BRIDE
The St. Johns of Stonerock • by Jules Bennett
Police chief Cameron St. John has always loved his best friend, Megan Richards—
and not just in a platonic way. But there's too much baggage for friendship to turn
into romance, so Cameron sets his feelings aside...until Megan's life is threatened
by her dangerous brother. Then Cameron will stop at nothing to protect her—and
ensure their future together.

#2406 HIS PREGNANT TEXAS SWEETHEART
Peach Leaf, Texas • by Amy Woods
Katie Bloom has fallen on hard times. She's pregnant and alone, and the museum
where she works is going out of business. Now Ryan Ford, the one who got away,
walks into a local eatery, tempting her with his soulful good looks. Ryan's got secrets,
but can he put Katie and her child above everything else to create a lifelong love?

**YOU CAN FIND MORE INFORMATION ON UPCOMING HARLEQUIN® TITLES,
FREE EXCERPTS AND MORE AT WWW.HARLEQUIN.COM.**

HSECNM0415

When Harper had gone back to work a few days after
the funeral, Ryan had offered to be the one to get up in
the night with Oliver so that she could sleep through. It
wasn't his fault that she heard every sound that emanated
from Oliver's room, across the hall from her own.

Thankfully, she worked behind the scenes at *Coffee
Time with Caroline*, Charisma's most popular morning
news show, so the dark circles under her eyes weren't as
much a problem as the fog that seemed to have enveloped
her brain. And that fog was definitely a problem.

"Do you want me to get him a drink?" she asked as
Ryan zipped up Oliver's sleeper.

"I can manage," he assured her. "Go get some sleep."

Just as she decided that she would, Oliver—now clean
and dry—stretched his arms out toward her. "Up."

Ryan deftly scooped him up in one arm. "I've got you,
buddy."

The little boy shook his head, reaching for Harper.

"Up."

"Harper has to go night-night, just like you," Ryan said.

"Up," Oliver insisted.

Ryan looked at her questioningly.

She shrugged. "I've got breasts."

She'd spoken automatically, her brain apparently stuck somewhere between asleep and awake, without regard to whom she was addressing or how he might respond.

Of course, his response was predictably male—his gaze dropped to her chest and his lips curved in a slow and sexy smile. "Yeah—I'm aware of that."

Her cheeks burned as her traitorous nipples tightened beneath the thin cotton of her ribbed tank top in response to his perusal, practically begging for his attention. She lifted her arms to reach for the baby, and to cover up her breasts. "I only meant that he prefers a softer chest to snuggle against."

"Can't blame him for that," Ryan agreed, transferring the little boy to her.

Oliver immediately dropped his head onto her shoulder and dipped a hand down the front of her top to rest on the slope of her breast.

"The kid's got some slick moves," Ryan noted.

Harper felt her cheeks burning again as she moved over to the chair and settled in to rock the baby.

*Fall in love with A FOREVER KIND OF FAMILY
by Brenda Harlen, available May 2015 wherever
Harlequin® Special Edition books and ebooks are sold.*

www.Harlequin.com

HSEEXP0415

Love the Harlequin book you just read?

Your opinion matters.

Review this book on your favorite book site, review site, blog or your own social media properties and share your opinion with other readers!

Be sure to connect with us at:
Harlequin.com/Newsletters
Facebook.com/HarlequinBooks
Twitter.com/HarlequinBooks

HARLEQUIN®

A *Romance* FOR EVERY MOOD™

Stay up-to-date on all your
romance-reading news with the
Harlequin Shopping Guide,
featuring bestselling authors, exciting new
miniseries, books to watch and more!

The newest issue will be delivered right to you
with our compliments! There are 4 each year.

Signing up is easy.

EMAIL

ShoppingGuide@Harlequin.ca

WRITE TO US

HARLEQUIN BOOKS
Attention: Customer Service Department
P.O. Box 9057, Buffalo, NY 14269-9057

OR PHONE

1-800-873-8635 in the United States
1-888-343-9777 in Canada

Please allow 4-6 weeks for delivery of the first issue by mail.